KU-760-740

DISASTROUS

DISASTROUS

E.L. Montes

DISASTROUS
E.L. Montes
Text copyright © 2012 by E.L. Montes

All Rights Reserved. This book may not be reproduced, scanned, or distributed in any printed or electronic form without permission from the author. Please do not participate in or encourage piracy of copyrighted materials in violation of the author's rights. All characters and storylines are the property of the author and your support and respect is appreciated. The characters and events portrayed in this book are fictitious. Any similarity to real persons, living or dead, is coincidental and not intended by the author.
The following story contains mature themes, strong language, and sexual situations. It is intended for adult readers.

Cover designed by David Goldhahn

www.davidgoldhahn.com

Edited by Theresa Wegand

This book is dedicated to my family. There are not enough words to show my gratitude. Thank you for all the love and support.

PROLOGUE

Grabbing my wrist, he begged me not to go. With the blood pulsing through my veins, my rage quickly boiled. Turning to face him, I shoved the palm of my hands against his chest. I was surprised by my own strength. Although he was bigger than I was, I was able to force him to stumble back a few steps, and he landed on the wooden desk. He managed to balance himself, but he didn't move. His sorrowful eyes were staring into mine, *pleading.* Those eyes that I once fell for, that I trusted, that allowed me fall under his spell— those eyes now only filled my stomach with such vile disgust.

Collecting my thoughts was impossible. My mind was racing a thousand miles per hour. I'd never felt so much pain in my life. I gave him one last look, but he did and said *nothing.* His eyes were saddened, but I didn't care. I wanted to get away! I turned away from him and ran as fast as I could. I could hear him yelling my name.

Snatching my purse from the table without looking back, I struggled to unlock the front door. I managed to open it with a shaky hand, tripping down the first few steps, realizing at that moment my feet were bare. Carelessly, I ran down the driveway and reached my car. I shoved my hand into my bag to collect my keys, but I couldn't find them. *Shit!* He was by the door. Rushing in the process, I was able to locate them and jump into the driver's seat.

Looking up, I found him on the bottom step, yelling, begging me to stop. My heart was pulsing at such a rapid speed I felt nauseated and lightheaded. After turning on the ignition, I raced out of the driveway and onto the street. The speedometer reached ninety-five miles per hour. My hands were sweating, and my heart was pounding so loudly I could barely hear myself breathe.

After twenty minutes, I was far enough to pull over by the curb, checking my rearview mirror; he was nowhere in sight. I made sure the doors were locked. Then burying my face into my hands, I screamed and burst into sobs, allowing all the rage and betrayal to pour out. How could I have believed and trusted him? How could I have been so stupid; this whole time he was warning me, but I was blind and didn't care ... I wanted the good and bad ... all of him.

Knowing at that moment what he truly was, I realized that everything was just lies. *Aarrgh!* I looked down, trying to catch my breath. Through blurry, watery vision I caught sight of my cream silk nightgown spotted in bright red blood.

My thoughts were uncontrollable. I was trying to make it all go away, and I pounded my fists against my temples, but all that managed to do was inflict additional pain. *Why me?* My chest felt tight, and it was so hard to breathe I was hyperventilating. After a few minutes of taking long deep breaths, I was able to control the airflow through my lungs. Then it all came back to me: the day I met HIM.

CHAPTER ONE

The month of April was so beautiful this year: clear skies, bright green grass, and a cool breeze perfect enough to wear a light jacket. It was my last day of class before my summer break began, and for some unexplained reason, Professor Johnson required the entire class to attend the last day, even after we'd submitted our final exam and paper. He was blabbing about what we learned in the entire semester of our Contract Law class. I knew I earned my 4.0 GPA, so I ignored his unnecessary lecture.

Staring out the window, I continued to admire Harvard's landscaping as the students and faculty scattered around. This had been a tough year, and I was just happy to be taking a break. The last few months had been nothing but an emotional roller coaster. Finally I was at a point where I could wake up without crying, go to school without zoning out, and enter a public place without the aching memories.

My thoughts were interrupted when I heard a round of applause. I joined in as I knew the class was finally over. The students began to pack their bags. I quickly placed my laptop and textbook into my backpack and headed for the door. Professor Johnson was standing by the entryway saying farewell to everyone.

I knew it would be difficult to walk by him without being pulled in for an intellectual conversation. So I attempted to hide my face by lowering my red cap. There were a few students in front of me, and I tried to blend in and sneak out, avoiding eye contact. I was almost out the door when Mr. Johnson shouted my name twice. A few students turned around, flashing sympathetic smiles. I couldn't say I didn't hear him. Slowly I turned on the balls of my feet and flashed a full-toothed grin. In return, I was faced with the stupid, goofy smile I was beginning to dislike. *Ugh!*

When I reached his side, he lifted his finger, indicating for me to wait a minute. *Great!* He pulled me aside and had the audacity to keep me waiting. After he gave a few more farewells, we were left alone in the huge classroom. Facing me with another big smile, he began to walk towards his desk.

I followed, dragging my feet, all while forming a handgun with my finger and thumb and aiming it at my head. Then I pulled the trigger. *Okay*, so that may seem a little childish for a twenty-four year old, but I didn't want to be bothered that day.

He took a seat behind his desk and handed me a sheet of paper. Raising an eyebrow at his amused grin, I looked down at the document. I was dumbstruck when I saw the letterhead. It was from The Law Office of Marcus DeLuca! I continued to read the letter when I realized it was addressed to me.

Dear Ms. Sullivan:

Thank you for applying to our summer externship. As you are aware, our firm chooses four law students each summer from Harvard Law. Each student will be placed in one of our four legal departments.

After reviewing your resume and references, we would like to invite you to interview for an opportunity to be a part of the externship program.

Kindly make arrangements to be at our office on Friday, April 27, 2012, at 9:00 a.m., at the above address, Suite 2500. You will be meeting with me and possibly Mr. DeLuca if he is available.

Unfortunately due to our fast-paced environment and busy schedule, this date cannot be rescheduled. If for any reason you cannot make this date, kindly call our office for a courtesy cancellation.

I look forward to meeting you. Thank you for your time and cooperation.

Very truly yours,

Lisa Harper

Human Resource Manager

Stunned, I read the letter two more times. I couldn't believe it! I looked up at Professor Johnson, who still had that smirk on his face. I shook my head in disbelief. "Um, Professor Johnson, this is terrific, but I didn't sign up for the externship position. I thought it was only for third-year students." He adjusted his crooked wire glasses and cleared his throat.

"Well, Lisa Harper is really good friends with my wife. So I asked my wife if she could do me a favor and put in a good word for you. Mia, you're the best student I've had in my twenty years of teaching. You're attentive; you submit your work on time, and you earned a 4.0 GPA your first year! You deserve this more than any third-year student."

Oh, that was nice. I guess he's not so bad after all.

"Professor, I truly appreciate this, but knowing that there's a possibility that I'll be interviewed by Mr. DeLuca is nerve-racking. How am I going to pull this off?" The thought made my stomach twist in knots. Marcus DeLuca was the youngest, richest, and most successful lawyer in Boston. This was a dream come true; it was also a foot in the door. Everyone who had been an extern for the DeLuca firm had either been hired or highly recommended for other top firms.

"Mia, you'll be great at the interview. Yes, you'll be a little nervous; that's normal, but once you're in there, you'll fly through that interview like it's nothing. Look, today is Tuesday; your interview is Friday. Take a break tomorrow, but stop by my office on Thursday. We can practice interview questions so that you're better prepared." He got up from his chair and walked over. Stopping when he was a foot away, he lifted the palm of his hand and patted my head. I felt like a six-year-old. "You're going to knock this interview out the park. Trust me." He crossed his arms and smiled, this time *less* irritatingly. Why was he being so nice to me?

I lightly smiled. "Thank you, Professor Johnson. I have no idea how to repay you for this." He shook his head.

"Oh, Mia, it's my pleasure, *really*. I have so much faith in you. I know one day you're going to be a very successful woman."

I hoped so.

****

Before going home, I decided to stop by a local boutique. I had to find something appropriate for this interview. I was sure sweatpants, a t-shirt, and a Harvard baseball cap wouldn't do. My fashion sense had simmered down the last few months, especially when I began law school. I didn't have much of a social life. Maintaining a 4.0 GPA was not going to happen while out drinking and partying every weekend. Don't get me wrong: I do have a fashion sense; I am a girly girl, but I do love my sweats and t-shirt days. Nothing in my closet at that moment was appropriate for a professional interview, *especially* with the number-one firm in the city.

I was greeted by a tall, enthusiastic blonde. "Hi! Welcome to Fabulous Boutique, is there anything I can help you with?" She was very pretty. Her hair was cut in a short bob; she had bright blue eyes and red lipstick that went well with her fair complexion. She was dressed in a black, fitted dress, a nude belt, and matching pumps.

Instantly, I felt embarrassed by my appearance. Lowering my head to examine my own ensemble, I wrapped my arms around the middle of my stomach in an attempt to hide, but it was no use. In defeat, I dropped my arms and brought my gaze back to her. She had a huge Cameron Diaz smile which was *actually* contagious. I smiled too. "Yes, um, I have an interview on Friday, and I need to find something that's professional."

She waved her hand in the air, "Oh yes! We have a great selection in our 'successful' section. Come follow me. Are you a six?" Following her towards the far right of the store, I was distracted by the number of collections they had in such a small place.

"Yes, I'm a six, sometimes a five; it depends." I followed as instructed and passed a mannequin. The plastic figure was wearing a black and beige waistline pencil skirt with a sheer nude blouse. The collar of the blouse was tied in a bow, and a matching beige purse hung from the mannequin's arm. It was pretty cute. "Something like this?" I pointed at the mannequin.

"Oh yes, I'll prepare some outfits for you to try on. It's best if you purchase a few so you have plenty of options," she said. And so I can spend money.

She skimmed through the racks as I stared at her selections, wondering how badly my thighs or hips would look in the skirts and dresses she'd chosen. I was blessed with curves and although I learned to accept them, not everything looked good on these hips.

She walked over to another section where she located a few blouses. Placing an emerald green blouse in front of me, she glanced from the thin silk fabric to my eyes. "Oh! This matches perfectly with your eyes, such beautiful eyes!" Looking down at the blouse then back at her, I smiled and gently shrugged.

"What's great about our boutique is that a lot of these pieces go well with each other, so it's easy to prepare a few outfits with just four or five pieces of clothing," she chanted as she continued to rummage through the hangers.

She turned to face me with another Diaz smile; you could tell she enjoyed this kind of stuff. "*Okay*, we can start with these, come let me show you to the dressing room." Reaching for my arm, she dragged me to the far back of the store.

This should be fun.

****

Melissa, the boutique clerk, was very useful and showed me different ways to wear the outfits that I purchased. After an hour with her, I had two dresses, four skirts, and six blouses, as well as two pair of shoes, a purse, and some jewelry to add to my collection. I was also five hundred fifty dollars poorer, but whether or not I got this position, I still needed the clothes for other interviews. Well, at least that was the logic I used when I swiped my credit card.

I managed to squeeze myself and all of the bags through the narrow apartment door. As soon as I entered the living room, sleepy blue eyes popped up from behind the sofa. Jeremy looked worn out as he rubbed his lids with the back of his hand. His eyes widened at the pile of bags I was carrying. Then he flashed a gorgeous grin.

"Celebrating summer break?" He nodded at my filled hands. I dropped the bags on the hardwood surface. Shopping is exhausting! Walking around the couch, I threw myself beside him and let out a huge draining breath.

"No, I went shopping for an interview I have on Friday." I turned to look at him; he had an amused expression.

"Interview? With whom?" I was a little hesitant, not sure if he'd be excited or upset with the news.

Biting my lip, I blurted out, "The DeLuca firm." Nervously chuckling, I watched as his lips slightly parted, and his cheeks lifted into a stupid boyish grin.

"Mia, that's awesome! I do too. I just received the letter today in the mail. My meeting is Friday at 9:30 in the morning. Wait, I thought they only accepted third-year students?"

In a way, this didn't surprise me. Jeremy's father designed the DeLuca firm's building, and his father had a way of using the advantages of knowing powerful individuals to help out his son.

I shrugged. "Professor Johnson put in a good word for me. I'm sure I won't get the position, but it's nice to be invited." He placed his hand on my shoulder and gave me a reassuring smile.

"Mia, I'm sure you'll get it. I'm actually *not* surprised you have the interview, *so* you know what this *means*!" he sang.

I knew I should be worried. "What?"

He jumped from the couch while stretching his arms in the air. He wore only boxer briefs, and with his curly blond hair a mess, he still managed to look adorable. He'd been working out a lot more this semester for the summer, and his hard work had paid off. I glanced at his ripped abs. The firm muscular lines caused the pit of my stomach to twist.

Swallowing, I tore my eyes away. The last time I'd had sex was two months ago, and it was with *Jeremy*. It began after my life changed seven months ago; he was there to comfort me, *fully* comfort me. Of course it was meaningless, drunken sex. We were able to do it and act as if nothing had happened.

Jeremy had never been in a relationship longer than a month. So in between his breaks, we would rekindle our sexual relationship. It actually worked out for us; though two months ago, I told him I didn't want to anymore.

I watched him turn and walk towards the kitchen. He opened the fridge door, grabbed a carton of orange juice, and drank from the container. I shook my head. *Boys will be boys*. He held the carton out to me, and I shook my head again. "So what does this mean, Jeremy?" I hated when he kept me in suspense for this long.

"We're going to celebrate tonight. Let's go to Club21." He sat beside me again. Within a second, he spread his legs and grabbed his package. "And besides I need to find a one-night stand because *Thor* needs some loving!"

I burst out laughing. "Thor? You named your package? Since when?"

He smiled. "I didn't. One girl told me in the sack that I looked like one of the Hemsworth brothers, so I stuck to it." He shrugged and took another swig of the orange juice.

Bringing my hands to my mouth, I tried my very hardest to stop the laughter. "Oh my God, *please* tell me she was hammered." Jeremy was handsome, no doubt, but to compare him with the one and only Chris Hemsworth? She had to be drunk.

He pouted. "Just a little. Besides, I have to get action somehow. You cut me off on that, *remember*?"

Dropping my hands, I glared at him. "Jeremy we discussed this. In order for me to try and heal from the loss without *your* help, we can't have sex anymore." He nodded his head, agreeing, and I continued. "Besides, don't you want me to help you find the hottest chick in the club tonight?"

His lips curled, and he nodded again. "You're right. You're a better sidekick than any of the guys."

Getting up from the couch, I walked over, grabbed my bags, and headed to my bedroom before shouting, "See! There's a good sport, so I should be ready around ten?"

I walked into my bedroom when I heard him yell. "*Yeah*! And don't be taking like five hours getting ready either!" I laughed and shut my door. It was only five, so I could take a nap. I hung up all my new clothes and laid out a dress, accessories, and shoes for the night.

****

At 9:45, I was dressed with my hair and makeup done. Walking out of my bedroom, I decided to bother Jeremy. Not bothering to knock, I opened his bedroom door. To my surprise, he was lying on his bed in the same boxer briefs. "Jeremy!" His startled eyes peeked over the open lid of his laptop. "What are you doing? It's fifteen minutes to ten!" Cocking my head, I glared at him as I threw one hand to my hip.

Removing the laptop from on top of his stomach, he placed it beside him and sat up. "Come on now, you know it only takes me fifteen minutes to get ready. I'll hop in the shower now." He stood from the bed. After a few steps, he froze and eyed me up and down. It was an erotic stare down, and my legs uncomfortably began to tremble. "What?" I asked, straightening my posture but keeping my hand on my hip.

With a slow and steady stride, he walked over. When he reached me, he was so close I could reach out and run my hands down his beautifully formed abs. *He was sexy*, but I didn't see him that way—not anymore.

Leaning in, he rested his hands against the inner doorway, my head trapped between his biceps. As if he weren't near enough, he moved in closer to the side of my face. "How could you possibly help me find the sexiest girl in the club tonight when I'm staring at her right now?" He erotically purred the words in my ear.

He was *delusional*! He knew better than to make sensual comments like that when I was already in heat. My initial reaction was to smack his arm, and I did it so fast, loud, and hard it made him jump and grab his bicep. "Jeremy! Quit that nonsense, get in the shower, and take me out! You owe me two drinks and a shot for that!" He smiled with his gleaming aqua blue eyes.

"Okay, okay, give a man a break. At least I tried. I am serious though; you look hot! I'll be pissed if I hear you got laid tonight and I didn't." Grabbing a towel, he headed for the shower.

Shaking my head, I made my way to the living room, threw myself on the couch, and grabbed this month's People magazine.

Twenty minutes later, Jeremy was standing in the living room in his fitted black pants and white button-down shirt with the top two buttons unhooked. His sleeves were rolled halfway up his forearms. His blond hair was damp from the shower but more maintained than earlier. He was wearing black shoes; although, I knew he'd rather wear sneakers. Club21 has a strict no-jeans-and-sneakers policy; it's *also* harder to get into.

I hurried to my bedroom to take one last glance in the mirror. I decided to leave my hair down. It was parted in the middle, so the golden brown waves fell down the sides of my face and along my shoulders. The dress was a little short and tight, but it flattered my curves. The nude four-inch pumps allowed the radiant blue dress to pop; a bold gold chain necklace and matching bracelet completed my outfit. I smiled at my reflection, mentally thanking Melissa for the tips.

CHAPTER TWO

In thirty minutes, we were in the Midtown Center City Boston nightlife. There was a strip with restaurants, bars, and nightclubs, but the place to be was Club21. After finding parking, we walked down the strip side by side, taking in the spring breeze. The stars in the night sky shone so beautifully on such a clear evening. When we reached the building, it had a ridiculous line that extended to the other end of the corner. It was a Tuesday night!

Then I remembered that day began the summer break for most universities, and many students were out celebrating. Luckily Jeremy's father was CEO of McCullen's Architecture & Designs. Mr. McCullen's firm built and designed Club21, thus my earlier comment about Jeremy's father: due to his connections, his son was welcome right in with his guests.

We reached a tall guard by the entrance. He was standing behind a platinum podium, wearing a black, fitted t-shirt, and his arms and chest were extremely huge. You could see every fat vein popping out of his biceps. I swear if he flexed an inch his shirt would have ripped. He looked up at Jeremy and smiled. "Mr. McCullen, you should have called. I'm afraid we don't have any VIP sections available, but I'm sure I can reserve a table for you near a bar." Mr. Husky seemed polite and professional with his strong Boston accent.

Jeremy smiled in response. "Not to worry, Tony. A table for four will be fine; I have two other guests who will join us, David and Michelle. Can you make sure they're on the list?"

David was a childhood friend of Jeremy's. I only saw him and his new wife Michelle when we got together at Club21. They were more his good friends than mine. Tony jotted down the names, and let us in; the place was throbbing with a loud hip-hop beat.

Mr. McCullen had done such an amazing job with this place. It had a luxurious, modern design. The dance floor was large enough to accommodate roughly one hundred people comfortably. There were six glass bars surrounding the club. Each bar had a different color fluorescent light gleaming through. The high ceilings were covered in white silk drapes, and the VIP rooms were on the second level overlooking the dance floor. Each of the rooms had a glass wall, so VIP guests could look down to view the entire first floor. Some of the curtains were closed for privacy, and others were open.

I'd previously seen that the rooms were large enough to fit twenty people each. They were equipped with an oversized white sectional and a black ottoman. I had the pleasure of visiting a few of them, and they were all decorated the same way. Each room also was completed with a beautiful chandelier and dim blue lights. On warmer nights, guests were allowed to enjoy the oversized L-shaped underground swimming pool and deck out back.

Jeremy grabbed my wrist and led me to the back near the blue bar. Beside it was a U-shaped sofa with a table in the middle. We slid along the seat until we met in the middle. Before getting comfortable, we were greeted by a tall brunette. She wore a black, fitted dress and black pumps. Her hair was slicked back into a low ponytail. "Hello Mr. McCullen, what can I get for you and your guest?" she asked.

Jeremy glanced at me and I nodded. He knew what I wanted; he just wanted to double-check. "A Cosmo for her and a Grey Goose and tonic for me, thank you." The waitress smiled and headed to the bar.

We didn't have a VIP room, but the table was private enough and tucked in the corner near the bar. We were also able to view the stage and dance floor. It felt good to finally be free from reading case after case, studying, and dealing with the grief I suffered the past seven months. I just wanted a *drink*! Although I didn't go out a lot, I made sure every Friday, either on my own or with Jeremy, to have a few glasses of wine to mellow out after a long week. This time I wanted liquor, not wine; I wanted to feel free, good, and relaxed.

The waitress returned with our drinks and three shot glasses.

I look at Jeremy confused; I didn't hear him order shots. "Mr. DeLuca sent these over; he said he'll be by once he greets a few people," the waitress blurted and then left.

Raising an eyebrow at Jeremy, I freaked the hell out. "Mr. DeLuca who?"

He smiled. "Okay, so I kind of never told you that I know Marcus. He owns this club, and my father designed a few things for him." He shrugged his shoulders and took a sip of his drink.

My eyes grew narrow. "You kind of never told me? And what about the externship? I knew you met him before and your father designed his office building, but I didn't know he owned this club and that you guys were close."

"Mia, we're not best friends. We've had a few drinks before … mostly here when you were *hibernating* for the past seven months."

"And the externship position?"

He bit down on his bottom lip nervously. "Well, Marc told me I have it. They just have to do the interview; it's mandatory." I rolled my eyes. I can't believe this! Now I'm going to sit here all goo-goo gaga over this dude because my best friend failed to mention that the guy we are interviewing with on Friday not only owns this place but he fucking knows him personally! Great! I grabbed my drink and chugged it down. "Whoa, calm down, Mia! He's cool; trust me. He's not like these stuck-up snobby, rich kids you see at school."

He had to be *kidding* me. "No, he's instead the richest and top lawyer of Boston! Jeremy, I'm not ready for this. This is my career we're talking about. Yours is obviously set! The last thing I want is for my possible future to meet me in a club over drinks. I wanted to get *drunk* tonight and make a *fool* out of myself. Now I have to behave!" He didn't move or say anything—just looked at me with those blue eyes and a sympathetic smile. God! There's no point; he would never understand. His entire life was rolled out in front of him like a red carpet. I spotted the waitress and lifted my glass. She nodded in response and worked her way back to the bar again.

I was so nervous. Just be yourself, Mia. Everything is going to be okay. I took a few deep breaths. My empty glass was replaced with another Cosmo, I thanked the waitress and she left. I took small sips this time. Jeremy grabbed my hand, "Mia I'm sorry, okay. Trust me he's cool." His touch quickly calmed my nerves. He was right; I'd be fine. I was overreacting as I usually did when it involved my future. I took a few more sips and calmed.

After what seemed like forever, I was on my fourth Cosmo and third shot. I was extremely relaxed. Still no DeLuca, but we finally met up with David and Michelle. Michelle is from England, and her accent is pretty cool, though a little hard to adjust too. She met

David in her hometown when he traveled there for business. David does some work for an advertising firm and travels a lot. They fell in love, and she followed him here. Three years later they were married and had a four-month-old baby boy.

The boredom that overtook me when Michelle spoke of diaper changes and different formulas that their son couldn't keep down was beginning to kill my buzz. I finished my fourth Cosmo and waved my hand at the waitress for another drink.

"So yeah, other than that, our little one is an angel." Michelle giggled while reaching for her cell phone. She began to search for something. *God,* she was going to show me pictures, *please no*! Sure enough her screen was in front of me with the image of a big green-eyed baby. If it weren't for the blue shirt and hat, I would've mistaken him for a girl. He was cute but nothing to go all *aw* about.

I smiled and said what every new mother wants to hear. "He is the cutest thing I've ever seen!"

With a bright smile, she placed her phone back into her clutch. "Thanks! He is, isn't he?" I nodded and glanced over at the dance floor.

Thankfully, David asked his wife to dance, and she accepted. Jeremy stood up and walked toward a woman near the bar. They'd been eyeing each other for twenty minutes. They exchanged a few words, and then he led her to the dance floor. I was left alone by myself with no drink. To pass the time, I grabbed my phone out of my clutch. Scrolling through it, I noticed no new emails, texts, or missed calls. The disappointment of having no one contacting me made me feel lonely. *Where* the hell was my drink!

I decided to read old text messages between Jeremy and me. The last text I received from him was an hour ago when David and Michelle arrived and were all over each other.

GET A ROOM! GROSS! :-/

I laughed to myself again. My response was a simple LOL.

I was scrolling through my phone deleting junk emails, when I was presented with another drink. This time I didn't look up at the waitress as I thanked her. I grabbed it and took another sip. *Ah*, it was even tastier than the first one. In the middle of indulging my, *oh so good* Cosmo, I heard the waitress' startled voice, "Um, good evening, Mr. DeLuca. Would you like your usual?" Choking on my alcohol, I managed to keep my eyes on the glass. I heard a low, deep voice with a slight Boston accent. "Yes, that's fine. Thank you." I finally had the courage to look up. The waitress hurried to the bar: this was the fastest I'd seen her move the entire night.

The man standing before me was definitely God's gift to women. He was tall, tanned, and had the most gorgeous big brown eyes I'd ever seen. His dark brown hair was neatly brushed with a loosened strand that lay on his perfectly thick arched eyebrows. He smiled at me with his full lips and perfect white teeth. He had one deep dimple on the right side of his cheek. I wanted to melt, but I held my composure. He was even more stunning in person. I'd seen pictures of him on his law firm's website and in advertisements, but I'd never had the opportunity to meet this beautiful man in person.

He didn't speak; instead, he slid over the chair until he was almost beside me. Gently placing my glass down, I hid my shaky hands under the table, laying them on my lap. I straightened my shoulders as he leaned in. Nodding at me, he lifted his right eyebrow. He must have sensed I was nervous because his smile broadened, and he seemed to be amused by his thoughts.

"Hi, I'm Marcus DeLuca, and you *are*?" He asked while reaching for his drink that magically appeared out of nowhere. I was instantly enthralled by his adorable smile; it was like a chain reaction, and I couldn't help but flush in response. *Oh my God*, I felt my cheeks turn a burning red. I cleared my throat and prepared to respond.

"Hi, I'm Mia, Jeremy's friend." I tilted my head and glanced towards the dance floor where Jeremy was grinding behind a brunette this time. He had ditched the blonde. I glanced back at Mr. Hottie who nodded then took another sip of his drink. The strong liquor from his glass smelled to be whisky or brandy. I wasn't sure which.

He put down his drink on top of the table and unhooked the single button on his navy blue suit jacket. I stared at him in awe: one of the side effects of my fourth or was it fifth Cosmo? Whatever, but the Cosmo must have had me feeling this way; he was so hot! I wanted to run my hands through his hair and suck on those lips. *What the hell was I thinking?* I shook the thought immediately away. He was staring at me suspiciously. Did he suspect my thoughts? It was beginning to feel extremely warm in there. Fanning my face with my hand to cool off didn't work. My face burned, and I was uncomfortable from the heat.

"Are you Sullivan? Mia Sullivan?" he asked, folding his hands on-top of the table.

Biting my lip, I chanced a quick glance at him again. "Yes, how did you know?"

"Oh, ah, Jeremy mentioned you a few times. Also I texted him earlier to see if he knew you. I've heard a lot about the highly recommended, first-year law student, Mia Sullivan." He playfully smiled. It was adorable.

I took a deep breath. "Yes, that's me. I ... I didn't apply. Professor Johnson decided to apply on my behalf. He handed me the acceptance letter for the interview this morning actually." His eyebrows creased. He grabbed his drink, and before taking a sip, he nodded his head, indicating the "I see" look. I'm not sure if it was a positive or negative response, but it made me wonder if I shouldn't have mentioned that Professor Johnson submitted the application. What if he thinks I don't want the position, or what if he doesn't take me seriously?

"Hey, there you are! I see you met Mia!" Jeremy interrupted my thoughts. His white shirt was damp, and his face was glistening with sweat. At least I wasn't the only one who felt warm. "Yes, we met." DeLuca's smile was replaced with a serious expression. I wondered, "Oh *shit*, did I screw up my only opportunity for this externship?" I felt queasy. "So Marc, sorry I can't hang, but I kind of have this chick that wants to hook up." Jeremy pointed his thumb to the brunette standing beside the bar. Marcus glanced over his shoulder then back at Jeremy expressionless.

Jeremy's smile faded when he turned his head in my direction. "Mia, I know you had too many drinks tonight, will you be okay getting home? I'm going to take a cab back to this chick's place. Also David and Michelle left like ten minutes ago. Are you going to be okay taking a cab home? I can wait for one with you if you like." He was mumbling.

I narrowed my eyes. What the *hell* makes him think I'll be okay on my own? You're my friend, *Jeremy.* You're supposed to make sure I get home okay. I wanted to yell at him and I would've, if Gorgeous DeLuca weren't sitting next to me. "I'll drive her,"

Marcus replied nonchalantly. I glanced at his drink. He must have read my mind after he followed my gaze. "This is the only drink I've had all night. I'm fine. I can drive her home. Go ahead, Jae; get out of here." Jeremy's excitement was pathetic. He practically ran out with the brunette after thanking DeLuca and placing a quick kiss on my cheek. *Oh*! I'll get him tomorrow! I plan on it.

Gulping down the rest of my last Cosmo, I grabbed my clutch and slid over the sofa. I felt fine until I stood up and all the blood rushed to my head. I instantly felt dizzy, and the room seemed to spin. I felt unbalanced with my heels, but Marcus placed his hand on my elbow, which allowed me to keep steady. I looked at him, and his face was still serious. *Great*, he must have been angry, having to babysit a drunken law student.

"Hey, you don't have to take me home. I'm fine with taking a cab. Thanks anyway," I said, slowly removing my arm from his grasp.

He tightened his grip. "No, I'm taking you home. What kind of man would I be if I let you go home completely drunk in a vehicle where a cab driver could possibly take advantage of you?" Looking over his shoulder, he quickly eyed me up and down. "Especially in that dress," he hissed while dragging me through the crowd.

My stubbornness instantly kicked in. Who the *hell* does he think he's talking to me in that tone? And what's wrong with my dress?! I yanked my arm from his rough grip. "And what? Shall I get in the car with you, a *stranger*! What if *you* take advantage of me?" I yelled over the loud beat of Beyoncé's voice singing *Single Ladies*.

He shook his head and laughed then grabbed my arm again. This time it was tighter than before, and he practically dragged me to a side door with a sign that read EMPLOYEE'S ONLY written in white bold letters. The loud pounding sound of the music was drawn out, and the bright light from the hallway made me squint. We walked down an endless hallway. I was stumbling along, trying to keep my balance.

"You can't even stand up straight on your own, and you want to get in a cab? Didn't you hear about those four females in Boston within the last year? All four were too drunk and were driven in a cab alone but never found again!"

Trying to pull on his grip was useless. "Yes, I heard! And I can't stand straight because my heels are too high, thank you very much!"

I rolled my eyes. I quickly made my judgment on DeLuca: he was an asshole, and that was that! *Ugh*, I didn't even know if I wanted to work for this guy.

He shook his head, "I don't understand why women put themselves through that torture." Looking over his shoulder, his eyes seductively traced my entire body, then he fixed his gaze back in front of him, "and you'd look just as good in that dress in flats." He mumbled as he continued down the hallway. I wasn't sure whether to take that as a compliment or not.

When we finally reached the end, there were two very tall, overly built men standing by a metal door. The one dressed in black pants and a navy blue muscle tee reached in his pocket and pulled out a set of keys. "Hey Boss, you want me to pull the car up?" the guy asked as he looked at me.

"No, we can walk to the car. Finish the job. Meet me back at the house when it's done and with the details." Muscle tee nodded and handed the keys over to DeLuca. The other man wearing a button down light blue shirt opened the door and looked out into the private parking lot. "Good to go," he said as he held the door open for us.

We walked out to a breezy night, but the cool air felt good against my warm skin. I breathed in the night air as he continued to lead me across the parking lot. We were finally in front of a black, shiny, tinted Mercedes. *Of course*. He unlocked the door and helped me into the passenger seat. I was drunk, but I managed to remember to strap on my seatbelt. He closed the door and walked around to the driver's side. He got in and pressed a button for the ignition. It was so quiet that if it weren't for the dashboard lights, I wouldn't have known the car was on.

He looked at me, "So where to?"

I was suddenly exhausted and nauseated. "You don't know where I live?" I mumbled.

"Why would I?"

Rolling my head along the headrest, I turned to look at him. "Do you know where Jeremy lives?"

Gorgeous brown eyes stared back into mine. "Yeah,"

Yawning, I was super tired. "We're roommates."

With furrowed brows, he said, "Oh, he didn't mention that."

"I can tell." He reversed the car and pulled out of the driveway.

CHAPTER THREE

Bang, Bang, Bang. "Mia, open up! Miaaaa!" *Bang, Bang, Bang.* I was awakened by a loud noise. The rude interruption startled me. I looked around and realized I was home in my room on my own bed. Thank God. My heart slowly returned to a normal pace. I was in my panties and bra with last night's dress lying beside me. Managing to sit up, I felt dizzy. Uh, it felt like I was hit with a hundred-pound-weight ball.

"Mia, open up!" Jeremy's voice trailed from out front. Jumping out of bed, I quickly threw on a t-shirt then headed for the living room. When I opened the door, I was greeted with a relieved grin. Jeremy said nothing as he walked by and headed straight for the guest bathroom leaving the door wide open as he undid his fly and peed. "Ahhh," he moaned. I slammed the front door and walked towards him. He shook *Thor* twice, then zipped back up, and headed for the couch.

I rolled my eyes as I entered the bathroom. I had to flush the toilet because he always forgets to do that small task! Sitting down, I released all of the alcohol I'd consumed the day before. Feeling queasy as I stood to flush the toilet, I hesitated before washing my hands. Once the urge to throw up passed, I joined him on the couch. Jeremy's eyes were shut with his head slumped back onto the sofa's armrest. "So, where are your keys?" I asked suspiciously, but I knew the answer already.

Slightly lifting his head, he opened one eye. "I don't know. I lost them somewhere. I searched everywhere possible." He mumbled.

Both eyes were open, and he sat up at my glare.

Leaning over him as I stood by the end of the couch, I raised my hand to chastise him. "Jeremy, this is the *third* time we've changed the locks due to your irresponsible behavior. You lose your keys, and I get stuck with making the phone calls and waiting all day for the maintenance man to replace the lock!" With both hands on my hips, I waited for his explanation. He had none.

He rubbed his head, disgusted with himself *or* with my attitude. "I *know*, I *know*, I'll make the phone call. I promise." With his right hand against his chest and his left palm in the air, he pledged this time he would.

I scowled at him. "We both know that it will take months before you call. *Ugh*, I'll just do it later." I decided there was no point in continuing to argue, so I headed back to my bedroom and searched for my sweats. He followed me and jumped on my bed. Before I could even remember it, he was holding my vibrator up with a crooked smile.

"*So* I take it you didn't get laid last night."

Embarrassed, I jumped over the bed and snatched my toy that was swinging in his hand. After I secured it in my drawer, I made a mental note to clean it later. I refused to clean my toys in front of him. It would have just given him something to tease me about for the next few weeks, and I had no idea where his hands had been. I didn't remember using it either!

He laughed out loud but instantly snapped out of it when he met my evil glare. By the time I found my sweats and put them on, Jeremy was comfortable on my bed with the back of his head leaning against my pillow. I scooted beside him and shifted under the covers. "So, how was your night?" I asked, trying to focus on anything other than the memory of Jeremy swinging my toy in the air with a wicked grin.

His hands covered his entire face, and he mumbled underneath his palms. "It was terrible! I followed this chick all the way to her place, but when we got there, she fell asleep! I was too tired and drunk to hop back in a cab, so I just crashed there. I left this morning before she awoke."

I burst into laughter, and he peeked at me through his spread fingers. He wasn't amused, which made me laugh harder. "Oh, Jeremy, Jeremy, Jeremy, so I take it *Thor* didn't get any action either?" I teased, and I could tell he didn't appreciate my sarcasm by his narrow eyes. I slapped his arm, "Oh don't be so lame."

Turning on my side to face him, I held my head up with my hand. He spread his arms over his head to stretch then brought his hands behind his head. I wasn't uncomfortable with Jeremy beside me in bed. Jeremy spent many nights here, not just for sex. Before our relationship became more than just friends, he would lay beside me in bed to comfort me.

On days when I thought I would cry alone the entire night, he was there. He was a really good friend. Our relationship may have seemed awkward to an outsider, but he was *my* Jeremy. I didn't see us going any further than we had. We were just comfortable with one another. I knew more about him than any female, and he knew more about me than…well more than anyone.

"So how was your night last night? I mean with being driven home by DeLuca and all." He yawned and closed his eyes.

Shit! I snapped back to reality. I'd totally forgotten Marcus drove me home. I began to gather my thoughts of the night. I remembered bits and pieces: getting into his car … his waking me up when we were in front of the building. What *else*, oh yeah I knew he came in and guided me to my bedroom. Then I undressed. *Oh no*! I could feel the blood drain from my face. I undressed in front of *him*. *What the hell!*

What else happened? What else happened! My head hurt from straining to remember. I remembered being mad, but for what reason? *Ugh*, I walked over to my drawer and pulled out my vibrator. OH MY GOD! Did I pull out my vibrator in front of him? I think I'm going to be sick! I don't know what happened next! *Wait*, I think I was too upset and tossed it. I didn't use it, but did he see it? The blood rushed back to my head, and I quickly felt nauseated.

"So are you going to tell me, or am I going to have to ask him myself?" Jeremy teased with his eyes still closed. Good, he couldn't see the red-faced, nauseous expression I was wearing.

"Uh, nothing happened: he drove me home, led me to the door, and then he left. I locked the door and went to bed." Hopefully that would keep him from asking any questions about what I did or did not do with Marcus. He nodded, and before I finally came up with another topic to discuss, he was fast asleep snoring.

I adjusted my pillow and shifted to lay on my right side, giving Jeremy my back. My stomach was in knots trying to recollect last night's events. How could I have been so stupid and childish? The one thing I didn't want to happen had happened! I made a complete fool of myself in front of not only a striking man but in front of a powerful, intelligent and *way*-out-of-my-league man.

Should I even show my face at this interview Friday? *Ugh*, I buried my face into the pillow. Hopefully he won't be there to interview me, and if for some God-only-knows- reason I get this externship, I'll work in a department far away from DeLuca so I won't have to see him again.

****

I woke to the sound of the doorbell ringing. Forcing myself out of bed, I stumbled across the hardwood surface and opened the door. I froze when I saw him. His eyes were tense, his stance so masculine, his jaw line tight and strong, his full edible lips slightly parted, and his broad shoulders overpowered my energy. I took all of him in, studying every inch of this perfect man in awe before speaking.

"What are you doing here?" I breathed.

Seductively biting his bottom lip, he dragged his teeth across it. I melted. *I* wanted to drag my teeth across those lips too. "I'm here for you, Mia. I want you, and I want you now," he growled. I gasped in air, aroused by his demand. Before I could respond, he wrapped me in his arms and crushed his lips on mine.

His kiss was so fierce and hard; his tongue overpowered mine. It was soft and moist. I felt the blood heat through my skin. My knees weakened, and I would have fainted to the ground if it hadn't been for his strong arms holding me in place. His fingers were tangled in my hair, and he gently tugged at it. Pulling my head back to look into my eyes, he aggressively said, "Bed, now!" I nodded in response.

"Mia, Mia, wake up, Mia." Jeremy nudged my leg, waking me from my sleep.

"*Hmm*, leave me alone; I was having a good dream," I whined, throwing a pillow over my head.

"Mia, Marcus is here for you." I yanked the pillow off.

"What?" I wasn't sure if I'd heard him correctly.

"He says you left your purse and phone in his car last night; he's dropping it off to you. I told him you were sleeping, *but* he wanted to hand it to you himself." Jeremy stood over my bed, biting into an apple.

I turned to look at the time. It was 5:30 p.m. I'd slept all day! "Okay, um, I'll be out in five minutes." Jeremy shrugged and walked out, closing the door behind him. I jumped out of bed and ran to the mirror standing by the corner of my room. Oh my God! I looked terrible: black eyeliner and mascara were smeared all over my eyes, and my hair was a wild mess.

Thankfully my bedroom had a private entrance to our main bathroom. I rushed in and quickly took a shower.

Fifteen minutes later, I was bathed, had my teeth brushed, and managed to put an outfit together with skinny jeans, black flats, and a fitted white t-shirt. I brushed my hair into a ponytail and threw on a pair of silver hoop earrings. On my way out I noticed a grey summer scarf on top of my dresser, and I quickly wrapped it around my neck.

Taking a deep breath, I headed out. At first I didn't see anyone in the living room. When I heard Jeremy laughing, I knew they were in the kitchen. Marcus was sitting on a stool by the island with his back facing me. Jeremy looked up at me. "Five minutes, huh?" I grimaced at him, and he responded with a crooked smile. Marcus turned his head. Oh he was even more gorgeous while sober. I couldn't believe I'd just had a dream about him!

He stood up from the stool and reached for something on the counter. Then he made his way towards me. He was wearing a black, fitted, very expensive suit; his shirt was a crisp light blue; his black silk tie was loosened, and the top two buttons of his shirt were undone.

When he finally reached me, he extended his hand. My clutch was lying on his palm. I reached for it, and my fingertips lightly brushed against his skin. Remembering his hands touching me in my dream made my insides tighten, and my face warmed at the thought. I looked up at him, and he seemed amused. "Thank you. I appreciate your going out of your way to bring me my belongings." I nervously smiled.

He flashed that dimple again, and my smile widened. "Have you eaten Mia?" The question puzzled me, *eaten*?

When I thought about it, I realized that I hadn't eaten since yesterday, and my stomach was aching with the realization. "No."

"Well, will you join me for dinner? I haven't eaten since noon and would love for you to accompany me. There's a little Italian restaurant a block or so away from here that we could walk to. It's a very nice evening." I didn't know what to say. I was still confused about what happened last night and in my dream.

Oh God. Well maybe I can get some answers. Looking past his shoulders, I tried to catch Jeremy's attention for guidance. He wasn't paying attention, though. Marcus followed my eyes and turned to face Jeremy who was busy texting away. "Jae, I'm going to take Mia out to feed her real Italian food. You want to come?"

Jeremy looked up from his phone and smiled, "Nah, man, if this text goes well, I think I'm going to have a visitor tonight." He wiggled his eyebrows.

"Very well then, see you soon, if not Friday." Marcus grabbed my elbow and dragged me out the front door.

Before leaving, I snapped my head around to Jeremy; he waved at me then returned to his text. What the hell just happened!

I breathed for the first time since leaving my apartment when we stepped outside. It was still light out, and the cool air was perfect. There was no need for a jacket, but if I were wearing one, I wouldn't have felt uncomfortable either. I relaxed once the light breeze swiftly blew by. Marcus was beside me near the curb, but he kept his distance from me. Looking down as we walked, I managed to speak. "So where are we going?" I asked, trying to avoid the uneasiness I was feeling. He, on the other hand, seemed calm.

"It's called Romano's. It's a small mom-and-pop shop, nothing fancy, but the food is amazing. Everything is homemade, even the pasta."

"*Mmmh*, that sounds good. I don't remember seeing it around here, is it new?" I asked, since I was brave enough to finally look at him. Even his side profile was gorgeous. Tracing his features with my eyes, I noticed the perfect line of his nose, his plump lips, and the perfect structure of his jaw line. I could have stared at him for hours and not gotten tired of that face. He wet his lips before responding, causing the muscles between my legs to tighten. Looking away, I proceeded in a faster pace, trying to distract my thoughts.

"No, it's been there for almost twenty years. It's a very small place. You've probably passed it a few times on your way to school but never noticed it."

Nodding, I remained silent for the rest of the walk.

We approached a small brick corner building. On the door handle hung a small blackboard sign with Romano's written on it with white chalk in cursive. He opened the door and let me in. It was a very tiny place; it held about twenty small round tables, maybe fewer. The place was empty, but each table was draped in white linen and decorated with a few lit tea lights. The dark wood floors matched the chairs, and the exposed brick wall gave the place a warm feeling. The lights were dim, and if I hadn't just walked in from outside, I would've thought it was at least ten o'clock at night. It was a very lovely place.

A small bell rang when the door closed behind Marcus. My eyes searched for a hostess or waiter. A moment later, a short overweight man appeared through a double swinging door from a room in the back, which I guessed was the kitchen. Marcus swiftly passed me and headed towards the man. The older man's face brightened at the sight of DeLuca. He raised his arms to greet him with a huge hug.

"*Ciao, come stai?*" The older man's voice was loud and enthusiastic.

"*Bene, e voi?*" To my surprise, Marcus spoke clear Italian. I didn't understand a word he was saying, but it sounded sexy.

"*Mi sveglio ogni giorno ... chi è questa bella donna*" The man looked at me with a huge grin while motioning his hand in my direction.

Marcus looked over his shoulder at me and smiled before returning to the man and replying, "Un mio buon amica."

The man nodded and waved his hand for me to come over. "Oh, ben venuto su ho a sedere alcune speciali."

The man turned and began to walk away. Marcus waited till I met up with him; he placed the palm of his hand on my lower back. The very small gesture felt intimate, and I was sure he didn't mean anything by it, but the touch sent a burning ache through my veins. I concentrated on anything else but that touch as we followed the man. We were led up a flight of stairs and into another small room full of tables and chairs set similarly to downstairs. We walked across the room till we were in front of glass doors. The man slid the door open and led us onto the balcony that overlooked the park across the street.

There was a small table with two chairs on the tiny balcony. He motioned for us to sit down, and with a strong Italian accent and broken English, he struggled to speak to me, "Friend of Marky, friend of mine. Please, enjoy." He was such a cute man, short, with full grey hair that was neatly brushed back. He wore a black t-shirt tucked into his black pants with his belly overlapping his belt. He also wore a gold chain necklace.

I smiled at his friendliness. "Thank you." He nodded with a huge grin and headed out the door.

"He's a very nice man." I turned my attention to Marcus whose stare was gentle and passionate.

"He was good friends with my grandfather. My dad used to bring me and my brother here all the time as kids. I haven't been here in a long time, and since I was in the area, I figured it would be nice to visit."

The older man returned with laminated menus and a pitcher of water. He poured water into our empty glasses. He asked a question, and Marcus looked at me, "Would you like some wine?" I shook my head rather too quickly. It made him laugh, knowing that I consumed enough alcohol last night to last me an entire week. He responded to the man who then left.

I glanced down at the menu. Thankfully everything was printed in English.

My stomach growled. I looked up at Marcus, wondering if he noticed. Surprisingly he wasn't staring at the menu; he was staring at me. It felt *strange*. "Do you know what you want?"

Wetting his lips seductively just like in my dream, he answered, but something told me he wanted something more than his meal. "I always order the Pesto italiano pasta."

Looking down at the menu and back at him, I tried to pretend his stare didn't faze me. "Oh, do you recommend anything for me?"

He slightly tilted his head. "I recommend the lasagna or the eggplant parmesan." *Oh God,* he was adorable with his crooked grin; suddenly I was hungry for him and not food.

What was wrong with me!

Bless the older man's soul when he interrupted my sensual thoughts. He placed before us two plates of salad, a basket of bread with a side dish of olive oil, and some type of seasoning. The man ran off again. I grabbed my fork and dug into the salad, not waiting for Marcus to go first. I was too hungry to be polite and not dig in.

We sat in silence as we ate our salads. Halfway through, I looked up at him, and he was staring at me again. "Is there something wrong? Every time I look at you, it feels like you've been staring at me the entire time."

"I have." He grabbed his glass and sipped his water, not taking his eyes off me.

"Why? Is there something on my face?" I picked up a napkin to wipe my lips.

"No." He chuckled. "I like staring at you. You're a beautiful woman, so it's hard not to stare." My stomach fluttered. Underneath the table, I pinched my hand to see if this were real or a dream. Nope, I felt the sting against my flesh; this was definitely real.

"Thank you," I whispered. To distract myself, I grabbed a piece of warm bread and dipped it into the olive oil. I took a bite; oh it was good. I took another bite. When I looked up, he was smiling at me. "What?"

"Do you want to talk about what happened last night? Maybe you can relax after we do." I stopped chewing. *What?* Oh no, something bad happened, I must have slept with him and don't even remember. *What a waste!*

Looking away nervously, I whispered, "What happened last night?" Turning my head, I tried to distract myself by admiring the trees in the park.

I could hear him adjust his body in the seat. "Well, for starters, we didn't sleep with each other." My eyes snapped to his.

"Oh thank God!" I cried in relief.

"But you wanted to; you asked me too."

"You're kidding, right?"

His all-white, perfect-toothed grin engulfed his face. "No, you were completely hammered last night. I helped you up the stairs and into your room. When we entered your room, you asked me to help you out of your dress. You were complaining about how tight it was, so I unzipped it for you. You sat down on the edge of the bed, so I could take your shoes off. After I did, you ran your fingers through my hair, saying how soft it was. You also mentioned how much you thought my lips were sexy." He smiled, remembering my foolishness. I wished I could fly away, maybe even make a clear escape by throwing myself off of the balcony, but I was too stunned to move, to even speak.

He continued, "You tried to kiss me, but I didn't want to kiss you like that. So I pulled away. You were very angry at the rejection. I remember a few curses, and then you stomped over to your drawer, pulled something out, and tossed it to the side of your bed. I'm not sure what it was. You then you threw yourself in bed. You lay there and fell asleep. I covered you with the blanket, and then I left."

Embarrassed by his brutally honest account of last night's events, I couldn't look at him. I also had the feeling he was just being polite and pretended not to know what I took out of my drawer. Lowering my head, I focused on my fidgeting fingers.

I could feel the heat of his stare, but I didn't dare to look up. "I apologize for my behavior last night. Please know that's not me. I don't even drink liquor." Nervously laughing once, I continued to mumble. "I'm more of a wine person. Last night was just a celebration of the start of summer break. I assure you it will never happen again." My voice was so low I'm not sure it was audible.

Bravely I peeked up through my long lashes, catching when his smile faded.

"I hope that's not true. See I wanted to kiss you last night, *very* badly, but not while you were incapable of remembering it." He bit his lip and then continued, "I want to get to know you better, if that's okay with you? I want to know about you, where you're from, your family, everything." He paused for a mere second. "For some unexplained reason, I'm drawn to you, and I can't stop thinking about you. All day at work today during a conference call and during my deposition, you were the only thing on my mind." His lips curled into a crooked smile.

Speechless, I opened my mouth to say something but couldn't find the right words, so I closed it. I thought he wasn't interested, especially the way he acted last night. "So what are you saying exactly?"

CHAPTER FOUR

"I want to date," Marcus said. "See where it goes. I've *never* dated before, and I don't know how it works, but you're the kind of girl that a man should treat like a woman, not as a one-night stand."

Baffled by this entire conversation, I blurted out the first thing that came to mind. "You've never been in a relationship before?"

His eyes grew serious. "I never had *time* for a serious relationship."

Glaring at him, I leaned in on the table. "But you have time to date *me*?"

His expression relaxed. "I'll *make* the time for you, to get to know you better."

I said everything in one quick breath as I always do when I'm mad or nervous, "And what if I'm not the woman you think I am? What if one of us takes this more seriously than the other? One of us could end up hurt. What if I get the externship position at your firm? How will people look at us, at me? How will it interfere with my position if it doesn't work out with us? I don't know if I can deal with all of that." I was extremely nervous.

Laughing once, he dragged his hand through his hair, thinking before speaking. "Stop over-thinking every little outcome. But to answer your questions, *yes* you're exactly what I thought. *No one* will end up hurt. You *will* have the extern position; there's no question about that. Don't worry about what others may think. If, *and* I mean *if,* it doesn't work out between us, your position will remain; your work life and personal life are two separate issues."

"Not when your work and personal life are combined. I don't know, Marcus. I've seen two separate sides of you so far. Last night you seemed angry and quite the asshole." He raised an eyebrow. "*Sorry*...and then today you seem to be polite and a gentleman."

Relaxing his shoulders, he leaned into the table, folding his hands. "Last night my anger was not directed towards you; I was angry at Jeremy for leaving you behind. He was willing to allow you to take a cab alone at that hour. It upset me; that's all. I apologize if I offended you in any way."

I stared at him for what seemed like a long time, trying to think this through. We didn't say anything for a few seconds, just stared at each other. In less than twenty-four hours everything had changed. He was a very handsome man but a busy man as he himself said. What did he want from me? Why me? Fortunately, the older man reappeared, ready to take our order, Marcus gave him our selections, and he rushed away.

"Can I think about it?" I needed a clear mind to analyze this on my own time, not while he was staring at me with those big brown eyes.

"Of course." Leaning closer, he studied me. "How about we change the subject? Where are you from, Mia? I can tell you're not from Boston from your accent."

I giggled. "*My* accent? I'm from Philly, and we Philadelphians do not have accents, whereas Boston natives do."

He shook his head, smiling. "How long have you been in Boston? Did you come here for Harvard Law, or were you living here prior to your attendance at the university?"

Why was he so formal? I'm not on a damn interview, or maybe this is the interview!

"I moved here with my brother when I was fourteen years old. He was ten years older than me and took care of me after our father passed away. It was emotional for us, so we left. He was hired as a detective, and he purchased a home here and took care of me." I took a sip of water to distract myself for a moment. I didn't want to cry. It was still too soon; every time I talked about my brother I'd get a little emotional.

"Sorry to hear about your loss. If you don't mind my asking, how did your father pass?"

Taking a long gulp of water before answering, I shifted in my seat. "He was a Philly cop. He was shot and killed while responding to a robbery at a local gas station. When he appeared on the scene, he was alone. He phoned in on the radio, letting them know it looked clear and that he was going in to question the clerk. But when he entered, the robber was still there: a nineteen-year-old boy. He was startled when he saw my father in uniform, and his initial reaction was to pull the trigger."

He raised his eyebrows, not expecting that answer. "Wow, I'm so sorry to hear that." The atmosphere between us became too serious. This was a subject I liked to avoid when people asked, because no one could understand why I had no one in my life. I had told these stories a few times before, but that time it felt different. I couldn't quite explain why.

"Your mother?" he continued to question.

Clearing my throat, I thought to change the attention onto him, but I caved in. "I don't know who my mother is. After giving birth to me, she left my father, leaving my brother and me in his care. I'd heard different stories, but the main one was that she suffered from depression and couldn't deal with being a parent, *and,* while on the subject, I don't know anyone from my mother's side of the family as well. My father was an only child. His father passed when he was young, and my grandmother died when I was nine of breast cancer.

"So after my father passed, it was just my brother and I. When my brother died in October, I took it very hard." I stopped myself and tried to make a joke out of my self-pettiness. "Well, I guess I'm a loner, all by myself." I nervously giggled, taking another sip of water, wishing I'd ordered that wine instead.

His eyes widened in shock. I thought that maybe he'd see that I was emotionally messed up and rethink this getting-to-know-me-better bit. "Your brother passed too?"

"Yes, *but* that's a subject I rather not discuss. It's been a few months since his death, and I'm still taking it very hard." He nodded in response, knowing not to touch that subject anymore. I managed to hold back my tears when talking about my brother, a first since his passing. "So you mentioned a brother. Is he older? Younger?" I asked, trying to steer the conversation away from me.

He squirmed in his seat now that the tables were turned. "Uh, yeah, he's older but not by much, by four years; he's thirty-three. Uh, it was just he and I growing up. We have a close relationship. When my father passed, I was just beginning my freshman year in high school. My mother took it very hard and forced my brother and me to have a good relationship. At that time, we hated each other." He laughed, thinking back. "It worked. I guess mothers know best, huh?"

I shrugged my shoulders; I wouldn't know. "Oh, sorry, I didn't mean—," he said.

"Don't worry about it. You know, I think I will have that wine."

"Yes, I agree." He called for the older man.

After a couple glasses of wine, we forgot about the touchy subjects and discussed other things, such as Marcus taking over the firm from his brother who began it all. His brother quit practicing law and started a private company. We didn't discuss this company much. He also mentioned how within a year after taking over the firm, he managed to double the size and clientele and tripled the profit.

We also talked about Harvard, which he also attended. He remembered Professor Johnson as his instructor. He made me feel a little more comfortable when he explained that Professor Johnson was attached to him and made similar comments about one day him being bigger than the average attorney. To know that Professor Johnson had an eye for knowing who would succeed made me feel at ease. Marcus also translated between Mr. Giuseppe and me, and I grew more fond of the old man the more we talked and laughed throughout the evening.

Pushing my plate aside and wiping my face with a cloth, I felt overstuffed. "Ugh, if I eat or drink anything else, my stomach is going to explode." I laughed and Marcus joined in.

"Yeah, me too."

We sat and talked a little before Mr. Giuseppe cleared our table. Marcus asked for the check, but the old man refused to take any money. He said that Marcus was family, and he wouldn't take no for an answer. Marcus told him he'd leave a tip for the cook, and Mr. Giuseppe approved. We rose from our chairs, and I watched as Marcus pulled out his wallet, opening the flap and revealing several hundred-dollar bills. He placed three of the bills on the table, and we left. It was darker out, but the lights from the park made it feel earlier than it really was.

"Would you like to walk through the park? I know it's a longer way to get you back home, but I figured we could walk off what we just ate, and I can spend some more time with you." He truly had the most beautiful smile I'd ever seen.

Smiling at him, I said, "I would actually like that." We walked side by side to cross the street. We entered the empty park. A nice breeze gave me a slight chill, and he took off his jacket and wrapped it around me. I thought it was such a sweet gesture. He leaned closer and placed his arm around my shoulder. I was close enough to smell his cologne; it was a sweet smell mixed with his own glorious body's scent. It was delicious. I leaned my head against the side of his chest, and we continued to stroll through the park.

We didn't say anything, just enjoyed each other's company. I was comforted by his scent and his strong grip around me. I could breathe his aroma all day and not get tired of that sweet smell. My thoughts began to turn on me as I imagined him ripping my clothes off and laying his naked body on top of mine. It gave me the chills. I shivered at the delicious thought, and he rubbed his palm against my arm to warm me. If he only knew what caused me to shiver ...

When we reached the front of my building, I surprisingly didn't want to go in. I enjoyed a beautiful night with Marcus, and he was leaving. I'd be alone, thinking of him in my dreams. He stood in front of me, and I couldn't help but move in closer and inhale his scent. "You smell so good," I whispered, unable to control my thoughts.

He cupped my cheek with his hand and lifted my face till our eyes met—his dark brown eyes to my emerald green. His thumb gently rubbed against my cheek. "Your eyes are so beautiful; you're beautiful," he whispered back. "Promise me you'll think about what I said about us spending more time together." I nodded while my eyes remained locked to his.

His eyes danced along my face, as if admiring me. Then without a moment's notice, he ducked his head, tilting it to the right. He was going to kiss me. I could feel the electricity going through my veins, and he hadn't even touched me yet.

I closed my eyes, anticipating his mouth. My heart raced as I felt them: his soft warm lips against mine. I felt his mouth open, and he slid his tongue into mine. He was gentle, sucking on my bottom lip and returning his tongue back inside in soft circular motions. I wanted more, so I deepened the kiss, forcing my tongue in as far as I could go. He moaned and pulled my hips to his.

I dragged my fingers through his soft, thick hair and tugged lightly. He groaned again, and I felt his erection pressing against my body. Just thinking that my kiss could have that effect on him made me want him more. I rose on my tiptoes, so I could further the kiss.

His left hand was at my waist, pressing me against him, and his right hand was in my hair, his fingers wrestling through my ponytail.

His mouth tasted of wine and salt, and I craved him. I'd never wanted a man so much. I would've taken him right there in the middle of the sidewalk if I didn't care that others were watching. I was lost in his spell, and at that moment I *didn't* care if anyone watched.

He broke from the kiss first at the sound of the door closing behind us. I looked up, and there was my third-floor neighbor. I scowled at the old witch, disliking her even more for interrupting my moment.

She walked down the stairs and glanced at us suspiciously. Marcus gave her a polite nod, and I shot an annoyed smirk at her. She continued down the street, walking her pug. I touched my lips to calm the soreness of the kiss. Once my neighbor was out of earshot, he snapped back in my direction with intense eyes. "*Mia,*" he breathed. I tried to catch my breath as well.

As if I needed any more distractions, I felt my phone vibrate against my back pocket. I took it out to see a text from Jeremy.

Jeremy (10:22pm): Where are you?

Me (10:23pm): On my way up.

Shoving the phone back in my pocket, I sighed heavily. "I have to go." He nodded. I was midway through shrugging his jacket off when he grabbed my arm to stop me.

"Keep it, that way you can have my scent near you, and hopefully it will make the decision about us easier for you." He flashed that dimple and gorgeous smile I was beginning to love and leaned down to plant a small kiss on my forehead. Without another word, he strode to his car which was parked only a few feet away. I watched him get in before I entered the building. *What* just happened?

Hopefully it was dark enough that he couldn't see from the rear-view mirror my stupid, girly, ear-to-ear grin. He tasted so good, his lips were so soft, and he was such a great kisser. I was sure I'd replay that kiss in my mind the rest of the night. Was that his plan to kiss me so passionately that I had no choice but to want more? Well it worked. What was I supposed to do? He gave me the best kiss I'd ever had and then left me deprived.

After taking a few moments to calm my racing heart, I entered my apartment with thoughts of Marcus, but they were instantly placed on standby. The brunette from the club last night startled me as she peeked from over the open refrigerator door. She straightened and slowly closed the fridge. She didn't move, and her expression was one of a deer in the headlights. Jeremy rushed out his bedroom door and nodded, which meant it was my cue.

"What the fuck is going on here!" I yelled, throwing my clutch and Marcus' jacket on the dining room table.

"Please, baby, let me explain." Jeremy was holding his hands up to stop my movement.

"Oh don't 'baby' me, who the fuck is this?" I dramatically turned my body and waved my arm in her direction. She was shocked and confused; her eyes went from Jeremy and to me and back several times. The realization that she was naked came to her, so she quickly covered her breasts with her arms.

"Uh, you ... You have a girlfriend?" she stuttered at Jeremy.

"Try fiancée, sweetie! You have ten seconds to throw your shit on and get the fuck out of my apartment!" I glared at her. She didn't move, and I placed my hand on my hip. "NOW!" She ran to Jeremy's room and back out, throwing her dress over her head. Rushing by me, she grabbed her purse and phone from the dining room table and hurried out the door barefoot, not saying a word or apologizing. I looked at Jeremy and rolled my eyes. He ran over to me, kissing both of my cheeks.

"You are a true talent, my dear Mia!" He placed his arms around my shoulders and led me to the sofa. I lay back and rested my head against the arm of the couch with my legs thrown across his thighs.

"I take it she wasn't good enough for you?" I asked, knowing the answer. Jeremy had a habit of mixing me up in his sex life. If a female became *too* clingy, he was instantly turned off. It all started a year ago when he brought home a girl who wouldn't leave; he'd run into my bedroom, begging me to get her out. Ever since it'd become a ritual: he would nod, and I'd know he wanted her out. If he immediately introduced us, then I'd know he wanted more time with her. I knew it was disgusting, and it was even worse that I played along, but he was my best friend. He was my *only* friend.

He slapped my thigh, "You have no idea! The minute we were done, she started comparing our facial features and told me how cute our babies would be. G*eez,* can I ever find a non-psychotic female?"

"You're a pig!" He truly was disgusting! I threw my arms over my head.

"Whatever, I couldn't wait for you to get home. You were out pretty long. Were you with DeLuca the entire time?" He reached for the remote and turned the TV on.

"Yeah, we had dinner at a little Italian restaurant called Romano's. Have you heard of it? It's literally one block away from the university." Desperately trying to avoid questions about Marcus and me, I thought the subject of the restaurant would steer us away from it.

"Uh, yeah, I walked past it a few times. I thought it was closed though; I've never seen anyone go in and out of that place." He flicked through the channels until a comedy, The Hangover, was showing. We didn't say anything after that and just enjoyed each other's company while laughing at each scene.

Once it was over, I slowly moved off the couch, trying to avoid waking Jeremy from his sleep. Grabbing my clutch and Marcus' jacket from the table, I entered my room.

After changing into boy shorts and a tank top, I was finally nestled in my comfy bed. I was pulling my phone out of my bag to charge it when I noticed two text messages. Both were from Marcus: one an hour ago and one less than five minutes ago. Before I opened the text messages, it took me a few seconds to realize that he must have programmed his number into my phone while at work. Looking at the text, I couldn't help the huge grin on my face.

Marcus (10:40pm): U were on my mind all day, n u will surely be on my mind all night. TY for a lovely evening and a kiss I will never forget.

Marcus (11:50pm): Sweet dreams, baby.

I waited before responding, not able to wipe the smile off my face. I wanted to give him something to think about all night.

Me (11:53pm): I will surely have sweet *wet* dreams of that kiss all night.

Marcus (11:53pm): You're killing me.

Me (11:54pm): Good night, Marcus ☺

Marcus (11:55pm): Good night, Mia.

****

Last night was the best sleep of my life. Dreaming of Marcus' lips, body, and scent put me at ease. Then the thought that I could have it all in reality put me in a greater mood. I woke up, sang in the shower, and made breakfast. I also placed a plate of pancakes, eggs, and bacon for Jeremy in the microwave and headed out the door to meet Professor Johnson to go over the interview questions. It was a beautiful day out, so I decided to walk instead of drive. The university was only a fifteen-minute walk away. The entire stroll he was on my mind. I couldn't remember the last time I'd woken up this happy. It was early, but I decided to send him a text anyway.

Me (8:35am): G.M., I slept very well last night. I hope you did as well? ☺

Before entering Harvard's building, I switched my phone to vibrate mode and shoved it in my back pocket. I headed for Professor Johnson's office. His door was open. When I walked in, he was sipping on coffee and reviewing the newspaper. He popped his head up at the sound of my footsteps and smiled. Taking the seat in front of his desk, I returned his gesture with a brighter smile than usual. "So Mia, are you ready for this interview tomorrow?" He placed the paper down and took another sip of coffee before placing the mug on top of his desk.

"Ah, yeah, I think I'm ready, but it's nice to go over these interview questions. I appreciate you taking the time to go over this with me, Professor."

Almost an hour later, Professor Johnson went over my resume, asked a few questions, and quizzed me on the firm. I didn't know much about Marcus DeLuca himself, just what was in a small biography written on the firm's website. Johnson said it would be smart to do some research on him as he always does research on the owner or CEO of the company he interviews with.

Having that extra knowledge of charities he had sponsored or awards he'd received, gave it an extra touch. I thought it would be a good idea for me *personally* as well. I thanked Professor Johnson again before heading out the door and wishing him a happy summer.

Reaching for my phone, I knew I had messages because it had vibrated against my behind during my meeting. I had three messages: two from Marcus and one from Jeremy.

Marcus (8:40am): GM Beautiful. I slept well thank you.

Jeremy (9:10am): Thanks for the breakfast, Mia, you're the best. Luv ya ;)

Marcus (9:22am): Have lunch with me today. I can send a driver to ur place. I have to see u.

I quickly respond to Jeremy with a simple "you're welcome," and then I replied to Marcus.

Me (9:34am): Lunch sounds great, let me know where to meet u, I can drive there.

Marcus (9:35am): You choose.

Me (9:36am): Marcie's at noon? I love that place.

Marcus (9:37am): Sounds good to me. Looking forward to seeing that beautiful face.

Me (9:38am): ☺

CHAPTER FIVE

"Good morning, my lovely friend." I jumped with delight on the small armchair located at the corner of the living room, giving me a view of Jeremy and the entire apartment behind him. He was unknowingly tracing his tongue along his bottom lip, concentrating on a game that he was playing on his game console. He quickly glanced at me and then back at the big screen. "You're in a good mood," he said while thumbing the controller. "What do you have planned for today?" he asked.

Jeremy and I had a very close relationship, and we hardly kept any secrets from one another, but I decided to keep this Marcus thing from him just because I didn't know where it was going yet. "Oh, I'm meeting a friend for lunch downtown and maybe do some shopping afterwards down there while I'm at it." I watched the screen and saw a Batman and Joker fighting each other. I wasn't certain which one he was because there were other comic book characters fighting in the background. I shook my head.

His character died, so he placed the controller down waiting for a new game to reboot. He eyed me suspiciously. "Friend? What friend?"

Shit, I'd forgotten we have mutual friends and that I didn't hang out with anyone except with him. I slightly caved in. "*Okay,* so I met this guy, and we are just going out for lunch, that's all." He wasn't buying it; adjusting his body on the couch, he was now facing my direction with an amused grin.

"What's this guy's name?"

I looked away because I couldn't stare him in the eye. I'm the worst liar. "I rather not say because we're just friends getting to know one another." Biting my bottom lip, I bravely looked at him, hoping he'd leave it at that.

He frowned. "Is it Marcus?" His expression shocked me.

"No! It's not, and why did you say it like *that*?" I thought he and Marcus were friends.

"He's a cool guy and all but wouldn't be good for you." He faced the flat screen to restart his game.

"Not that I care because it's *not* Marcus, but if it were, why wouldn't he be good for me?" The question was delivered a little harsher than I expected. You could feel the tension building between us. He knew something and didn't want to say, but I was nosy and would continue drilling until I collected my information.

My tone of voice set him off. His ears were bright red, and he seemed to be biting his tongue. I knew that look: the steam was building, so he'd blow up pretty soon if I kept pushing his buttons, but didn't care. I stood from the chair and crossed my arms, giving him a nasty stare. "It is Marcus, so what!" That did it. He got up, throwing the controller on the couch.

"Jesus Christ, Mia! Did you fuck him?" His cheeks turned the same fire-engine red as his ears.

What the hell was his problem? I gripped my hip with my one hand and waved my other at him like he was a five-year old. "That is none of your business!" I stormed to my room and slammed the door. The nerve of him! Did I *fuck* him? *Why* was he so against Marcus? I paced back and forth in my bedroom to calm my nerves.

The door swung open, and Jeremy was standing by the doorway irate.

"First of all, it is my business because you're my *friend* and I don't want to see you hurt. Second, have you thought about the rest of the summer when you're working for him and how it would affect *you*? Third, I *highly* recommend you do some research on him and see the *stuff* that he's into, because, so help me God, Mia, if you get hurt in any way and I find out that he was involved, there's no telling what I would do." He slammed the door behind him and left me in the room speechless by his outburst.

What did Jeremy mean, "if I'm hurt in any way," and what's this research thing about? What kind of stuff is Marcus into that could possibly harm me? My mind was racing, and I had so many doubts. This was what I didn't want to happen, and yet a kiss from him had made me weak. There I was getting ready to meet him for lunch while my best friend was angry with me in the other room.

I threw myself onto the bed, trying to go over the past few days. My friendship wasn't worth losing. What if Jeremy were right? Maybe I would get hurt in the end. Was Jeremy jealous or just being a concerned friend? I had so many unanswered questions. There was only one way some of these blank holes could be filled: Google. Jumping off my bed and slamming into the chair, I started up my laptop.

There were lots of articles on Marcus DeLuca: on his firm, his achievements, his charities, and his successful verdicts on many criminal cases, mainly involving the mafia. I looked at many websites and spent twenty minutes trying to find something until the headline of one Boston newspaper caught my attention. It was short and to the point.

JIMMIE DELUCA QUESTIONED ON
MAFIA DRUG DEAL

21 December 2011

Written by Samantha Jones

Jimmie DeLuca was taken in for questioning Monday morning regarding a drug deal at a local warehouse in Midtown Center City. For many years, there have been allegations that the DeLuca brothers, Jimmie and Marcus DeLuca, were and still are involved with the illegal acts of the Sorrento Mafia Family. Sources close to the brothers have denied all allegations, and there has been no evidence to charge them with any crimes.

Shortly after Jimmie DeLuca was taken into Boston Police headquarters, his younger brother Marcus DeLuca came to the rescue as his

attorney. The detectives had
no   evidence   to   arrest
Jimmie, and released him,
not even ten minutes after
Marcus DeLuca arrived.

Anyone who knows the DeLuca
brothers knows that Marcus
took over his brother's firm
five   years   ago.   When   he
became   involved   with   the
firm, he began to represent
the   Sorrento   family   and
cleared   their   names   from
many   accusations   involving
drug   deals,   money
laundering, as well as gun
trafficking.

Whether   these   accusations
against the DeLuca brothers
are   true   or   not,   it   does
raise one question: What is
their   true   involvement   with
the Sorrento family?

End of Article. SJ

I continued to research and found similar articles but with
Marcus brought in for questioning a few times. After researching for
what seemed like forever, I blankly stared at the monitor for a while,
trying to wrap my head around what I'd just read. Was this what
Jeremy meant? There was nothing incriminating about it. They were
taken in for questioning, but they were never charged with a crime.

I'd heard that the Sorrentos were very dangerous and definitely
not a force to be reckoned with. I'd heard stories about murders,
corrupt cops, and drug deals involving the Sorrentos and that anyone
who crossed their path was either family or an enemy. In the Italian
mob, there are no friends: you're considered family even if you

aren't blood related. The thought that Marcus could be involved made my stomach turn.

Though growing up with a cop as a father and a detective as a brother, I knew that the media portrayed things as worse than they really were.

I was stuck. Should I believe the media, or would hearing him out be a better idea? Should I cancel this lunch date, or go and flat-out tell him what I read? Due to the fact that I was very pushy and needed information to make a decision on anything involving my life, I decided to meet him for lunch and ask all the questions that I needed. One thing I'm grateful for is that I can read people very well, courtesy of my brother. If it so happened that I felt he wasn't trustworthy, I'd walk away.

I took a shower and threw on a navy blue maxi dress, beige flip-flops, and a matching messenger bag. My hair was in a low ponytail, and I accessorized with gold hoop earrings and a long gold necklace with a horseshoe charm. It was my favorite piece of jewelry. Michael bought it for my twenty-fourth birthday last October before he passed away.

Every time I wore it, I felt like he was nearby, protecting me. I glanced in the mirror, looking at my reflection. My big green eyes filled, but I held back my tears, not wanting to ruin my makeup. I held the horseshoe up and pressed the charm against my lips. Giving it a kiss, I whispered a small prayer for him to protect me always.

Walking out of my bedroom, I didn't see Jeremy anywhere. He had to be in his room unless he left while I was taking a shower. I felt terrible about our fight and refused to leave the apartment until we made up. We never fought, ever.

I knocked on the door, and since he didn't answer, I pushed it open. He was lying in bed with his eyes closed, listening to music. I walked over to him. He must have sensed me because his eyes popped opened. Sliding in next to him, I placed my head on his chest; he wrapped his arm around me after he took off his earphones. "I'm sorry, Jeremy. I don't want to fight like that ever again." I tightened my arm around his chest.

Sighing, he squeezed me a little tighter. "I'm sorry too, Mia; I had no right to go off like that. It will never happen again. I promise. He's a good guy ... I've just heard stories about him; that's all. Who am I to judge?" He laughed once and placed a kiss on the top of my head.

"Thank you, and just so you know, I didn't have sex with him. I just led you to believe it to get you mad." I nervously peeked up at him.

"I knew you didn't; I was mad that you lied to my face. By the way, you're a terrible liar." I laughed and he joined in. We said our goodbyes, and I went out the door ready to question DeLuca.

Relieved to find street parking, I pulled into a spot and dug for change to place in the meter. After I scrounged three dollars in quarters and dimes, there was plenty of time for lunch and light shopping. Admiring the midtown of Boston had never bored me with so many successful individuals wandering around in their business attire. They seem to move at a fast pace, rushing to a busy work schedule. Tourists wandered at a slower pace taking pictures by the Charles River and other historical sites.

I reminded myself that one day that would be me: an up-and-coming attorney running around and busting my ass until I made partner at a top firm. I let out a deep breath, knowing it would all be worth it in the end. I would have to sacrifice having fun and being spontaneous until I was at the top of my career. Hey, I'd done that so far in my life to be at the top of my class, what were a few more years?

Reaching the building, I pulled the door handle; it wouldn't budge. I shook it a few more times, nothing. I was stunned when I finally saw an OUT OF BUSINESS sign on the door. Great, what was I supposed to do now? Quickly searching for my phone, I dialed Marcus' number. He picked up instantly. "Hello, beautiful."

"Uh, hi, uh I'm standing in front of a closed Marcie's." I giggled.

"Yeah, I found that out earlier. I had my assistant make reservations at another restaurant if you don't mind?"

"Okay, where shall I meet you?"

"Well, if you turn around you will see a tall, well–dressed, and handsome young man walking in your direction." He laughed. I turned and spotted him instantly. He was right: he was sexier than I could've ever imagined. He wore an all-black, high-end suit, fitted perfectly against his clearly fit body. The light, salmon-colored shirt and matching silk tie looked perfect against his tan complexion.

Even though most men would not dare to wear pink, there was something about a man who could pull it off. Marcus DeLuca could definitely pull it off. Everything about him screamed masculine, powerful, and bold from the roots of his hair down to the stride of his walk.

When he reached me, his eyes were on mine with a wide smile. He pulled me into an embrace and held me. I hugged him back, surprised by his warm, public display of affection. He pulled away and planted a small but soft kiss on my lips. "You look very beautiful, Mia." Still stunned, I whispered, "You too." His brows rose with humor. "Shall we eat?" he asked. I responded with a simple nod, unable to say anything else.

I nervously asked him how his morning was as we headed towards the restaurant. He went on about a boring conference call with a judge, but my mind was wrapped around how we walked side by side with his arms around my shoulder. Shamelessly I liked the feeling. It was odd, but it felt intimate: something I wasn't used to. I'd only known him for a couple days; I had no idea who this man was. Yet I had this connection with him that I couldn't describe. Then I thought of Jeremy and the articles, and I pulled away. I could tell by his expression that he knew I felt uncomfortable, so he kept his arms at his side for the remainder of the walk and continued with his discussion.

After the longest fifteen minutes I'd ever endured, we entered the restaurant. Of course it was a five-star place. We were immediately seated in a private booth. I settled in my seat across from him. Everything about him was irresistible. My eyes met his, and I lowered my glance to his lips: those lips that he teased me with last night, making me want him, allowing me to fall in a trance I couldn't control. I had to get to the bottom of things before I got lost in him again.

"We need to talk. I have a few questions for you." I made it a point to sound stern.

He waved his hand before him. "By all means, Mia, ask away. I mean it, whatever you want. Don't hold back."

I scowled at him suspiciously, but before I could begin my interrogation, we were greeted by a waitress I recognized. She saw me, and her eyes widened with a smile. "Hi, Mia, how are you? What are you doing here?" She was overly ecstatic.

"Ah, hi, Melanie, I'm here with a friend. Marcus, this is Melanie; we had a few classes together in undergrad." Marcus politely shook her hand; she flushed when she noticed him. She stuttered and mumbled something, but it wasn't clear enough for me to understand. She took our drink order and hurried away uneasily.

I looked back at Marcus once she was gone. "So you were saying?" He leaned into the table, folding his hands before him patiently waiting.

"Okay, I'm going to just get to the point. What is your connection with the Sorrento family?"

"It's strictly an attorney-client relationship," he stated nonchalantly and a little too quickly—maybe even a little too rehearsed.

My stare grew narrow as I studied him. "So all the allegations about you and your brother being involved in illegal acts with the Sorrentos are false?"

His face turned serious. "If I tell you that, then I'll have to kill you." My mouth dropped open in horror. "*Jesus*, Mia, lighten up; it was a joke. Yes, all of it is false." He laughed. I didn't find it funny.

Mmmh, the questioning began. "Why do you want to date me? I mean you can obviously snap your fingers and have any woman you want. I just don't get it."

Melanie came over with our drinks and placed them before us with shaky hands. Marcus had ordered water and I'd ordered wine. He had known me for three days, and each day I'd been drinking. Surely he must have thought I was an alcoholic by then. We quickly chose something from the menu, and she hurried off.

"I like you," he simply answered while taking a sip of his water.

"You don't *know* me, what could you possibly *like*?"

He leaned in closer and his smile faded. His eyebrows creased together, and his eyes grew serious. "That night in the club when I saw you sitting there alone, I knew you were out of your element. You looked so innocent and pure. Then when I walked over and saw you up close and you looked up at me with those long lashes and beautiful eyes, it was like a breath of fresh air. You're something I've needed for a very long time. You seemed honest and humble."

He reached over, placing the palm of his hand on top of mine. "You see, Mia, for a long time I haven't had anything like that: honesty, innocence, and pureness. After seeing it through your eyes,

I never wanted or needed it more in my life. Then when I took you home that night, after placing the covers over you, you looked up at me and said something like you were used to being alone. Then your eyes watered, but you held back the tears. Your eyes were filled with sorrow, sadness, and emptiness. I thought to myself, *How could she be this sad?* I wanted to lie down next to you, hold you, and take away all your pain."

My mind was scrambling to find the right thing to say, but I couldn't think of anything. I was breathless, unable to think or speak. What do you say to that? He held my hand a moment longer, and then I retrieved it and put it in my lap, but he didn't move. "Marcus, I am an honest person, yes, but I am not innocent or pure. I'm *emotionally* messed up. Do you understand that?"

"Please just give me a chance. I don't know what it's like to date, but I want to try."

Looking away for a moment, I tried to focus on anything but those eyes. "My heart is telling me to give you a chance, but my head is telling me that you're dangerous and I'll end up hurt." I finally met his eyes again.

He momentarily looked down as if there were some truth to what I said. "I wouldn't hurt you, Mia." Then his sincere eyes stared back into mine. It took me a few minutes to process those words. I thought of how I'd felt with him the night before. This could work. I just couldn't get emotionally involved, so if it didn't work out, I could just simply walk away.

Taking a deep breath, I nodded my head. "Okay, I'll give whatever this is a shot." A relieved grin spread across his face.

Melanie brought out our hot meals, and we dug right in. The more I thought of Marcus and me as a potential item, the better I felt. I didn't know where it would go, but for the last few years, I'd held back and sacrificed so much. Maybe I should do this for me. I deserved to have a little fun even if it was just a summer fling. I would just have to stay emotionally shut down. I couldn't fall for him, or I'd never be able to live it down.

Marcus interrupted my thoughts, "What are you doing this weekend?"

"Ah, I really don't have any plans. Why?"

"Come away with me for the weekend. I have a shore house in the Bahamas. It's on a private beach. We can have the entire weekend to spend time with each other—get to know each other better. We can leave tomorrow morning."

Surprised by his boldness, I took a minute to let what he said sink in. "Marcus, I don't know; isn't it too soon to go away somewhere with each other?"

"No, I have a six-bedroom shore house. You can sleep in a room on a different floor from me with the doors locked if that will make you feel better." He joked.

"I can't. I have my interview tomorrow." I shrugged apologetically.

His smile returned. "It's done, I told Lisa that I met you at Club21 and that I gave you the interview already. She was shocked, of course, but you start Monday morning." He reached for my hand. "Come on, Mia, the moment you feel uncomfortable I will drive you to the airport myself." He gave me a reassuring smile, flashing that adorable dimple.

I couldn't believe I was considering this. "Okay, what time should I be ready?"

He sat back in his chair with his shoulders straight and a sign of triumph in his eyes. "The plane leaves at 10 a.m. I'll pick you up at 9 a.m."

"Don't we have to be at the airport two hours before the plane departs and go through baggage claim and security?"

He slightly tilted his head amused. "My firm has a private plane; we don't have to go through all that hassle."

Of course, he had a private plane! I wanted to roll my eyes but refrained from doing so. Instead I settled for a simple nod. The rest of the lunch ended pretty well. I tried to pay for it, but he refused. I didn't argue with him; he was too aggressive about it and shoved his credit card at Melanie before I could reach for my bag.

Before we went our separate ways, he embraced me in a hug; this time I hugged back and kissed him on the cheek. I figured I should play with him and have a little fun. "I'm off to do some shopping. After all I have to make myself simply irresistible for this weekend." I blew him a kiss and walked away.

I didn't turn when I heard him yell. "You're killing me, Mia!" I giggled.

I had an hour to spare and went to a few shops. I purchased a couple bikinis, dresses, and lingerie. Even though I wasn't sure if I'd be using any of them, I thought having a few sexy undies wouldn't hurt. Right? Reaching my car with seconds to spare before the meter ran out, I jumped in and noticed an officer a foot away. I quickly pulled out and decided to go to the spa. I was in a desperate need of a manicure, pedicure, and wax.

****

Feeling the massage chair vibrate against my back and thighs was very soothing. Every girl should enjoy a spa day at least twice a month. I rested my head back as my feet were scrubbed and massaged and my toenails polished with a bright pink color. After my nails were done, I walked back to the waxing station. Embarrassed by my lack of grooming, I lay there.

Susi lifted her head from between my legs; her eyes were filled with fear *or* shock. I wasn't sure which one. "When you last time wax?" I shrugged apologetically. She waved her finger. "Tsk, Tsk, Tsk. You no let grow like this, understand?" I nodded and threw my head back humiliated. Okay, so I'd neglected my sacred place, but no one had seen it in over two months.

****

Jeremy skeptically watched as I slowly walked across the living room with my legs spread opened. "What happened to you?"

"I got a wax." I grumbled passing by him; he was by the kitchen island.

"Oooh, can I see?" He dropped the grin when I snapped an evil glare.

Lying in bed, I wondered if the pain would go away by morning. How red faced and embarrassed would I be to have Marcus staring at me while I walked like I'd been horseback riding? I heard my phone go off, so I reached for it.

Marcus (4:25pm): Thank you, Mia.

Me (4:26pm): For what?

Marcus (4:26pm): For today, for this weekend. I promise I won't let you down.

Me (4:27pm): I hope you don't, Marcus.

Marcus (4:27pm): Did you purchase anything good ;)

Me (4:28pm): Oh you'll have to just have wait and see,
DeLuca.

Marcus (4:29): I look forward to it! ;)

A nice cold shower soothed the soreness from my wax. The redness went down a lot, and I was walking normally by nine o'clock. Thank God! I decided to pack my bag for the weekend, only leaving out what I'd be wearing in the morning.

Feeling guilty that I hadn't worked out in three days, I set my alarm to go off early so that I could fit in a good run in the morning. I threw on my yoga pants and a spandex sleeveless shirt so that I could jump right out of bed and just brush my teeth before my run.

I stepped out of my bedroom, and Jeremy was still playing his stupid game. I noticed he ordered pizza. Great, I should really cut back on the carbs. The past three days, I'd consumed more calories with alcohol and pasta than I had in months.

Then I remembered I needed to tell Jeremy about my weekend trip. I was nervous about saying anything, afraid of how he would react. I grabbed a slice of pizza and headed over to the couch. To my surprise, he didn't seem shocked at all and even mentioned that he hoped I'd have a great time.

A half an hour later, I was in bed.

CHAPTER SIX

Jogging cleared my mind and relieved all my tension. I had a mixed variety of music on my iPod, and as soon as the shuffle switched from Lady Gaga's "Marry the Night" to Limp Bizkit's "Rollin," I picked up the pace. The wind was the perfect temperature against my damp skin. I felt like I was in control, and it was just me and the road.

Passing the university, I stopped near a tree to catch my breath before lying on the grass. I did a few sets of sit ups along with lunges and squats. Then I stretched against a bench and began the jog back to my apartment at an easier pace.

I ran in place while waiting for the red light to change when I noticed Romano's restaurant. I smiled to myself. Marcus was every girl's dream: he was successful, a gentleman, and absolutely, ridiculously HOT!

I'd known men like that ... *well* not as handsome as Marcus, but they were all confident assholes. Although spending that one night with him at Romano's made me truly believe that he might just be different.

He wanted to spend time with me, and who was I to not let him? It couldn't hurt to give it a shot, could it? By agreeing to this weekend trip, I knew that something more than just getting to know each other would occur. I couldn't resist his smile and his scent. Just thinking of him without his clothes on boggled my mind. A man brushed past me and ran across the street. I dismissed the thoughts of Marcus and continued with my run.

I was a couple blocks away from my building, so I sprinted. Stopping in front of the stairs, I took ten long minutes for a good stretch. My face was dripping with sweat, and I could feel the heat and blood rushing through my veins. It felt good.

Using the tree for support, I placed my right leg behind me and slowly bent my left. I repeated this, stretching on the other side. I sidestepped away from the tree, lifted my hands over my head, and reached for the sky very slowly, stretching my arms over to the right side and left side of my body.

I rolled my neck then bent over, reaching for my toes and aligning my back and legs. Slightly spreading my legs apart, I caught a glimpse of the bottom part of jeans and men's white sneakers directly behind me.

The legs bent, and a set of big, brown eyes met mine. "Well good morning. You'll have to let me in on your running schedule, so I can make it in time for your stretching." That now-familiar smile peeped through my legs. I jerked up and quickly brushed a few loose strands of damp hair away from my face. Then I turned to face him.

"You're early." I stumbled back a few steps.

He eyed me up and down with an entertained, crooked grin. "And you're sweaty. I *love* it." He winked.

My eyes traced every inch of him; the casualwear suited him very well. This was the first time I was able to witness his firm biceps through his fitted, white, short-sleeved shirt. His loose, straight jeans flattered his waistline. He shoved his hands in his front jean pockets causing the muscles of his forearms to flex. His platinum Rolex was wrapped comfortably around his wrist. "I hope you don't mind that I've arrived a little early; I wanted to make sure you wouldn't bail on me." He chuckled.

Bringing my attention back to his eyes, I blinked a few times. "Um, no, it's fine; I just went for a quick run. I hope you don't mind waiting while I take a shower and get ready. I can make you some coffee if you like?"

"Please lead the way." His smile widened. We entered the building and walked up to the second floor. I was sticking the key in the lock when Trevor from the fourth floor approached me. He's a very good-looking guy. He'd also tried on numerous occasions to ask me out, but I never dated anyone in my building. That was my number-one rule. Trevor handed me an envelope with a huge smile. "Good morning, sexy, my month's rent," he said.

"Ah, early as usual, Trevor, thank you." I smiled as I grabbed the envelope.

"Dinner Saturday?"

"*Trevor.*" I narrowed my eyes.

Lifting his palms to surrender, he laughed. "Hey it was worth a shot. You can't blame a man for trying?"

"No, you can't, unfortunately she has plans with me for the weekend." Marcus just had to butt in. Oh my God, I rolled my eyes and opened the door. They both eyed each other, refusing to back down: Trevor with a cocky expression and Marcus with an amused grin. Trevor broke from the staring contest first and waved goodbye. I smiled at him and waved back. I walked into my apartment as Marcus followed.

"So you manage the building?" He asked casually as if the small episode in the hallway didn't happen.

"No." I walked to the kitchen and pulled out my selections of coffee. I slid three different kinds on the island before him, and he pointed at the extra bold strength. I placed his selection in the one-cup coffee maker, retrieved a mug, and hit the button to brew the coffee.

"*So* you just collect the rent from tenants as a favor for the landlord?" He settled onto a stool.

"I'm the landlord, Marcus. This is my building." Placing cream, sugar, and a spoon before him, I grabbed his cup and set it down next to the items. When I looked up at him, his face was unreadable. He grabbed the mug and spoon, scooped two sugars, and poured a little cream into the cup. "I have to hop in the shower. Will you be okay while I get ready? You're welcome to turn on the television. Please make yourself at home."

He glanced at his Rolex. "Actually I have to make a few phone calls. It's only eight fifteen; please, take your time." I smiled at him and then noticed that I didn't embrace him with a hug or a kiss. Forcing myself to be brave, knowing he wouldn't reject me in any way, I walked over to him, placing one hand over his and my other hand at the back of his neck. Reaching up to him, I set my lips against his cheek. His head slowly turned, gently brushing my lips, but I pulled away.

"I won't be long. The sooner I'm ready, the sooner I'll be able to spend an entire weekend with you." Turning on my heels, I walked away. That should give him something to think about for the next hour. I felt pleased with myself.

Taking my time in the shower, I washed my hair and rubbed body wash all over three times. This was more than my usual routine, but, hey, I had to smell irresistible. After I was done, I dried myself thoroughly and slathered every inch of my skin with lotion.

I threw on my green halter top, summer dress, and gold wedge heels. I ran back to the bathroom and towel dried my hair. While it was still damp, I applied mousse and worked my fingers through my hair, deciding on the wavy-teased look. When I was done, I took my time with my makeup to make sure it was flawless. The last touch to my face was a hint of lip gloss.

It was nine o'clock, so I grabbed my travel bag and headed for the living room. Marcus was still in the kitchen on the phone. He looked over his shoulder when he heard me enter. Placing my bag on the island, I opened the refrigerator and grabbed half of a grapefruit. Not wanting to disturb his call, I stood across from him. I could feel the heat of his stare as I placed a spoonful of grapefruit into my mouth. When my eyes finally met his, he mouthed, "You look beautiful." I smiled, reveling in the attention.

He went on with his conversation, not taking his eyes off me once. "That's fine … yes … no, it can wait until Monday. I still have three weeks before the deadline. Okay. Yes, I have my Blackberry if you need me to review anything that is absolutely urgent. Other than that, Marvin can take care of any documents that need to be out today. Thank you. Bye." He ended the call, which was made on a touchscreen. I heard him say he had his Blackberry with him, so that led me to believe he had two phones. I wondered why. Maybe he was one of those people who prefer to have a work phone and a personal phone. I never understood the concept of having two phones. It's too much to keep up with. It's like having more than one social network: too exhausting.

He slid off the stool and walked over to stand behind me. I shivered at his nearness, feeling his face on the side of mine. "You smell delicious." I should after washing up as much as I did.

"Thank you." I whispered.

"Are you ready to go, or do you need more time?" Gripping my hips, he turned me to face him. He was so close, invading my space, but I didn't mind, not one bit. "Yes, I'm ready. Marcus?"

"Mmmh?" he mumbled while rubbing the back of his fingers against my cheek, along my jawline, and down the nape of my neck. I felt a warm, tingling sensation from his touch.

"I don't do this, at all, you know—go away for an entire weekend with a man I don't know. Can you just bear with m—" He stopped me in mid-sentence, cupping my chin and rubbing his thumb along my bottom lip.

"Mia, if I ever make you feel uncomfortable, just tell me and I'll step back. I will not make you do anything you don't want to do. Do you understand?" I nodded. "Good, let's go enjoy a weekend on the beach." He took my hand and led us to my bag, which he grabbed with his free hand. We walked through the living room, but before we got to the door, I stopped.

"Wait, I need to leave a note for Jeremy." I ran back to the kitchen and wrote on a post-it note magnet on the fridge. *Will be back Sunday, stay out of trouble. Take the trash out! Call if you need anything. Love, Mia.*

Remembering that my driver's license was in my car, I walked over to it after leaving the building. He stood and watched me enter and exit my vehicle, and then I hit the alarm button. "What?" I asked at his wry expression.

"That's your car? You drive a convertible Mustang?"

Shaking my head, I grabbed his hand and smiled. "Yes, that's my *car*." I teased.

He shook his head laughing. Most men have the same expression when they see my car. He opened the passenger door for me. I got in his car and buckled up. We took off as soon as he was in.

"Can I ask you a personal question?" He placed his hand on my bare knee. It felt nice.

"Yeah, of course, isn't the whole purpose of this trip is to learn more about each other, *personally*?" I turned to see the side of his face, the side with the dimple.

He gently smiled before responding. "You don't work, right?"

"No." Not sure what he's getting at.

"Yet you own a four-story building in a really good neighborhood, and you own a-top-of-the-line convertible Mustang. How could you afford something like that?"

"I sold my soul to the devil." He laughed. "No, all jokes aside, when my father passed, he was prepared with a large life insurance policy. It was split between my brother and me. Of course, I was too young at the time. My half was placed in an escrow account where it accrued interest. Anyway, long story short, I was given access to the money on my twenty-first birthday. Instead of splurging on clothes, I invested in stocks.

"I found that building two years ago and thought it would be perfect; it was a huge fixer-upper and needed more than just TLC. I made an offer and worked on it for a year. I'm happy with the outcome. I splurged on a building and a car. I don't buy lavish clothing and go on expensive trips. I watch what I spend and live off the money from my tenants."

He took a long look at me at the red light. "Very impressive, did your brother do the same—invest in properties?"

"Not really, my brother invested in stocks as well; he made out better than me actually. When he passed, he left me everything in his will. I donated half to the Boston and Philadelphia Police for Families of Fallen Officers. The money is given to families that were not fortunate enough to have the same privileges that I had. Most people don't think to prepare their families in case of an unexpected death. My father was always adamant about saving money and looking into the best life insurance policies; it was like he knew one day it would happen sooner or later. My brother had the same mentality."

"They seem like very smart men." He gently squeezed my knee and took off when the light turned green.

"Thank you, they were. My father and Michael left me with the same mind-set."

His soft grip on my knee stiffened, and he quickly removed his hand, placing it on the steering wheel. "Michael?" he asked alarmed.

"Yes, Michael Sullivan, did you know him?" His facial features changed; he seemed lost in thought, worried even.

"Ah, nope, didn't know a Michael Sullivan." *Mmmh.* Maybe the name sounded familiar for a second.

He remained silent for the rest of the ride. Did I say something wrong? Everything was going well; at least I thought it was. We reached the airport and parked in a private lot. When he turned off the ignition, he shifted to face me. "Excuse me one minute. I need to make a phone call before we go."

I nodded, not sure what else to say; he was acting a little strangely. He stepped out of the car, and I remained seated. The parking lot was empty. He was far away so that I couldn't hear his conversation but could see his facial expressions and gestures. He seemed upset, his hand ran through his hair several times, and he paced back and forth. He seemed tense about something. He glanced at my direction twice and looked away. About five minutes later, he walked over, his stride powerful and strong, but his face seemed troubled. He reached my door and opened it. I looked up at him but didn't get out of the car because he seemed to be keeping me in.

"Mia, *fuck*, I'm sorry. *Um*, they need me at the office."

"Oh." Looking down, I tried to hide my disappointment. "That's fine, Marcus, maybe some other time." Meeting his gaze, I forced a smile. He didn't say anything for a moment, but he didn't move either. Pressing his lips together, he shook his head.

"No, you know what? They'll be fine without me. I promised you a nice weekend, and that's what I'm going to give you." He offered his hand, and I grabbed it. His smile told me he wanted to go, but his eyes seemed uncertain.

Sliding my legs out of the car, I hesitated. "Are you sure, Marcus? I seriously don't mind; you can go. I understand you're a busy man." He shook his head and pulled me to my feet.

"Not this weekend—this weekend it's all about you." Biting my lip, I tried to hide my pleased grin.

****

The private plane was better than I'd imagined. It had a modern design with the utmost in technology and comfort. The flight from Boston to the Bahamas felt shorter than it actually was. I guess the comfortable chairs, smooth ride, and the conversation Marcus and I were having mostly about his firm allowed me to enjoy the trip.

We were greeted by an SUV and a driver when we landed at the airport. "Are you hungry?" Marcus asked, placing his hand into mine.

"Actually I'm starving," I said.

"Would you like to eat at a nearby restaurant, or wait till we get to the house? It's about a thirty-minute drive from here."

"Mmmh, I can wait."

"Are you sure?" He raised an eyebrow.

"Yes, positive." He gave my hand a slight squeeze, and we entered the SUV.

CHAPTER SEVEN

I'd never been in the Bahamas. Sadly I'd never left the U.S. My father took Michael and me as kids to Disney World and sometimes to the Jersey shore for the summer. We never visited the Caribbean. Luckily, I had a passport. I had gotten one right before Michael passed. Jeremy and I had planned to go to Mexico that month. Of course, we didn't go. Who could enjoy a vacation knowing the entire time you'd be miserable? We promised to do it again sometime but never talked about it again.

The Bahamas was like no other place I'd ever seen; it was beyond beautiful. I was like a child as I continued to admire my surroundings from the passenger window. There were so many locals and tourists wandering around taking in the scenery. Everyone was laughing and having a good time. Caribbean music flowed through the air from a nearby festival. Vendors sat patiently in their booths selling seashell jewelry, knick-knacks, as well as portraits with palm trees and beaches.

The light breeze from the ocean made the eighty-five-degree weather tolerable. I was thrilled to be here and grateful that Marcus invited me. "Marcus, thank you," I said while watching a little boy standing by the curb, waving at me with the biggest smile. I waved excitedly back as his mother picked the little boy up into her arms and waved before walking towards the festival.

I could feel him staring at me as I glanced out the window. "You've never been to the Bahamas?"

"No. It's beautiful."

"Yes, it is."

We reached a huge metal gate. The driver's window lowered; the man up front punched a code into a keypad which opened the gates. We wended our way along the driveway; surrounding us was a beautiful landscape of unique flowers, palm trees and beautifully manicured grass.

What caught my immediate attention was the traditional Bahamian home centered at the end of the driveway. The home was two levels with a wraparound upper terrace. It was stunning. It looked like something out of painting or a high definition photo from a welcoming brochure that would read on top, "A place to enjoy and relax." I stepped out of the car before Marcus or the driver could open the door. As I made my way around the vehicle, I stood speechless admiring the home. Turning to face Marcus when I felt the warmth of his body beside me, I was greeted with a boyish irresistible grin. "You like?" He asked, entertained by my reaction.

"Marcus, it's breathtaking."

"Come, I'll show you the rest; there's lots to see." Wrapping his arm around my shoulder, he led me to the double front doors.

When we entered the home, we walked into a huge foyer which led to an enormous living room. The high vaulted ceiling gave the home an elegant presence while the all-glass walls gave it a modern touch. Every room had a view of the beautiful beach through the ceiling-to-floor glass walls. The living room was filled with oversized furniture: a sectional, a coffee table, side tables, and two recliners.

The dining room was stunning with a long wooden mahogany table set for twenty people. The kitchen was my favorite with the tall white cabinetry and top-of-the-line stainless steel appliances that were complete with the blue and grey glass tile backsplash and a kitchen island.

The first floor had two additional bedrooms that were connected to a joint bathroom, another guest bathroom, and an office/library. The second floor had three additional large bedrooms each with a bathroom and balcony overlooking the ocean. The master suite was another favorite. It was bigger than my entire apartment.

In the middle of the master suite sat a California king mahogany sleigh bed decorated beautifully with a brown silk comforter along with blue, white, and brown accent pillows. The entire right side of the wall was all glass, overlooking the beach. You could step out to the terrace where a hammock, table and two chairs were neatly placed.

On the left side of the room, a doorway led into a sanctuary spa-style bathroom. A Jacuzzi was in one corner surrounded by brown and beige marbled tiles. A steam shower big enough to fit six people was set beside the tub. On the opposite side was a long two-sink vanity. The sinks were the shape of large white bowls with stainless steel modern fountains. Above the sinks were two matching oval-shaped stainless framed mirrors. The toilet sat alone behind a wall. Behind a sliding door was a walk-in closet. I was surprised by the lack of clothing, but then again it was a vacation home.

"You can sleep in here, Mia; I'll take the room next door." Marcus said, giving me the master suite.

It was beautiful, but I could not possibly take his room. "I couldn't. I'll be fine in another room."

"No, you'll sleep in here, and that's final." I nodded.

"Come. Let's get you fed." Grabbing my hand, he led me back down to the kitchen. He sat me down onto a stool by the island. I folded my hands as I watched him take out chicken breasts, mushrooms, butter, olive oil, some seasonings, and flour. "Are you *cooking*?" I asked astonished. He walked over to a cabinet and removed two wine glasses. "Yes, I'm cooking for you."

Slamming my hand against my chest, I let my mouth drop open. "Wow, I'm surprised, Mr. DeLuca, *you* can cook?"

"I guess you'll be the judge of that."

I laughed. "Did I tell you that I'm starving? Maybe we should have pizza on standby, just in case." He shook his head.

Removing red and white bottles of wine from the hidden wine refrigerator behind one of the cabinet doors, he held both up to me, and I pointed to the red. Opening a drawer, he removed an electronic wine opener. Then he poured the red wine into both glasses. He walked over to me and set my glass down. Leaning over, he placed his soft lips against my forehead; the gesture made me smile from ear-to-ear. "Sit back, relax, and watch me cook, *baby*."

Walking back to the opposite side of the island, I thought of him cooking naked. Now that would be something. He removed a few more items from the cabinet and washed his hands before preparing the food.

Every muscle in his arms and chest flexed with each chop and slice, making him even more attractive. "Who knew that watching a sexy man cook could be such a turn-on?" I grabbed my wine and took a few sips.

He looked at me with a crooked grin. "So you think I'm sexy, huh?" Slowly I nodded and continued gulping down my wine. "So I smell good, and I'm sexy. Good to know."

"And I'll let you know if you can add "great cook" to that list as well." I winked. He laughed. It was an adorable laugh. He seemed so carefree and worriless, as if he were in his element: enjoying his surroundings, cooking, and drinking wine. Watching him like this, I didn't see him as the powerful attorney of Boston. I saw him as a twenty-nine-year-old man enjoying life.

After slicing two chicken breasts in half, he lightly rubbed flour on the four pieces. A little salt, pepper and other seasonings and they were placed on a plate. Placing a pan over medium heat on the stove, he poured a little olive oil and two scoops of butter into it. He took a few sips of wine, waiting for the butter to melt.

I felt buzzed from the one glass of wine since I drank it on an empty stomach. As if reading my mind, he walked over to the fridge and removed a small tray of cheese, crackers, and grapes. He placed it in front of me and popped a cube of the cheddar cheese into his mouth. He winked before returning to the stove. The grapes were mouthwatering, and my stomach growled after I teased it with just a few. I look up embarrassed, but from what I could tell, he didn't notice.

While eating a few crackers, I watched him stab the chicken breasts with a fork and place them into the sizzling pan. I poured each of us another glass of wine. "So how did you learn to cook?"

He smiled. "My father was very big on cooking. He loved it. Every Sunday he enjoyed spending time with my mother, and he helped her prepare a huge feast. On days my mother felt sick, he let me help. I wanted to help. He made it seem like so much fun the way he would throw salt behind his shoulder before placing it in a recipe or grab a whole chicken, wobbling it across the counter, making chicken noises. He was always happy in the kitchen." His eyes gleamed with the memory of his father. You could tell he'd been very close with him. I imagined Marcus as a little boy with dark brown, messy hair and big brown eyes and the most adorable dimple, sitting on a counter laughing at his father's goofy ways.

"You seem to have lots of good memories of your father."

He nodded as he worked his way around the kitchen. "I do. I couldn't have asked for a better father; he made us his priority, and family meant everything to him. The best memories I have of him were in this house." He flipped the chicken breast in the pan, revealing a golden crisp top, allowing the other side to cook.

I glanced around the house again, it seemed so new. I recalled that he mentioned his father passing away when he was in high school. "*Really?*"

"Yeah, he would bring us here several times during the summer. Sometimes my brother didn't want to come, so he would just bring me. I can remember as far back as five years old, and we would go on the beach, collect seashells, watch movies in the den, and play games." He smiled. I didn't remember seeing a den, but noticing a door in the far right of the kitchen, I assumed it led to the hidden room.

"The house seems so modern, did you remodel?"

"When my father passed away, my mother wanted to put it up for sale; she said it was too difficult for her to come here because of all the memories. I begged her not too. I told her I wanted to keep it. She didn't want to at first, and my brother didn't care for it. I had so many memories with him here I couldn't give it up. She didn't sell it, but we never came back here. On my eighteenth birthday, I had access to my share of my father's estate, and my mother gave me the keys. I flew here the first chance I had. It was abandoned, uncared for. I extended the home to make it bigger and modernized it with the exception of the den, of course. I didn't touch one thing in that room; it's exactly how my father left it, except for the TV. The old one was broken, so I purchased a new one."

He placed a lid onto the pan after he poured the mushrooms and Marsala wine into it. He lowered the heat and placed diced red potatoes into the oven after he seasoned them. "Wow, have your mother and brother come back to see it?"

"Um, a couple times, yes."

"You must come here a lot to keep up with it." I watched him wash his hands again as I took a few more sips of the delicious wine.

"Actually, I haven't been here in over a year. It's been really busy at work. I hired a live-in maid who keeps up with it. I let her know when I coming; she stocks the fridge and visits family until I leave. I usually don't like company; I never bring anyone up here."

"So you never brought a girl to your shore home?" I questioned with narrowed eyes.

"Besides my mother and you? No, I haven't."

"Why not?" If Jeremy owned a shore home, he would have brought dozens of girls at a time. What made DeLuca different from other men?

"This is my getaway spot where I can run from my hectic life. This place is very personal to me. I never thought to bring a woman here ... until you." Uncertain if that was true, I narrowed my eyes then decided to leave it at that.

He offered me his hand. "Come, I want to show you something. Dinner will be ready in twenty minutes." I grabbed his hand and followed as he led me to the door at the far right of the kitchen. When we entered, it felt as though we walked into another home. The den had outdated ocean blue rugs, white paneled walls, and high ceilings. A white brick fireplace was the centerpiece of the room. An oversized black leather sofa was on one side of the fireplace, opposite from two matching recliners. In the middle of the furniture was a glass coffee table. A built-in oak bookcase on the right side of the fire place held books and board games.

Sliding my hand away from his, I wandered the room, admiring how warm it felt even with the white walls. It was outdated, but it felt homey. I slid my shoes off and rubbed my toes on the soft carpet. Walking over to the bookcase, I picked up a metal picture frame; the picture showed a tanned man with a full head of silky black hair, wearing white linen pants and a matching shirt. His arms were wrapped around two boys: a little, brown-haired, tanned boy and a lighter and taller boy with light brown hair. The taller boy held up a hook with a fish half his size. The little boy held a fishing rod. All three were smiling aboard a boat.

Marcus walked up beside me. "That's my father, my brother, and I. I was eight and Jimmie was twelve." He smiled to himself, remembering the day. "My brother and I had gotten into the biggest argument about who would pose with the catfish for that picture. My father solved it by flipping a coin. As you can see, I lost."

"Your father was very handsome; you look just like him." I looked up at Marcus who smiled. He took the picture from my hand, placing it back in its place. "Thank you, I get that a lot."

"I take it your brother looks like your mother?" I asked, drifting away from him.

"Yeah, on top of the fireplace, there's a family portrait of the four of us." There were several frames on top of the mantel. I found the one of the four of them, and I reached for it. Jimmie had greenish eyes and light brown hair so different from Marcus. Mrs. DeLuca was absolutely beautiful. She had big green eyes, light brown, wavy hair, fair skin, and a beautiful smile with a dimple on the right side of her cheek. I smiled, acknowledging where Marcus got his dimple from, but he looked just like his father with the tanned complexion, dark, thick hair, brown eyes, and thick arched eyebrows.

"What are your mother's and father's first names?" I asked while placing the frame exactly back where I found it. I turned to find him behind me, looking at the picture as well.

"James Vincent DeLuca, my brother is a junior, but we call him Jimmie. My mother's name is Theresa DeLuca."

"Who were you named after?"

He laughed before answering. "I was named after my mother's father, but my middle name is the same as my father's, Marcus Vincent."

"Marcus Vincent DeLuca? *Mmmh?*" Smiling at him, I leaned in and whispered, "I like it."

The sides of the eyes wrinkled as his smile grew wider. "Do you now?" he said, placing his arms around my hips and pulling me in. Unable to control myself, I wrapped my arms around his neck.

"Yes, very much." Leaning up on my toes, I breathed him in, and his smell was intoxicating. "Which cologne do you use?" It had a clean citrus scent.

"That will be my little secret from you." When he leaned down for a kiss, the buzzer to the stove went off. He shook his head and rested his forehead against mine. "Perfect timing, huh? Come on, I know you're hungry. Let's eat then head to the beach."

Excited about the beach, I practically ran behind him. He set up our dinner plates with, chicken marsala, roasted red potatoes and garlic asparagus. He patiently waited as I took a bite. It was tender and bursting with flavor. "*Mmmmmh*, Marcus this is so good." As I looked at him, he smiled with relief and poured us another glass of wine. We enjoyed our delicious dinner, wiping our plates clean.

I washed the dishes and headed to my room to change into my swimsuit.

After deciding on my turquoise bikini, white cover-up and matching flip-flops, I grabbed two beach towels and headed down the stairs. Marcus was nowhere in sight, so I went out the sliding doors and headed towards the beach.

It was absolutely beautiful. I smiled as I laid the two towels onto the white sand. Stripping off my cover-up and tossing my flip-flops aside, I made my way towards the ocean. The sun beamed against my skin, and my feet burned from the hot sand. When I finally reached the edge of the water, I allowed the cool water to splash along my freshly polished toes.

I sighed in contentment. There is always something peaceful and calming about the beach. The way it allows you to take in its beauty. It's like the ocean knows all of your deepest, darkest secrets and thoughts. It doesn't judge you; instead, at that very moment, all the pain and sadness you feel just drifts away along with the waves.

After what seemed like a long time, I turned around to see if Marcus were near, and there he was walking towards me in knee-length black swimming trunks. They were hanging low on his waist, teasing me as they revealed the V shape on his hip bones; his abs were perfectly ripped and tight. They were the most perfect abs I'd ever seen. His chest and broad muscular shoulders screamed for my hands to rub all over him.

His aviator sunglasses hid his dark eyes, but his smile showed approval of my bikini. He picked up the pace as the sun beamed against his golden tan, and the beautiful scenery behind him made it seem like he was posing for a high-end magazine.

When he finally reached me, he didn't say anything. Instead he pulled me in his arms and kissed me hard and passionately. I was already out of it mentally when I noted the image of him walking towards me, but once his lips met mine, I lost complete control of myself. I allowed him to take over my mind and body; and whatever he wanted I was willing to do, so his kiss took over me in a way I couldn't explain.

I tried to reach up to further the kiss, but he was too tall, and my toes sank into the sand. His lips spread into a smile at my failed attempt. Slowly bending, he brought me down with him. He sat on the sand, and I nestled on his lap, straddling him. I was able to deepen the kiss as I rustled my fingers in his hair. His arms were strong and secure around me.

Now that I was sitting on him I felt in control. I took over, trying to overpower him. I bit down on his bottom lip, and he moaned. The vibrant sound from his throat hardened my nipples. He traced his hands along my curves; his touch made my lower belly twist with excitement, and I arched into him. I'd never wanted a man this much.

Marcus DeLuca had to be a dangerous man because I was caving in too soon; it was just too soon to feel this attachment, to feel and want him so desperately. When something seems too good to be true, it's exactly that.

CHAPTER EIGHT

I pulled away from the kiss, trying to catch my breath. I couldn't see his eyes, so I snatched off his sunglasses then grabbed his face with my hands. I looked into his eyes, trying to find his reason, the reason why I was there. All I saw was sincerity in his eyes.

His chest was pulsing as he took in some air. "Mia, you're so beautiful. Seeing you in this bikini, I can't control myself." I sighed, leaning my forehead against his. "You're killing me." He whispered to me, closing his eyes and caressing his thumb against my cheek.

"And you're killing me, Marcus." I shook my head. That kiss was too much, too passionate. A kiss like that was meant for two people in love, not meant for two people getting to know each other. I stood, and his eyes squinted with confusion.

Turning from him, I walked further into the ocean, deep enough for the waves to splash my thighs. Crossing my arms, I stood there and watched the blue waves angrily dance in the distance.

Marcus was beside me instantly. He gently grabbed my hand and turned me to face him. "What's wrong, Mia?" He asked with worried eyes.

It was hard for me to explain my feelings without it coming out the wrong way. Waving my hand in the space between us, I said, "I don't know, Marcus. I don't know what this is, you know?"

He nodded. "Yeah, I don't know what this is either, Mia." He sighed. Leaning closer, he grabbed my face. "I've never felt this way for anyone, but you have to trust me when I say we'll be fine." He leaned in and kissed me. This time it was softer and warmer.

I wanted to trust him, but it was so hard when I was always let down. Pulling away from his kiss again, I shook my head. "I don't know if I can do that." I turned and quickly made my way back to our towels without looking back. My feet sank into the sand with every step.

I reached our towels and grabbed my cover-up, pulling it over my head. When it was completely on, Marcus was already in front of me. His shoulders were hunched forward with his hands on his hips. He was looking down, shaking his head and trying to catch his breath.

I crossed my arms, waiting for him to say something, and after a moment he looked up. "Why?"

"Why what?"

"Why can't you trust me?" I bit my lip, contemplating whether to just let it all out. Screw it. I'm the type of person that needs to say how I'm feeling. I can't keep it bottled up inside, even if it sounds wrong.

"I've only known you for what, four days? And I'm already telling you things I've never told anyone. *And* those kisses the first night and today—those were not ordinary kisses, Marcus!"

"I know." He leaned in to me, but I brought my hand up to stop him.

"Let me finish. Then you can talk." Placing his hands back on his hips, he gave a small nod. "Trusting people in general is hard for me. You have to understand I came from a life where it's normal for the people you love and trust to just disappear. I don't know what a mother's love is, my father was taken away from me at a very young age, and the one person I had left, the one I ran to for every problem, every heartache, he was ..." I fought to hold back my tears when speaking of Michael. I dropped down on the towel Indian style. I felt him beside me, not saying anything just listening. I continued without looking at him.

"When I was in college, I met a man who told me all the right things. I was young, gullible, and I believed everything he said. After a year in a relationship with him, I found him with his wife and six-month-old daughter in a nearby park. When he saw me, he pretended as if I didn't exist. It took me a long time to get over it, but I did eventually.

"My senior year of BU, I met another guy. He was also smooth and knew how to manipulate me. Then I caught him in my dorm room with my roommate. After that I told myself I would never get attached, never allow myself to take another man seriously, and I haven't. Yet here you are, another man with all the right things to say, and I'm slowly falling for every word. I just got to the point in my life where I accepted being alone not only in a relationship but *alone*. I have no family. My only friend is a guy I live with, and I'm okay with that." I turned my head to face him, trying to show him in my expression that I was sincerely fine with it.

Biting his lip, he shook his head. "Mia, I'm sorry you've been hurt. I really am, but please don't make me pay for other's mistakes. I don't know where this is leading, but I want to see where it goes. I feel that we could be something, but I can't prove myself to you if you don't let me try." He shifted closer, placing his arm around my shoulder and pulling me in. I laid my head on his chest. "Can you just try? Not just for me but for us? We could have something special." Lifting my chin with the tips of his fingers, his eyes met mine. His stare deepened with reassurance. "Can you do that, Mia? Can you at least try?"

Letting out a deep breath, I closed my eyes. "I'll try, but if you screw up once, I don't care how small, I'm out. Do you understand?" Shooting my eyes open, I gave him a pointed glare.

He laughed once. "And if you screw up?"

"I won't." I smiled.

"Okay then, we won't screw it up. Sounds simple enough." We smiled at each other. I laid my head back on his shoulder, and it dawned on me. I'd be working for him until the end of July. The thought that this was not the first time he'd slept with a co-worker left an unsettling knot in my stomach.

"Marcus?" I asked unsure if I should even ask what I was thinking.

"Yeah?"

"I know I don't have a right to ask this, but how many females who worked for you have you slept with?" I closed my eyes when I felt his arms tense around me. I knew it. How stupid could I be? He's a handsome man: successful and powerful. How could he resist having his way with all the women who flirt with him at the office? "The only reason I'm asking is because I start working for you on Monday, and I don't want any unexpected surprises." I bit my lip. Sometimes I don't know when to just shut up.

"Well, to be honest … only one," he said softly.

"One? Does she still work for you?" I was surprised. I thought it would be dozens.

"Yes, Mia, but it was strictly a sexual relationship, nothing more. It ended a few months ago, and she knows that our relationship is nothing but business now."

I shrugged; I could work with that. "I can understand that. I was in a sexual relationship, too, for several months, but we decided to stop, and we remained friends."

"Friends?" He asked.

"Yeah friends." I snuggled into his embrace.

"I thought your only friend was Jeremy?" *Shit!* Why can't I keep my mouth shut! What do I say? *Screw it!* It's going to get out sooner or later, why not sooner, right?

Taking a deep breath, I strove for honesty. "That's right, he's my only friend." Marcus slowly removed his arm from around my shoulder. Lifting his knees, he laid his forearms on them, allowing his hands to dangle in front of him. He needed space to collect his thoughts. I turned my body to face him.

"Wait, so you're saying that you and Jeremy? Jeremy and *you* had a sexual relationship?" He seemed dumbfounded. I took another deep breath as I knew this would be hit or miss.

"Yes." He shook his head in disbelief. I quickly continued to explain. "It wasn't like that in the beginning. It started after my brother passed away. I'd never felt lonelier in my life, and he was there, helping me with all the funeral arrangements and the grief. It just *happened*. Then I thought it wasn't fair for him or me to continue something that was holding us back from other opportunities. I wanted to try and start dating and seeing people, and so did he. We have a strictly friendship relationship now. We're more like brother and sister." I laughed, trying to lighten the mood; it didn't work. His head snapped at me, and he stared with a disgusted expression.

"A brother who you'll fuck?" he asked, his voice dripping with scorn.

Whoa! That stung, I didn't mean it like that, and why would he say it in a hurtful way? I didn't know how to respond to that. My heart dropped at the tone of his voice and the anger of his stare.

He stood up and stormed away towards the house.

Should I have lied? I couldn't do that, not when we were trying to get to know each other. I wasn't going to hide myself. He either accepted me as I was or *not at all*. My heart began to pick up its pace, and the more I thought of his words, the angrier I grew.

Not thinking twice, I stood and marched back into the house. My mind was boggled, and I could feel my face heat as my heart sped with anger. I entered through the sliding doors by the kitchen, and he was at the island, pouring himself a strong drink. When I entered, he shot me a sinful glare before gulping his drink down and pouring another one.

"Who are you to judge me? You know what, Marcus? I'm an honest person, and I thought the purpose of this trip was to get to know each other!"

He sarcastically laughed once. "Yep, and I think you pretty much summed it up." He lifted the glass before him and nodded in salute before taking another swig of his drink.

That pissed me the hell off. I took in a deep breath and blurted out everything without thinking twice. "Fuck you! You want to know who I am, Marcus. Well, here it goes! I am temperamental, over-sensitive, and outspoken. I'm honest! I cry at stupid love movies, and I'm a sucker for a romantic novel. I don't allow people to walk all over me, I have *trust* issues, and I have insecurities. I've slept with four men in my entire life! And the one thing I don't do is take *shit* from men who try to act like they're better than me as if they don't have any hidden skeletons! I'm not keeping shit hidden, how 'bout you? You can fuck off. I'll find my own way home. Have a nice *fucking* life!"

I stormed out the kitchen, holding back the tears. I was completely outraged! My hands and legs were trembling from the adrenaline. Running up the stairs and missing a few steps in the process, I finally entered the bedroom.

I grabbed my overnight bag and packed the few clothes I had laid out. I couldn't see with all the angry tears running down my face. I didn't want him to see me like this. I had to rush out of here.

Not even thinking to change into jeans and a shirt, I threw the bag over my shoulder and turned to face the door, but he was there standing in the way, blocking the exit. I looked down, hiding my tears. "Move," I choked.

"I'm sorry," he whispered.

"Move," I managed to sound clearer.

"Please, Mia, I'm sorry."

"Marcus, please don't make me repeat myself." Not saying another word, he stepped aside. I began to walk towards him. Before I passed the door, he softly took my arm to stop me. I hesitated at his touch.

He reached for the strap of my bag, and with one brush of his hand, the bag fell to the ground. He lifted both of my hands to his face and lightly brushed my knuckles along his lips.

"I'm so sorry, Mia. Please don't go. I was completely out of line. I'm an asshole."

I didn't say anything as I kept my head lowered, still feeling hurt. He wrapped my arms around his neck and pulled me in closer. Leaning his back against the inner entrance of the doorway, he lowered his head and nuzzled my neck. His lips vibrated along my collar bone when he spoke again. "I *beg* you, don't go. I'm sorry, baby." His bare chest felt warm, and his scent drew me in. With my eyes closed, I brushed my cheek against his. The stubble of his growing beard felt nice against my skin. I began to feel weak. He pressed his lips along my cheekbone, trailing soft kisses along my cheek until he reached my lips.

My initial instinct was to fight him off, but as he slid his tongue into my mouth, I couldn't resist. I let go, allowing him to possess me, to take over me emotionally and physically. The taste of bourbon mixed with salt from my tears blended surprisingly well, and I desired more. Intensifying the kiss, I was lost once again in his hex. Even after we just fought, I felt safe in his arms and wanted to stay there.

It wasn't until my head was pressed against the soft pillow that I realized he had carried me over to the bed.

His hands remained holding my face, my fingers rustled through his thick hair. The weight of his body on mine caused my heart to race. We were on his bed, and I felt comfortable with what might happen.

Lifting my right leg, I forced his hip deeper against me, feeling the hardness of his erection deep between my legs. Oh, well now … The thought that I could have that impact on him made me wet and excited.

He traced his hand down and cupped my breast. I moaned, and he ground his erection against me once again. I wanted him inside me, so I tugged at his hair as our tongues continued to entwine with one another. His hand continued down my curves until he reached the bottom of my cover-up; he slowly brought it up. I pushed away from his kiss and yanked the cover-up over my head. He sat up, kneeling between my legs breathlessly. Looking down at me, his eyes were dark with arousal. He sucked his bottom lip, and I want to lunge at him. "Mia. You're so beautiful."

"So are you. Now come here." I pulled at his arms, and his sculptured abs pressed against my stomach. Looking at me, he rubbed my cheek with his thumb.

"Are you sure you want to do this?" he whispered.

Reaching my fingers up, I brushed aside a lock of hair that lay over his eyebrow. "Yes, I want you more than you'll know." Pressing my hand against his neck, I brought him down to me.

He pulled back. "Give me a minute." He jumped out of bed and left the room. Where was he going?

He quickly ran back into the room, holding up a roll of condoms dangling from his hand. Ah … good boy. I giggled when he shrugged and tossed them onto the side of the bed. I look at them; there had to be at least six. How many did he plan on using?

He lay back on top of me, and my mind drifted back to him. Leaning down, his lips touched the side of my neck, and I got goose bumps. His lips were so soft and moist, tracing kisses along my collar bone down to my chest. He pulled both strings to my bikini top, allowing my breasts to break free, yearning for his attention.

Reading my mind, he cupped my bare breasts and lowered his head to them, twirling his tongue around my sensitive nipples. The sensation made me eager, and I pulled on his swimming trunks with my toes. He looked up at me with a wicked grin. "Now, now, be patient. I'm not a selfish man," he whispered.

Pouting and letting out a deep breath, I relaxed and allowed him to take control. He continued to fondle my breasts, teasing and making them ache with each lick. I moaned and slightly arched my back. It felt so good. Traces of heat were left after each kiss with his lips, all the way down to the middle of my belly.

I refused to plead as I knew that the wait would be well worth it. His lips reached my hip bone, and he traced his tongue along it as he went lower. Pulling the strings off my bikini bottom, I spread my legs, allowing him access to my most secret place. I moaned when he licked my inner thigh, anticipating what was next. I felt his lips part into a smile when I squirmed. My back arched deeper as he twirled his tongue in and out, up and down. "Marcus," I moaned as he rubbed me with his fingers to enhance the sensation.

"You taste so good, Mia." He groaned. The pleasure was building with each thrust of his skillful fingers and tongue. I couldn't take it anymore. I was about to explode.

Spreading my arms aside, I gripped the bed sheets and fully arched my back, tossing my head into the pillow, and yelling his name as my orgasm erupted. I panted and kept my eyes closed. When I caught my breath, he removed his finger and gripped my thighs. He continued to lick between my folds, groaning, until my heart rate lowered.

When I finally glanced down at him, his eyes were dark, ready for me. I prepared myself as I watched him quickly remove his trunks, and I saw the large erection spring to life. He kneeled between me, spreading my legs wider. Reaching over, he grabbed the roll of condoms and tore one off, throwing the others aside. My heart sped as I watched him bring the foil between his teeth and tear it open.

I watched his every move as he brought his hand down and placed the condom on the tip of him, slowly rolling it back. I wanted him more than ever. He was perfect in every way: his face, his body, his thick hair, and the power he had over me. I wanted all of Marcus DeLuca: the good and the bad. I so desperately wanted the bad. I wanted him to be rough, not gentle. I needed hard, wild, crazy sex. He leaned over me with a narrow-eyed stare. "You ready for me?" He seductively groaned.

"I want it hard." I panted, surprised by my own boldness. He flashed a wicked smile and brought his hand to the back of my head, gripping a fist full of hair. There was a slight pain in my scalp, but it was a good pain. "Oh baby, I'm going to fuck you so hard you're going to beg me to stop," he said through clenched teeth. The threat excited me, and instantly I was aroused again, ready for him.

He slowly filled me with his hardness. I gasped, and he moved in and out at a slow rhythm. "Fuck Mia, you feel so good," he whispered. Each movement gave me goose bumps, and it hardened my nipples. He slowly tugged my hair, pulling my head back, and he crushed his mouth against mine. I melted in his arms, never feeling more needed or wanted. "*Hard*, I want it hard, Marcus," I moaned through our locked lips.

With my words, he pulled my hips closer to his, not moving away from our kiss, and he picked up the pace. He pulled away and thrust hard, repeating it over and over again. Each time he pulled away, he forced his hips harder into me. I moved my hips with his; our bodies were in perfect unison with each rhythm. With each thrust, he was deeper inside of me, making me forget everything: our argument, the pain, the emptiness, and the sadness I dealt with during the past few months. My mind was completely empty, and I'd never felt freer.

In one swoop, he was kneeling on the bed still inside me as I sat on him with my legs wrapped around his hips. My back leaned against the headboard. The minute we were up, he pushed deeper inside me, moving at a faster pace. My body felt overheated with pleasure, and I cried out each time my back slammed against the mahogany surface.

My body gave in, not able to take it anymore, and I convulsed around him as I came for the second time. He didn't stop; he continued at the same pace, grunting with pleasure as he felt me weaken in his arms. "Marcus, *please,* I can't take it anymore," I moaned. I could feel the pressure building up again within my lower belly. I couldn't do it to myself. At that moment, it was painful but pleasing at the same time.

"Beg me to stop," he whispered as he nibbled on my earlobe.

"Please *stop,*" I quietly begged as the pleasure of his lips caressed my neck. With my words, he thrust three more times before he exploded deep within me, groaning my name.

We stayed seated that way for what seemed like forever, catching our breaths. Finally, he lifted his head from my neck, planting a kiss on my swollen lips. My smile widened, and I giggled. He raised an eyebrow. "What's so funny?"

"So that's what they call the Energizer Bunny?" I laughed. He chuckled and lowered me into the bed so that we were lying side by side looking at each other. I held my head up with my hand and watched as he stared at me mesmerized.

With his hand, he caressed my body from the side of my breast to my hip and back up, slowly tracing my curves. "You are the most beautiful woman I have ever seen."

"I truly doubt that," I said as I rolled my eyes. He's gorgeous; I'm average.

"Why are you so insecure? You're beautiful from head to toe. Any girl would be jealous of you. Your curvy body, beautiful big green eyes, and those lips—those lips are juicy and delicious." He smiled as he caressed his thumb against my bottom lip before placing a small kiss against them.

"I don't know. It's a female thing, I guess." I shrugged. Leaning in, I laid my head against his chest. I listened to his heartbeat which was soothing. We lay in silence and fell asleep in each other's arms.

****

I had more orgasms in three days than I'd had in my entire life. We had sex in every area of the beach house: the living room, kitchen, bedroom, shower, even on the beach. We were able to goof around and play games but also have deep conversations. I felt closer to him than I had with any man. The weekend was ending, and I was beginning my new externship position the next day. I was nervous. What if he's different around me? How will he act? Will he be the same goofy, sexual, and fun Marcus that I have grown to know? Of course he'll have to be professional and the powerful man at work, but will he dismiss me and pretend I don't exist? I knew that if that were the case, I would have to suck it up, but it still left a slight twinge in my belly.

I looked over at Marcus who was on a phone call as we drove to the airport. He made such a commitment to me over the weekend by shutting off both of his phones the entire day. He gave me his full attention by day only to turn it back on at night to make sure there were no emergencies. I was thankful for that as I knew he was a busy man. He ended his call and placed his arm around me. He must have sensed the worry in my eyes. "What's wrong?" he asked, placing a kiss on the top of my head.

"I was thinking about how this is going to work at the office."

"What do you mean?" His lips remained on my head as he mumbled beneath them.

"Well, you know. We're just getting to know each other, so maybe we should keep this private until we feel as though we can take it to the next step?"

He remained quiet for a moment. I wished I could read his mind. I wondered what he was thinking. "Is that what you want?" He ran his fingers through my hair.

It was obvious that was what he wanted. "Yes, I'd like to keep it strictly professional around the office. I wouldn't want people to think any less of me."

He sighed before responding. "Okay, we can keep it strictly professional for now."

****

Four hours later, we pulled in front of my apartment. I was tired and had to get myself ready for work the next day, but I was disappointed the weekend was over. Surprisingly, I was feeling attached and almost pouted because of the distance we would have. I shook that thought out of my head and stepped out of the car door that Marcus had opened for me. I reached up and gave him a tight hug. I truly did not want to let go. His scent was so sweet and his body so strong I felt safe and warm with him. He returned the hug gently, lifting me up from the ground. When he placed me back down, we embraced with an intimate kiss.

"Thank you, Marcus, for everything. This entire weekend was amazing." I pulled back with my arms still wrapped around his neck.

"Thank you for coming and giving me a chance. You don't know how much it means to me that you were willing to do this." I smiled and gave him one last kiss before walking into the building.

When I entered my apartment, there was a strong nasty smell in the air. I walked over to the kitchen to see that the garbage can was completely full. Ugh! I can't believe Jeremy! He only had one task while I was gone and that was to take the trash out, and he just dismissed it altogether. I lifted the bag from the trash can and tied it. I went back down the stairs to throw it in the dumpster by the alley.

When I reached the entrance door to the building, I could see through the side glass that Marcus was still out front. He was talking to a man. The man was handsome with a full set of salt and pepper hair. He looked older than Marcus but by no more than ten or fifteen years. He was also shorter by four inches. Though he wasn't muscular and tall, his stance was that of a powerful man. He puffed on a cigar and waved his hand while he talked. Marcus looked upset. I couldn't make out what they were saying, so I cracked open the door to eavesdrop.

"What? Have I not *fucking* taught yah brother or you nothing? You don't chase pussy; the fucking pussy chases you." The man's voice was loud and raspy with a strong Boston accent.

Marcus shook his head. "What? Yah fucking following me or something now!"

"Jimmie was looking for yah, and so was I," he said, shrugging while taking a puff of his cigar.

"That cock-sucker knew I was on vacation!" I was surprised to hear Marcus curse. I was wrong about his light Boston accent. He seemed angry, and I could tell that when he got angry his true Boston roots showed.

"Vacation, huh? Since when do you take vacation?" Marcus didn't answer. Instead he bit down on his lip to keep from exploding. The man continued. "Well, he said you were planning on coming back, yah know, to finish the job. We tried calling yah, but you wouldn't answer. It took every inch of my fucking bone not to get on a plane and fly to the Bahamas to drag your ass back here. When yah say yah gonna finish a job, yah fucking finish the job, Marky!" The older man growled pointing his finger into Marcus' chest, emphasizing the last few words.

Marcus looked down at the man's finger. Then returned his gaze and inched closer into him. "I would have *loved* to see that!" Marcus grunted.

The man looked back over his shoulder. Another man that looked awfully familiar was standing behind him now. "Look at this fucking tough guy!" He said to the familiar man while pointing his thumb at Marcus. Returning his attention to Marcus, he shoved the cigar back in his mouth, and lightly slapped both of his hands onto Marcus' face. "Marky, Marky, Marky." He mumbled through the cigar. "You talk back to me like that again, and I'll slice that fucking pretty face of yours. You *understand*?" He nodded, waiting for Marcus to respond.

Marcus stern face turned into a huge smile, and then he laughed—he truly *laughed*, really loud. "Sure Uncle Louie, you fat cock-sucking bastard, you'll have to get past my mother first; you know how overprotective she is of her boys." Uncle Louie laughed and nodded as he removed his hands from Marcus' face and took the cigar out of his mouth. He blew the smoke in Marcus' direction, but Marcus didn't flinch.

"You're right. How's that mother of yours anyways? Is she still lonely at night?" He winked.

"My father would turn in his grave if he heard yah talking like that about his wife."

Uncle Louie chuckled and patted Marcus on the shoulder before walking to the black SUV that was parked behind Marcus' car. The tall man followed and opened the back passenger door for him. Before entering the vehicle, he shouted out to Marcus. "I'll be by tomorrow to go over the next job. No fucking excuses this time, Marky!" He entered the vehicle, and it sped away. I watched as Marcus slammed a closed fist on top of his car and yelled a few curses before getting in and speeding away.

I stood in place for a few minutes before going out to make sure Marcus was far enough. I went out and walked to the alleyway next to our building. I dumped the trash and practically ran back in. What was that conversation about? And what did that Uncle Louie mean, talk about the next job? What was Marcus into? What I did know was that conversation had *nothing* to do with a legal case. He did call him uncle, so I guessed he was related.

Deciding to put aside my thoughts of Marcus and Uncle Louie for the moment, I searched my clothes instead to figure out what I would wear for my first day of work. It didn't take long for me to choose the light grey, high-waisted pencil skirt with a sky blue blouse and nude pumps. That would certainly have Marcus thinking about our little weekend all day at work the next day; well at least I hope so. After ironing my clothes and gently placing them on a hanger, I hopped in the shower.

****

It was nine o'clock when I heard the front door open. Jeremy's grin widened when he saw me on the couch. "Hey, Mia! How was your weekend?" he asked as he placed his keys on top of the table and walked over to me. He kissed my forehead before taking the empty space beside me. "I see you've gotten a nice tan."

I smiled like a school girl, remembering my weekend. "It was so much fun. I love the Bahamas! We should go there together before the summer is over."

He shrugged as he reached for the remote. "Sounds good to me; I haven't been to the Bahamas in a couple years."

"So are you set for tomorrow?" I asked as I stretched my legs over his thighs.

"Yeah, I'm kind of excited. You want to drive down together? Or do you have plans after work?"

"No, that sounds good. Well I'm going to bed; I'm exhausted. Good night."

"Okay, I'm going to watch TV for a while before calling it quits. Good night, Mia."

He asked me about my weekend and that was it. He didn't ask me about Marcus or any scoop regarding what happened. He's such a guy! Sometimes on days like this, I wish I had a girlfriend: someone I could call and confide in, someone that can give me advice and tell me if I'm making a stupid mistake or a good move. Other days I wish I had a mother: a mother who would wipe away my tears, a mother who would encourage me to do well, and a mother whose words could soothe a broken heart. God! I only get this emotional and sensitive when my time of the month is approaching. So I know it's coming soon. Oh well, off to bed I go.

CHAPTER NINE

My alarm was set for six thirty-five in the morning; although, I knew I could sleep in for another half hour. I woke up and used that time for a morning workout. I wanted to make sure I was flawless today; first impressions are everything. Well, it was my first impression for the office, and I wanted to look good for Marcus. The memories of my weekend with him forced me to stay in the shower a little longer than necessary.

When I finished my shower, I dressed in the clothes I'd laid out the night before, and I took extra time doing my makeup and hair. I styled my hair in a low ponytail with my bangs swept to the side of my face. I completed my look with medium white gold hoop earrings and a simple thin necklace with a diamond pendant my father purchased for me on my fourteenth birthday. I glanced in the mirror and congratulated myself on a job well done.

It was eight fifteen a.m., and I was ashamed to admit my disappointment when I didn't receive any text messages from Marcus. I felt a deep twist in my stomach, thinking that he might not be interested in me any longer. I was not going to allow that to ruin my morning though. When I walked out to the kitchen, I was shocked to see that Jeremy was ready. He was dressed and had two travel mugs of coffee in his hands. He walked over to me and handed me one. I couldn't help but smile at how handsome he looked in his all-grey suit, sky blue shirt and matching tie. We matched.

"What?" he asked after taking a sip of coffee.

"Nothing, I was just thinking you're going to make one handsome lawyer one day." He shot me a crooked smile, and we walked out of the building.

We decided on his car and headed toward Midtown Center City. Traffic wasn't too bad, and we made it to the parking lot with ten minutes to spare. Jeremy had come for the interview, so he knew where we were going. I followed as we entered into a sky high building. The design and décor had Jeremy's father's name written all over it. I'd seen a lot of his work and could point it out in a heartbeat. He was definitely a creative man and knew how to satisfy a customer. The lobby of the building was beautifully designed with all-white marble floors and black-and-platinum fixtures and furniture.

We walked to the visitors' table where we gave our names and IDs to a good-looking young man. He handed us badges that gave us access to the building until August first, which was the last day of our externship. We entered the elevators. Jeremy pressed the button for the 25th floor and swiped the badge along a scanner, just as he was told to do by the young man at the front desk. The ride up was a smooth one, and to my surprise I didn't feel nauseated as I usually do on elevators.

Upon entering the 25th floor, we were presented with double glass doors with DELUCA & ASSOCIATES engraved in frosted letters. Jeremy opened the door and, as always, allowed me in first. There were cherry hardwood floors, and the blond receptionist was seated behind a high desk in the center of the room. On the right side of her desk there were two chairs, a sofa, and a coffee table for guests. The same exact arrangement was on the left side of her desk. We walked towards the receptionist whom Jeremy instantly found attractive. I could tell by his flirtatious smile. He leaned his arm over the desk and winked at her; she blushed immediately. *I* rolled my eyes.

"How may I help you?" she asked him a little too seductively.

"We're the new summer externs, and I would *love* to take you out." He leaned in closer onto the desk and flashed a huge grin. Her face turned a darker shade of red, and she looked down shyly to compose herself. She finally looked up.

"I would *love* that too. Mr. DeLuca is waiting for all the externs in the small conference room. Head down that hall, the first door to the left. Oh and here's my number—call me after work some time." She winked, and I almost barfed.

Jeremy grabbed the piece of paper and placed it in his jacket pocket. I rolled my eyes at him again. He caught my reaction this time and placed his arm around my waist. He walked beside me as we headed towards the conference room. "Jealous, *much*?" he asked.

"Ha! You wish. You're a pig. You couldn't even wait to settle in the new job for five minutes before trying to get your dick in someone's skirt!" He didn't respond just smiled at me; he knew I was right!

"You're such a *womanizer*." I breathed.

As we entered the door, he slapped my ass: his response to my comment. I turned and punched his arm. He rubbed his throbbing bicep. *Well at least I hoped it was throbbing.* He looked down at me with a crooked smile. I couldn't help but laugh in response. In the middle of our goofing around, I heard someone clear his throat. I turned around to see who it was. There he was, Marcus, sitting at the head of the conference table; he looked tense and very upset. Sitting beside him was a red-headed woman. She stood from her seat and gave us a polite smile. Jeremy and I made our way towards them.

"Nice to see you again, Jeremy, please have a seat, and you must be Mia? I'm Lisa Harper, very nice to meet you." She offered her hand and I shook it. Marcus and Jeremy said their hellos before Jeremy sat next to him on the opposite side of the table across from Lisa. I was left with no choice but to either take a seat next to Jeremy, next to Lisa, or on the other end of the table directly across from Marcus.

"It's very nice to meet you as well, Ms. Harper, Marcus." I shot him a nervous smile and a slight wave of my hand. He nodded in response, not taking his eyes off me as I made my way around the table to sit next to Jeremy. I felt so uncomfortable. Marcus seemed angry, or was this just the mask he wore at work?

I didn't dare look in his direction, but I could feel the heat of his stare. I knew this would be awkward. I should have known something was up when I didn't receive a text from him this morning. Screw that shit! I can play this game as well. I'd show him he didn't intimidate me. I straightened my shoulders and folded my hands on top of the table, avoiding eye contact with him.

"We are just waiting for the other two externs before getting started. They should be here any moment. Please help yourself to coffee and pastries by the coffee table over there." Lisa pointed behind Marcus. Both Jeremy and I thanked her but declined the offer.

The next few minutes were horrendous as Lisa and Jeremy spoke, and I sat there twirling my fingers. I could see from my peripheral vision Marcus grabbing his phone and dabbing his thumbs on the keys; it looked like he was sending an email or text. I felt my phone vibrate against the table. When I glanced at my screen, I saw the text was from him.

Marcus (8:56am): What the hell was that?

Me (8:56am): What?

Marcus (8:57am): Your little entrance with Jae!

It took me seconds to respond. Is that what he was upset about? Jeremy and I were only kidding. We were goofing around like we always do.

Me (8:57am): We were just joking around.

Marcus (8:58am): I didn't like it! At all!

What do I say to that? I'm sorry for clowning around with my best friend? *What the hell is his problem?* I just stared at my phone for a few seconds, not knowing how to reply. He seemed very angry, but I couldn't believe it was over that. I was trying to gather my thoughts to find the right words to respond. Luckily, the other two externs walked in, and I quickly put my phone away. That would buy me time to think of something to say. They said their hellos and took their seats before Marcus began talking.

"Good morning, everyone, as you may already know, I'm Marcus DeLuca, and this is Lisa Harper. She is my right hand. Any issue you may have, you go to her first, and if it's something she's not able to handle, she will bring it to my attention to be solved. The four of you were carefully selected for the summer extern positions. As you are aware, we have four separate departments. Each department is handled by a partner of the firm.

"Each of you will be assigned to one of the departments, working closely with the partner. Jeremy, you'll be working with Jason Peirce in the civil department. Tasha, you'll be working with Cynthia Evers in the contracts department. David, you will be working with Tracy Long in the antitrust department, and Mia, you will be working with me in the criminal department." I looked up, shocked. No one seemed to notice or even care that I'd be working hand in hand with Marcus. Well except for Jeremy whose foot slightly nudged against mine.

"I'm sure all of you will do a great job. Lisa already has discussed your pay rate, and you'll be getting paid on a weekly basis. At the end of your term, a letter will be sent to the university signed by the partner you have worked with. The letter will discuss which cases you've worked on and the hours you have put in. That will be all for now unless anyone has any questions. Okay then, Lisa will you take the externs and introduce them to the partners they will be working with? Mia, you can follow me, and I will get you settled in."

Marcus stood up and walked toward the door. I quickly jumped from my seat, but Jeremy grabbed my arm before I turned to leave. "Want to do lunch today?" he asked.

I glanced over my shoulder to see Marcus staring at me and waiting by the doorway. "Uh, I'll shoot you a text and let you know." I quickly grabbed my belongings and rushed to the door. I walked directly behind him as I followed in his direction. Not watching where I was walking, I almost tripped over my own heels.

Luckily Marcus didn't notice as he entered a room. When I walked into the oversized office with floor-to-ceiling windows overlooking the city, I was in awe. Marcus' office was completely different from the rest of the building. It had a masculine, antique look to it. His desk looked like it was a dining room table that had been used at a ranch. He had a rustic style coffee table with oversized chairs and a large bookcase which held numerous volumes of law books, both of which had the same wooden texture as his desk. I loved it; it felt warm and peaceful. There was a small bar on the right side of the office, small antique statues on the tables, and artwork on the walls.

He closed and locked the door behind me and sat at one of the oversized chairs by the coffee table. He motioned with his hand for me to join him. I slowly walked over and sat across from him. He was quiet for a while longer. I wasn't sure if I should break the silence, but when I was going to, he cleared his throat. I watched as he placed his elbows on his knees, then he joined his hands together and slightly lowered his head as if it were difficult for him to speak. "It's *not* like me to be a jealous man, Mia. *Fuck*, I'm never jealous. Though for some reason, when you walked into the conference room with Jeremy's arm around your waist and when he slapped your *ass*, it took *every* part of me to not stand up and knock him the fuck out."

"*Marcus*," I breathed his name so low I wasn't sure if he heard me.

"No, let me finish." I leaned back against the plush chair and allowed him to continue. He remained with his head lowered. "See, even if it weren't Jeremy, if it was a total stranger, I would've still felt the same because, for some reason, you make feel that way, and *now* that I know the history between you and him, it made it that much harder to control myself. I'm telling you now that I didn't like it." He lifted his head finally, his eyes meeting mine.

I swallowed before speaking. "I'm sorry you feel that way, and I would never want to make you feel uncomfortable *or* jealous, but I cannot stress this *enough* to you: Jeremy and I are *just* friends. That's how we goof around Marcus. It was completely innocent. If you want whatever this is between us to work, you will have to *trust* me."

"*Trust?*" He said the word as if testing how it sounds. I stood up and walked over to him and bravely sat on his lap, wrapping my arms around his neck. He didn't flinch away from me; that was a good sign. He just stared at me confused by something, maybe his own feelings?

"Marcus, this weekend was absolutely perfect. Let's not ruin it?" I leaned in and kissed him long and hard. At first he stiffened as if he was going to pull away from the kiss, but he didn't. He slid his hand up my thigh, feeling underneath my skirt, making his way to my hips. His touch made my skin burn with heat. I changed my position so that I was straddling him. I kneeled, enclosing his thighs between my legs. He leaned back on the chair and lifted my skirt up to my waist. I ran my fingers through his hair, allowing him to unbutton my blouse.

One minute I was in his arms kissing him, touching him, and the next I was standing up, and he was quickly adjusting his clothing. He looked up at me and waved his hand to indicate my appearance. I was confused until I heard a knock on his door and a man's voice yelling for him to open it up. I was so lost again in our kiss, I didn't hear the knock on the door the first time.

Marcus yelled to give him a minute when he marched over to me and began to quickly re-button my blouse. It took me all but a few seconds to shake the trance and adjust my skirt. I smacked his hand off and tucked the shirt back into my skirt. He walked over to the door and glanced back at me. Once he saw that I was back in order, he opened the door. A man stormed inside and walked passed him.

"What the fuck is going on with you, Marc?"

The man was so upset he was pacing back and forth and didn't notice my presence. Marcus slammed the door and walked over to him. I examined them as they faced each other. The man was slightly taller than Marcus; he had an athletic built. He looked like he worked out but was more slender than Marcus. He had a buzz haircut and green eyes. His complexion was lighter than Marcus'. He was very good-looking. After careful observation, I recognized him from the photos in Marcus' shore house. It was Jimmie, his brother. He was older than in the pictures and his hair was shorter, but it was definitely him.

"I'm busy. What do you want?" Neither of them looked my way.

"What do I want? I get a fucking phone call from you on Friday with important information. When I tell you to back down from it, you said you would, but you go anyways!" Marcus' eyes grew bigger, and slowly he turned his head in my direction. His brother followed his eyes. When he saw me, he looked back at Marcus and rolled his eyes.

"Um, hi, I'm Mia, the new extern." I didn't know what else to say. This was beyond awkward, and what made it worse was the long silence within the room.

"She works with you? That's just fucking great!" His brother threw his arms in the air. I was completely unaware of the reasoning behind this reaction. I was also offended. Did he know about me *and* our weekend? Did he think of me as the kind of girl who always slept with her boss? He glared at Marcus before walking towards me. Extending his hand, he gave me a tight smile.

"Hi, I'm Jimmie, Marc's brother." I looked up at him and then looked at his hand, questioning if I should take it. He impatiently extended his arm further which, in turn, gave me no choice but to grab his hand. He lightly tightened his grip and shook it twice before releasing my hand. "It's nice to meet you, Mia. Do you mind giving my brother and me a minute?"

Swallowing, I nodded lightly. *"Sure."* I grabbed my belongings from on top of the coffee table and walked towards the door.

"Mia," Marcus said. I turned to face him. "Uh you can take the office next door on the right. It's one of the attorney's, but she'll be out the remainder of the summer for maternity leave. So you can work from there." I nodded and walked out of his office. When I shut the door behind me, I let out a deep breath, not realizing I was holding one in. I quickly walked to the door on the right of Marcus' office. I entered and swiftly made my way behind the wooden desk and sat in the chair.

Whoa that was weird! I steadied my breath and glanced around the room. It was spacious but way smaller than Marcus' office. It felt empty as well: no art work, no pictures, and no personalization. It only had a desk, a table in the corner with two chairs, and an empty vase in the center of the table. A bookcase that was semi-filled with legal books occupied half of the one wall. That was it. I turned my chair to look out the window. At least there was a beautiful view to the city skyline.

"What the hell do you want?" I jumped when I heard Marcus' voice. For a second, I thought he was in my room, but the sound was coming through the wall. Oh my God, the wall! I could hear their conversation. I rolled the chair closer, so I could get a better listen. Then I felt stupid for eavesdropping. I was going to go back to the desk when I heard my name.

CHAPTER TEN

"What's going on with you and Mia?" His brother's voice was stern.

"None of your business."

"Seriously? None of my business!" His brother was angry. There were a few seconds of silence before he spoke again, this time with a calmer tone. "Come on, Marc. You know I don't like arguing with you. You're my baby brother, and we're in this together. *You* told me you were going to back off. We can't deal with *any* interruptions right now. You do understand that, *right*?" There was another few seconds before someone spoke.

"Yeah, I understand," he sighed. Marcus' voice was lower, but I could still make out what was said.

"Good. Let's just focus on this job. Okay?"

"Yeah, whatever you say, *boss*." Marcus said sarcastically.

"Come on, Bro, don't be like that. This is just as hard on me as it is on you. We are *so* close to finishing this job. I just don't want some chick to ruin it all."

"She's not just some *chick,* Jimmie; there's something different about her."

"Look, Bro, I can understand that, but your timing is way off. Let it go now before you get too deep into something you can't back away from." Nothing was said. I heard footsteps on the hardwood floors stomping across the room then the sound of the door opening and closing.

After a few more seconds, I heard a loud bang and something shattered, as if glass were thrown across the room. "Fuck!" Marcus yelled.

I quietly rolled back to the desk. When I was safely secured behind the desk, I crossed my arms on top of the table and laid my head on my wrists. *What the hell was that about?* Does this mean that Marcus and I can't be together? Does his brother have so much control over him that all it takes is a mere snapping of his fingers and Marcus does what he's told?

If that's the case, then that means we can't have more than just an employer-employee relationship. Why is it when I finally really like a guy, who makes all my problems and fears go away with a simple kiss or touch, he's taken away from me? I should be used to having important people taken away from me by now, but no matter how many times it happens, it still hurts.

I spent the next three hours contemplating whether I should go to his office and let him know everything I heard, or if I should just leave it alone and see what he would do. So far, he hadn't come over to check on me, to go over any files, not even to discuss what my duties would be.

He hadn't left his office either. I wondered what he was thinking. I kept replaying the conversation between him and his brother over and over in my head, but nothing made sense to me. If everything he said to me over the weekend was true, then he wouldn't listen to his brother, and we'd continue our relationship, but if he listened to him then …

My phone vibrated against the wooden desk. It startled me, and I grabbed it in the hope it was Marcus, but it was only Jeremy.

Jeremy (11:58am): Lunch?

Me (11:58am): Sure, meet u in the lobby in 2 mins?

Jeremy (11:59am): K

I inhaled and exhaled one deep breath before standing up. I grabbed my purse and headed towards the door. It felt like it was going to be a long day. Slowly turning the knob and exiting out the door, I quietly shut it in the hope that he wouldn't hear me exit. When I turned around, Marcus was walking out of his office too. *Great!* We just stood there looking at each other, confused and anxious with desperate looks between us.

My heart was beating rapidly. He looked so lost. I just wanted to reach out and touch him; instead, I pulled myself together and walked past him. He grabbed my arm and pulled me to face him. "What's wrong?" His eyes were searching mine, trying to find something. His answer? Our relationship? Our feelings for one another? I didn't know what he was searching for.

I looked down at my elbow that his hand was gently holding and then looked back up at him. I yanked away from his grip.

"You tell me." I couldn't hold it in. I'm the worst with crap like this.

"What are you talking about?"

"I heard you and your brother talking." He took a few steps back to collect what he just heard.

"What do you mean you heard us talking?"

"You guys were pretty loud, and the conversation came through the walls. I couldn't hear *everything*, just bits and pieces, but from what I did hear, basically I'm considered an *interruption,* and therefore we cannot be *together*." Okay, so I lied. I didn't want him to know that I could hear everything from his office. He'd probably move my desk.

He looked up at the ceiling and closed his eyes. He's thinking? It seemed like he'd been thinking for the last three hours. "Mia, I'm sorry you had to hear that." He brought his head back down.

"So what does this mean?" I crossed my arms.

He shook his head. "I don't know." He just stared at me, not saying anything after that comment. It was like he was waiting for me to come up with a solution to our problem.

It pissed me off. "Well, when you figure it out, let me know. I'm meeting Jeremy for lunch." I turned and walked away, slightly swaying my hips to show him what he'd be missing. I thought he would run after me and ask me to go to lunch with him instead, but he didn't. It took so much of my willpower not to look back. I didn't, and I felt like the biggest idiot. Why didn't I just tell him how I felt? Sometimes my head takes over my heart, and I'm left with unanswered questions.

Jeremy and I decided on a small diner up the block from the building. It was extremely packed, so we had no choice but to sit at the counter. He went on and on about how much he loved the partner he was working with, how *cool* he was, and how much he'd taught him in just the few hours they spent together. I couldn't help but feel jealous. This was supposed to be my future, my career, and here I was swooning over my boss instead of preparing myself for my future. I had to get my head out of this fantasy and bring myself back to reality.

"What's up with you? You haven't touched your salad." He asked as he dipped a fry into the ketchup he squirted onto the side of his plate then tossed it into his mouth.

"Oh nothing, just not hungry, I guess. I was really busy this morning with all the files Marcus gave me that I can't even think about food." I lied. I was starting to get good at this lying stuff. Maybe I should have made a career out of it; oh right, I was. Jeremy, of course, was oblivious and popped another fry into his mouth, and then he continued to talk about how awesome his first few hours were. Blah! Blah!

****

When I walked back into "my" office, I saw that Marcus had left a few files on my desk with a typed note that read, "Review each file and the discovery. Each file has a post-it note of what needs to be done. If you have any questions, contact Lisa. Thanks, M.D."

Great! I guess this means we are strictly off limits. He's such an *asshole*! He could have at least given them to me in person. So our working relationship will be us avoiding each other and placing work back and forth on our desks. Just awesome! I shook my head and exhaled. Screw it, I was there to build my resume and gain experience; I might as well get it over with.

The first file I grabbed was labeled *State vs. Johnny Di Angele.* The post-it note required that I review the file and discovery and locate case law similar to this case regarding self-defense. It was a murder case. I pulled the discovery out of the file and began doing what I was told to do.

The Di Angele case was very intriguing. Our client was at a local bar with a friend; they got into an argument. He left the bar alone and began walking home. Another man held our client at gunpoint for his wallet. Our client, when pulling out his wallet, decided to grab his pocket knife instead; he quickly jabbed the knife into the robber who was standing behind him and ran for it. The robber pulled the trigger and shot our client who fell and passed out. There were no witnesses and no surveillance cameras in the area. A nearby neighbor heard the gunshot and called police. When the police arrived at the scene, both our client and the robber were taken to the hospital.

The robber was stabbed in the chest, and he lost too much blood. He was pronounced dead by the time he arrived at the hospital. Our client was treated for his injuries and questioned. After he was interrogated, they arrested him, and he was charged with first-degree murder. The case was dropped down to third-degree murder at the preliminary. There was a jury trial scheduled for the end of next month. I hoped I could sit in on the trial and watch the case unfold; that would be cool. After an hour I had researched a few cases similar to this case, prepared memos, and began working on the next file.

I was so consumed with the research and work I'd done that I didn't realize the time. I heard a knock at the door and told whoever it was to come in. Jeremy popped his head in.

"Ready to go? It's after five, and I tried calling you." I looked around for my phone then realized it was in my purse.

"Oh, I'm sorry, Jeremy. Give me two minutes." I pulled together the files I worked on that day and piled them on top of each other. I shut the computer down, grabbed the work and my things and headed for the door. "I have to put these files in Marcus' office. I'll be back." I knocked on his door. Thankfully he didn't answer which meant he wasn't there, so I walked in and placed them on top of his desk with a post-it note that read, "All done. Thanks, M.S."

This time on our drive back home I was talkative; we were discussing how interesting the criminal law field is. I didn't mention the case itself, but I did tell him about all the case law I'd researched in self-defense murder cases. The work kept me so busy I didn't have time to think about Marcus. Now, that I was almost home, and my thoughts weren't occupied by work, my mind raced back to him. I started thinking about our weekend and how he asked me to give him a chance to trust him and that he wouldn't hurt me. I'm not one of those girls that are clingy and try every way to get a man's attention, but I just had to get one thing off my chest before I shut him out emotionally. I grabbed my phone out of my purse and sent him a text.

Me (5:45pm): You asked for a chance. You had your chance. Now it's gone.

The minute I sent it I wanted to take it back. My heart started pounding when all of his possible reactions to my text came to mind. Would he be angry? Or would he even care? I hated those mind games when two people started dating. Sometimes I wish I could read minds, so that the truth is always put out there. Then I would never have doubts or second guess a person's facial expression or a comment that I may have taken out of context.

We arrived at the apartment, and I was exhausted. It was my turn to cook that night, and I really didn't want to. I convinced Jeremy we should have pizza, which was not hard to do since it's his favorite food. I placed the order and told him to watch out for the door, so I could take a long shower. I ran the shower and tested the temperature. It was still cold, so I walked back into my bedroom to grab a new towel.

I tested the water again; this time it was nice and warm. I hopped in and scrubbed away all of the day's tension. *Ugh*, what was I going to do about DeLuca? If my brother were still alive, he would have been the perfect person to talk to about this. He always gave me great advice about men. I told him about everything—well everything *minus* my sex life; that would've been too awkward.

I grabbed the shampoo and massaged it into my hair. Afterwards, I leaned my head back and allowed the warm water to rinse out the suds. The water felt really good, and my tension was slowly releasing. I massaged conditioner in my hair, and I lathered the body wash one more time on every inch of my body.

Cutting the shower off, I walked out onto the tile floor. Heading towards the bathroom sink, I started my nightly routine: brushing my teeth, flossing, and untangling my hair. For my final touch of the day, I rubbed night cream on my face and neck. I tightened the towel wrapped around me and opened the bathroom door. My eyes popped out of my head when I saw Marcus sitting on my bed, staring at me.

"W-what are … H-how did?" I stuttered, not able to complete a question.

"Jeremy told me you were taking a shower. I asked if it would be okay to wait in here." I was frozen, but managed to step out of the bathroom and into my room. I couldn't read his facial expression. His face was smooth; he didn't look upset, but yet he didn't look happy. I leaned against the dresser next to me to hold myself up.

"What do you want?"

"I received your text. I came over as soon as I got it."

"*Oh?*" I gulped in air, not knowing what else to say. I didn't expect him to fly over here; a simple reply would've done.

"Yeah." His face was still unreadable.

"So?"

"So I came here to talk in person."

"So talk." I instructed while crossing my arms. He lifted his shoulders to sit up straight and moved closer to the edge of the bed.

"I'm sorry you heard the conversation between my brother and me. I'm also sorry that I shut you down when you asked me what it meant for us. I'm not usually the caring type, except with my family, yet with you I am, and I'm definitely not the scared type."

"Scared?" I asked.

"Yes, scared, Mia. I've known you for only a week now, and I have these suppressed feelings for you. It's hard for me put it all together. I've never felt like this; it makes me feel weak and out of control knowing that I can't *put* it all together."

"Are you used to putting everything together?" I asked, dropping my hip and tightening my crossed arms.

"Yes, that's what I do for a living. I analyze every little piece of evidence until I make sense of it. But with you, I *can't*." I saw where he's going with this.

"It's okay. I get it, Marcus. You feel we don't make sense together."

"No! You don't get it. We make *perfect* sense together, but there are so many reasons why we *shouldn't* be together. I keep trying to go over it in my head, weighing my options on what's best or what should be done."

"Best for whom exactly? *You?* Me? *Us?* Or what's best for your brother?" This visit was starting to piss me off. "It's really not difficult at all, Marcus. You either want to be with me or you don't."

"I *want* to be with you. You know I do. But I *can't*."

"So why are you even here? You could've simply ignored my text, and I would've taken the hint, Marcus." My hands moved to my hips; I was really getting annoyed. So I did what any woman would do: ripped my towel off and let it drop to the floor. *Okay*, maybe not every woman.

I stood there long enough to show him what he'd be missing. His eyes began to trail up and down to view every inch of my curves. They grew dark with desire. I started to slowly walk towards him, looking straight into his eyes. I was only inches away from his knees, but I didn't touch him, instead I slightly turned, walked past him and into my closet. I could hear him exhale as I entered the sliding doors.

I knew he was behind me; I could feel him staring. I pretended that he wasn't there, so I bent over to the lower drawer, knowing damn well my panties and bras were in the top drawer. I roamed through my sweats and shirts. Ah, I grabbed a pair of fitted yoga pants and a white fitted t-shirt. Slowly I put them on with my back facing him.

His mind would go crazy knowing I wasn't wearing any underwear. I turned around and slightly jumped, acting as if he scared me. He was leaning against the inner entryway of the closet door with his arms crossed. I didn't move. I just stared at him. He was so handsome, and his dark brown eyes looked lost and confused. I instantly felt guilty for how I was acting with him. It wasn't fair to him.

"Look, Marcus, I'm sorry. I shouldn't be inconsiderate of your feelings and your work. If you brother feels as though this is a busy time in your life and you don't need any distractions, then I understand. Can we at least be friends?" He didn't say anything for few seconds. He finally began to move towards me; I was a little taken back. I didn't know what he was going to do. When he was a foot away, he reached up and tucked a piece of damp hair behind my ear.

"The thing is, Mia, you see," he hesitated and placed my face between his hands while caressing both of my cheeks with his thumbs. "You see the thing is with or without you, you'll be a major distraction. All I do is think about *you*. So why can't I be with you, knowing that you'll have the same effect on me either way? I can't *just* be friends." I nodded in agreement. He made a valid point. He breathed out a crooked smile and pressed his forehead down to mine.

"So what does this mean?" I whispered with hope. My heart picked up pace with anticipation.

"Be my girlfriend." *Girlfriend*? I couldn't help but laugh.

"What's so funny?" He asked amused.

"Girlfriend sounds so high *school-ish*. Don't you think?" He laughed out loud.

"Okay, well, be my woman-friend, my lover, my partner—whatever you want to call it. I don't care. Just be *mine*."

"So you're saying you want us to be exclusive and label this relationship?" I pointed my fingers between us.

"Yes." I bit down a smile at that comment.

"What about at work? What will we be considered at your office? What will people think?"

"Don't worry about what others think. I'm not going to hide my feelings for you. If they ask what our relationship is, I'll simply tell them you're my girl—no woman-friend." He smiled. I smacked his shoulder and giggled.

"Okay, so I guess we're exclusive then?" I asked, double-checking.

"Yes. Now come here." He pulled me in and kissed me long and hard.

CHAPTER ELEVEN

The next morning I awoke feeling sore but refreshed. Marcus and I spent another magical night together, and I couldn't help but smile at the realization when I opened my eyes. I stretched my arms over my head and looked over beside me. He fell asleep with me last night, but he wasn't there. When I glanced at the alarm clock on my nightstand it was ten minutes to seven. I reached for my phone and noticed a text from him.

Marcus (5:30am): I had to go home to get ready for work. You looked too peaceful to wake up. It was tempting though. I miss you already. See you in the office, babe. ;)

No one would have been able to wipe the grin off my face. This was how he made me feel: like a teenage girl. I threw my head back into the pillow and stared at the ceiling. Last night was absolutely wonderful. Three times in one night had to be a world record for sure—well at least in my sex life it was. It was like we needed it desperately. I could feel his stress, and he could feel mine. The minute our bodies connected, all of our problems and issues were wiped away and solved.

We didn't talk about work or family or anything depressing. Instead, we talked about our favorite movies, foods, hobbies, and shows. We laughed and made fun of each other. I snuck pizza into the bedroom once Jeremy was asleep. We ate and talked some more. To be able to see a side of him that he said most people didn't see made me feel special. I had a feeling we were going to be good for one another.

The alarm went off, so I jumped out of bed. Once my feet hit the ground, I regretted moving so quickly. My thighs and hips felt sore, like I'd been doing lunges and squats all night. Before hopping into the shower, I stretched my legs. I didn't know how much longer I could put up with this soreness. A nice hot bath would soothe the pain. I walked into the shower and completed my morning routine, which was similar to my nightly one. I applied my makeup, blow-dried my hair, and headed to my closet to find something to wear.

When I walked into my closet, I looked on the floor where my yoga pants lay, the ones that Marcus ripped off last night. I laughed at myself. My closet would never be just a closet anymore; it would now be a steamy memory added to the ones we'd also made on our weekend trip.

Today I decided to wear a simple V-neck black dress. It fit perfectly around my curves, but it wasn't too tight. My red pumps matched the color of my glossy lips. I wondered what Marcus would think of me with red lipstick; I usually wore a nude lip gloss. I shrugged my shoulders and headed towards the kitchen. Jeremy was not out of his room yet, and we still had time to spare. Only because I was in an *awesome* mood, I made us coffee and cheese omelets.

"You made breakfast?" Jeremy asked with an eyebrow raised as he walked into the kitchen, looking more handsome than yesterday in a navy blue suit.

"Yes, I'm in a good mood this morning." I said giving him a full-toothed grin and sliding the plate to his end of the island. He stopped it with his hand and settled down on a stool.

"Did DeLuca sleep over? And you were *extremely* loud last night by the way." I tossed a fork in his direction. He caught it and I rolled my eyes.

"*Oh* please, how many times have I had to endure the loud screams of your female friends' orgasms?" I placed his mug in front of him and walked back to the other side of the island, deciding to eat standing up. He looked up at me and winked.

"My bad, I know how to please the ladies. What can I say?" Ugh, barf alert! I shook my head and continued eating my breakfast. To be honest, the few times I'd had sex with Jeremy, I was drunk. I really don't remember if I faked my orgasms or not, but I decided to keep that to myself, not wanting to hurt his feelings.

"So you guys seem to be getting serious, huh?" He said while taking the last bite of his omelet.

"Uh, yeah, he actually asked me to be his *girlfriend*." I hesitated on the word "girlfriend," not sure how it sounded.

Jeremy choked on his coffee. "Excuse me, did you just say girlfriend?" He cleared his throat and continued when I nodded. "Wow, you guys are taking things a little too seriously."

I bit my lip. "Do you think it's too soon? I mean I really like him *a lot*. I feel happy around him."

Jeremy's expression grew unreadable, which was a first, since I knew him so well. His every crease or wrinkled expression wasn't new to me, but this was definitely new. It made me a little nervous. "Mia, you deserve to be happy, really, and if Marcus makes you happy, then, no, it's not too soon."

"I barely *know* him." I expressed.

"No one ever knows a person right away. You could be with someone for ten years and learn something new about them. People are always changing. Don't let that scare you."

"Wow." Taken back by his sincere words, I was shocked.

"What?" He said, standing then placing his dishes in the sink.

I laughed once. "I never had a serious conversation with you. It's different. You're usually goofy or telling a dirty joke. It's nice for a change. Thank you."

"Yeah, well don't get used to it. You look hot by the way." He smacked my ass.

"And he's back!" I yelled, pointing my finger in the air. We laughed and headed out the door.

****

"Good morning, Jeremy and Mia," Stacy, the blond receptionist greeted. "Mia, Mr. DeLuca is in the small conference room. He would like you to go there first."

"Thanks Stacy. Jeremy, see you later!" I smiled and winked at him. He was busy flirting with Stacy.

Quickly I made my way back to the small conference room. The door was open, so I stepped right in. My body came to a complete stop, frozen for a few seconds, analyzing what I was witnessing. Marcus sat at the head of the table, same as yesterday. This time a brunette was sitting on top of the table facing him. She was looking down playfully, talking and laughing, and Marcus was amused by whatever she was saying. His smile grew bigger at the sight of me. "Hey, baby!" The woman looked over her shoulder to glance at me. Marcus stood up from his chair and made his way in my direction.

He embraced me with a hug and kiss. The woman stood up beside Marcus' seat, facing our way.

"Uh, good morning, babe." I said. He grabbed my hand and led me back to where he was just seated.

"Mia, this is Stephanie; she's my assistant. She was out yesterday. Stef, this is Mia; she's one of the new externs and my girlfriend." Stephanie eyes widened. She looked shocked.

"I didn't know you had a girlfriend, Marcus. Ah, hi, it's nice to meet you." She extended her arm. I did as well, and we awkwardly shook hands.

"Yeah, it's kind of new." There was really nothing else I could say; it was true. We were new, and I knew her reaction would be the same as everyone else's that worked in the firm. She nodded and looked at the both of us. I felt small, knowing that she was probably thinking, "*Why her*?" Marcus was oblivious to the whole thing. He was just standing there with a huge smile on his face. For some reason, I didn't know why he was so happy. Was it because this was the first time he introduced me as his girlfriend? *Or* was it because of whom he introduced me to.

"Well, I'll get to my desk. Mr. Di Angele will be here in about twenty minutes. I'll bring him back once he arrives."

"That would be great, Stef, thanks." She waved at me and then walked away.

"So, *babe,*" he playfully said, slouching down so that we were at eye level, "you look beautiful as always. *Mmmh,* and those red lips." He leaned in to kiss me, but I pulled back. "She's the one you slept with." His brows pulled in.

"H-how did you know?"

"I'm a girl, Marcus. We know." I shook my head and began to walk away.

"Wait, babe. Come here. You're mad?" Hearing the desperation in his voice, I turned to face him. I had no right to be mad. The feeling I had was probably the same exact feeling he felt about Jeremy and me. But I'd just seen the hurt in Stephanie's eyes: she was devastated. She loved him.

"No, I just wish I was warned. I knew she still worked for you, but as your assistant? That's, I don't know, going to be hard for me to get used to."

"The same way it's going to be hard for me to know that Jeremy sleeps in the same apartment as you every single night." I sighed. "I'm sorry. I shouldn't throw Jeremy in your face."

"No you're right. How about we just leave our past sexual relationships in the past and just focus on us? We have to trust each other, right?"

"Agreed," he said while bringing that gorgeous dimple back to life. His large strong hands wrapped around my face as he lowered his head and pressed his soft lips against mine. After a few seconds, he leaned back from the kiss and smiled. "Oh, I almost forgot. Come over to my house next Sunday for dinner with my family."

That caught me off guard. It was so random. "What? Your family?"

"Yeah, we all have dinner every Sunday. We usually take turns in each of our homes. Next week is my house. I'd like to introduce you to them." He seemed ecstatic about the idea.

"*Oh*, I don't know, Marcus, what about your brother?" I would love to meet his family, but if they were anything like his brother, I'd rather not. He leaned in and ran his fingers through my hair, and the tension immediately evaporated.

"I spoke to my brother this morning, and my family will love you. I promise."

"How did your brother take it?" I bit the corner of my lip, anticipating the rejection.

"He'll get over it." His hands trailed down my lower back, and he pulled me closer to him.

"Why doesn't he like me?" It hurt to think that his brother thought so little of me.

He shook his head. "It's not *you* per se. He just thinks you'll be a distraction."

"A distraction from *what*?"

He shut his eyes and heavily sighed. "Mia, I can't tell you that." And that was the moment when I realized he was in something deeper than I thought. Marcus had just admitted to me that there was another part of his life he couldn't tell me about. The question was whether I was willing to live that way. Then I thought of Jeremy and our talk this morning when he said that you could be with someone for ten years and not fully know them.

I gave him an understanding smile. "Okay Marcus, but you'll have to tell me one day. I'm not saying tomorrow, but one day, even if it's a year from now, promise?" He nodded.

****

The rest of the morning went well. We met with Mr. Di Angele, and he *loved* me. He was impressed with all the case law I found relevant to his case; he even went so far as to ask me to be present at his trial. Marcus, of course, said it was fine. I was thrilled.

After the meeting, we went around the office, and he introduced me to a few attorneys, the partners of the firm, and some of the paralegals, all who learned that we were dating. At first it was awkward, but after the third person, it started to sound nice being introduced as an item.

I was a little disappointed that Marcus couldn't have lunch with me. He already had plans, and Jeremy asked Stacy out for lunch, so I was left to fend for myself. I decided to grab something from the deli up the block and hide in my office.

Halfway through my sandwich, I was getting ready to send a "thinking of you" text message to Marcus when I heard his office door open and close. Two sets of footsteps stomped across the floor. Then there were low voices. I couldn't hear what was going on, so I dragged my chair closer to the wall to have a better listen.

A man's voice began speaking first. "So Marky, are you going to finish what you started with this job, or are you going to bail on me like you did Saturday?" The man's strong Boston accent and similar raspy tone allowed me to place the voice as Uncle Louie.

"When do you need me?" Marcus made sure his tone was lower. I'm guessing since he knew I heard his last conversation, he was trying to be safe. I thanked myself that I didn't tell him I could hear *everything*.

"Next Friday night, meet at the warehouse, usual time."

Marcus loudly sighed before answering. "Fine."

"What are you so beat up about, huh?" The loud sound of a chair squeaked which allowed me to believe that one of them took a seat.

"*Nothing*. Is there anything else I can do for you, Lou?"

"Nope, just make sure your ass is at the warehouse next week. If you're a minute late, your ass will be deep down the Charles river, if yah know what I mean."

"Sure, sure, whatever you say, Lou."

"Sunday dinner this week?"

"Nope, you know we don't do those anymore."

"That's just a damn shame. I still ask your brother every week just in case. I always look forward to your mom's cooking, especially her famous lasagna."

"Yeah, me too. Anything else, Lou?" Marcus asked clearly irritated.

"Why do I have the feeling that you want to get rid of me? And all through lunch you referred to me as Lou. What are we not family anymore, Marky?"

"Sorry, I've been a little distracted."

"Yah forgiven for now. Well, I'll let you get back to work. I know you're a busy young man. See you next week, Marky."

"Yep, see you then L— uh, Uncle Lou." The sound of the door closing was the last sound that emanated through the walls. I rushed back behind the desk and popped the earphones into my ears. Did he cancel the Sunday dinner, or was that just something he said to Lou to keep him from coming? I was getting the feeling that Uncle Lou wasn't really family, but if he wasn't related to him, then who was he?

Marcus walked through the door, breaking my thoughts. He smiled at me, and I pulled the earphones out of my ears.

"You didn't go out to lunch with Jeremy?" He asked, making his way to me.

"Nope, he had a lunch date with Stacy." I frowned.

"Aw babe, I'm sorry. If I could've gotten out of this lunch appointment, I would have, but I canceled on this guy last week." He reached my desk and shook his head when he saw the half-eaten sandwich on top of its wrapper. "Look at you eating by yourself; I feel terrible now."

"Don't worry about it. Seriously I'm fine. It was kind of relaxing sitting here, surfing the web, listening to music. It was okay. I promise." He eyed me suspiciously then grabbed my hand. With one swift movement I was lifted from the chair, turned, and placed on his lap after he took my position on the seat.

The entire exchange happened so quickly I couldn't help but giggle. It was funny. He laughed at my gasping reaction. I love his laugh; it sounded so carefree and young. He was so adorable like this, so I hugged him. Smiling at me, he ran his fingers through my hair. He looked so happy. I had a feeling it had something to do with me.

A few moments ago, he sounded annoyed and dismissive with Lou, but here he was smiling, and his eyes seemed to fill with peace and contentment. Searching his face, I tried to find a flaw, and I couldn't find a single one. His olive skin, straight white teeth, perfect long nose, and his beautiful eyes, *oh* those eyes. They were dark brown, no special color of blue, green or hazel: large dark brown eyes filled with so many secrets, pain, and suffering. Though at that moment all of that seemed to be hidden behind his pupils, and only happiness was gleaming through.

"What are you thinking?" He asked, rubbing his hand along my arm.

"I'm thinking that if we keep this up, we'll never get any work done in here."

He laughed once. "Yeah, you're right. Let's get to work."

"Marcus?" I asked before stepping off his lap. He froze and looked up at me. "Will you sleep over again tonight?" I almost regretted asking when he hesitated.

"I have something to do after work. I don't know how late I'll be. You'll probably be asleep already."

I nodded. "Okay, no problem."

"Hey." He lifted my chin to meet my gaze. "How about next Friday I sleep over, and then you spend the rest of the weekend at my place before the family dinner? How does that sound?"

I held back my smile, so he couldn't see how excited I was. "Okay, that sounds nice." I really wanted to jump up and down with joy but managed to hold on to my composure.

The rest of the afternoon we actually managed to get work done. We sneaked in a few kisses, touches, and flirting, but that was bound to happen. The more time I spent with Marcus, the more I liked him—really liked him.

A week ago when we met at the nightclub, I thought he was an arrogant asshole. Now that I was actually getting to know him, he was the total opposite. He was sweet, funny, and caring. He talked a lot about his family. You could tell he cared for them deeply. At first I felt a pinch of envy: he had this huge family that looks out for him and would do anything for him. I had no one. Then I felt stupid for feeling that way; I was happy for him—happy that he had a family to love and care for.

CHAPTER TWELVE

"I can't believe Stacy and I have so much in common. Can you believe that?" Jeremy couldn't shut up about Stacy the whole ride home. We were in my car, so I was driving. He went on and on about how funny she was, her taste in music, hobbies, video games, the whole nine yards. He seemed excited about her; it'd been awhile since he was overly excited about a girl, and I couldn't help but laugh.

"So someone is falling hard, huh?" I teased.

"Uh, falling hard? No, I don't fall hard. She's pretty cool. I never met a hot chick that actually likes to play video games and loves sports! Do you know one?"

"I don't know any girls, Jeremy."

"Right, anyway, well she does. I just think it's cool. That's all." He shrugged. Rolling my eyes at him, I fixed my gaze back onto the road.

"Anyway, well she invited me to her parents' vacation home down the shore next weekend. I told her I was in."

"You're going to meet her parents?" This was a major shock to me.

"Hell no! Her parents are away for an anniversary trip to London or France, whatever. She has the place to herself. So you know what that means!" He clapped his hands together and began rubbing his palms. I knew exactly what he meant. He was going to get laid.

"You're a pig!"

"Hey, you love this pig." I saw his huge smile in my peripheral vision.

"Yeah, yeah, you know I do." I still thought he was a dirtbag regardless.

Seeing a spot on the corner, I perfectly parallel parked my car. We exited the vehicle and made our way to the apartment. Jeremy, of course, was still talking about his weekend plans. I was sidetracked when I noticed a black SUV parked directly across from the apartment building. It sat underneath a tree. The shadow from the leaves did not allow me to pinpoint who was sitting in the driver's seat, but there was definitely someone in there.

An unmarked vehicle was not unusual in our neighborhood because we live near a park, but I remembered a similar SUV the night Marcus dropped me off after our trip. All the windows were tinted except for the windshield. Whoever was sitting up front was wearing a black shirt and sunglasses. The arms were muscular, so I knew it was a man, but I couldn't make out the face.

Getting a better look without allowing the driver to know I spotted them was going to be hard. It was probably nothing, but what if someone were spying on Marcus. *Spying on Marcus?* What the hell was I thinking? Who would spy on him? My imagination sometimes got the best of me. Deciding to let it go, I entered the building with the mind-set that if I saw the vehicle again tomorrow, I would definitely keep a closer eye on it. It was Jeremy's turn to cook, so I went into the shower to begin my nightly ritual.

Twenty minutes into my shower Jeremy yelled out. "Mia! Can you get that? I'm taking a shit!" *Seriously?* What the hell! Why are guys so blunt about crap like that? He could have just simply said he's in the bathroom? The doorbell rang again, so I quickly wrapped the towel around my chest.

Running as quickly as possible without slipping on the hardwood surface, I lifted the heels of my feet to look through the peephole. It was Marcus. Excited, I rushed to unlock the door and swung it open.

"You came!" I threw my arms around his neck. His fast reflexes grabbed the towel that was beginning to slip off.

"Do you usually walk around the entire place in a tiny towel?" He seemed annoyed. I pulled my head back to look at him.

"No, I was in the shower. Jeremy was using the bathroom, and he asked me to see who it was."

He cocked his head to the side. "He was using the bathroom while you were taking a shower?" The question was low but stern.

"Marcus, we have two bathrooms. What's your problem? I'm excited to see you, but you don't seem so thrilled to see me." The implication behind his questioning began to steam my blood vessels.

His face relaxed. "I'm happy to see you, baby. Can I come in?" When I moved aside, he entered, and I locked the door behind him. Not saying a word, I lightly jogged on my tiptoes back into my bedroom. He followed me, and I could hear my bedroom door closing.

"Who was it, Mia!" Jeremy shouted.

"It's Marcus!" I shouted back with an annoyed tone. I took it back immediately; it wasn't Jeremy's fault. Then I felt guilty for taking my anger out on him. When I turned around, Marcus had an apologetic smile. When I rolled my eyes and crossed my arms, he lowered his head.

"I'm sorry." He whispered while remaining by the door.

"Yeah, well, don't do that again. I'm not fond of accusatory remarks, especially when I didn't do anything to deserve it." Clearly annoyed, I stomped into my closet and threw on a long t-shirt. When I walked back out, he hadn't moved.

"Do you still want me to stay?" He slightly lifted his arm, and I looked down at his hand. He was holding a small duffle bag. Not noticing the bag before, I felt guilty for giving him attitude. He was making the *time* to be with me like he said he would.

Walking over to him, I grabbed the bag and placed it on top of the dresser. Gliding my hands through the sleeves of his jacket, I slid it off, placing it on top of the bag. After locking my door, I reached up and placed my hands behind his neck. He looked down at me, searching my face to see if we were okay. It made me want to kiss all of his worries away. So I leaned up to kiss the wrinkle between his eyebrows. The moment my lips touched him, his skin smoothed and his shoulders relaxed.

"Of course I want you to stay." Gripping the collar of his button-down shirt, I began walking backwards, leading him towards my bed. We didn't take our eyes off each other. My legs met the edge of the plush surface. As I lay on top of the bed, he stood at the edge staring down at me. I smiled at him playfully, throwing my arms behind my head. "Well? Give me a show."

Raising his eyebrows with amusement, he licked and bit the edge of his bottom lip. My eyes traced his hands as he slowly unbuttoned his shirt revealing a white t-shirt underneath. The light blue button down hit the ground. He looked at me. I raised an eyebrow. "That's all you got?" He laughed once before he grabbed the back of the collar and pulled the t-shirt over his head, throwing it on the floor beside the button down. Not hesitating, he began to un-hook his belt. He bent slightly to drop his pants, and his abs flexed when he stood back up.

Now he was only in his boxer briefs, and my eyes traced every inch of his defined muscles until they met his eyes again. He began to lean over me, but I protested. "Ah uh, you're missing one more piece of fabric." I sang, pointing my toe at his boxers. He looked down at them and then back up at me.

Shaking his head, he flashed me a full smile. He was not following directions; instead, his hands landed on my thighs under the seam of my shirt. The soft cotton fabric wrinkled as he traced his hands beside my hips and up the side of my belly. Throwing my arms up so he could take the shirt off, I laughed when his hand lightly touched the side of my ribs near my underarms. He sat back, his dimple deeper than I've ever seen, excited to discover this new reaction to his touch. "So someone's ticklish, huh?" He teased.

"No! Marcus, don't even think about it." He brought both of his hands over my arms with a wicked smile. I yelled, "No! Marcus, don't!" He did anyway, digging his hands under my arms. I squirmed underneath him, pleading with him to stop while laughing as he continued to torture me. "Marcus, stop, please!" Tears were streaming down from my eyes. "Oh my God, I'm going to pee on myself. Please stop!" He threw himself beside me, bursting into laughter.

Annoyed I jumped on top of him. "Oh yeah, you think that's funny?" I brought my hands over his arms, and he snorted.

"Babe, I'm *not* ticklish."

I raised an eyebrow. "Nowhere?"

"Nope, sorry, but I'm so happy to know you are."

"Ha, I don't believe you. Everyone is ticklish."

Plopping his hands behind his head, he flashed a crooked smile. "Give it your best shot." Skeptical but curious, I wiggled my fingers under his arms: no squirming, no movement, nothing. He just had a smart-ass grin across his face, and his eyebrows rose indicating that he told me so.

"*Okay.*" Tossing my hair to the right side of my shoulder, I leaned down towards him. "How 'bout here?" Pressing my lips against his ear, I gently sucked on his earlobe and planted a small kiss.

"No, but that feels good," he whispered.

I smiled. "Oh *yeah*? What about here?" Tracing my tongue down the nape of his neck, I planted a kiss at the collar bone. He moaned.

"You're getting close." He chuckled. The sound of his laugh made smile.

Sitting up, I looked down at him. "You make me happy." It was such a random comment, but I couldn't help it. Staring at him, I couldn't believe that he was mine. Even in such a short period of time, I was beginning to fall for him. That scared me the most. My biggest fear was to fall so deep, that it would be too hard for me to accept if things were to go wrong. I could feel my eyes water at the thought, but I held back my tears. It was too soon to feel this way. The last thing I needed was for him to think I was a clingy psycho and that he should run.

Sitting up on his elbows, his smile faded. "Mia, since the day I met you, I've been nothing but happy." Then very slowly his lips curled into a wicked grin. "Though, if you keep walking around in tiny towels, I'll have no choice but to punish you." He teased, smacking a hand on the back of my ass.

"Marcus!" Swinging my hand to smack his arm, he grabbed my wrist and pulled me in. Gripping the back of my neck, he forced my lips onto his and kissed me. Knowing my weakness, I allowed him to take over and please me in ways that only *he* can.

****

The next two weeks couldn't have been more perfect. Well, except for the smart remarks from the secretaries in the office. The remarks were never directed to me, but I heard the snickering every time I walked by. It was difficult to adjust to females touching Marcus every time they spoke with him. It was actually disgusting how they blatantly threw themselves at him. Marcus would gently remove their hands from his arm or chest. He did it even when he didn't notice I was watching. *Good boy.*

Stephanie, his assistant, had toned down her narrow glares and eye rolling. She didn't know I could see her grim looks when Marcus would embrace me in a hug, a kiss, or even when he made an endearing comment towards me. Marcus was clueless about her reactions, and I chose to keep it that way. I didn't want him to worry about some assistant that couldn't keep her smug stares to herself.

It was the last thing I needed to worry about as well when I had the upcoming family dinner. Marcus hadn't stopped talking about it. At first I thought it was canceled after hearing his conversation with Lou, but I put two and two together and realized he didn't want Lou to be there.

It was Friday, and Marcus promised to come over that night. I was excited because Jeremy was leaving straight after work with Stacy to go to her parents' shore home. That meant I had the entire apartment to myself, and I planned to take advantage of it. The last three days I had done nothing but make arrangements to ensure that this would be the most perfect night.

I just needed Marcus to stay away for a couple hours, so that I could have everything ready. It felt like the longest day of the week. What made me more eager for this evening was that Marcus and I hadn't been together the past few days. Our time together was spent only in the office. He'd been busy in the evenings a lot. We talked over the phone and sent a few texts messages, but that's all. I wasn't complaining. I'd take what I could get as long as I could see him.

"Hey, babe." Marcus poked his head through the door. Looking up from my computer screen, I smiled at him.

"Hi, baby. Is it five yet?" Grabbing my phone, I looked at the time to answer my own question.

"Yes, uh, I'm going to be a little late tonight. I have something that I *have* to do." He carefully said, expecting me to be angry.

Perfect! This would give me plenty of time to set everything up. "Okay, what time do you think you'll be over?"

"Ah, maybe eight. Is that too late?"

"No, it's perfect. I can give you the spare key, just in case I'm in the shower or something." Standing up, I dug into my purse. Locating my key chain, I slid the spare key from the ring, walked over and handed it to him.

"Okay, babe. I'll shoot you a text when I'm on my way." Leaning in, he quickly kissed me and hurried away.

CHAPTER THIRTEEN

Dinner was ready, dessert was in the oven, the table was set for two, and a couple bottles of wine were being chilled. The apartment and bedroom were set up just like I'd imagined. I stood in the living room admiring my masterpiece. Smiling at my work, I did a final check. The candles were lit, the lights were dim, and rose petals trailed into the bedroom. The new red satin sheets were neatly spread across the bed, and some cuffs that I purchased were lying on top. I'd never done anything like this before, and in a way I was nervous. He *may* pretend to think it's silly, but I knew he wouldn't actually think so. I glanced at the clock. It was only seven; he should have arrived within the next hour or so.

Running towards the bathroom, I began to doll myself up. My makeup was flawless: I decided on the smoky-eye look. My hair was teased and wild; and the pink lip gloss definitely made my green eyes pop. I looked in the mirror, and I barely recognized myself. I looked HOT! The black lace corset enhanced my curves. The matching lace panties lay perfectly on my rounded ass, and the red pumps I wore gave the outfit the finishing touch.

Super excited about the night, I went into the kitchen to take the pie out of the oven. The flaky golden crust looked delicious. My stomach growled. I was starving. Skipping lunch may have been a bad idea, now that I thought about it. Now that everything was ready, I sat back and waited for Marcus to arrive.

Me (8:35pm): Hey babe, u on ur way?

Me (9:00pm): Everything ok?

Me (9:38pm): I'm starting to get worried.

Me (10:15pm): Please call or text me.

Me (11:25pm): Babe?

Marcus (12:00am): I'm so sorry, on my way now.

Was he *fucking* kidding me! I was seriously upset. No, I was
irate. No, better yet, I was furious! I'd been worried the past four
hours, thinking something happened. I'd called him, leaving him
voice message after message. And what did I receive? A text with a
simple, "I'm sorry, on my way." What kind of *shit* is that? *Arrrgh*!
Stomping over to the beautifully decorated table, I grabbed the wine
bottle out of the bucket that was filled with water from the melted
ice. I poured myself a glass and drank, and drank some more, and
then some more.

After the entire bottle was finished, I began the second one. It
was almost two in the morning with no Marcus. I was so angry with
him at that moment that I didn't even want to see him. *Screw* him!
Deciding to lock the top lock since he couldn't get in without that
key, I stood to make my way to the front door.

Whoa. The entire room was spinning; too much wine at such a
fast pace wasn't doing me any good. Blinking a few times so the
spinning could stop, I managed to have a clear view. Wobbling over
to the door, I stopped when the door knob began to jiggle. He'd
arrived. Just awesome! When the door opened, he froze, gawking at
me with a huge grin from ear to ear.

"*Baby*." He breathed, pleased with my appearance.

I rolled my eyes. I was too angry to blush over his reaction.
"Don't you *baby*, me." I said, waving my finger at him while
slapping my free hand on my hip.

His expression dropped instantly. Closing the door behind him,
he didn't take his eyes off me. "I'm so sorry. I am really, really,
sorry."

Waving my hand in the air dismissing his apology, I stomped
over to the island in the kitchen and poured myself another glass of
wine. "I don't want to hear it, Marcus; I'm beyond angry right now.
So save your apologies for someone else." Taking a gulp of my
drink, I watched through the glass as he looked around at the rose
petals on the floor and the table perfectly set up for two.

He sighed, and his eyebrows pulled in. "You did all this for
me?" he whispered.

"No, Marcus, I usually do extravagant shit like this once a
month. You happened to walk in at the right time!" He looked down,

clearly disappointed in himself. Plucking my shoes off, I made it a point to not stop there. Maybe it was the wine on an empty stomach, but I wanted him to feel crappy for standing me up.

"Yes, I did it for you. I've been planning it for three days. I cooked you dinner—even made dessert. I didn't eat. At first I was worried sick, thinking you may have gotten into a car accident or hurt. Then I got a text from you at midnight, four hours after you said you would be here!" Slapping both of my hands against my chest, I slightly lost balance but managed not to fall. "And you walk in here at two in the morning, and what? Am I supposed to welcome you with open arms? *Oh*, Marcus, I missed you; please eat my food and fuck me." I looked at him through hazy eyes, waiting for him to respond.

He traced the top of his teeth with his tongue, and then his lips curled to the side. His jaw tightened. He was angry now. "Okay, I think you've had enough to drink." With one step he was beside me, reaching for my glass. I yanked it away before he could grab it; some of the red wine spilled on my hand and onto the granite counter top. "See what you did!" he said.

Annoyed by his crap, I yelled, "Fuck you. Why are you still here?"

His eyes widened. "*Seriously*, Mia? You're going to talk to me like that? Give me that!" He gripped my hand. We began to wrestle back and forth with the glass. The rest of the wine spilled all over the floor and onto our clothing.

Realizing that I was not giving up, he gave in, letting me have it. Angry with the entire debacle, I slammed the stem on the island, causing the glass to shatter. His veins protruded off his forehead. It pissed me off even more that he was angry. He had no right to be angry! I was the only one who should be mad.

"I said I was fucking sorry! What the FUCK! This entire little scene isn't necessary, Mia. You're acting like a child!"

Did he just seriously say that? "I'm acting like a child? *I'm* acting like a child!" Stepping back to the table, I turned and grabbed the covered food. Lifting the plates, I slammed them to the floor. All of the food and broken glass splattered across tiles. "Is that fucking childish enough for you. Get OUT!" Breathing heavily, I pointed toward to the door.

Hovering over me, he yelled, "FINE!" His face was red with anger. He stormed away, grabbing his keys on the side table by the entrance and then slammed the door behind him. The loud thumping noise brought me back to reality. I slid down the wall, dropping to the ground, sobbing. Throwing my face into my hands, I couldn't believe what just happened. *What had I done?* I was probably acting childish, and there was no excuse, not even liquor. Somehow the liquor gave me the courage to act stupidly.

Even though I was still furious with him, I had to wonder what was so important that made him six hours late. He was so secretive, and it was getting hard for me to deal with.

I probably sat there for fifteen minutes before I heard the front door slowly open. I didn't have to get up to see who it was. I just knew it was him. Who else would it be?

"Mia?" His voice pierced through the kitchen, and I lifted my hand, so he could see where I was. He walked around the island and spotted me. His face dropped, and very slowly he inched over to me. The front of his sneakers tapped against my toes, and he bent down to my level. He lowered his head to me. "I'm so sorry ... about everything ... being late. You had every right to be angry."

I wiped the moisture of the tears off my cheeks and sniffed. "I'm still mad at you."

Letting out a deep breath, his brows pulled in. "I know. I'm really sorry."

"Why were you late? Why didn't you text me right away or call? I was worried sick about you."

"I was on a job. I couldn't get out of it. I really tried, baby. I really did. I was stuck and I couldn't answer you 'cause I was too busy."

Wiping the snot with the back of my hand, I sniffed again. "What job?" Pressing his lips together, he gave me the look that I'd learned way to soon. He couldn't tell me. "Oh, that's right. It's a *big* secret." I rolled my eyes and stood. He stood up with me and grabbed my arm to keep me from moving.

"Mia, please, I'm really sorry. I don't want to go to bed angry. Please forgive me. I promise I'll make it up to you."

I couldn't believe I was caving in to those eyes. It was more because I was extremely tired and hungry, and the corset was sucking the life out of me. I nodded at him and walked toward the bedroom. He followed.

"I'm so sorry, babe," he said, shaking his head when he saw the new silk sheets neatly spread over the bed. I didn't say anything; I was too exhausted. Instead I shifted my body, asking him to unhook the corset. Once it was off, I let out a deep breath; it felt so good to take it off. We crawled into bed, lying on our sides, staring at each other in complete silence.

"Mia?" he whispered.

"Yeah?" I asked as he reached his hand over and gently brushed his fingers against my face. The gesture was so soft and simple, but it felt right. It felt like a relief, and as much as I wanted to still be mad, I didn't have the strength.

"I'm sorry—"

"Let's forget about it, okay?" He nodded once in agreement. Bringing his head in, his lips gently kissed mine. It felt different. We usually kissed forcefully, hard, and powerfully. This time he was gentle, stroking his tongue in soft movements and carefully holding my head. His touch always broke me, and I quickly forgot about our fight. I wrapped my hands around his neck and pulled him in closer.

Breaking from the kiss, he took off his clothes, and I yanked my lace panties off. Grabbing my face with his hands, he continued to kiss me indulgently. I spread my legs, and he made his way between them, instantly filling me with his hardness. I gasped. This was the first time we didn't use protection, and it felt so good when he moved his hips in a slow rhythm that I couldn't fight him off.

Gripping my hands with his over my head, he continued at the same pace, not missing a beat. We stared at each other as our bodies molded perfectly against one another. Sex with him was usually rough and hard. But this, this was different: we were making love. His eyes searched my face; he seemed lost and afraid. Usually he would flash me a wicked smile or make a naughty comment. It was like we both couldn't breathe, mesmerized with one another. I moaned when I felt myself building, ready to let go. With him I wasn't just me; I was *his*.

Both of our bodies trembled at the somehow new sensation; he leaned down, his lips meeting mine. "*Mia*," he whispered. He thrust his hips against mine, my insides tightened, and he groaned against my bottom lip as he exploded inside of me. My body instantly reacted to his convulsion, and I whispered his name as my orgasm reached its peak. Still inside of me, his body slammed against mine, and he threw his head into the nape of my neck. "I *love* you." It was barely a whisper, but I heard it.

I was afraid of those three little words—afraid because I felt the same. It was too soon. We'd just had a huge fight just a few moments before. Wasn't it a bad sign to be arguing at such an early stage of a relationship? He was saying he loved me. We'd only known each other for a couple weeks. Was it really love, or was it lust? Pretending not to hear him, I didn't say anything. We just stayed in that position, listening to sound of our own breathing, until we drifted into a deep sleep.

****

The smell of fresh brewed coffee woke me. The side of the bed Marcus had occupied was now empty. Stretching my arms over my head, I squealed with delight. Glancing at the small alarm clock, I saw that it was seven in the morning. It was Saturday. I was never up this early on a weekend. My eyes, feeling heavy, began to close again. They re-opened at the sound of a loud thumping noise coming from the kitchen. It sounded like he was cooking. Unwillingly, I rolled off of the bed. Noticing his t-shirt thrown on the floor, I bent over, grabbed it, and tossed it over my head. Dragging my feet to the bathroom, I lifted the toilet lid and slumped on the seat. I could hear a few more thumps in the kitchen. *What* was he doing?

Finishing, I stood and flushed the toilet. Making my way to the sink, I jumped at the sight of myself in the mirror. My overly teased hair was a mess. My smoky eye makeup was all over the place, and the mascara left dry drip marks on cheeks from crying. He'd woken up to *this*! Grabbing a hair tie from the side drawer, I tossed my hair into a high bun, attempting to calm the medusa look.

Turning the faucet on, I adjusted the hot and cold until the water turned a satisfying warm temperature. I grabbed the facial cleanser and squeezed the gel onto my hand, rubbing my palms together till it foamed. I scrubbed my face and rinsed, making sure I repeated it two more times till there were no more traces of smeared makeup. After brushing my teeth, I headed for the kitchen.

Marcus' back was facing me as he hovered near the stove. Looking around, I noticed everything was clean: the shattered glass from last night was no longer on the counter top or the floor, and the rose petals that I placed on the floor were all gone.

The table was still set for two but with new plates. What time did he wake up? We went to sleep a little after three in the morning, and it was only seven. Did he ever sleep? He turned around when he felt my presence and smiled. "Good morning, babe." Lightly jogging over to me with a spatula in hand, he gave me a quick peck on the lips and led me to sit at the table. "I made breakfast."

"Thank you." He opened the microwave and took out a mug. Running back to me, he handed me a cup of coffee, placing sugar, cream, and a spoon in front of me as well. I smiled and began preparing my cup. He kissed my forehead before heading back to the stove. Taking a few sips of coffee, I watched him as he hurried back and forth from the stove to the island, placing the bacon, eggs, and pancakes on separate plates. Walking over, he grabbed both plates from the table and made his way back to the island. He prepared our plates, piling them high.

When he placed the food before me, the smell of bacon made my stomach growl so loudly he looked down at me with a raised eyebrow. "Hungry?" he asked, sitting in the chair across from me.

"I didn't have lunch or dinner yesterday." I whispered. His face fell with understanding.

"Yeah, I'm sorry about that. Want some orange juice?" I shook my head, digging into my food.

He laughed. "I love that about you. You're not embarrassed to eat in front of me. Most girls would pick at their food."

He said the "love" word again. I froze for a second and then continued with my food.

"You're a loud cook." I grumbled through a mouth full of pancakes.

"Yeah, I'm always jumping around in the kitchen."

"This is *so* good." The satisfaction was so unbearable my eyes watered with delight.

"Whoa, slow down, we have plenty, and your stomach will get upset." I looked up through my lashes. I didn't realize I was gulping the food down. Breathing a half smile, I wiped the side of my lips with my hand and continued at a slower pace.

I was completely stuffed and couldn't move, literally. I watched as he washed the dishes. Once he was finished, he walked over to me. "So what are the plans for today? What do you want to do?" Glancing over at the microwave's clock, I saw that it was not even eight yet, and now that I was full, I just wanted to crawl back in bed for a long nap.

"Chillax," I said, shrugging my shoulders.

"Chillax?" His eyebrows rose. "What does that mean?"

"You know, chill and relax." He pressed his lips together, forcing down his amusement, but he couldn't help it.

"Is that a Philly thing?" He laughed.

"No, it's a *me* thing, I think? Maybe it's a Philly thing as well. I don't know. Come on." I stood up and grabbed his arm, making my way to the bedroom. I threw myself on the bed, and he followed beside me.

"So is this what you want to do all day?" he asked, brushing my hair with his fingers.

"You have a better idea?" I yawned, and he smiled at me.

"Yeah I do, but I can wait until you wake up. Get some sleep. Then you have to pack a bag. We're going to my place for the rest of the weekend." I smiled at him. This would be my first time at his place. It was exciting, but I needed my sleep first. Closing my eyes, I drifted into a sleep, beginning my dream of the one and only man I was falling for, and he lay next to me at that very moment.

It was pitch dark, and I couldn't see where I was going. It was hard to know where I was. I stretched my hands in front me, trying to feel my way around. It was an open space. I kept walking, but I wasn't getting anywhere. An orange flame caught my attention; it was flickering straight ahead. I followed it, picking up the pace, desperate to walk into the light. The closer I got, the bigger the flame got. I was outside now in front of a huge field. There was an old farmhouse burning. The flames were huge, covering every inch of the home. I was standing at least a yard away, but I could still feel the heat burning against my face. I began to walk back into the darkness. Maybe was safer in there, but I stopped when I heard a familiar voice yelling my name.

Straining my eyes to get a better glance in the distance, I noticed the person running out of the house covered in black ashes. "Michael!" I screamed. He fell to the ground. Running in his direction, I could feel the strength of the heat from the flames. Forcing myself through the pain, I continued to run until I reached him. My brother was barely recognizable: half his face was burned. Falling to my knees, I pulled him into my arms. Screaming for someone to help, I rocked him as he lay on my lap. "It's okay, Michael. I'll get help. Please don't leave me. Please stay with me." I sobbed, throwing my head into his chest. I couldn't feel him breathing. I didn't want him to leave me again, so my cries turned to screams.

At the sound of a low raspy cough, I sprung my head up. He was alive. He was mumbling something. "What is it, Michael?" I leaned my ear closer to his lips, so I could hear him.

"Promise," he whispered.

"Anything, promise what?" I asked urgently.

"Promise me you'll stay away from him?" I turned my head, and my eyes met his. We were only inches away from one another.

I was confused. "Away from whom?" I asked, shaking my head.

He slowly turned his head to the left, looking by the house. I watched as he gradually lifted his hand to point, but when my eyes followed its direction, I froze. Marcus was standing by the burning house, holding a container of gas in one hand and a box of matches in the other. His legs were spread apart, his shoulders were hunched over, and his eyes were dark. What scared me the most was the wicked smile that spread across his face.

"Mia. Mia, wake up!" I was awakened by the sound of Marcus' voice and a slight nudge to my shoulder. My eyes popped open. My breathing matched my rapid heartbeat. My throat and mouth felt dry. "You were having a bad dream. You were screaming and crying." He looked worried. Sitting up, I leaned against the headboard. *It was just a dream; it was just a dream*, I repeated over and over in my head until my breathing and chest calmed to a normal pace. "Are you okay?"

Looking at him, I wanted to cry. I wanted him to hold me to keep me safe, but he was the person I was afraid of at that moment. My nightmare was about him. I needed him to go away for a few moments. "Marcus, my throat is really dry. Can you grab me some water, please?" He nodded and jumped out of the bed, leaving the room.

Dropping my shoulders in relief, I buried my hands into my damp sweaty face. Oh God, I hadn't had a dream about my brother in months. Finally I did, and he was warning me about Marcus. I took a few deep breaths to control my anxiety, and Marcus stumbled back to my side, handing me a glass. I snatched it out of his hand and chugged the water. *Ah, just what I needed.*

After I was done, I placed the empty glass on the nightstand. Marcus was kneeling on the bed, cautiously watching me. I wanted to cry or run. Instead I jumped over to him, wrapping my arms around him. He hugged me tightly, not questioning me about my dream, just holding me. How could my brother warn me to stay away when I felt the safest with Marcus? I knew my dream was more about my feelings of being afraid. So I said the one thing I didn't want to: I told him how I felt. "*Marcus?*"

"Yeah, baby?" he said while kissing the top of my head.

"I love you, but I'm scared." I whispered.

His shoulders relaxed while letting out a heavy sigh. "I love you more than you'll know, and I'm scared too." Closing my eyes, I tightened my arms around him. Here we go, it was either up or down from here. It would definitely be a roller coaster, but I was willing to take the ride.

CHAPTER FOURTEEN

Marcus' house was absolutely beautiful—everything you could dream of and more. It was probably as large as his beach home. The entrance was similar as well with a metal fence. He had to plug in a code before it opened. The driveway was surrounded by overgrown trees and an amazing landscape. The miniature mansion was a brick colonial home with white pillars and an oversized front porch. The interior was decorated and styled in a manner similar to his office with dark hardwood floors, light colored walls, antique oversized furniture, and modernized kitchen and bathrooms.

"Your house is beautiful." I said, twirling around in his bedroom, the final stop of the tour. "You live here alone?"

"No, my brother and his daughter live here with me."

"Your brother has a daughter? You have a niece?" He'd never mentioned that before.

"Yes, she's eight, going on twenty." He laughed while grabbing my bag and unpacking my clothes into an empty drawer.

"Oh, is he married?"

"He was. His wife was killed in a car accident a few years ago."

"Oh." I whispered, feeling stupid for asking the question. His brother was raising a little girl all on his own. That had to be hard. But then I thought of my father raising us on his own, and he'd made it seem so easy. "What's her name?"

"Brielle. She's adorable. We call her Elle. *She* is very entertaining. You'll meet her later on today." I nodded. I wasn't used to being around children. I wasn't sure exactly how she'd react to me; I felt nervous. "Want to go for a swim?" he asked.

"Okay." I smiled.

"Cannonball!" Marcus was in midair: knees pulled into his chest, arms wrapped around his legs. His round-shaped body slammed into the pool, and water splashed all over the patio and the lounge chair I was lying on.

"Marcus!" I laughed.

His head popped up from under the water, his hair was soaked, and his smile was irresistible. "Come on!" The last hour he had been trying to persuade me to do a cannonball. I'd never done it before, and I was scared I'd slip and break a bone. I knew I was a sissy, but growing up, I never broke a bone in my body. I guess that was one of the benefits of living with two overprotective men. Standing up and walking towards the edge of the pool, I dipped my toe in the water. It was warm. Biting the side of my bottom lip, I wondered if I should just do it.

He watched as I took a few steps back. I tried to do it twice but stopped before actually jumping. I knew he was skeptical, thinking it wouldn't happen just like the other two times. Taking a deep breath, I ran for it. When my feet hit the edge of the pool, I jumped, hugging my legs into my chest. My eyes were shut tight. I took a deep breath when I felt my behind hit the water. Then I was underwater. Opening my eyes, I smiled because I made it without getting hurt.

Untangling my legs, I waved my arms until I was above water. Marcus was swimming in my direction. I couldn't take the smile off my face. It was so much fun! He reached me, grabbing my face with both his hands. "I told you! You did great!" I giggled. He was so happy that I did it that it made me laugh.

"It was fun! I want to do it again," I said. He laughed and kissed me. Of course, the cannonball could wait. I'd rather kiss my man.

Wrapping my legs around his waist and my arms around his neck, I tightened my grip. I wanted to be closer to him. It's like I was addicted; I could never have enough of him. He was everything I wanted and everything I needed. My dream had just been portraying my fears of allowing him in. Since I told him I loved him this morning, all of my fears went away. No relationship is perfect. I knew that. I also knew that we'd have issues that we'd have to resolve along the way, but it was all worth it. As long as I had him by my side, we'd be okay.

"Ahem." We were interrupted by someone clearing his throat. Marcus and I both turned our heads to see his brother standing at the edge of the pool. He was holding the hand of a little girl who was wearing a bright pink swimsuit. She was absolutely adorable with long brown hair, green eyes, and an olive complexion.

"Uncle Marc?" she asked while slapping her free hand on her hip. Her smile showed me she was teasing.

"Elle! You wanna join us in the pool?" Marcus asked, still holding me.

"Only if it's PG-13." Jimmie said, looking at the both of us with a slight grin. I pulled away from Marcus embarrassed.

"Hi, Mia," he said.

"Uh hi, Jimmie." Swimming over, I met them at the edge of the pool. I looked up at the little girl. She bent her knees and offered her hand to me. Surprised by her gesture, I grabbed her tiny hand, and she smiled.

"Hi, I'm Brielle Marie DeLuca. You can call me Elle." Her cute girly voice made me giggle.

"Hi, I'm Mia Sullivan. You can call me Mia; it's nice to meet you." Elle stood back up, both hands on her hips. I could see why Marcus said she was eight going on twenty. She was a grown woman trapped in a child's body. "Have you ever cannonballed?" I asked her.

"Psssh, cannonballs are for amateurs. I just learned how to do a backflip. Want to see?" She asked with her eyes widened.

"No, Elle, that's dangerous, and, Marcus, you need to stop teaching my daughter all of those tricks. If she hurts herself, I'm going to hurt you!" Jimmie warned. Marcus' laugh sounded from behind me.

"Yeah, okay, I would love to see that, Jimmie. Elle, let's leave the flips for when your dad's not around." Now beside me, he winked at her.

Pouting, she crossed her arms. "Daddy! Come on! *Please*?"

"No, and that's final." She sighed, throwing her arms to her side. Kicking her sandals off, she walked back a few steps, ran, and cannonballed into midair. Marcus swam over to her. Once her little body was back up from under the water, Marcus picked her up and sat her on his shoulders. Her giggles were contagious, and I joined in.

"Well, I'm going to go throw some burgers on the grill." Jimmie walked away. I watched him head toward the grill by the patio farther away from the pool.

"Mia, do you think you can convince my Uncle Marc to take me to the carnival that's coming up next month?" Marcus shook his head, so I would say no.

"I think I can do that for you, Elle." I smiled at Marcus.

"Oh you think you could, huh?" He asked with a crooked smile, more gorgeous than ever.

"Mmmmhuh." I mumbled. He smacked his hand against the water, splashing it in my direction. I yelled and splashed back, and thus began a splash war.

"Okay, okay! I'll take you next month, but Mia has to come too." He took Elle off his shoulders and placed her next to him. Her head bobbed in the water as she jumped up and down with delight. "Yes!" she squealed. Swimming in my direction, she threw her arms around me. I gently lifted her to my side. She gave me a quick peck on the cheek. "You're my new best friend!" I laughed. I was starting to love this little girl. *Who wouldn't?*

"So, Mia you're beginning your second year of law school?" Jimmie awkwardly began to make small talk. Elle and Marcus were still in the pool. After a half an hour of jumping in, I grew tired and hungry. I was sitting at the patio when Jimmie joined me, laying a plate full of well-cooked burgers before me. I grabbed one and took a bite.

"Yeah, I just finished my first year. You went to Harvard as well?" I asked with my mouth full.

"Yep. What inspired you to be an attorney?" He took a swig of his soda.

"Uh, I was always interested in the legal field. Both my brother and father were in law enforcement, so I guess I got it from them."

He nodded. "I see."

"What made you get out the field?" I was curious to find out what he truly does.

"Uh, just wasn't into it anymore. Marcus is really good at it. I, on the other hand, sucked," he said laughing. "I would never admit that to him though." He raised his eyebrow warning me to keep quiet; I smiled.

"So what do you do now?"

"It's complicated to explain. I'm a freelancer. I work from home for companies. When their systems are down, I can access any info via my network and assist any time of the day."

"Oh, that's interesting. And it must be nice to work from home." Chewing the last bite of my burger, I took a sip of water.

"It's okay, I guess." He looked at Elle and Marcus who were now running in our direction. "Hey, I wanted to apologize about the first day we met. I'm not that type of person, just so you know."

Smiling at him, I felt a bit relieved. "Thank you." He nodded. Elle ran into his arms, and he hugged her. They were too cute together. He seemed to be a really great dad. It made me think of what type of father Marcus would be. I wondered if Marcus wanted kids in the future. It was too soon to think like that, but it was good to know. Marcus struck me as a family man. The way he was with Elle and the way he talked about the family dinner all week, I knew he would make a wonderful father one day.

"You okay, babe?" Marcus swung his arm over my shoulder as he took a seat right next to me.

"Yeah, I'm great." Reaching for a burger, he shoved it into his mouth. He must have been starving; the last thing he ate was the breakfast he made this morning.

"Excuse me. I have to go to the bathroom." I stood up.

"You want me to go with you?" he asked. I looked at him with a strange look.

"I think I can handle going to the bathroom on my own." I giggled at him, after he slumped back into his seat. Then I thought maybe he wanted to do something else. Leaning down, I whispered in his ear, "Unless, you had something in mind."

Wetting his lips, he flashed a wide smile and nodded. "I like your way of thinking."

We both stood and headed toward the sliding door as Jimmie shook his head at Marcus' boyish grin.

****

The rest of the day went by smoothly. We spent a lot of time with Jimmie and Elle. We had dinner and played some games: Scrabble and Monopoly. Then Elle forced me to play a dance game on one of her consoles. I couldn't say no to her, so I proudly humiliated myself in front of both men. They just laughed and watched us play. Elle knew all the dance moves to each song, so she beat me. After we were finished for the night, Marcus' phone rang. He stepped into his office to take it.

"Mia, you have good moves." Elle said as she jumped to sit beside me on the couch.

"Me? You're the one with the moves." I lightly tickled her, and she giggled.

"Well, it's way past my bedtime. See you tomorrow." Throwing her arms around me, she kissed my cheek then ran to her father. Jimmie lifted her until her lips met his, and she gave him a quick peck on the lips. "Good night, daddy!" She yelled.

"Good night, princess. Sweet dreams." She ran up the stairs. Jimmie laughed to himself then turned to face me. "She really likes you. It's hard for her to get attached to someone, especially females."

"She's a great kid, Jimmie." I smiled.

"Thanks. Well I better go to …" He looked up at Marcus before finishing his sentence. Marcus looked concerned.

"He wants us to go in tonight." Marcus' expression was unreadable.

Jimmie sighed, placing his hands on his hips and lowering his head. "You'll have to go on your own tonight, Marc. Melissa is off tonight again." Marcus looked at me then back at Jimmie. I didn't belong here. It felt awkward, not knowing what they were talking about.

"It'll be done a lot faster if you are with me." Marcus grew impatient.

"I'm sorry, Bro, but I can't leave Elle without a babysitter."

"I-I'm here. It's not a problem. I can make sure she's okay." They both looked at me, speculating. Jimmie glanced at Marcus. They looked at each other for a long time. Finally their eyes were back on me. "Seriously, she's in bed anyway. I'll let her know that you guys had to run off, and if she needs anything she can come to Marc's room."

Jimmie pulled his brows in. "Are you sure? If it's too much trouble …"

"No it's fine. Go do whatever you guys have to do. If it's faster for Marcus to get back home, I don't mind." I glanced at Marcus; he had a soft smile.

"Thank you, Mia. Marcus, I'll be in the car." Jimmie walked away. Marcus kneeled before me. He grabbed my hands with his. Looking up, his eyes were filled with distress.

"Where do you have to go?" I whispered, searching his face for an answer.

Slightly shaking his head, he pulled his brows in. He was thinking. I wish I knew what was going on in his mind. Reaching out, I placed both my hands on his cheeks and rubbed my thumbs against his cheekbones. Shutting his eyes, he sighed.

"I'll be back soon. Thank you for watching Elle." Leaning up, he kissed my forehead, then lowered and kissed my lips. Before I could question him any longer, he was gone.

After poking my head into the fourth bedroom, I finally found Elle's room. She was lying in bed, knees up, and head leaning against a pillow. Her thumbs were tapping against a handheld. She looked up when I entered her room.

"Sorry to bother you. I just wanted to let you know that your father and uncle had to run out. So if you need anything, I'll be in Marcus' room. Are you okay?"

Placing the handheld on the nightstand, she sat up Indian style facing me. "Why do they always go out so late?" she asked.

"Does it happen a lot?" Making my way to her bed, I sat on the corner, lifting only one leg to face her.

"At least once a week. Last night Uncle Marc begged my daddy to go with him, so he could finish faster, but my babysitter, Melissa, is off this weekend. She gets one whole weekend off a month."

"Do you know what they go do?" She shrugged. *Of* course she didn't; I don't even know why I asked her.

"Well, Elle, I'm heading to bed. If you need anything, let me know. Okay?" Smiling at me, she nodded. Elle flopped back in her previous position and grabbed her handheld again.

CHAPTER FIFTEEN

It had been four hours since the guys left. Ever since then, I'd been pacing back and forth in the bedroom, wondering what the hell was taking them so long. Glancing at my cell phone for the twentieth time, I threw myself on the bed and stared at the ceiling. I'd been holding back from calling or texting him. It was so hard to do when I was worried sick. What were they doing?

Whatever it was, I knew it was bad, and something told me it had a thing or two to do with Lou. The mere sound of that man's voice gave me the creeps, let alone his name. I could feel Marcus' uneasiness in his voice and posture when he talked to Lou. Jimmie and Marcus were in something way deeper than I could imagine, but I didn't know what it was and why it was so hard to just walk away from.

"Mia?" Elle's frightened little voice froze my thoughts. I leaned up on my elbows as she hurriedly ran over to me. Her eyes were almost in tears, and the tight grip she held on her blanket allowed me take her into my arms.

"Did you have a bad dream?" I asked as she curled up in a ball on my lap. She shook her head and looked up at me.

"No, I heard noises downstairs from the living room. I don't think Daddy or Uncle Marc is here. Someone's in the house." I froze. What do I do? Taking a deep breath, I tried to hide my fear for her sake.

"It's okay. I'm pretty sure it's nothing. I'm going to check to see what the noise is. Lock the door behind me, and if I'm not back up in ten minutes, call the police. My cell phone is right here," I said, pointing at the nightstand. "Do you think you could do that?" She nodded her head. "Good, it's going to be okay. Don't worry. I'll be back soon," I said, giving her a reassuring smile.

She followed me to the door, locking it behind me. I turned the knob to make sure it was secured. I couldn't hear anything, but Elle's room was farther down the hall near the staircase. Making my way down the hallway, I tiptoed, so that if anyone *were* here, he couldn't hear me. When I reached the top of the staircase, I hesitated, waiting to hear something before making my way down.

I waited three long minutes. There was no noise, so I decided to go back to the room. I slowly turned on my toes. When I heard a loud thump, I quickly turn backed toward the stairwell. I bent to see if there was anyone at the bottom of the steps. My heart picked up its pace. I could do this; it was probably nothing. Slowly tiptoeing down the stairs, I heard a few more thumps and a voice mumbling.

At the end of the stairs, I followed the voice. When I reached the front door of Marcus' office, I sucked in my bottom lip and bit. Taking a deep breath, not knowing what to expect, I opened the door. His office was dark, and the only light was from the lamp in the far right corner. I jumped when I saw Marcus lifting his head from behind his desk. He was slouched and lying on one arm, while the other hand held a half empty bottle of brandy.

"Marcus, you scared me." Relaxing my shoulders, I made my way toward him. When I got closer, I noticed that his eyes were blood shot. He could barely keep them open. "Did you drink all of that?" I asked, reaching for the bottle in his hand. He pulled back in his seat and chugged another swig of the drink, then slammed the bottle back on the desk, making a thumping noise. Now I knew where the noise was coming from.

"You are so beautiful." He whispered in a raspy tone.

"What's wrong, baby?" I asked, worried. He seemed lost. I'd never been around him this intoxicated, so I maintained my distance. You never know what to expect from a drunken person.

Taking another sip from the bottle, he smiled. "Nothing's wrong with me. I'm great!" He threw his hands in the air, laughing.

"*Marcus*, let's go to bed, okay?" I whispered, hoping my low voice would lower his.

"You know what *fucking* pisses me off?" he said, dismissing my plea.

"What, baby?"

"When people say, 'Don't worry about it; it will get better,' or I love this one um, 'Things happen for a reason.'" He burst into laughter. I just stared at him lost.

"Yeah, that pisses me off too, Marcus," I said, trying to side with him.

He looked up at me with his brows pulled in. "See that's why I love you so much." He shook his head. "You don't deserve me, Mia. You deserve someone so much better than me." Carelessly he stood up, dipping side-to-side as he made his way toward me. He tripped over an area rug and fell into me. I stumbled back but managed to keep us from falling. The liquor from his breath and clothing was so strong I couldn't bear it. He chuckled at himself and straightened his posture, pulling me into him.

Looking into my eyes, he seemed to search for answers. "Why do you love me?" he asked.

I looked at him troubled by his question. "*Marcus,* you should know. You're funny, sweet, and a gentleman. I love how you talk about your family. I know they mean everything to you. And today watching you with Elle, I know one day you'll make a wonderful father."

"You think all that about me?" he asked, disgusted. I nodded. "I'm an evil man. You only know half of me. If you knew the other half, you would *run.* I'm far from perfect, Mia."

Grabbing his face, I managed a stern tone. "Hey, no one's perfect. I love you no matter what. You hear me?" He looked away. I grabbed his face and pulled him back to look at me; his eyes softened. "I love you, Marcus, perfect or not, but obviously whatever you're into is breaking you. If you don't let me in, I won't be able to help you."

Pressing his lips down, he looked like he was going to break. His eyes were watering, his face was red, and he let out a heavy sigh. "Mia, I'm—"

"That's enough, Marcus." Jimmie stormed into the room. He snatched the bottle of brandy from Marcus' hand and tossed it into a trash bin beside the desk.

Startled by his entrance, I mumbled, "Jimmie, Elle is in Marcus' room."

"I know. I went to look for her when I didn't see her in her room. She told me that she heard noises, and you went to find out what it was. I'm sorry about this, Mia. I'll take him into one of the other rooms," he said, throwing Marcus' arm around his shoulder. Then he wrapped his arm around Marcus' waist to hold him up.

"No, no, take him to his room. I can't leave him like this."

Jimmie nodded once. He managed to help Marcus walk up the stairs and down the hall. By the time we reached the room, Marcus pleaded for the bathroom. Jimmie placed Marcus in front of the toilet. Marcus hugged the toilet and began to throw up. His face was red, and veins popped out of his neck and temples each time he vomited. Jimmie leaned against the sink, legs and arms crossed. He looked exhausted.

"Jimmie, it's okay, I'll take it from here. Go ahead and go to bed." Looking up at me, he thought for a moment, and then his shoulders relaxed.

"Are you sure?" he asked, looking back down at his brother. I followed and watched as Marcus continued to vomit and groan.

"Yeah, I'm sure." Glancing at his brother once more, he shook his head and walked out, closing the bathroom door behind him. I waited a few seconds before I went by Marcus' side.

"How you feeling, baby?" I asked, rubbing the palm of my hand on his back.

"Like crap," he said, choking on his own vomit.

"Yeah, well you smell like crap too. Do you want to take a shower?" He shook his head.

"I know you don't want to do anything right now, but you'll be doing me a favor if you take a shower. Also you'll thank me tomorrow morning. I'll take one with you."

Lifting his head from the toilet bowl, he groaned, "Fine."

Testing the temperature of the faucet, I turned the shower on. I walked back to Marcus; he was leaning against the sink cabinet. Sighing at him, I began to take his clothes off. Starting with the easiest, I tossed his boots off. Luckily, he wore a button-down shirt, so I just quickly unhooked the buttons and removed the shirt. It was exhausting taking off clothes for a drunken man. His arms weighed three times as much. After I wrestled and struggled with his jeans and boxers, he was completely naked.

Tossing my t-shirt and shorts off, I kneeled before him and placed his arms around my shoulders. I tried lifting him once, but he didn't bulge; I tried again, nothing. "Baby, you have to help me a little. Try to stand up for me." Groaning, he obliged. We slowly made our way to the shower, and he sat in the tub instead of standing. I adjusted the showerhead, so the water could hit him. He leaned his head back against the tile wall and shut his eyes. His head gently rolled from side-to-side as he moaned. I grabbed the washcloth and soap. Kneeling across from him, I nestled between his legs.

"Mia?" His eyes were still closed when he called my name.

"Yes, Marcus?" I asked while rubbing the cloth over his chest. The water dripped over his head rinsed the foamy suds away.

"I'm sorry." I didn't respond just continued to wash him. What was I going to do with him? I loved this man so much, but I had no idea what to expect in this relationship. Could I handle more nights like this? Was this an ongoing event? I'd save my questions for the morning, because when he woke up, I'd be questioning the hell out of him.

****

"What do you think of this dress for today, Mia?" Elle twirled around, modeling a yellow sundress with white flowers. I smiled at her. It was the sixth dress she tried on so far.

"I love it. They are all very pretty, Elle, but if I have to choose one for today, I would have to say that one." She squealed with delight and ran back into her closet.

Marcus was still asleep. It was almost noon, and I didn't have the heart to wake him. When I woke up that morning, I took a shower and dressed, meeting both Elle and Jimmie in the kitchen. We had breakfast together.

Jimmie and I didn't mention anything about last night. Maybe it was because Elle was with us. I realized I truly misjudged Jimmie when we first met. He was nothing like I thought he was. He's a family man, just like Marcus, a loving and devoted father to Elle. At times, he seemed to drift off, thinking, trying to hide the loneliness in his eyes, but once he looked at Elle, it all went away. Jimmie, just like his brother, was a very handsome man, I wondered why no female had come and stolen his heart. He still may have been grieving from the loss of his wife. If I had any female friends and if any of them were good enough, I would have definitely try to play matchmaker.

There was a knock at the door, and a gentle female's voice followed. "Where's my precious granddaughter?" A petite woman walked through the door. She was dressed in a fitted summer dress and wedge heels. Even with the heels, she still looked tiny. Her long light brown hair and gleaming green eyes radiated with her soft fair skin. Elle ran from the closet and jumped into her grandmother's arms. Mrs. DeLuca hugged her tightly with closed eyes. When she re-opened her eyes, she finally laid them on me.

"Well, Elle, who's your friend?" She asked with a huge grin while straightening her posture.

"Grandma, this is Mia. She's my new best friend and Uncle Marc's girlfriend." Elle grabbed her grandmother's hand and dragged her over to me. I stood from the bed and offered my hand.

"Hi, Mrs. DeLuca, I'm Mia. It's very nice to meet you." She gently smacked my arm away and pulled me into a tight hug.

"Oh, call me Theresa!" She tightened her arms. "It's so lovely to finally meet you. You're all my son talks about lately." She pulled back, looking me up and down. Her face was beaming with satisfied delight. "And I can see why now. You're gorgeous!" Smiling, I placed my hand against my belly. I wasn't sure why. I was embarrassed by the compliment, and I thought maybe by doing that it would hide me.

"Thank you." It was all I could say.

"So where's my son? I haven't seen him in weeks." She tilted her head.

"Oh, he's still sleep—"

"I'm right here, Mom," Marcus said, rubbing his eyes with the back of his hand. His hair was a mess, his eyes were still blood shot, and he was only wearing pajama bottoms. Most people would look terrible after chugging down a bottle of liquor, but Marcus DeLuca is not most people. He was still good-looking. She turned with joy and ran over to her son.

Theresa was so tiny in his arms. He embraced her with a tight hug and bent over to kiss her cheek. Then he stood up straight, looking in my direction. His gentle smile met mine. His mom was still clinging to his waist.

He looked down at his mom and smiled. "Mom, you act like I haven't seen you in ages."

"It feels that way. Do you know how it feels to have both your boys all grown up? One minute they come to you for everything; the next they don't need you."

Marcus playfully rolled his eyes. "No, Mom, I don't know how that feels, but we still need you, especially for Sunday dinner." He laughed.

She nudged him in the rib with her elbow. Stretching out her arm towards Elle, she called out, "Come on my little helper, Grandma has a lot of prepping for dinner tonight."

"Can I help?" I blurted, not ready to be alone with Marcus yet.

Her eyes widened, and her dimple remarkably appeared when her lips curled up her cheeks. "Of course, darling, I would love your help." She walked past Marcus and patted his arm before making her way down to the kitchen.

When I followed behind her, Marcus stepped aside to block me from exiting. Looking up at him, I crossed my arms. "Mia, can we talk? I know I messed up last night." His chest moved in and out as he breathed impatiently.

All I ever wanted to do was talk, but he always shut me out, giving me half-assed answers. With his family coming, I'd rather have a talk after they leave.

"We can talk, but *after* the dinner. Right now I'm going to help your mom, then have this dinner with your family, and then *you* and I are going to have a nice long talk."

"Are we okay?" he asked desperately.

To be honest, I wasn't sure. Considering last night's drunken binge and being stood up the night before when he was six hours late, I needed answers, but he was always shutting me down.

"We'll talk later, Marcus."

Closing his eyes shut, he stepped aside to let me by.

CHAPTER SIXTEEN

I was placed on dicing duty: chopping the potatoes, tomatoes, and veggies. Elle was on rinsing duty: she stood on a stool by the sink rinsing all the fruit, meats, and vegetables. Theresa was busy preparing the meatballs and other items for the dinner tonight. She moved so fast in the kitchen I wasn't sure she needed help at all. Jimmie was watching a game in the living room. I laughed with his mom as she talked about raising two boys who were four years apart. She had plenty of stories about the two of them. His mother was loud for someone so little. She also moved her hands wildly as she talked.

Theresa began going down the list of all the family that was coming that night. It was a lot! I never knew anyone with such a huge family, and they got together once a week for dinner! She went down the list, warning me who to stay away from, who was the sweetheart, who would bust my "balls," and which of Marcus' cousins would try to hit on me, even in front of Marcus. She said not to worry about them though; they'd just be teasing Marcus for fun. I tried to keep up with them, but there were too many. On Theresa's side of the family there were four brothers and two sisters. Marcus' father had three sisters and one brother. Their brothers and sisters had kids who also had kids! It was exhausting just to think about.

"So, Uncle Marty is the pig?" I asked, describing him exactly as she described him to me.

"Yeah, but don't worry about him; if he makes you feel uncomfortable, I'll throw him out," Marcus said jokingly as he walked in the kitchen. He was freshly showered, his hair was tamed, and he was dressed in a fitted black t-shirt and jeans. He was back to his normal self. Picking up a knife from the counter, he stood beside me. Grabbing a carrot, he began to chop it. He smelled so good this close compared to last night when it smelled as if he'd bathed in liquor. I watched him as he pushed the chopped carrots aside with the pile of diced veggies I'd already done, and grabbed another one.

Not able to resist, I put down the knife I was holding on the cutting board. I leaned up, wrapped my arms around him, and pulled his face down to kiss the side of his cheek. Turning to fully face me, he pressed his forehead against mine with his eyes closed, and kissed the tip of my nose. I giggled and he smiled. We were okay for now. But I couldn't let him go the entire night thinking we weren't. It wasn't fair to him. When we turned back to our chopping, I looked up; his mom was staring at us the entire time with a huge smile. Smirking at her, we continued to go down the list of the family.

After cooking all day, the table was set, and the food and dessert were done. Thank God I didn't decide to choose cooking as a profession because it was too exhausting. We had enough food to feed fifteen households and then some. With an hour to spare, I decided to shower and get dressed for the dinner. Marcus was occupying his mother and niece in the kitchen, so I knew I could have some time to myself.

Managing to quickly shower and dress, I took my time on my hair and makeup: nothing extravagant, just a simple blush, mascara and lip gloss. I wore dark blue skinny jeans, white flats, and a fitted white t-shirt. Once I was finished, I made my way back down the stairs. The moment I entered the living room, I noticed the entire house was full. Looking around nervously for Marcus, I slowly passed an overweight man. He jumped as I brushed past him.

"Whoa! If you wanna feel me up just say so, cupcakes," the short fat man said while smiling.

"Oh, um, I'm sorry; I wasn't trying to feel you up. I was just, uh." Nervously I chuckled. After a second glance, I was able to place a name with a face. "You're Marty?" I asked.

His smile grew wider. "The one and only sweetie, and *you* are the new love of my life?"

"No, she's the one and only love of *my* life." Marcus cut in, wrapping his arm around my shoulder.

"Huh, would you look at this guy!" Marty yelled over his shoulder while pointing at Marcus then placed his hand against Marcus' shoulder. With his free one, he shook hands with Marcus. "You're a lucky man here, Marky!" Then Marty's expression grew serious, and he leaned into Marcus' ear. "Hey, have you heard about the rats Louie has? There are rumors that FBI agents have been snooping all around the warehouses," he whispered.

Marcus shook his head. "No, Uncle Marty, we'll talk more later in private."

Marty nodded his head, and Marcus led me to other family members, leaving me with more questions to ask later. After being introduced four times, I began to ease a little. His entire family has the same sense of humor and animated characteristics as his mother. They made me laugh with all the jokes they had and stories they told of Marcus' childhood.

Marcus joined in with the teasing of others. He was so loose and himself around his family. I'd love seeing him like this: around them he was worry and stress free. He was like this with me until he'd get a phone call from "him" for another job. Then his entire demeanor changed.

After dinner, everyone talked and joked over dessert and wine. The kids played in the backyard, chasing each other around. I sat back and watched all of them. I never had a big family, not even on Thanksgiving. It was no particular holiday, and yet this family was together just because. I couldn't be more in love with them. They were all about spending quality time together, and that's what they cherished the most.

Marcus threw his arm around his oldest cousin, Romeo. "So Rome, you ready for school in the fall?" he asked him with a huge smile on his face.

"I'm freaking out, man." Romeo laughed.

"Hey, you'll do fine. Mia's starting her second year." Romeo looked at me and smiled. He was starting law school, and I might see him around campus.

"Yeah, the first year was hard: a lot of studying and less partying. Well at least for me, but if you focus, you'll do fine. If you need any help at all, I have no problem helping you study."

"Really? That's awesome. Thanks, Mia." Marcus patted Romeo's shoulder before he walked away.

"Thanks for that." He said, sitting beside me. "So, what do you think of my crazy family?" he whispered, leaning in so no one could hear him.

Turning, I brought my lips to his ear and whispered back, "They are the best family I have ever met. You're very lucky to have them." The side of his eyes wrinkled when he smiled. I kissed his cheek, and we continued talking to his family.

****

"Mia, don't forget me on Wednesday!" Theresa yelled from the front porch. A few minutes earlier, she'd plugged her number into my phone and mine into hers. She insisted that we have lunch downtown, just the two of us. If it were any other person, I would've been nervous, but she was so sweet it was hard to resist.

"I won't, Theresa. See you then!" I yelled, waving my hand. She was the last to leave. Marcus closed the door after he said his goodbyes.

The entire day was draining. After cleaning the kitchen with his mother's help, I felt beat. Elle fell asleep under the dining room table. She was playing hide and seek with her other little cousins. They never found her. Jimmie crawled underneath the table, lightly picked her up, and carried her to her room. Marcus and I stood alone by the foyer. He looked down at me. My serious expression let him know that I didn't forget about our talk. Pressing his lips together, he closed his eyes, and then let out a heavy sigh. "You ready to go to bed?" I nodded in response.

We made our way up the stairs, not saying a word. When we reached the room, I heard a loud beeping sound from my phone: the same tone it makes when warning the battery is too low. Walking over to the nightstand, I unplugged Marcus' phone and plugged mine in. When I unhooked his phone from the charger, it lit up, showing he had a message from Stephanie. Looking over my shoulder, I noticed he was by the dresser taking off his clothes. I'm not sure why it came over me, why within those few seconds I thought of it, but without second guessing, I quickly swiped the screen and opened the message.

I felt a punch to my chest and lost my breath. Heat boiled up in my veins and radiated all over my body till flames reached my face. This *bitch* sent him a picture of herself in nothing but a bright pink lace bra and a matching thong. It was a side profile of her entire body, posing with one hand on her hip with the other hand holding the phone toward a mirror, clearly taking the picture herself. Lifting the phone in disbelief, I turned around to face him. He was pulling down his jeans. Finally turning in my direction in nothing but his boxers, his eyes met my evil glare.

Startled by my quick change in demeanor, he asked, "What?"

"So, you're still seeing Stephanie." My tone was hoarse, holding back the tears.

His expression was puzzled. "What? No! Why would you even think that?"

Lifting up the phone, facing the screen to him, my tears fought against my will and escaped down my face. "Really, Marcus? Because if a woman sends a guy a half-naked picture of herself, it tells me that they are clearly FUCKING!" I threw the phone at him. He lifted his hands to block his face. The phone slammed against his forearms and fell to the ground. *Damn it,* I missed!

He reached over and grabbed the phone. When he saw the image on the screen, his face turned red with rage, and his eyes almost burst out of their sockets. Looking up at me, he slowly took a few steps forward, holding his hands up. "Babe, listen to me. I am not seeing Stephanie. I have no idea why she sent this to me. I swear." His expression was still angry, but his tone was soothing. He was trying to calm me down.

Growing agitated by that notion, I yelled, "Okay, call her then!" Crossing my arms, I waited for his reply.

"Okay, I'll call her right now." He dabbed through his phone. I was calling his bluff: he wasn't calling her. After he touched another button, a ringing tone sounded in the room. He placed the call on speaker. *Good.* He looked at me, biting his lip, but I didn't stop him. I tapped my foot against the floor, waiting impatiently. I wanted to hear what she had to say.

"*Hey.*" She picked up! Not only did she pick up but she sounded seductive and happy as if she were waiting for his response. I hated her. I'd never hated anyone in my entire life, until then.

"Why the fuck are you sending pictures like that to my phone, Stephanie!" Marcus yelled, clearly pissed. *Good.*

"I-I ..." Shocked by his outburst, she grew silent.

"Huh?" he asked annoyed.

"I've missed you," she whispered.

He sighed. "Stephanie, you know that the two of us were never serious. I'm with Mia now. I *love* her. You can't do that again, do you hear me?" He lowered his tone but remained firm.

"Y-you love *her*?" Stephanie's voice broke. Then she whimpered over the phone. I rolled my eyes. *Ugh,* I don't even feel sorry for her. Who sends a naked picture of herself to a man who was in a relationship? To man that she *knew* was in a relationship! She knew how happy we were; she saw us in the office. Why would she try to break that up?

"Yes, I do. Look I think it would be best to transfer you to a different department."

"I think that's best," she mumbled. Then I heard a long beeping tone. She hung up.

Marcus tossed his phone on the bed. Looking up at me, he waited for me to say something. I was so pissed off I couldn't say anything. Instead, turning on the heels of my foot, I stomped in the bathroom. Stripping my clothes off, I turned the shower on and threw myself in.

I didn't care to wait for the temperature to warm. I didn't care that the freezing cold water stung against my skin when I entered the shower. I didn't care that my lips trembled, and I surely didn't care that this was the third shower I'd taken today. Leaning my head back, I allowed the water to massage my aching head. It was literally pounding. There was too much to handle these past few days. It was hard to keep up!

Marcus stepped in and wrapped his arms around me. Annoyed by this, I rolled my eyes. I needed privacy for ten damn minutes! He couldn't leave me the hell alone? I wanted to scream from the top of my lungs. I relived every emotional moment I'd felt: our first fight, his saying he loved me, my not being sure of my feelings, the dream of my brother, my waking up and finally telling him I love him, his leaving last night and coming home a drunken mess, and just now the thought that he may have ... had been with Stephanie after I confessed my love to him.

All of it, every bit of emotion erupted in the only way I knew how. I cried, and I don't mean just tears. It was the sobbing, can't breathe, choking-back-my-own-tears cry. It was embarrassing and pathetic, but I didn't care. He turned me around, placing his hand on the back of my head, pulling me to his chest. As much as I wanted him to leave me alone, I wanted him to stay and hold me. These conflicting feelings were so stressing. How could you love someone when he was the reason for the mixed feelings?

"What's wrong, Mia? Talk to me," he whispered. Leaning my head back, I looked up at him.

"It's just so confusing." I confessed.

Wiping a strand of soaked hair behind my ear, he pressed his lips together before asking, "What is?"

"You, me, *everything* ... In the last two weeks, we've had so many wonderful moments, and then we had really bad ones too. You're hot one minute, and then you're cold the next. Sometimes I look at you, and you seem so lost. I want to ask you what's wrong, but I know you'll just hold back. I know there's another side to you that you refuse to tell me about."

Not saying a word, he just looked at me, waiting for me to go on, or maybe he was thinking about what I was saying. I decided to continue anyway. "Then last night, the way you were completely *drunk*. Do you do that often?" I tilted my head, pleading with him with my eyes to tell me something. He looked down. I didn't say anything, not wanting to disturb his thoughts. He seemed to be contemplating whether to confess. When he finally fixed his gaze back to me, he opened his mouth then closed it again. "Marcus *please*, I won't be able to help you, unless you tell me something. If you love me, you have to let me in."

Nodding, he brought me down with him. We were both seated in the tub facing each other. The now-warm water was hitting the space between us. Looking up at the shower head, he let out a deep breath. Lowering his head, he focused on his legs. He continued to grip and un-grip the calves of his muscles, trying to focus on something other than me. I was going to say something, but he began to speak.

"I do drink a lot." He blew out another breath, and still not looking up, he continued, "Only, after a job. It's only once a week, mostly like last night, but if it's a simple job, then I'm good. When it involves ... When I have to hurt someone, it fucking fucks with my head."

Mouthing a small thank you prayer, I was happy he was finally talking to me about this. I tried to push my luck. "What do you mean job?" I asked.

His knee began to slowly bounce. It was a nervous gesture I hadn't noticed before. "I work for Lou Sorrento. You know who that is?" he asked, finally meeting my eyes.

Lou Sorrento was the Italian mafia boss for the Sorrento family. I'd neither seen him in person nor pictures of him online, but I'd heard of him. I was able to put everything together: Uncle Louie is

Lou Sorrento. *Why hadn't I thought of that before?* I nodded at him, biting my bottom lip to hide my fear and anger—anger because he lied to me. When we met up for lunch that one day, he told me he had nothing to do with the Sorrento family. So I sat there patiently and listened to what he had to say.

"Well, I started when I was young after my father was murdered. See Lou and my father knew each other since they were in diapers. I haven't told you, but my father was always involved with the mob. His father was in it, and growing up, that's all we knew. He wanted different for my brother and me. He made sure we were in the best private schools and had the best tutors. He even owned a small successful financing business. My father made sure to always stay low key, never buying extravagant things that looked like it was more than what his business was worth."

He rubbed his temples with his fingers and continued. "Well, after my father's death. I took it really hard, got into a lot trouble in school. I was almost expelled." He laughed once at the memory. "My mother couldn't handle me, so she asked Lou if he could put me in my place, you know. He said to me, 'Marky, if yah angry, yah taking it out on the wrong man, yah know? Come work for me; you can earn some money on the side and take out that frustration on those who deserve it.' So I did. It started off as doing some loan-shark stuff, beating a few men, collecting money that was owed to Louie.

"My father left us money, but after my mom paid off the house, debts, and the shore home, there wasn't enough to pay for college. Louie offered to pay off my tuition. Then he started getting deeper with drug and gun cartels. That's what I handle now. When there's a trade, I and sometimes Jimmie go make sure everything goes through smoothly. When it doesn't, you can guess the rest." Looking up, his eyes began to search mine, anticipating my thoughts.

Shocked by his sudden confession, I felt speechless. Looking into his eyes, I tried to think of something to say. "Why can't you just get out?" I whispered.

He shook his head. "It's not that easy, Mia. There's a lot more to this story, but that's something I can't explain to you right now. You just have to trust me." Shrugging, he gave a small, gentle smile.

"Why did you lie to me when I asked you about your involvement with the Sorrentos the day we met for lunch?"

He sucked his teeth. "Come on, Mia, would you have given me a chance if I disclosed that information to you after we just met? I wanted you to get to know me, not that side. I wanted to show you there was another side of me—a *good* side."

It's true I wouldn't have given him a shot whatsoever, and even though it had only been two weeks, I couldn't give up on him because I was madly in love with him. Not wanting to press my luck, or force him into saying anything he didn't want to say, I reached for his hand and spread my fingers in between his. Looking up I said, "Promise me something?"

Placing his hand to my face, he caressed my cheek with his thumb. "Anything." He exhaled.

"Promise me that you'll never drink like that again. If you feel terrible or fucked up in the head after a job, come to me. You don't have to talk about it. We'll just lie there together. Okay?"

A confused, soft smile appeared on his face. He gripped the back of my neck, pulling me in. His moist lips kissed my forehead. "What am I going to do with you?" He mumbled through his lips. Shrugging my shoulders, I lifted my chin and kissed him.

CHAPTER SEVENTEEN

It was the week of Fourth of July. It was two and a half months since Marcus and I met. We'd been going strong, spending a lot of time together, especially with his family. A lot can happen in two months, especially if you're not careful. Oh God, why wasn't I careful? I was so stupid. Pacing back and forth, I waited till the timer went off. This was the longest three minutes of my life. My underarms were beginning to feel damp. Searching the bathroom cabinet, I found and grabbed a deodorant. I quickly rolled it under my arms. A loud buzzing noise startled me, and I dropped the deodorant into the sink.

It was time to look at my results, and I was scared. Taking a deep breath, I grabbed the small stick and glanced down. My heart slightly dropped. Sure enough the small digital printout said it loud and clear: PREGNANT. I leaned over the counter to keep from fainting. Suddenly I was nauseated, and I didn't think it had anything to do with the change in my hormones. Why and how did I allow it to get this far? These are the consequences of not taking precautions. It was no one's fault but my own. I didn't plan it, but I didn't prevent it from happening. Ever since Marcus and I made the mistake of not using the protection the first time, it never came up to use it again. *Oh God*!

Finally letting out the air I was keeping in for what seemed like forever, I looked at myself in the mirror. *What was I going to do*? The past couple weeks, my body felt different. I just knew I was pregnant, but as I stared at myself, I still looked like me. I could feel the tears beginning to swell in my eyes. What would he think about this? A small part of me feared that he'd be thrilled, but why was I scared about that reaction?

A light knock on the door broke into my thoughts. "Mia, you ready? Elle is growing impatient." Marcus voice pierced through the door. Grabbing the test and the now-empty package, I shoved both into my purse. Glancing one last time in the mirror, I inhaled and open the door.

Marcus eyed me curiously. "What were you doing in there anyways? You never lock the door." He asked.

I wanted to throw myself in his arms, cry, and tell him our news. But I couldn't, well, just not at that moment. I wasn't sure myself how I felt about the entire situation. "I'm not feeling well." I managed a slight lie; holding my hand against my stomach, I looked up at him. "I didn't want you to walk in on me if I threw up."

He slightly pouted. "Aw babe, you got a stomach bug or something?"

Oh I have a *something* alright. "Maybe." I shrugged.

"Wanna stay home? I can take Elle to the carnival myself. I'll try to be back in a couple hours."

Waving my hand, I quickly replied, "No, no, I promised Elle I would go. Besides I feel better now, it comes and goes."

He stared at me with a raised eyebrow. "Sure?"

"Yes, I'm certain." Not really, but it wasn't the time to tell him.

During our ride to the carnival, Elle and Marcus played the "I spy with my little eye" game. My mind was too distracted to join in. Staring out the window, I watched other people drive by in their cars. Some drivers were alone, others were laughing with passengers, some were even singing along to a song. I wondered as I saw their faces fly by if any of them were struggling with the same issues I was: second-year law student, pregnant by a man with a double life.

During the last two months, we spent lots of time together. Jeremy had been staying at Stacy's house a lot. I didn't like staying home alone, especially knowing that the black SUV was parked outside. I hadn't mentioned anything to Marcus about it. The days that Marcus was at my place, it was never there. I'd never seen it near his place as well, so I didn't want to worry him with my speculations. I was sure it was nothing, but something about that vehicle gave me a bad vibe.

At the office, I hadn't run into Stephanie. The day after the picture message she was moved to another department. Marcus' new assistant was a sixty-year-old woman. Marcus still felt bad about the entire situation. Several times a day he'd hand me his phone, giving me permission to go through it, but I *trusted* him even with all the females in the office flocking over to him. I didn't want to base our relationship on having to be a part-time probation officer. I always declined. There had to be trust in a relationship, especially with a little one on the way. Looking down at my belly, I tightly wrapped my arms around myself.

It was going to be hard going to school full time, studying, maintaining my 4.0 GPA, and dealing with pregnancy hormones. I had to tell Marcus, but I didn't know how. Should I set an appointment to see how far along I am and then tell him, or should I just come out and say it?

My biggest fear was rejection. I knew he'd make a great father, but what if he didn't want to be a father? Was I prepared to be a single mother? Regardless if he accepted it or not, we'd only known each other for two and a half months; others will think the worst. Knowing Marcus he would say, "Stop worrying about what others may think. Who cares about them?"

It's true I shouldn't worry what people will say. There is always someone judging you, no matter how good a person you are. Hell you could be a saint, and still there would be that one person who'll despise you. That was fine, though being judged by his family? That was something I wouldn't be able to handle. I had grown to love them so much. It would hurt me to lose them all.

"We're here!" Elle squealed. She jumped up and down in her seat. Marcus laughed at her. After parking in a spot, we exited and walked to the entrance.

The sun had set, and the light breeze made a beautiful evening for rides. Bright lights from the roller coasters and booths illuminated the entire park. It was extravagant and over the top. It made me feel like I was ten years old again. My father took me to one similar to this, though it was smaller and at a local supermarket parking lot.

"Daddy, look! Can we pleeease go on the Ferris wheel? Please!" I'd pulled on my dad's hand, and he chuckled at my enthusiasm. Glancing down, his radiant brown eyes beamed at me. I loved the way the sides of his eyes wrinkled when had a huge smile. It was one of those smiles that led to his famous small raspy chuckle.

"It goes really high, Mia, are you sure?"

"Oh yes, daddy, please?" I begged, pressing both my hands together and tucking them toward my chin.

"Okay." He emphasized with amusement.

Biting my lip, I couldn't hide my excitement. We walked to the ticket guy. My dad gladly handed over our stubs, and the man let us pass. I practically squealed when we entered the cart. It slowly moved a few feet forward to let a couple in the cart behind us. It continued to move bit by bit until we were all the way on top. Stretching my neck, I looked over to see below us.

"Wow, daddy, the cars look so small from here. And look at all the people; they look like dwarfs!" I giggled.

"Mia, you're one brave young lady; I'll tell you that much." Turning to face him, I beamed for two reasons: one, he kept his promise and brought me to the carnival; two, he referred to me as a young lady and not a little girl.

Tucking myself under his arm, I squeezed tightly. "Thank you, daddy, this is the best day ever!"

Sighing at the memory of my father, I held back my tears. It was ten years ago since his death, and I still loved him more each day. The older I got, the more I cherished those memories. His love and care for me made me the woman I was that day. He taught me to be strong, outspoken, and never trust easily. After losing two important men in my life, I built a wall, not allowing anyone in. Once Marcus stepped into my life, that wall slowly crumbled. Finally I'd found a man that I could trust.

Since Marcus had confessed some of his second life, he'd kept his promise. Although, he worked more than one night a week now, he hadn't come home drunk like that night. Instead after a job, he would lie next to me in bed and tightly hug me. I'd run my fingers through his hair until he fell asleep. Keeping that small promise to me allowed all my fears about us to vanish. I knew we'd be okay, and there was nothing to fear. I knew that I shouldn't keep this big secret to myself.

"You okay, babe. You've been really quiet." Marcus wrapped his arm around my shoulder.

Turning my head to him, I smiled. Staring into his concerned expression warmed my heart; he was everything I wanted, needed and more. "Yeah I'm fine, so what do we do first?"

"Ferris wheel!" Elle yelled. I laughed at how much she reminded me of myself.

After a few rides and games at the booth, we were beat! Marcus had Elle thrown over his shoulder. She was fast asleep as her head and arms swayed side-to-side when he walked. He held an oversized stuffed animal horse on his other arm. I held another two medium-sized stuffed animals. All three Marcus won for her.

When we reached the car, Marcus gently placed her in the backseat and secured her seatbelt. Only the two medium-sized stuffed animals I held fit in the trunk, so the large one lay in the backseat next to Elle. When we got into the car, Marcus took his phone out of the glove compartment. Turning it on, he glanced at it and sighed heavily.

"Shit." He said while glancing at a message.

"What?" I asked praying it wasn't Lou. I really wanted to talk to him when we got back home.

"I have to go in. What time is it?" He looked up at the dashboard, and I followed his eyes. It was ten o'clock.

"I have plenty of time." He said relieved and tapped his fingers against his screen. Rolling my eyes, I huffed. Not realizing it was a loud sarcastic exhale, I was surprised when he turned his head. His eyebrows pulled together. "What's wrong?"

Crossing my arms, I looked out the window. "Nothing."

He blew out air. "Come on, Mia, what's wrong? Talk to me."

Arms still crossed, I turned my head to look at him. "Can you cancel today? I need to talk to you."

His expression went from irritated to concern in a nanosecond. "What about?"

Looking anywhere but his eyes, I tried to come up with an excuse about why I wanted to wait. "I want to be alone, in private."

"Mia, what's going on? You've been quiet all day, distant even. Did I do something wrong?" He spoke nervously.

"No! No. You didn't do anything. We just need to talk. It's important," I whispered the last sentence. It was important. I didn't want to talk about this with Elle in the backseat, not knowing how he would react.

"Okay, let me see if I can get someone to go in for me tonight." Grabbing his phone, he dabbed a few keys. I hoped he could. I couldn't keep this in any longer.

****

I woke up, startled by the sound of footsteps in the bathroom. Instantly knowing that Marcus was home, I jumped out of bed.

Apparently this job was too big to have some amateur handle it. He promised as soon as he got in, he would wake me so we could talk. The nightstand clock read three in the morning. How did he have so much energy to do anything?

Sliding my feet into house slippers, I made my way into the bathroom. The bright light in the bathroom caused my eyes to squint. When my eyes were finally focused, I caught sight of Marcus. He was slumped over the sink, washing his hands. His jacket was thrown on the floor beside him. He looked up at the mirror, feeling my presence. When he saw my reflection in the mirror, he rolled his eyes, and shook his head. I was taken aback. I never get this reaction from him.

Not turning around to face me, he snarled, "Mia, go to bed."

"You said we could talk when you got home." I muttered.

Adding more liquid soap in his hands, he continued to roughly scrub them. "Mia, tomorrow, it's late. Go to bed."

It took me a few minutes to process his demeanor. He'd never spoken in this tone with me. It's like I was irritating him. I started analyzing today, wondering what I did or said to deserve his attack. The water stopped running, and meeting my gaze in the mirror, he didn't move. His expression was unreadable.

"Are you okay, Marcus?" At my concerned words, he lowered his head. I took a few steps toward him, and he immediately shot his head up.

"Don't come any closer, Mia. Just go to bed!" He snapped.

My heart dropped. He just yelled at me—*really* yelled at me. What did I do? Has he found out what I've kept from him? Does he know? He couldn't know. There's no way he could have found out. Does he suspect that I am?

Trying so hard not to cry, I could feel my lips tremble. The hormones, lack of sleep, and exhausting day did not allow me to hold them in. I burst into tears. When he saw that he hurt my feelings, he quickly ripped off his shirt, throwing it into the sink.

Running to me, he wrapped his arms around me. "I'm so sorry, Mia! I just didn't want you to see."

"See what?" I asked sniffing. Pulling away from him, I looked at the white t-shirt he was wearing, it was spotted with blood. Rubbing his chest, I search to find his wound. "Oh my God, you're hurt."

Grabbing my wrists to stop me, he stepped back still holding my hands together. "No, it's not mine," he whispered.

It's not his. It's not *his*. Then whose blood is on his shirt? Pushing him aside, I walked toward the sink. Grabbing the collar of the button-up, I lifted it till it was at eye level. The entire front of his shirt was drenched in splattered blood. Gasping, I dropped it. The fabric slowly fell and landed on my feet. I could feel the dampness of fresh blood against my skin. Disgusted, I kicked it away.

I turned to face him. His eyes were filled with horror. Was it fear of what he'd done or what I would do once I found out what he'd done? "Whose blood is it, Marcus?" I asked, not able to hide the anxiety behind my tone.

He tried to make his way over to me. I brought my hand up, forcing him to halt. I couldn't have him near me, not then, not when I needed answers. "Marcus, this is not one of those questions that you can avoid with a simple hug or kiss. Do not come near me! Whose blood is this?"

Lowering his head, his shoulders dropped. He was defeated. He knew there was no getting around this. He brought his hand up, pressing his fingers against his forehead. He seemed to be thinking. What was there to think about? Irritation began to possess every inch of my body. "Whose is it, Marcus!" I snapped.

Finally looking up, he pressed down on his lips. His breathing began to pick up, and I could see his chest heaving up and down through the thin cotton fabric, which was now covered in smeared blood. "I-I … It was a bad exchange. Mia. I … There was nothing else I could've done."

I gasped, bringing my hand to my mouth. Looking in his eyes, I wanted him to say it, to clarify it. "You *killed* someone?"

His eyes were begging me to understand. I couldn't stop staring at him in fear, in shock. He was standing there, my Marcus, the man I had grown to love and know, yet he was covered in blood and asking me to understand a "bad exchange." I began to feel nauseated and lightheaded. Stumbling back a few steps, I leaned against the sink. Clenching my hand along the edge of the granite top and placing my other hand against my stomach, I glanced at the floor. I looked at his shirt beside my foot. It was covered in so much blood, another man's blood. He could have been someone's husband, father, or uncle, someone's son or brother.

Tears began to flow down my cheeks. I began to sob, feeling sorry for a man I didn't know, yet I could feel the sorrow of his loss, of his family's loss. The picture of Marcus standing in front of a man and blowing his brains out came to mind: blood and skull splattered all over. The thought instantly brought vomit to my throat; not able to hold it, I ran to the toilet. Once I opened the lid, I threw up.

"Mia, baby." Marcus was at my side, rubbing his hand along my back.

"No! Get away from me!" I pushed him away with my hand, as I continued, straining to throw my guts up. Tears fell from my eyes. Once I was finished, I rested my head on my arm, which was wrapped around the toilet seat. The taste of the vomit in my mouth made me want to do it again. After a few seconds, I managed to stand and walk over to the sink. Marcus was leaning against the wall, looking at me desperately. I ignored him and brushed my teeth, trying to erase the taste. After rinsing my mouth twice, I stormed into the bedroom.

What was I supposed to do? I couldn't even look at him, let alone stay in the same room as him. I walked over to the drawer he said was mine and in one swoop grabbed all of my clothes, dumping them onto the bed. Walking back, I opened the second and third drawers and did the same.

Marcus walked over to me and reached for my wrist. Pulling away, I walked past him and headed for the closet. I spotted my small suitcase and rolled it over to the bedroom. When I walked back in, Marcus was placing my clothes back in the drawers. "Marcus, what the hell are you doing?" I yelled.

"You're not going anywhere, Mia. I won't let you. Please, you have to talk to me. Let me explain," he begged.

"Marcus, I am tired of this!" Dropping the suitcase to the ground, I lifted my hand to my chest. "I can't do this anymore: the late nights, your second life. I love …" The tears began to take over again, and I was practically sobbing. I wasn't sure if I was even understandable. "I love you so much, and it will hurt for me to leave, but I have to do what's best."

He ran to me, keeping his distance, not sure if I was ready for him to touch me. His eyes were lost and confused. "Please, Mia, don't leave me. I-I know I fucked up. I had no choice, Mia. Please, you're the only person that I live for." His voice broke at the last words.

"You don't understand. It's not about me anymore, Marcus. I have a bigger responsibility to take care of and think about now. It's way bigger than both of us, and I'm not ready to bring that around this." I said, waving my hand at his bloody shirt.

Looking down at his shirt, he brought his gaze back to me. "Please, *Mia,* don't do this; I need you."

"Someone else needs me more." I said, pressing my hands against my belly.

CHAPTER EIGHTEEN

He looked down at my hands, back up into my eyes, and then down at my hands again. His head slightly tilted to the side. After a few seconds, he caught on and gasped taking a step back. Slowly his gaze met mine again. Tears begin to sting his eyes.

"Y-you're pregnant?" He breathed the question in shock. Not saying a word to him, I just simply nodded. This was not how I expected to tell him; this was not how I wanted to tell him. Yet there we were. Before, my fear was of his reaction; now, my biggest fear was of knowing I'd have to do this alone because I wouldn't allow my child to grow up in this environment.

He swallowed hard and stepped in closer. He looked at me to see if it was okay. I didn't move, so he inched in some more, meeting my eyes again to see if I'd retreat. I didn't move. Cautiously he brought his hand and placed in on top of mine. Sliding my hands away so that he could touch, he gently caressed my belly. A gentle smile formed on his face; looking up at me, his eyebrows furrowed. Slowly he lowered his head toward mine. I wanted to kiss him desperately; I wanted this moment to be special, to be a happy moment for the both of us. When his lips almost brushed mine, I pulled away completely smacking his hand off of me.

Within that second, I regretted my reaction when I saw the hurt of my rejection on his face. It made my stomach twist in knots. Leaving him would not only hurt me but it would cause so much pain to him. I didn't know if I could handle that, but it wasn't about me anymore. I needed to focus on what was more important, and that was the safety of my unborn child, our unborn child. I had this instant connection with my baby, this need to protect it.

"Mia, please, let's be a family. Please don't leave me. I promise I'll do better." He begged.

Hope filled me. I would do anything to have a family. "Will you leave then? Will you stop working for Lou?" Searching his face, my spirits begin to lift. Maybe he'd finally leave it behind. If he loved *us* enough, he would, wouldn't he?

"Mia, I … I can't do that right now." He swallowed.

Hurt and rage filled my every bone. Tilting my head, I studied him. "Why not? Don't you love me? Don't you want this to work? I can't raise a child in this environment, Marcus! I won't allow my baby to end up like you!" I didn't mean to say it that way. I just wanted him to understand—understand why I wanted him to leave. I loved him so much, and I knew those words hurt him deeper than anything. The look on his face … It pained him to know what I thought of him.

We didn't say anything to each other for a long time. We just stared at one another, both of us breathing heavily. Lost, confused, anxious, and scared, I didn't know what to say next. So instead I brushed past him with my suitcase, laid it on the bed, unzipped the lid, and began to throw my belongings in it.

Trying to hold back my tears, I couldn't. It was hard to see what I was doing through blurry vision. When I finally packed the last piece of fabric, I closed the suitcase. Anxiety overcame me, and I felt faint. Leaning against the bag, I sniffed and tried so desperately to calm my breathing. I grabbed the handle to the bag and turned around. Marcus was standing in the same spot, this time facing me, staring directly at me with those big, warm, sad, brown eyes. Tears slowly dripped down his cheek. Shocked to see this, startled by this reaction, I couldn't move; I just stared at him.

"I had to do it." He finally spoke in a low husky tone. "It was either him or me." I didn't move or speak out of fear, shock, and curiosity. I allowed him to talk. "I walked into the warehouse, thinking it would be like any other day. Eager to get back home to you, I just wanted it to be over with. It was me and two other guys, Larry and Vinnie. They usually go with me on these jobs. It was a drug trade with a Chinese cartel." He continued to talk, not moving or taking his eyes off of me. I sank down onto the edge of the bed, waiting nervously for what he would say next.

"We've done plenty of business with them before. So it wasn't anything new, same shit: we go in, make the trade, count the money, and seal the deal. Though this time, it was different. There was a new guy in their group. I found him suspicious the moment I saw him. I don't like new people, especially in this line of work. You always have to be cautious, but I wanted to hurry the deal to get home. My guys began to unload the bags of drugs into the back of their truck. I watched everything that was going on, keeping my eyes on my guys, the truck, the other group, and the new guy who was eyeing me down.

"I felt uneasy, so I focused more on him. He didn't like that I was intensely paying extra attention to him. I watched as he whispered something to his boss. His boss narrowed his eyes at me, and I knew something was going to go down. I felt it. The boss made his way to me, standing only inches away. By this time my guys were attentive and were beside me, feeling the vibe as well. He asked me if I was a cop. I was completely shocked by this. I'd previously done jobs with him. I told him no, and he asked me if I was wearing a wire. I lifted my shirt to show him I wasn't. The new guy wasn't convinced. He began to chant something in their language, and I grew irritated. So I made an offensive comment that he didn't like.

"Before I knew it, guns were drawn and shots were fired all over the place. My guys shot the other two men. The new guy had attacked me at that time. We wrestled, punched, and tackled each other until he reached for his gun. He pointed it at me. At that moment, I thought I was done. Your face was the only thing that came to my mind—that and the thought of leaving you behind, the thought of never being able to hold you again, to kiss you again. I didn't want to go without a fight. So without thinking, I quickly punched him and reached for the gun and shot him in the head. It was him or me, and I chose *me* because of you."

I was speechless, listening to him and his story. He spoke in detail of the night, of the fact that he almost lost his life. My heart picked up its pace as I began to realize that I almost lost him. He was inches away from being gunned down and killed. He would have been the third man in my life that I loved so dearly to have been taken away from me. Fresh tears began to form in my eyes, and I wanted to hold him and let him know I wouldn't go—let him know that I would stay no matter what.

Though I wanted to reach out and comfort him, I pulled back because this was the main reason why I had to go, why I should take my unborn child and run. It would hurt less to leave than to stay and wait up every night, wondering if he'd be home soon or if I'd get a call that he was dead. I shuddered at the thought. I wondered if I were brave enough to walk out of there even after his confession.

Slowly rising from the bed, I grabbed the handle of the suitcase and began to walk towards him. When I was inches away from him, I reached up and touched his face. My thumb caressed his cheekbone. He looked so tired and defeated.

Tracing my hand on the back of his neck, I pulled him down to me. His soft lips touched mine, and I gently kissed him. Tears streamed down my face as this would be our last kiss. He gently sighed at my embrace, but I pulled my head away. His eyes shot open, searching my face. "Goodbye, Marcus," I whispered. His eyes filled with pain, and his breathing began to pick up.

"No!" He yelled. Gripping my hips, he pulled me into him. "No, please don't leave me, Mia. I need you. I can't live without you. Please!" His arms were tightly wrapped around me. I couldn't breathe. I tried to pull away, but he pulled me in tighter. "No! Please. Please. I can't …" His voice broke. Then before I could pull away again, he began to sob. He buried his face into my neck. I could feel the moisture of his tears against my skin. It broke my heart to see and hear this strong, powerful, masculine man this vulnerable and broken.

I began to sob with him, dropping the suitcase onto the ground. I wrapped my arms around his neck. "Please, Marcus, let me go. I love you so much, and this is hard enough …" I couldn't finish. He tightened his arms around me like I would disappear any second.

His head dug in deeper into the nape of my neck, and he sobbed, crying out for me not to leave. "Mia, please, you're the reason for me living. You're the reason I want to wake up every morning, and you're the reason for my existence. Before you, I didn't care if I was killed. I woke up every morning miserable, wondering why I was here. I was so close to taking my own life right before I met you because I thought I was useless. Then when I met you … You're everything, Mia Without you, there's no reason for *me*. Please." He choked.

Taking in everything that he just said, I closed my eyes as tightly as I could and squeezed my arms around him. He tried to kill himself before? If I left and there was no reason for him, did that mean he'd try to again? The thought made my heart shatter into a million pieces. A world without Marcus DeLuca wouldn't be a world at all. He thought he was useless and therefore tried to take his own life. *Oh*, I wanted to make him feel okay. I wanted to take all the pain and misery away from him.

He'd been through so much, and this was all he knew, but it wasn't what I knew. Was I ready to deal with this? I loved him so much. At that moment, even though I knew I must protect our child, I would rather deal with the consequences of his second life than see him broken down and hurt.

Lifting my head to face him, I cupped his face with my hands. His eyes were blood shot. His eyelids are swollen and wet. "I'm sorry," I whispered, bringing his lips to mine. He was hesitant at first. I'm sure he was afraid that it was a goodbye kiss. My mouth slightly opened, allowing his tongue to slide in.

He hungrily kissed me, tasting me and brought his hands to my face. Before I could deepen our kiss, he pulled back, looking into my eyes. "You're not leaving me?" His tone was uneasy and shaky.

"No, baby, I'm not. I'm sorry," I whispered.

Letting out a long deep breath, he closed his eyes, pressing his forehead against mine. "Oh, Mia, I'm sorry. I'm so sorry. I fucking love you so much." Reaching back for my lips, he didn't move from them.

Bending down, he gripped my thighs and lifted me, wrapping my legs around his waist. Not breaking from the kiss, he walked over while carrying me to the bed. My body sank into the soft mattress. He ripped off our clothes, and before I knew it we were both naked. He pressed his body against mine, and the warmth of his body sent shivers down my spine. He placed his elbows on either side of my face and dug his hands under my head. Bringing his head down, he began to trace long kisses all around my face: on my forehead, my eyes, my nose, my cheeks, down my jawline and my chin. He bestowed warm kisses on every inch of my face until he reached my lips.

"I love you, Mia." He mumbled against my lips.

"I love you too, Marcus." I moaned. Feeling him on me, his lips on mine, and his warm responsiveness, I was able to forget at that moment about everything and just allow him to take control. I gasped when he spread my legs with his thighs and filled me with his length. I wanted him as badly as he wanted me. He met my hips, and his every thrust was at the perfect rhythm and speed. He took his time, allowing us to enjoy each other, to savor this moment, not wanting this moment to disappear.

Tracing his hand down my neck to my aching breast, he plucked and teased my nipples with his thumb. I moaned on his lips, and he wouldn't take them away from mine. His hand continued to trace down to my belly, down my hip and along my thigh. He could touch me a thousand times, and each time I still felt the electricity of his touch as if it were the first time.

Gripping my thighs, he lifted them, and I wrapped my legs around his waist, allowing him to go deeper inside of me. I grunted at the sensation. He groaned, and the vibration of the tone trembled against my lips. Biting my bottom lip, he began to move at a slightly faster pace. Our bodies melded into one another, allowing all of the feelings of almost losing each other to be relieved the only way we knew how, by making love.

Every emotion began to build, and my body trembled as I cried out his name and convulsed. Within a matter of seconds after I exploded, he did as well, groaning with relief.

Panting, I threw my head back into the plush mattress and shut my eyes with satisfied pleasure. I felt a tear fall down my face. Though I wasn't crying when I opened my eyes, Marcus was staring at me, his face seriously deep in thought with one drip mark down the right side of his cheek. Reaching up, I wiped the watermark off his precious cheek and leaned up to kiss him long and hard. He didn't want to let go, and neither did I.

The rest of the night we held each other tightly, afraid that one or the other would walk away.

****

"Ava." Marcus whispered while tracing small circles around my belly button. He was slumped on his side as he held his head up with his hand. I lay flat on my back, watching him trace all sorts of objects on my belly with his finger. It was very early in the morning, and we hadn't slept since he walked in at three this morning.

Arching my brow, I wasn't sure if I should be offended. "Huh?" I asked, wondering if he was calling me someone else's name.

Looking up, he gently smiled. "Ava Marie DeLuca if it's a girl." I couldn't help but grin widely at him. The past three hours we made sweet love, kissed passionately, and held each other, but neither one of us had brought up our baby.

"Ava? Hmm. I like it." I said. "And if it's a boy?" I asked curious as to the name; I had one in mind already.

"A junior, of course." He laughed. I raised my eyebrows. Don't get me wrong I love Marcus' name, but it wasn't my first choice.

Laughing at my expression, he said, "What? You don't like my name? What did you have in mind?" He chuckled.

"No, I love your name. I was just ... Well ..."

He stopped his finger tracing and gently pressed the palm of his hand along my belly. His brows creased. "Go ahead, Mia. Tell me what name you have in mind."

"Michael Marcus DeLuca." I never expected to have a child, *ever,* and I wasn't that type of girl that already had her children's names picked out before she even got married. Though, the moment I knew I was pregnant, I just knew if it was a boy that I wanted to name him after my brother.

Marcus looked at me with gentle eyes, understanding the meaning behind the name I'd chosen. He smiled, lifting his head away from his hand and slowly lowered it to my belly. He gently traced small kisses there. I giggled with each brush of his lips on my ticklish skin. "I love it. Michael." His lips stretched into a smile along my belly button when he said our unborn son's name. I sighed in contentment.

He laid his head against my stomach, and his eyes met mine. As an instant reaction, I ran my fingers through his thick hair. His eyes were half closed. He must've been exhausted. I know I was. I knew he'd make a great father; he grew up with such a loving and amazing family and home. He's a wonderful uncle to Elle.

Would I make a decent mother? I didn't have anyone to pick up the traits from. At least Marcus was raised by his father until his teens. He always mentioned that his father made sure to put them first. I, on the other hand, didn't have a mother. I wouldn't know what a mother's love and care felt like. I would never abandon my child.

Marcus eyes widened, and I didn't realize I was frowning until I noticed the concerned look on his face. "What's wrong, Mia?" His tone was uneasy.

"I … Well I was just thinking. I know you'll be a really good dad. I was just wondering, will I make a half-decent mom?" That last part was spoken very low.

Sitting up beside me, he leaned against the headboard. Wrapping his arm around my shoulder, he pulled me in till my head lay on his lap. Brushing his hand against the side of my face, he made my worries drift away.

His touch was so comforting I was beginning to drift off into a deep sleep. Before falling asleep, the last thing I heard was, "You're going to be one of the best mothers I know." The smoothness of his voice allowed me to dream peacefully.

CHAPTER NINETEEN

We slept in until late afternoon that Sunday, not wanting to leave each other's side and exhausted from the vivid night. When we finally awoke, we had dinner in bed. Marcus ordered pizza, and we watched old eighties' movies while cuddling. He also emailed his new assistant and told her that we wouldn't be at work the next day. Marcus stayed up the rest of the night, searching for the best OB-GYN in Boston. He was beginning to get a little annoying. When I found one that I really liked, he would shoot him down if there was one bad review. When Marcus said, "No," the answer was "no."

I wanted to see Dr. Tracy Muller. She was known to be one of the top doctors in her field. There were numerous five-star reviews, but one previous patient gave her two stars, stating that when she was finally in labor, Dr. Muller was out of town. That review changed Marcus' opinion very quickly. I pouted after a while when he didn't allow me to pick one. I mean, after all, it's my body. I should feel comfortable with the doctor.

After three hours of fussing, pouting, and a lot of disagreeing, we settled on Dr. Lee. He was, after all, the number-one OB-GYN in the entire state of Massachusetts with excellent credentials, background, and reviews. The only issue I had was that Dr. Lee is a male. I wasn't sure how I would feel having another man exploring my personal … space. Marcus assured me that if I felt uncomfortable in any way, I could choose the next doctor, which put me at ease.

First thing Monday morning, Marcus contacted Dr. Lee's office, and after intense negotiations, we were scheduled for that evening. I truly thought Marcus wouldn't be able to get us in as Dr. Lee was booked until next year! Then again this was Marcus DeLuca; he could be very persuasive and persistent when he wanted his way. Since we had the entire morning and half of the afternoon free, Marcus wanted to take me out for a day in town. He didn't leave my side, holding my hand, hugging me tight, and kissing me every chance he could. Although this was his regular routine, somehow today it seemed different.

He made sure I ate well and consumed plenty of water throughout the day. When his phone rang, he ignored it. He gave me one-hundred-ten percent of his attention. At one point, when we entered a store and I wandered off to a look at some clothing, he shouted my name around the aisles frantically. When he found me, he embraced me with a tight hug and kiss. It was as if he thought that I was going to run away the moment we were apart. I assured him I wasn't going anywhere. He would just nod and slightly smile, but his eyes were filled with uncertainty.

When we finally entered Dr. Lee's office, I was in awe. The office was contemporary with high-end furniture and equipment. The entire building was extremely shiny and clean; I felt like I needed to take a sanitary shower before entering the building. Because of that, I added two points to my very own mental review. The super friendly staff and nurses made us feel welcome and comfortable, so I added another star. After meeting with Dr. Lee, I gave him a rank of five stars. I would never judge a male doctor again. He was gentle and made me feel comfortable throughout the entire process.

Peanut was the nickname we decided to give our little one. At six-weeks that's exactly what the image on the small black-and-white screen appeared as—a tiny peanut. Marcus couldn't wipe the grin off his face as we walked out of the doctor's office side by side with my arm wrapped around his waist and his one arm slung over my shoulder, holding the small picture of our peanut.

"I can't believe this little thing is our baby." He said still mesmerized by the photo.

Laughing at him, I grabbed the picture so I could have a better look. "I know, right. Our baby is already adorable."

He pressed his lips on top of my head and kissed me. "If our child looks anything like his mother, then yeah, he'll be one gorgeous baby."

I could actually imagine an adorable little boy or girl with Marcus' smile and dimple and my green eyes. Sighing with contentment, we stepped into the car.

"So where do you want to go now?" he asked, turning on the ignition.

I shifted my body to face him. "Marcus, I'm really tired right now. Do you think you could take me home?"

Caressing his thumb along my cheeks, he gently smiled. "Of course, baby. Elle will be happy to hear the news."

"Uh, Marc, ah, I don't want to say anything to anyone until the second trimester. You heard what the doctor said, 'There's a possibility of complications.' I just don't want to get anyone excited and then ..." When I didn't finish my sentence, he seemed to understand.

Nodding in agreement, "Sure, let's go home."

"Um, Marcus?" He turned to face me. I didn't know how to say this without hurting his feelings. "I would like to go home, to *my* apartment. It's not that I don't like being at your place. I just haven't been home in over a week, and I would just like to go *home*."

Nodding in agreement, he turned on the ignition. "Okay, we'll go to your apartment tonight, not a problem." What I really wanted was to be home alone. I needed *me* time, and I was exhausted, but I decided to just let him come with me. After the previous night's fiasco, I was sure he didn't want to leave my sight.

The ride home was in silence. I looked out the window, thinking how so much had changed within the last two and a half months. Who would have known that night at Club21 when I met Marcus that I would be sitting here right now with him, holding his hand, twirling his fingers with mine, discussing baby names for our first born? How would it work with us living-arrangements-wise? Would he move in with me? Would I move in with him? Would we stay as is in separate households?

The thought of home brought me to Jeremy. I hadn't spoken to him all week. We'd seen each other at work, but it wasn't the same. There was so much we needed to discuss. I know I told Marcus I didn't want anyone to know just yet, but maybe I could tell Jeremy. I wondered how he would react.

When Marcus finally found parking, my initial reaction was to look around to see if I found the black SUV. It was nowhere to be found. I wasn't sure why I felt uneasy about the stupid car. It could be a new neighbor's vehicle for all I knew.

Marcus made his way to my side of the car and opened the passenger door. Looking up at him, I witnessed the biggest smile on his face, and it was contagious. He was so happy. I giggled at his amusement. He gave me his hand, and I took it. Yanking my hand, he pulled me into him and kissed my forehead. "Marry me," he said casually.

"What?" I looked at him baffled.

Chuckling, he tightened his arms around my waist. His face grew serious. "I know it's not the ideal proposal, but I love you, Mia. I can't see myself with anyone else. You're my life. Now that you're carrying a small piece of me, I want you to be in my life forever. Be my wife. Please say yes. Marry me."

"No." His head cocked back with widened eyes and his lips parted, trying to come up with some response to my unexpected answer. I bit down on my lip to keep from laughing.

"No? Why?"

"That was a half-assed proposal, Marcus! I will not say 'yes' unless it's better prepared. You're lucky I'm giving you a second chance at this. Most men aren't so lucky." I arched my eyebrow playfully.

His face relaxed, pressing his forehead against mine, he laughed once. I looked into his wrinkled, joyous eyes. "You're killing me, Mia, but I love you so much."

We kissed again and walked towards my building. Jeremy's car was nowhere in sight, so I guessed he was at Stacy's again. I hadn't been home all week, so I wondered if he even took the trash out. If not, I wondered if my pregnant hormones could handle the scent of trash juice.

We entered the building and walked up the stairs. Marcus was playfully slapping my behind with each step. I giggled and smacked his arm away. It just inspired him to torture me some more, so he began to tickle the side of my ribs.

Trying to get away, I began to run up the stairs giggling. When I turned the corner of the second floor, I rushed over to my door. He was chasing me. Adrenaline pumping from our childish chase, I tried to hurry and search for my keys before he got close.

"Mia?" Startled to hear my name by an unfamiliar voice, I turned towards the direction from where it came.

A few feet from my door, a woman was seated on the floor, leaning against the wall. She slowly lifted herself up. I tilted my head to study her, wondering if I recognized her. She knew my name, but she didn't look familiar.

She had dark circles under her eyes and wavy untamed golden brown hair. She was well dressed in fitted jeans, flats, and a white blouse. After adjusting the strap of her purse on her shoulder, she fidgeted with her fingers. Looking down at her hands for a few moments, she finally looked up at me, but didn't move any closer. At this point, Marcus was beside me. He must have sensed my distraction or uneasiness because his hand was pressed firmly against my lower back.

"Yes?" I asked.

Inhaling a deep breath, she took a step forward, still keeping her distance. "Are you Mia Sullivan?"

"Yes, how may I help you?" It occurred to me that she was probably seeking information for any vacant apartments.

Slowly she made her way over to me, playing with her fingers the entire time. When we were only a few feet away, her eyes met mine, and she gasped. Lifting her hand to her mouth, her eyes began to water. "Oh my God, you're beautiful." She choked as tears dripped down her face.

Alarmed by her reaction, I turned to look at Marcus. Apparently he turned his head at the same time. We both stared at each other with the same awkward expression. I gave him a questioning look, wondering if he knew who she was or what she wanted, but he lightly shrugged in response.

Fixing my gaze back at her, I asked, "I'm sorry, do I know you?"

Closing her fingers into a tight fist against her lips, she lightly shook her head. She tightened her eyes closed then opened them again. They were the biggest, most beautiful green eyes I'd ever seen. The color was very similar to mine: a hue of emerald green. "I'm Sara Sullivan. I'm your mother."

Taking in what she just said, my mind began to fog, everything closed in, my heart dropped, and my head felt light. Then her face turned into a blurry vision, and before I could speak, everything went black.

"Maybe you should go." Marcus' voice was distant and faded.

"I know. I just wanted to make sure she's okay," a woman's voice responded. *Shit*! It wasn't a dream. Flashing my eyes open, I looked around frantically. Marcus was instantly at my side, dabbing a warm damp cloth around my forehead and face.

"Baby, how you feeling? You fainted."

Jerking up, I looked around, and after a second glance around the room, I spotted her. She was sitting on the edge of the couch across from me. Pulling my legs off the couch, I scooted to the edge to get a better look at her. She was biting her thumbnail. Her eyebrows were pulled in, and her knee was bouncing nervously. Cocking my head to the side, I examined her features: perfectly arched eyebrows, long, golden brown, wavy hair, heart-shaped face, small, round, button nose, and long lashes which accentuated her stunning green eyes.

Gasping for air, I raised my hand to my mouth in disbelief. I was unable to control my emotions, and tears streamed down my face. I was the *spitting* image of her. All my life, I wondered who I looked like. My father had light brown eyes and sandy brown hair; my brother took after his features. In pictures we were a family, but it looked as if I didn't belong. I'd never seen pictures of my mother. My father never described her to me or even mentioned her. All I knew was that she was the woman that ran out on our family.

"W-what are you …?" Unable to speak, I cleared my throat; it felt hoarse and raspy. "What are you doing here?" I asked with my fingers still spread along my lips.

Her legs stopped shaking. Lowering her head, she placed her hands to her lap, fidgeting with a gold ring around her index finger. After several seconds, her head slightly lifted, meeting my gaze. Biting down on her lip, tears began to swell her eyes. "I've been trying to find you for a couple months now. I wanted to see you, talk to you. I understand if you want nothing to do with me. I just want to explain everything to you, but if you don't want to talk with me, that will be fine—well not fine, but I'd understand." She had a high-pitched tone to her voice. She stood from her chair, and she grabbed the purse lying beside her seat.

"No, um, just give me a minute." Not exactly sure what I was doing, it was the first thing that blurted out of my mouth. Nodding, she sat back down. I quickly stood and rushed to the bathroom.

Once behind the closed door, I leaned against it. I exhaled deeply, staring at the ceiling, trying to find answers. What does she want? Why is she even here? Oh God! I let out another deep breath. I managed to move my shaky legs to the sink. I rinsed my face a few times, and the cool water helped soothe my heated skin.

I looked in the mirror, not able to stop staring at my features. The reflection I saw was a younger version of the woman sitting on my couch, proclaiming to be my mother.

A soft knock on the door startled me, but I didn't turn to see who it was. I could smell Marcus' scent. His light footsteps made their way to me, and then I felt his strong, warm hand against the middle of my back.

"Mia, you don't have to do this right now." His voice screamed with concern.

Turning to face him, I buried my face into his chest. His strong arms wrapped around me, and I felt safe. "Marcus, what am I supposed to do? She's here. She found me. I don't know anything about that woman. What am I supposed to say to her?"

Marcus sank down to meet me at eye level. Cupping my face, he lightly turned my head, demanding that I look at him. Through my lashes, I managed to view him past my blurry tears. "You do not have to speak with her. If you want me to, I can ask her to leave a number, and you can contact her when *you're* ready. Is that something you want to do?"

I wasn't sure what I wanted to do. It felt overwhelming. Never in a million years would I have thought that I would be standing before my mother: a woman who decided to leave her newborn daughter, ten-year-old son, and loving husband behind for reasons I never knew. I never asked questions growing up, well, maybe once. But after getting the runaround from my brother and father, I knew not to ask again.

I'd never felt anger towards her, yet at that moment I felt enraged. After twenty-four years she walks into my life now? After everything I'd been through, when I needed her the most, she wasn't there, and now she stumbled in front of my door wanting to talk. Suddenly, I wanted answers: I wanted to know where she'd been, what she'd done with her life, the reason for leaving, and *most* importantly, the reason she was back.

CHAPTER TWENTY

Sucking my bottom lip, I inhaled, and I placed my hands on top of Marcus'. Gently I gave him the best "it's okay" smile I could. Wiping my face to hide the evidence of my tears, I strolled out of the bathroom with my chin up and my shoulders relaxed. Well, at least I hoped they seemed relaxed. Marcus, of course, hurried behind me. When I entered the living room, she must've sensed my presence. She jumped to her feet with her purse clenched to her side and chewed her thumbnail nervously.

"Would you like some tea, water?" I asked in the best casual way I could.

Dropping her hand to her side, she masked a tiny smile. "Tea, please." Following me into the kitchen, Marcus set her at the table and arranged two chairs side by side to sit across from her. Taking my time, I thought of a million ways to start our conversation. The room was silent: the only noise was the steam emanating from the teapot.

Cutting the stove off, I prepared tea for three. Marcus likes his tea with lemon and sugar. I like mine with cream and sugar, but I didn't know how she would like hers. Uncertain, I placed her mug in front of her along with lemon, cream, sugar, and a spoon, allowing her make her own.

Marcus wrapped his arm securely around my shoulder when I took my seat beside him. Taking small sips, I peeked through my lashes and watched as she prepared her cup: two scoops of sugar and a splash of cream. I should remember that, shouldn't I? She stirred and lightly tapped the side of the spoon on top of the mug before gently laying it on the table. Biting her lip, she stared at her tea for a moment, not taking a sip, and not saying a word. She just focused on her mug as if something would magically appear.

The unbearable silence was broken when Marcus cleared his throat and shifted impatiently in his chair. My "mother" shot her eyes up at us and moved her shoulders, so she could sit straight up. I looked into her eyes and saw an older reflection of myself. "I'm sorry that this is unexpected and a shock. I don't know where to start." Her shoulders gently lifted into a slight shrug.

"How about what you're doing here?" Marcus blurted. Irritated by his response, I shot him an annoyed look. I knew he was there to support me, but this was hard on me and most definitely hard on her as well. I didn't need him adding to the tension and awkwardness in the room. He noticed my annoyance and nodded in a way of saying "sorry." Fixing my gaze back on her, I noticed that she had the softest, sweetest smile I had ever seen. She was clearly not affected by his rudeness.

"I've contemplated different ways to approach you. After finally finding you, it took me weeks and several scribbled letters before I worked up the nerve to meet you face-to-face. See at first I was going to leave you alone because Michael refused to let me see you—"

I cut her off at the mention of my brother's name. "*Wait*? Did you say Michael didn't want you to see me?" I didn't know my brother had contact with her.

"Yes, when I found out your father passed away, I went to the funeral. Michael refused to let me in. He said I didn't deserve to see him or you. I wanted to help him with you. I wanted to be a part of your lives. I apologized to him a million times, but he said he was going to take care of you and leave Philly. I begged and pleaded, but I didn't want to make a scene. So I left. A year after your father passed, I found out that he moved to Boston. I mailed several letters to the both of you, but he returned all of them unopened. After a few years of trying, I gave up. I know I shouldn't have, but I did."

I was in a daze from everything she was saying. I couldn't believe Michael kept this from me! Was he trying to protect me from her, afraid that she would leave again? Or was he afraid that I would choose her over him? I knew the second part wouldn't have crossed his mind, but I had heard him time and time again wishing I had a mother figure to teach and lecture me about things that he couldn't. I know he gave up his youth to raise me, and for that I would always be grateful, though I wonder if he ever regretted his decision.

I allowed her to continue without interruption. "I hated myself for the woman I was—the one I allowed myself to become, and I cried almost every night since I left your father and my two children.

He was the one and only love of my life. I'm not sure if he ever told you the story of how we met?"

I shook my head, and she proceeded. "I was young, very young. He was six years older than me, and now it may not seem that old, but at that time my parents hated it, hated him. I was fifteen, and he was twenty-one. Your father was a rebel: a young, handsome man. One day I was walking home after school. I began to walk along a crosswalk when a motorcycle flew by. Frightened about getting hit, I jumped back, lost my balance, and fell to the ground. He was immediately by my side, making sure I was okay, and he repeated numerous times that he didn't see me.

"The moment I laid eyes on him, I was mesmerized by his perfection. I thought I was dreaming. How could this beautiful man possibly be staring back at me with the same awe-struck expression? We instantly made a connection. He offered me a lift home. Every day after that, he would wait at the crosswalk with his motorcycle parked as he leaned against it, greeting me with a huge smile. He didn't even ask me out; he would simply walk me home, leaving his cycle behind, asking me numerous questions.

"After a month, he finally asked me on a date. He didn't know my age at first. He thought I was older than I was. I was afraid if I told him I was only fifteen, he would run away. I lied to my parents and told them I was studying at a friend's house." She smiled at her memory.

"After months of lying and sneaking around, I turned up pregnant." She looked down at her mug and took a small sip. I knew she was young when she had Michael, but I didn't know she was fifteen. I could only imagine what she'd been through: the fear of being a mother at such a young age.

Finally placing her mug down, she continued. "I tried to hide it from my parents. I was afraid of them. They were very religious and strict. After your father found out about the pregnancy, he demanded that I tell them. I finally worked up the courage, and they kicked me out. Well it was either abort, put my child up for adoption, or get kicked out of the house. When they found out I was pregnant by your father, there wasn't even an option. It was simply 'get the hell out.' Your father took care of me from the start, though. He signed up for the police academy. Once he was in, we got a tiny apartment, and he took care of me.

"It was hard, very hard at first, but eventually we got through it together. Though I felt like I was missing a part of me, I couldn't explain it. I had dropped out of school. I didn't work. I just stayed home: a housewife and a mother. I felt like, was this all? Is this what my life was supposed to be? When I had you, I loved you so much, but I wanted more. I know that sounds selfish and cruel, but I felt trapped. My whole life I felt trapped. My parents finally came to their senses and agreed to take me back, and I could help run the family business if I left your father.

"I was going to bring you kids with me, but you meant the world to your father. I couldn't break his heart that way. I knew leaving would be bad enough, and if I tried to take you kids as well, he would have never allowed it. He would have fought tooth and nail for you kids. So one night, I packed my bags, wrote a note for him, and left—never looking back, and never calling to check up on you guys." Sara, my mother, I didn't know what to call her, broke into quiet sobs.

I wish I could've blamed my tears on the hormones, but I knew I couldn't. She had said so much; I learned more about the whole reasoning behind her leaving. Now that I knew, I wasn't sure if I should be angry, content, happy, or relieved. Where did we go from there? How do you begin to build a relationship with someone after so many years of wanting and needing her, knowing that she *chose* to be selfish? Did she even want to build a relationship, or was this a way to help ease her guilty conscious?

Sara wiped her tears with the back of her hands and looked back at me. We stared at each other for a moment. Her eyes pleaded for forgiveness, and mine screamed with pain and understanding. So many things were going through my mind: more questions, wanting her to explain more of herself.

Just when I felt I was going to blurt out everything and tell her about all of my feelings towards her, the front door opened and closed. All three of us turned our attention towards the door, and Jeremy was standing there, staring at us questioningly. He slowly made his way in our direction.

It may have been the emotional roller coaster of the last hour I'd endured with my mother, or last night's mishap with Marcus, or the fact that my pregnancy hormones were getting the best me, but when

I saw Jeremy and his familiar, friendly face, I couldn't help but jump out of my seat and throw myself into his arms.

At first he was wary, and then when I began to sob in his arms, he tightened his embrace. He was my best friend, and I missed him so much. It felt like forever since we'd talked, *really* talked. I went to him for everything, and now that we had our separate lives, I didn't realize how much I needed him.

Pulling back, Jeremy slightly lowered his head to look at me. "Hey, what's the matter?"

Wiping the snot off my nose with the back of my hand, I looked at him. His piercing blue eyes were warm and allowed me to relax. "I'm fine. I just missed you. That's all."

He flashed his perfect smile while pulling me in and kissing the top of my head. "I've missed you too."

A screeching noise from the kitchen startled me. When I turned around, Marcus' chair was farther away from the table. And he was nowhere in sight. Before I could react, I heard a door slam shut. With our arms still wrapped around each other, we looked at each other, and without a second thought we unlocked our hold. Marcus was angry. I know him. He'd always been jealous of Jeremy, and my little "welcoming" display probably set him over the top. Sighing, I fixed my gaze at my mother who was still seated, staring at us.

"Maybe I should go. Do you think we could meet up sometime this week? I would like to maybe treat you to lunch or dinner. We could talk more?" She asked as she stood from her chair. Digging in her purse, she removed a pen and piece of paper. After scribbling something down, she made her way to me. "Here's my cell and home number. I moved here a month ago. My address is written on there as well." She handed me the info. I looked at it. *Should I give her my information as well, or should I just leave it at that and contact her when I'm ready?*

"Thank you. I'll call you tomorrow." She gently smiled and walked over towards the front door. I watched as she opened it, and looking over her shoulder, she smiled once again before leaving.

"Who was that?" Jeremy asked as he searched in the fridge.

"Long story, are you staying here tonight?" Now leaning over the kitchen island, he bit into an apple and nodded. "Well I have to fill you in on *a lot* of stuff. First, I'm going to check on Marcus."

I debated before opening the door whether I should give him some more time or not. We were doing so well today. *Ugh*, I hated this about us. We were always up and down. Though, no matter how many times we were down, I still truly loved him. He was everything to me, and I didn't want him to ever feel in any way insecure or jealous. The last thing I wanted was another argument. I didn't think I had the strength to fight back. Taking a deep breath, I walked into my room. Marcus was lying on my bed, hands behind his head, legs crossed, and eyes shut. I inched over to the edge and noticed he was listening to my iPod.

Kneeling on the bed beside him, I kept my distance. He popped opened an eye. Smiling, he took off the earbuds. With one hand still behind his head, he reached the other out to me. I took it, and he pulled me into him. I fell on chest and giggled. "What are you doing?" I asked, lifting my head to him.

"Chillaxing." I burst out laughing, my mixed-use words sounded funny coming out of him, especially with his slight Boston accent.

He raised an eyebrow, and his smile grew crooked. "You find that funny? You should hear how it sounds when you say it."

Slapping his chest, I yelled, "Hey!" Chuckling, he shifted his body so that I was flat on my back. He was on top of me with his stomach pressed against mine. He was searching my face, lost in thought.

I wondered sometimes what went on in his head: all he had seen, the secrets he kept, the dark path he'd chosen and refused to break from. Would he ever leave it? Would our love be enough for him to walk away from it? Or would this be his life even twenty years from now like his father's? If that were the case, then what was I doing? *Could* I truly live this way? His face grew sad, and he wiped the tears that I unknowingly shed, two simple drops that rolled down the side of my temples and onto the pillow.

"What are you thinking?" he asked. I didn't want to answer him. I didn't want to argue anymore. I just wanted to finally be happy, to be a family. I had to stop thinking about what tomorrow would bring and live for today. Tomorrow isn't promised, and I couldn't think of any reason why we shouldn't be together at that moment. The love he'd shown me was deeper than most. Right then, at that very instant, I couldn't imagine my life without him.

"Ask me again?" I whispered.

His brows creased questioningly. "Ask you what?"

"Ask me *again*." His eyes brightened when he realized what I was asking.

He leaned on his elbows, and his expression grew serious. Running his fingers through my hair, he wet his lips before speaking. "Mia, before you, I was lost. And the moment I laid eyes on your beautiful face, I knew … I just knew I had to make you mine. I found a woman that makes me *terrified* to love for the first time. Finally I found the *only* woman that I want to spend the rest of my life with. I'm not asking. I'm *begging* you if you would do me the honor of becoming my wife."

My heart swelled with each word. The love we had may not have been perfect, but it was love and no less. I had a beautiful, strong man, who was more damaged than I was, and throughout everything, we could still hold on even through the tears and laughter. How could I have given that up? Tears stung my eyes as I blurted out, "Yes."

"Really?" He asked uncertain by my answer.

"Yes, I'll marry you, Marcus. I know fifty years from now in your arms is where I'll want to be." His eyes sparkled with his smile. He breathed out in relief and kissed me deeply and passionately.

We allowed ourselves to forget everything because, at that moment, we were happy and nothing could ruin it.

****

After Marcus fell asleep, I spent some time with Jeremy in the living room. We watched a comedy, snacked on junk food, and talked about the past week. I told him everything that happened, minus Marcus' second life, but I spent hours telling him about my long-lost mother, the pregnancy, and the proposal. He was shocked, concerned, and happy for me. Jeremy was more worried about my career. I assured him that I was going to finish school, and even though it might take me an extra year, I was going to finish, no matter what.

He was very supportive and confident that I would be a wonderful mother. Although, I wasn't certain that I could, I vowed that I would try my absolute best to show unconditional love and support throughout my child's life.

The next few days were better than expected. Morning sickness, for some unexplained reason, occurred at noon and in the evenings as well! Every smell bothered me except for one: Marcus. He was thankful for that—afraid that I would end up hating him. He said he read an article that said some women began to hate or resent their partner during pregnancy. I couldn't see how that was possible. If anything, I felt clingier towards him. I wanted him around, and every time he left the room to even use the bathroom, I was emotional. It was super pathetic I know, but for some reason I had to be near him always.

That weekend, he surprised me with a beautiful ring. I knew he was going to get me one even though I told him I didn't need it. The look on his face was unforgettable when he handed me the small red box. He bit on his bottom lip, nervously awaiting my reaction, and his eyes gleamed with excitement.

When I flipped open the small lid, a glistening four-carat, princess-cut diamond brightened my eyes. Tiny diamonds wrapped around the platinum band. It had an antique style to it. I was surprised by how breathtaking a piece of jewelry could be. I was afraid to touch such an elegant piece, so he slid it on my finger. I'm such a simple person, never going crazy with jewelry, and although the ring was big and elegant, it was simple. I loved it.

Everything was going well, and we continued to keep the pregnancy hidden for a while. Marcus was a little upset that I told Jeremy about the pregnancy. So I allowed him to tell Jimmie, but that was it. We did announce our engagement to his entire family at Sunday dinner. Everyone was ecstatic, especially Theresa and Elle. Theresa began to plan the wedding at the dinner table.

Marcus and I tried to tell her we were in no rush and didn't want anything big. She refused to listen, claiming that a winter wedding would be beautiful, and the family was too big not to have a huge wedding. I didn't know how I would feel walking down the aisle with a huge belly. I allowed her to share her ideas. Once we announced the pregnancy, we could convince her to wait until after the baby was born.

Rumors began to spread very quickly at the office. Some were that I was knocked-up; that's why he was marrying me. That wasn't entirely false, but still. Others were that I was only marrying him for his *money*. That was completely false. I never thought of Marcus' money once. I never even thought about how much he or his firm was worth, because it was never my intention to get his money. It bothered me that people thought that of me. Marcus didn't allow any of the rumors to bother him. I envied that about him: how he just let it slide off his shoulders, not allowing any comment to affect him. I guess he was used to worse speculations spreading throughout the media, and simple office gossip didn't faze him.

After a couple weeks, it was the beginning of August and my externship was over. The first day spent without Marcus was dreadful, so I focused on spending time with Sara. We met up every day for the next few days. My mother explained that she mailed another letter, hoping that Michael would have a change of heart. When the letter returned from the post office, she began to search for a new address. That was when she found out about his death. It was a little difficult for her to find me since I wasn't listed, so she hired a private detective. That explained the black SUV. The entire time I thought it had something to do with Marcus. I was completely wrong!

We managed to slowly establish a relationship. I wasn't sure what type of relationship it was, but we were working on that. I finally felt that my life was coming together. I'd gained a beautiful family with the DeLucas. Jeremy and I still had our close relationship. Soon I would be a mother, and recently I gained my mother. At one point in my life, I was at my lowest and thought nothing could possibly lift me from the miserable grief I'd suffered. Now I could honestly say I was the happiest I'd ever been.

Nothing could go wrong.

CHAPTER TWENTY-ONE

"Oh, Mia, thank you so much!" Theresa jumped from the couch and rushed to the door as soon as I entered. Grabbing her purse, she was halfway out before I could answer. Turning back, she finished the rest of her sentence. "The last time she ate was this afternoon. She's in her room, playing her game. *Oh* and also I've been meaning to tell you I want to plan a surprise birthday party for Marcus' thirtieth."

I'd almost forgotten his birthday; it was the next month at the end of September. "Can I help with the planning?" Theresa is very big on events, but I really wanted to help her with this.

She smiled before answering, "Of course! I have to run. See you soon, and thanks again for watching Elle at last minute."

"It's not a problem, Theresa. Go. You don't want to be late." She waved and ran out the door.

Elle's sitter had surgery last week, so Theresa had been watching her. Though today she had to run to a doctor's appointment she had forgotten about, and she called me immediately when the office called to verify the appointment.

Luckily, I was home doing nothing, just stuffing my face with Oreo cookies: the only craving in my pregnancy thus far. At ten weeks, I hadn't gained any weight. I did feel bloated and had slight cramping, oh yeah and the "morning" sickness. Other than that, I'd been fine. Marcus and I were excited to share the news in a couple weeks with his family.

On my way to Elle's room, I heard a knock at the door. I thought it was weird. There were never any visitors except for during the family dinners, and Theresa had a spare key. Maybe she'd left something behind and forgot it. I made my way to the door, and I was shocked when I caught sight of Romeo, Marcus' younger cousin.

His shoulders were slouched over; his hands were shoved in the front pocket of his jeans, and his clothes were filled with mud. When he looked up, I gasped at the sight of his bruised face. He had a black, swollen left eye, the bridge of his nose was split open, and dry blood covered his nostrils and the side of his face. His lips were swollen and gashed open. "Oh my God, Romeo, what happened?" I reached out for him, grabbing his shoulders.

"He got himself into a little mess." I was so focused on Romeo that I didn't see Lou Sorrento standing just a few feet beside him. My heart dropped at the closeness. This was the first time I'd seen him face-to-face, and my anger began to slowly rise. He was responsible for Marcus' other life, and I knew he was responsible for Romeo's appearance.

Offering his hand, he brightly smiled. "Hi, I'm Lou. You must be the lovely Mia? It's a pleasure to finally meet you." Looking down at his hand, I didn't take it. He would have no respect from me. I didn't know what type of relationship he and Marcus had beside the obvious employment relationship, but I refused to show him any form of decency. His eyes widened with amusement, and then he rubbed the untaken hand against his chest. "Okay, I need to talk with Marky. He's ignoring my calls."

"Marcus isn't here, but when he arrives, I'll make sure to tell him you're looking for him. Goodbye." Pulling Romeo into the house, I quickly walked in. Lou stopped the door with his foot, pushing his way in and shut the door behind him.

My heart began to race. What's he doing here? Would Marcus be upset that he's in the house? Had he ever been in this house? "I think I'll stand here and wait for him. He needs to clear up the mess his *idiot* cousin made. I'm sure he wouldn't miss any of your calls. If you call him, maybe I could be out of your hair sooner."

Ignoring him, I walked over to Romeo, placing my hand on his face. He flinched in pain. "What did you get yourself into?" I whispered. Romeo couldn't look at me; he was too ashamed. He clearly was not going to answer me. I had no choice but to call Marcus. Glaring at Lou, I wanted to smack the smart-ass grin off his face. Walking over to my purse, I grabbed my phone and made the call.

After one ring he picked up. "Hey, babe." It sounded like he was in the car. I could hear wind blowing and other vehicles driving by.

"Marcus?" I failed desperately to hide the shakiness in my voice.

Knowing me very well, he asked, "What's wrong?"

Taking a deep breath, I tried to think of the best way to explain this. I walked over to the corner where no one could hear my conversation. "Romeo is here. He's badly beaten, and Lou is with him. Lou won't leave until he speaks with you."

There were a few seconds of silence before he yelled, "What the fuck!" A few thumping noises along with the horn sounding off rang my ears. I knew my man well enough to know that he'd just punched the steering a few times, upset. Taking a deep breath, he was silent for a moment before responding again. "Put Lou on the phone."

Hesitating for a second, I intently stared at Lou. He was seated on a chair in the living room, facing me. His legs were crossed, his elbow was on the armrest with a closed fist underneath his chin, and still he had that stupid amused grin. Clearing my throat, I spoke. "He's on the phone." He stretched out the hand that was lying on his lap.

I flashed a cocky look and smacked my hand to my hip. I further extended my arm with the cell phone. I was not one of his employees. He could very well walk his ass over and grab the phone. When I tapped my foot, he laughed once, shook his head, and stood from his seat. Striding over, he took the phone from my hand and placed it to his ear, not taking his eyes off of me the entire time.

"Marky." He grinned. Taking a few steps back, I watched him closely. He was only a few inches taller than me. He had a medium build, thick salt-and-pepper hair that was neatly brushed back, and light brown eyes that narrowed as he listened attentively over the phone. If I didn't hate him so much, I might've thought he was a good-looking man. Then I thought of all the pain Marcus and I had gone through because of him. I only saw him as an evil, malicious, disgusting man.

Speaking in a low, raspy tone, his eyes grew darker as he continued to ogle me. "What can I say? He came to me asking for work ... *no* ... he screwed up ... *big* time ... sixty ... yeah, sixty." Slowly he began to walk towards me, his eager eyes staring into mine.

For every step forward he made, I took one step back, until my back pressed against the staircase. My breathing sped up when he was only inches away from me. "Your woman's a feisty one, isn't she?" He slightly pulled the phone away from his ear and cringed. I could hear Marcus' loud tone throughout the phone but couldn't make out what was said.

Lou laughed and fixed his gaze back on me. His hand slowly moved from his ear over to the side of my face. Because I was frozen, he pressed the phone along my ear with the tip of his fingers sliding across my cheek. His touch shot shivers through my spine and caused the hair on the back of my neck to stand up. He frightened me, but I made sure not to show it. Pushing his hand away, I grabbed the phone. He took a few steps back.

In a raspy, dry manner, I managed to say, "Hello."

"Baby, I need you to do me a favor. Are you near my office?" Marcus' desperate tone forced me to be alert.

"Yes," I said, watching Lou as he cocked his head to the side, folding his arms on his chest. His stares were giving me the creeps. Swallowing, I focused back on Marcus.

"Okay, I want you to walk into my office and lock the door behind you."

"What?" I asked confused.

"Just do it. Tell me when you're in there and the door is locked."

I looked up at Lou. He was in the same position. I fixed my gaze towards Romeo. He was sitting by the couch, watching Lou. Was Marcus trying to keep me away from them? What about Romeo, shouldn't I lock him in the office with me? Confused by this sudden request, I wasn't sure what I should do. "Mia, are you in the office yet?" Marcus' impatient tone hurried my legs to his office, and I shut the door behind me. Locking the bolt, I turned the knob to make sure it was secure. "Okay, I'm in here. The door's locked. What now?" I asked.

"Good, at my desk by the top right-hand drawer, you'll find a key. Let me know when you find it. What the fuck! You cocksucker, move out the fucking way!" Road rage—he was trying to rush home. I glanced at the clock by his desk. It was rush hour. There was no way he'd be here anytime soon.

After I took a seat in the office chair, I reached for the top right-hand drawer. There were several files, no keys. Rummaging through, I tried to see if the keys were in between the files. I was alarmed when I noticed one particular folder. On the tab written in all caps were the words M. SULLIVAN. Why was there a file with my name in his desk? I lifted the file to have a closer look. That was when I noticed the key. Marcus interrupted my curiosity, "Mia, did you find the key?" Biting my lip, I wasn't sure what to do. Romeo was out there with Lou, and if I didn't hurry, he could harm him again. Taking a deep breath, I grabbed the key and placed the file back. I'd look at it later.

"Yes, I have it." I said, closing the drawer.

"Okay, beside the bookshelf, you'll see the large-framed mirror. Underneath the frame, you'll have to feel for a small keyhole to place the key in. Unlock the mirror and open it. Behind it will be a vault."

What the hell? As many times I'd been in this office and stared into that mirror, never once did I expect it to be a hidden passage to something. The mirror had a vertical gold frame, and it was taller than me. I assumed it was décor; I always admired how beautiful and luxurious it looked.

Kneeling before my reflection, I held the phone between my shoulder and ear. Feeling underneath the curvy detailed frame, I managed to locate a small keyhole. I dug the key in and turned it. A small clicking noise told me the mirror was loosened. Standing up, I pulled the mirror open like a door. Behind it was an all-black steel door with a keypad in the middle. "It's open," I whispered, imagining what could possibly be behind this door.

"Good, now you have to do this correctly, or the entire system will lock for twenty-four hours." He waited for my okay and continued, "On the keypad press the following code: pound-two-four-four-seven-pound. Once you hear the door unlock, open it and enter immediately. Don't be alarmed. The door will shut behind you. Let me know when you're in."

This was ridiculous; he should be here to do this. What if I get stuck in there? I didn't want to screw this up, and he trusted me with all of this. I sucked it up and took a deep breath. Doing as I was told, I punched the code into the pad and entered as soon as it unlocked. As he said, the door closed behind me. I was standing in a small, lit, narrow space with another door in front of me. I told him I was in and waited for the next instructions.

"You're doing good, baby. Just a few more steps and you'll be done. Now this entry is similar, though the code is different: pound-two-two-zero-four-pound."

I did as I was told, and the door opened. Hurrying through, I almost dropped the phone. When I looked up, I was shocked. It felt like I'd walked into an eight-by-ten, advanced storage unit. On one side of the wall, there were shelves filled with all types of guns: small, large, AK-47's, many different calibers. If you could think of a type, it was there. On the other side of the wall were neatly stacked bricks of money. Not just a few bills, no, there were rolls and columns of one-hundred-dollar bills wrapped in Saran Wrap. If my jaw weren't attached to my face, it would have fallen to the ground. I'd never had been around this much money. I knew Marcus was financially successful, though my mind steered more toward only a fraction of what was in this vault.

"Okay, Mia, now that you're in, I need you to walk over to the money stacked along the right side of the wall. On the metal table in the center of the room, you'll find a few black bags. Each small stack is worth ten grand. I need you to take six of those stacks and place them into a bag and hand it to Lou."

The "small" stacks were placed into two fabric bags. After exiting the vault and making sure it was securely closed as per Marcus' instructions, I placed the key back in the drawer. Marcus said he'd be home in twenty minutes. We hung up, and I was left in the room holding two heavy medium-sized bags worth sixty-thousand dollars. Taking a few deep breaths to calm my nerves, I stormed out of the office.

Romeo was nowhere in sight. Lou was sitting on the couch, and beside him was Elle, holding up her handheld game, showing her score. Lou had his arm wrapped around her shoulder. The image of him touching her disgusted me. "Elle, go to your room." Both of them snapped their heads in my direction. Elle first smiled, but it instantly faded when she saw the irate expression I had.

"But I'm showing Uncle Lou my game," she whined.

"Go to your room now!" I pointed to the staircase with a black velvet bag in my hand. She flinched at my tone, and her lip began to tremble. *Great*, I was becoming Marcus. I took a deep breath and tried in a calm manner to explain myself. "Please, Elle, go to your room. I need to talk to Lou … *privately*." He nodded at her, giving her the okay. Very quickly she ran past me and up the stairs, holding back her tears. I felt terrible. I didn't mean to snap at her. Shifting my anger back on the person it was meant for, I stomped over to him and tossed the bags on the couch where Elle just vacated. "You have what you want. You can leave now."

The smart smirk slowly turned into stern, thin lips, and his jaw tightened. Very slowly, he flexed his neck side-to-side, and a loud crack sounded. Standing up, his shoulder bumped into mine. Adjusting his suit jacket, he turned and lowered his head. His lips were inches from the side of my face, and he growled in a low, raspy, stern tone, "You know at first your little attitude was cute, but don't *fucking* think for one second that I will tolerate it." Turning, he grabbed the bags, and walked towards the door. Before leaving he yelled out, "It was a pleasure meeting you, Mia. We should do lunch." The door slammed behind him.

When all the air released from my lungs, I collapsed into the sofa, burying my face into my hands. The entire experience had been terrible. I just wanted to be locked in Marcus' arms. What happened with Romeo? Why did he owe so much money? *Aarrrgh!* I just wanted to scream at the top of my lungs. At the sound of the door creaking, I snapped my head up in its direction. Romeo was standing a few feet away with a frozen steak to his eye. I glared at him, and he looked down mortified. "You, in the kitchen, now." I flew past him and headed to the kitchen. He followed, and I directed him to sit by the table.

Elle had had a few scratches and dents, so I knew the first aid kit was kept inside the pantry. I placed the open kit on the table, and he looked at me with his light brown eyes. Except for the eyes, he bore a striking resemblance to Marcus: the same olive skin, perfectly thick arched eyebrows, and model-like silky, dark hair. He was definitely gorgeous even with the bruises. Now that I was closer, I was able to see a huge split from the middle of his forehead to the end of his eyebrow. It was about three inches in length and pretty deep. "Romeo, you're going to need stitches."

"No, I'm not going to the hospital. Can't you stitch it together?"

"No! I wouldn't even know how to. There are butterfly bandages here. I can use them, but if Marcus thinks you need a hospital, you have to go." He nodded. I began the cleansing process. Before I could even nurse the cuts, I had to clean his face and wipe all the blood, just in case there were any open cuts I missed.

I cleaned all of the blood with a wet cloth and started to nurse the cut on his lips. I needed to steer my mind away from exploding.

Not enjoying the silence, I began to question him. "What happened to you, Romeo?"

Shrugging, he hesitated before speaking. I wondered if he thought to tell me the truth. Then when he began, he spoke as if it was like a relief to get it all out. "Marcus warned me not get involved, but I didn't listen. I figured I could use the extra money before school starts. I did a few runs for Lou. I delivered a few small packages to certain groups, collected the money, and brought it back to Lou. He'd give me a cut. Today, I had to deliver a package to a Russian cartel. They teased me, saying I was too *pretty* to be a runner. I didn't like it, so I said a few words." He's more like Marcus than I thought. Since when does someone teasing you, give you the go-ahead to be cocky?

I brushed the cut on his forehead with an alcohol wipe. He sucked in air and winced. I bit my lip and apologized. Cautiously, I wiped his wound again. This time he pressed his lips together and shut his eyes. "So Lou didn't do this to you?" I asked, continuing to nurse him.

His eyes shot open. "No, the Russians did. They took the package, and left me on the side of the road. When I was finally conscious, I found my way back to Lou. He said he would take care of the Russians, but the package was worth sixty grand. That's when we came here."

"*You* brought him here, Romeo?" I thought Lou brought Romeo here, knowing it was the other way around, upset me even more.

"I had no choice, Mia. He threatened to *kill* me, saying if I didn't come up with the money, then—" We both jumped when the sound of the front door slamming alerted the room.

"Mia!" Marcus yelled my name from the front door.

"In the kitchen!" I shouted. Romeo straightened his shoulders, and his knee began to bounce nervously. I thought that was weird. Why would he be nervous? If anything he should be relieved Marcus was finally here.

Marcus stormed through the kitchen door. His shoulders were broad and rapidly moved up and down with his heavy breathing. His arms were slightly bent and secured on the side of his body. His hands were closed in tight fists, and the veins on his hands and arms were visibly seen from a distance. His face was red and damp with sweat. He glared at Romeo with an arched eyebrow and a straight face. This was the angriest I'd ever seen him. I just couldn't understand why he was so upset with Romeo. Lou was the one that deserved the evil look. Within three steps, Marcus was by us, pushing me aside. He leaned over Romeo, pressing his hand against the side of Romeo's face.

Yelling from the top of his lungs, he let him have it. "What the FUCK WERE YOU THINKING?" One hard smack across Romeo's face forced him slightly off his chair. I jumped.

"Marcus!" I breathed, shocked by his behavior. *What had gotten into him?*

He ignored me and continued to grill Romeo. "Huh?" Romeo lowered his head and began to cry.

"I'm sorry ..." Romeo choked.

"You're sorry? You're *sorry!* I told you, Rome! I *fucking* told you to stay away from this shit. But you wouldn't fucking listen, would you? Then you bring him to *my* house! Where my niece and my girl stay?" Veins popped out of his forehead and neck as he poked his middle and index finger into Romeo's forehead with each word, "HOW COULD YOU BE SO STUPID!" Marcus yelled the last insulting word so loudly spit flew all over the place.

Sniffing a few times, Romeo tried to control his weeping. "I promise I'll pay you back every dime."

Marcus leaned up, pressing his hands on his hips. "Pay me back? It's not about the money, Rome!" His arms flew wildly in front of him. After a few seconds of silence, he placed his hands back on his hips. "I didn't want you in this shit." Marcus lowered his head and brought one hand up to his forehead, rubbing small circular motions with his fingertips. It calmed him a bit, and he lowered his tone. "Do you want to end up like your brother? Like my *father?*"

Romeo burst into hard sobs, shaking his head. His body began to tremble with his cries. "No!" He moaned.

It felt like forever before Marcus spoke again. He stood over Romeo, watching him break. I was a mess in quiet tears by the island, watching the entire episode, stunned. Finally Marcus kneeled before Romeo. Sighing heavily, he looked up at him. "I spoke to Lou; you're out. He's not giving you any more work. I need you to promise me that you'll focus on school and *live* life the way you're supposed to live it. If you can promise me that, we're even. Can you do that?"

Romeo nodded.

"Okay, I can't send you home like this. I'll call your mom and tell her you're staying with me for a couple weeks. I'll make up some shit about shadowing me at the firm. Take the room on the third floor and get yourself cleaned up."

Both of them straightened and hugged in a tight manly embrace. Romeo muttered something while they were locked together. Marcus patted his back and assured him everything would be okay. It only lasted a few seconds, and Romeo flew out of the kitchen with his head lowered and went up the stairs. It took a moment for Marcus to compose himself. He looked everywhere else before looking at me. I watched as he put the first-aid kit away and pushed the chair back underneath the table. He also sprayed down the table with sanitizing spray and wiped it. It was his way of avoiding a breakdown.

When he reached the point where it was okay for him to acknowledge me, he didn't say anything. Instead he walked over to the island where I was. Burying his head into my collar bone, he sighed. I wrapped my arms around his neck. Pulling me in by my waist, we didn't say a word, just sheltered each other, feeling safe and relieved. The only thing that came to my mind was, "What is he thinking right now?" He always wanted to know my thoughts when he could sense I needed to talk or if he didn't know how to comfort me.

Marcus tells me how he's feeling when it involves me. He never holds back in telling me how much he loves me and how much I have changed his life. He never talked about how he felt regarding the stress and the emotional conflict working for Lou brought. He kept everything all bottled up. I was afraid one day he'd explode and when that day came, it might be on the wrong person.

He took my hand in his grasp, and we silently made our way up the stairs. I stopped in front of Elle's room. When I entered, she was lying on her bed, arms behind her head, watching a movie on her small flat screen. I felt terrible for how I acted earlier, and at that moment I realized the reasons behind Marcus' outbursts. He never meant any harm; he was just simply trying to keep me away from witnessing terrible circumstances. I apologized to Elle several times, and she assured me time and time again that it was okay. I promised to take her shopping the next week at the mall for a girls' day as a way to make it up to her. She quickly approved.

Marcus went ahead to his bedroom while I spoke with Elle. After she and I made up, I left her room. When I entered Marcus' bedroom, his back was facing me. He stood over the nightstand. Empting his pockets, he placed the items on the nightstand. Walking up behind him, I wrapped my arms around the middle of his stomach. I squeezed tightly against him, and he sighed, lowering his head and rubbing the back of my hand with his fingertips.

"Talk to me, Marcus," I pleaded, using the words that so easily worked on me. I pressed the side of my face on his firm back. He eventually turned in my arms and faced me as I still held him tightly. His hand gently cupped my face, and leaning down, he planted a small, tender kiss on my forehead. The feeling of his soft lips sent a warm sensation through my blood. My body instantly relaxed, and I closed my eyes.

"I can't do this anymore, Mia," he whispered.

My eyes shot opened. "Do what?" I searched his face. He can't do *us* anymore? The *job*, the *stress*, the second life, what can't he do anymore?

"This … Look at me. I'm slowly breaking … With a baby on the way and you … The thought of either of you hurt or even …" He didn't finish. He didn't have to.

"Marcus, then leave. Why are you still involved with the Sorrentos? Just *leave*." I begged. Hoping and wishing he could, I wasn't sure why it was so hard to walk away. Did he owe Lou Sorrento something? Was it money? I was sure he could pay him off with all the money that he had in the vault.

"You don't understand. I *can't* …" His hands firmed against my face.

"Why don't you talk to me, Marcus? I thought we were a team here. How can I possibly know what's going on up here?" Pointing a finger to his temple, I said, "If you don't let me in, I'll probably never understand."

He didn't say anything as always. He just stared at me for a long time as if holding back something he so desperately wanted to say. Instead of using his lips to talk, he forced them onto mine. Keeping my eyes open, I watched as his eyes were tightly shut. This was his way of coping? To *fuck* his way into forgetting? I wanted to be angry with him, to smack him away and tell him we needed to talk, that sex wouldn't solve his issues, but he grew hungry and twirled his tongue along mine. His slight moans made the pit of my stomach twist with sensation. Giving in, I closed my eyes and allowed him to take over. The moment I relinquished myself to him, he forced me onto the bed.

Aggressively, he ripped my clothes off as he stood by the edge of the bed. He watched me with his wicked glare as he threw his clothing to the floor, and my breath hitched at his violent stare. I wasn't scared. No, I knew he wouldn't hurt me. Instead I was extremely turned on by his instant need to take his frustrations out with wild, hair-pulling, lip-biting, moaning, groaning, crazy, incredible sex.

No, I didn't mind at all. I allowed him to bruise my hips with the firm grip he held at each thrust. I allowed him to hungrily bite my lip till we tasted the metallic flavor of blood as my flesh slightly tore. I allowed him to ball a fist in my hair as he cried out my name when our bodies joined.

He was in control. I *wanted* him in control, and he *needed* to be in control.

****

I woke up with Marcus hovering over me. He was in a deep, senseless sleep, snoring along my chest. The heat from his bare skin made my temperature rise, and I became instantly uncomfortable. I inched over, trying to avoid waking him. His breath hitched and then went back to normal.

He shifted his leg onto my upper thighs. My bladder felt completely full, and the pressure of his heavy weight made it feel as if it were going to explode. Scooting over a few more times, I managed to break free. He grunted then smacked his lips twice before returning to his loud snore.

Standing by the bed, I admired his beauty as he slept peacefully. He was lying flat on his stomach with only the right side of his face showing. His hair was an adorable mess, his lips were partly open, and his shoulders rose, evenly matching his breathing. His right hand was inches away from his face, his right leg slightly bent, while the left side of his body lay completely straight under the sheets.

His well-built back teased me as it flexed and perfected each muscular line as he inhaled and exhaled. Instantly, I became aroused again; even his back turned me on. *What* the hell was wrong with me? I could've stood there and watched him for hours. He was a stunning piece of art, and he was mine.

Sighing in contentment, I forced my eyes away. I felt a slight cramp from the full bladder. Tiptoeing, I made my way to the bathroom and gently closed the door behind me. I stopped and giggled at my bare reflection in the mirror. My hair was a tangled mess, and my lips were swollen and bruised. Pressing my fingertips against my sore lips, I laughed to myself, remembering what we'd just done a few hours ago.

The thought was rudely interrupted when I felt a pull on my bladder again. I hurried to the toilet. After I finished, I wiped myself. My body trembled at the sight of bright red blood on the toilet paper. *Oh my God! What's wrong with me? Is this even normal?* I wiped again—more blood and some cramping. I needed to call Dr. Lee.

CHAPTER TWENTY-TWO

With shaky legs, I managed to slip on a cream silk nightgown and headed for Marcus' office. I remembered leaving my cell phone on his desk after speaking with him about the money for Lou. I didn't want to wake Marcus in case I was completely overreacting. This could be normal. I think I read something somewhere … I think. Oh God, please make sure my baby's okay. I can't lose my peanut. Protectively I wrapped my arms around my belly, somehow hoping that if I shielded my baby, he'd be okay.

Taking a seat on the plush leather chair, I located my cell phone. Scrolling down, I found Dr. Lee's telephone number. It was late, a little before midnight. I knew he said that if I left a message stating it was urgent he'd contact me immediately. Dialing his number with the office phone on the desk, I waited for the beep at the end of his greeting. "Hello Dr. Lee, this is Mia Sullivan. I feel this may be an emergency. I'm bleeding, not heavily but a little more than just spotting. Please call to advise me on what I should do. Thank you." Hanging up the phone, I sat there tapping my foot against the bottom edge of the wooden desk.

I didn't know if I should I wake Marcus so he could take me to the ER, or if I should patiently wait for Dr. Lee's call? It hadn't even been five minutes yet, and I was dreading the waiting game already. I almost gave in when I remembered the folder! I pulled it out from the drawer and stared at the name before opening it. It was a regular-sized file folder. It was pretty thick with documents. Why would he keep a folder on me? The tab had a label with all caps printed M. SULLIVAN. Maybe it contained work information, but, then again, it wouldn't be kept in his home office.

When I opened the file, the first document was an eight-by-ten photo. It was a distant image of two men. It looked like they were talking in a park. The next document was the same two men in the park, but it was a closer image. I couldn't make out the other man, but I instantly identified Marcus. He was wearing his all-black suit, and the collar from his shirt was white. Since it was a profile picture, I couldn't tell if he was wearing a tie. He was standing slightly hunched over, one hand pointing in another direction and the other pointing at the man. Marcus uses his hands a lot when engaged in conversation. I could tell by his posture that he wasn't angry. He was telling a story of some sort.

When I turned to the next picture, my heart dropped. I was wrong, oh yes, very wrong. The image of the two was closer, and I made out the second man instantly: his familiar golden brown hair, his fair complexion and handsome profile. His eyes were familiar. The skin on the side of his temples wrinkled when he laughed. The brown leather jacket I bought him for Christmas two years ago was snuggled comfortably against his athletic build. This file was not on me. *No*, it was on Michael, my brother. Slowly I stood from the chair, grabbing the documents and pressing them against my chest. Walking around the desk in disbelief, I instantly felt faint, dropping to my knees. The documents I held fell before me.

Images of my brother and Marcus laughing, talking, patting each other on the shoulder were spread all before me. There were documents of meetings at a warehouse, transcripts of conversations between the two, between other mafia groups, regarding drug and gun deal arrangements. Overwhelmed by it all, I was engulfed by tears, allowing drops to fall over the papers lying before me. Marcus not only knew my brother but they were friendly with one another.

My brother couldn't have been involved with the Sorrento's mafia family. He was an undercover detective. *Wait!* He was an undercover detective! Did Michael have an assignment to go undercover with the Sorrentos? If that were the case, then he was closely watching Marcus as well. Was Marcus involved with my brother's death?

"There you are. I was looking all over …" Marcus walked through his office door. I snapped my head up when I heard his voice. He was staring at me curiously. His lips twitched to a slight crooked grin. "What are you doing on the floor, Mia?"

My chest moved rapidly as my heartbeat began to pick up the pace. I tilted my head, watching him. *No*, he couldn't have been involved with Michael's death. Shaking my head, I stared at him again. He took a few steps towards me. I flinched, and he froze at my reaction.

His now worried face searched mine, trying to find what could have possibly caused me so much pain. His eyes wandered from me to the documents. He cocked his head at the papers spread on the floor and inched over to them. Bending, he hovered over the pieces and picked one up to eye level. His eyes grew larger as his lips spread apart.

Marcus brought his eyes back to me. My eyes pleaded with his. He didn't explain anything—just stared in shocked at the information I'd just found. My hands were clenched against my chest. I tried to speak, but my tongue felt dry. He reached for me, but I pulled back. "No," I managed to spit out through the hoarseness of my tone. He cringed at my refusal. "No," I said again. "No. No. No. You lied to me, Marcus!" Shaking his head, he shifted to his knees so that we could be at eye level. "Yes, you lied to me! How could you? You knew Michael this entire time? Did you know about me before we met? Did you know who I was that night at the club?"

Blowing out a deep shaky breath, he shook his head. "No, Mia, I didn't know who you were." He looked down at the documents spread underneath him. "I did lie to you when you asked me the day we drove to the airport if I knew Michael—when you said your brother was a detective. I should have caught on, but when you said his name and your last name, I put it all together." He tried to reach for me, and I pulled back again, falling on my behind. "I'm so sorry, baby."

"You do not get to call me baby! I'm not your baby. I'm nothing to you!" A noise of pain released from his lips as his shoulders and head dropped. "Did you kill him?" My demand brought his watery eyes back to mine.

"No!" He shook his head violently, disgusted that I even thought it.

"Were you *involved* with his murder, Marcus?" I slowly began to rise, standing over him wanting answers.

"Mia, no!" He pleaded, his hands reaching up to grab my waist.

I smacked them away. "But you know who killed him, don't you?"

Exhaling deeply, he closed his eyes. Biting his lips, he gently nodded.

"It was Lou, wasn't it?" Just speaking his name out loud pissed me off. Slowly my rage began to build. When he gently nodded his head again, I reached my boiling point. "You go and work for him almost every other night, and then you come home to me?" My trembling voice slowly began to pick up in volume, *"knowing, he killed my brother!"*

Unable to breathe, unable to think, unable to make sense of anything, I smacked him. I was so *angry* with him. It hurt me to know this entire time he was lying. Everything, every emotion I felt, every single pain I dealt with since we met, I took it out on him at this very moment.

Balling my fist, I swung at him, and continued to punch him over and over, hitting his face, his chest, and his shoulders—anywhere that was visible. Dropping to my knees inches away from him, I continued to pound on his chest, and he let me. He didn't move, didn't try to get away, and didn't even *flinch*. It was as if he knew he deserved every inch of the pain.

"Why Marcus? How could you do this to me?" My wrist gave out, and in a slower motion I lightly punched his chest one last time before burying my face into it. Sobbing, I tried to find a normal way of breathing, but my cries were uncontrollable. Wrapping his arms around me, his weeping overpowered mine. "I'm so sorry, *Mia*. I never meant to hurt you. I never meant to ... *fuck*, please forgive me." No, I couldn't, not this time.

"I hate you, Marcus. I *hate* you so much." Those words hurt us both. Though that was what I felt at that moment. So I pulled away from him. I couldn't look into his eyes. Quickly standing, he hovered over me. I pushed him away. Walking over to his desk, I grabbed my phone.

Grabbing my wrist, he begged me not to go. With the blood pulsing through my veins, my rage quickly boiled. Turning to face him, I shoved the palms of my hands against his chest. I was surprised by my own strength. Although he was bigger than I was, I forced him to stumble back a few steps, and he landed on the wooden desk. He managed to balance himself, but he didn't move. His sorrowful eyes were staring into mine, *pleading*. Those eyes that I once fell for, that I trusted, that allowed me fall under his spell. Those eyes now only fill my stomach with such vile disgust.

Collecting my thoughts was impossible. My mind was racing at a thousand miles per hour. I'd never felt so much pain in my life. I gave him one last look, but he did and said *nothing*. His eyes were saddened, but I didn't care. I wanted to get away! I turned away from him and ran as fast as I could. I could hear him yelling my name.

Snatching my purse from the table without looking back, I struggled to unlock the front door. I managed to open it with a shaky hand, tripping down the first few steps, realizing at that moment my feet were bare. Carelessly I ran down the driveway and reached my car. I shoved my hand into my bag to collect my keys, but I couldn't find them. *Shit!* He was by the door. Rushing in the process, I was able to locate the keys and jump into the driver's seat.

Looking up, I found him on the bottom step, yelling, begging me to stop. My heart was pulsing at such a rapid speed I felt nauseated and lightheaded. After turning on the ignition, I raced out of the driveway and onto the street. The speedometer reached ninety-five miles per hour. My hands were sweating, and my heart was pounding so loudly I could barely hear myself breathe.

After twenty minutes, I was far enough to pull over by the curb, checking my rearview mirror. He was nowhere in sight. I made sure the doors were locked. Then burying my face into my hands, I screamed and burst into sobs, allowing all the rage and betrayal to pour out. How could I have believed and trusted *him*? How could I have been so *stupid*? This whole time he was warning me, but I was blind and didn't care. I wanted the good and bad—*all* of him.

Knowing at that moment what he truly was, I realized that everything was just lies. *Aarrgh!* I looked down, trying to catch my breath. Through blurry, watery vision, I caught sight of my cream silk nightgown spotted in bright red blood.

My thoughts were uncontrollable. I was trying to make it all go away, and I pounded my fists against my temples, but all that managed to do was inflict additional pain. *Why me?* My chest felt tight and it was so hard to breathe I was hyperventilating. After a few minutes of taking deep long breaths, I was able to control the airflow through my lungs.

The loud ringing of my phone pierced through my thoughts. Thinking it was Marcus, I was going to cut the damn phone off, but it wasn't him. It was Dr. Lee. "Hello," I answered urgently.

"Ms. Sullivan. This is Dr. Lee. I just received your message. Are you still spotting or feeling any cramping."

Choking over my tears, I burst out, "It's a lot of blood. It seeped through my gown—"

Cutting me off, he spoke in an urgent but controlled tone. "I need you to meet me at the hospital. I can make it there in fifteen minutes."

CHAPTER TWENTY-THREE

"Ms. Sullivan, the procedure could take anywhere from thirty to forty minutes. We are giving you general anesthesia. When you wake up, you will feel a little groggy. I want you to count down, beginning from one hundred."

"One hundred, ninety-nine, ninety-ei..."

I awoke feeling confused. Just a minute ago, I was lying in a cold operating room, counting backwards, and then I was in another room. A woman in navy blue scrubs was standing a few inches away from the edge of the bed. She was scribbling away on a piece of paper. My eyes felt heavy; it was exhausting trying to keep them open. The nurse must have sensed my attempt to stare. Looking from under her glasses, a warm gentle smile spread along her face. Placing the clipboard into a holder on the end of the bed, she walked to my side. "Hi, Ms. Sullivan, my name is Sandy. I'm the RN on this floor. You're in the recovery room. How are you feeling?"

Trying to locate my voice, I mumbled, "Uh, I feel really groggy and thirsty." She gently smiled and giggled.

"That's normal. Dr. Lee will be in to speak with you in just a few minutes. Your mother is speaking with him at the moment. In the meantime, I'll grab you some water." She left the room, leaving me in a daze.

A couple nights ago—that night I left *him*—I went in to see Dr. Lee. Some testing showed that my HCG levels were dropping, and Dr. Lee could no longer hear the heartbeat of my little peanut. I was miscarrying, and Dr. Lee recommended that I allow the fetus to pass on its own. When I followed up this morning, he said that only half of the fetus passed, and he strongly recommended a D&C to prevent an infection.

There was one problem. I could only be discharged if I had someone drive me home. The past few days I stayed in a hotel room, avoiding the outside world. The thought of home sent me into a depression. I couldn't go home because *he* would surely be there.

Then I thought of Jeremy. I wanted tell him everything, but I was afraid he would call *him*. I didn't even attempt it. Who could I have called? Where could I've gone? I didn't have any other friends, and the people that I was close with were all *his* family.

Then my mother popped in my head. When I called her, she didn't recognize my voice. I wasn't sure I would've been able to recognize my own voice either. It was raspy and unintelligible from the yelling, screaming, and crying I'd done the past few days: yelling at *him* after finding out what he'd kept from me, screaming from the top of lungs for feeling betrayed and neglected, and crying from the loss—the loss of our love, the loss of the trust, and the loss of our *child*. At that moment, I wished I was under again away from my thoughts. My whole life had caved in, and I wasn't sure I had the strength to recover from this.

Tears ran down the side of my temples as I lay there and wondered how something so perfect could completely turn into one huge *disaster*. I knew *he* had the right to know about our baby, but I also knew I wasn't ready to face him. Knowing that, I couldn't go home just then. I took my mother's offer and stayed with her for a while. It was the only place I knew he wouldn't find me. At one point, his arms were where I felt safe. Now I was running away from him to feel safe.

"Ms. Sullivan, *oh,* I'm sorry. I could return ..." Lost in my own sorrow, I didn't hear Dr. Lee enter.

I managed to bring myself to sit. "No, it's fine." Before I could use my fingers to wipe my own tears, Dr. Lee handed me a tissue. The gesture for some unexplained reason brought fresh tears to my eyes. Lowering my head so he couldn't see, I wiped the soft tissue against the moisture on my eyelids.

Pulling a chair beside my bed, he took a seat and opened a folder he held. "Ms. Sullivan, the procedure went very well. We were able to fully clean the cervix. There was no scarring or tissue damage. As discussed earlier, it was best to have the D&C, since only half the fetus passed. There will be bleeding and slight cramping that will occur for up to two weeks. I will prescribe you an antibiotic to prevent an infection and ibuprofen for any pain or discomfort. Here is a list of do's and don'ts of what to avoid within the next two weeks. Do you have any questions?" he asked as I took the sheet of paper from his hand. I shook my head, and he stood.

"Okay, your mother is waiting for you. I'll write up your discharge paperwork, and you're free to go. If you feel abnormal pain or are bleeding excessively, you should contact me immediately. Also, I'll need to see you in two weeks to follow-up, and, Mia, I'm very sorry." Nodding my head again because that's all I could do, I watched as he turned and walked out the door.

The nurse returned a few moments shortly after Dr. Lee left. She handed me a cup of ice water, and I gulped it, almost choking on the cold that was soothing my dry throat. She also gave me a bag with clothes that my mother brought for me. The bag contained jeans, a blue t-shirt, and flip-flops. The jeans and shirt were a little loose, but the flip-flops fit perfectly. When I was finished dressing, the nurse returned with a wheelchair. She wheeled me through the halls, and I kept my head lowered the entire ride.

Before the procedure, my mother was able to visit me. We talked for only fifteen minutes before I was taken to the prep room. We cried about the miscarriage together. She asked about *him*—if I wanted her to call him. I told her we were no longer together, and she didn't ask any questions after that. I guess she didn't want to seem too pushy. Maybe she felt she needed to earn the privilege of my confiding in her.

No matter how close our relationship develops, I would never disclose everything. There were things between him and me that were too personal and confidential that would always be just between the two of us.

The nurse locked the wheelchair in place once we exited the building and entered into the pick-up lot of the hospital. My mother was already up front in her old beat-up Toyota Camry with the passenger door opened. She rushed to my side, scooping her arm through mine. We walked to her car, and I got in. Closing the door, she thanked the nurse and took her place behind the wheel.

Shifting to place her seatbelt on, she quickly glanced at me. She sighed and leaned the side of her temple against the headrest. Reaching out her fingers, she tugged a piece of hair behind my ear. "Are you hungry?" she whispered.

The softness of her tone forced tears to spring my eyes. I shook my head. Food was the last thing I wanted or needed. Shifting away from her, I stared out the passenger window. The rest of the ride was in silence.

When we finally reached her tiny two-bedroom apartment, I just wanted to lie down and fall asleep again. When we entered her place, she hurried around to grab fresh towels and blankets. I stood in the living room. Well, it was the living room, dining room, and kitchen all-in-one. With my arms hugging my chest, I admired how she took a small place and made it welcoming and warm.

I wasn't sure how long I would stay. As much as I liked her place, it wasn't home. Though when I thought of *home,* my first thought wasn't the place I shared with Jeremy. It was *his* place, and my eyes burned as fresh tears began to form once again. How much could one person cry, not just here and there, I mean really cry for several hours straight? I had a feeling I'd spend the next few weeks crying, and the thought seemed exhausting.

Sara entered the small room and guided me to where I would be staying. The room could possibly have been the size of my walk-in closet. It only fit a futon and a dresser. I watched as she pulled the metal frame, transforming the sofa into a full-sized bed, making the already tiny room smaller. Placing the blankets and pillows she held on top of the bed, she glanced over at me and shrugged. "I'm sorry. I know it's not the best place to sleep." Shaking my head, I walked over and hugged her as tightly as I could. She returned the embrace.

"It's great. Thank you for everything, Sara. I appreciate your letting me stay here awhile." I whispered.

Pushing away, she held me by the shoulders. "Of course, Mia, it's the least I could do. I'm glad you're here … well, not under these circumstances. Get some rest. I'll see you in the morning." Leaning in, she pressed her lips against my forehead. I wasn't sure why that small motion brought *him* to mind. It was a gesture he always used, and when Sara closed the door behind her, I sank into the futon.

With soft sobs, I drenched the pillow until I drifted into a deep sleep, dreaming of him. I hoped that if I closed my eyes tightly enough I would wake in his bed, wrapped in his arms, laughing and giggling as he tickled my belly, bringing his lips close, singing our baby a lullaby. *Yes,* this nightmare was just a dream, and soon I'd awaken.

Unfortunately I was forced back into reality when I woke the next day. With burning, dry eyes, I stared at the ceiling the rest of the morning. Sara knocked a few times, but I didn't answer. I could hear the door screech open. She whispered my name, but I kept my eyes shut, hoping she'd go away. Eventually she did. I wasn't ready to face the real world. Instead I wanted to dwell in my misery. Here in this tiny box, I was safe and away from everything else. Nothing could hurt me in here—nothing but my haunting thoughts.

Sara grew impatient when day two came around and I hadn't moved from the bed. After opening the door, she sank down beside me. I opened my eyes when I realized she was not giving up. Her soft smile brightened her eyes. Her eyebrows pulled in, and her lips pouted at my resistance in acknowledging her with the same greeting.

"Sweetie, you can't stay in here forever. You haven't eaten a thing. How about you take a nice long hot shower, while I make us some dinner?" I wasn't hungry, nor did I want to take a shower. However her sad eyes grew in sorrow, and I didn't want anyone to feel sorry for me. So I caved in, lifting myself onto my elbows, and I nodded. Smiling a little brighter, she stood and closed the door behind her.

The warm shower soothed my aching body. Massaging the cloth along my skin, I stared blankly at one of the pink tiles in front of me. The day he opened up to me was in the shower when he told me about his involvement with the Sorrentos. Everything reminded me of him. After all the things we'd been through, I knew I'd miss everything about him: the way he would enter the shower uninvited, wickedly grinning as he would take over and wash me himself; those big brown eyes, the way they looked into mine; and the way he held me at night, tightly against his chest, whispering how much he loved me in my ear. Deep down I knew I would never get over him. He would always hold a special place in my heart. He would always be the love of my life.

****

My mother busied away by the stove as I sat on the tiny table for two. Gulping down water, I hadn't realized how dehydrated I was. As she slammed away on the pots and pans, I heard a small buzzing sound. The sound grew louder. Sara turned around giving me an apologetic smile. I eyed her questioningly. "I hope you don't mind, but your phone was going crazy all night, so I placed it on vibrate. It's on the charger by the window over there." She pointed to the window by the couch then turned and went back to her cooking.

I dreaded walking over to the phone. I knew what I'd find, and I wasn't sure I was ready to confront it. Taking a few deep breaths, I found the courage to stand and head toward the window. A small blue light flicked on and off as it did to notify me when I missed any calls or received any messages. I took the phone off the charger and sat on the couch. Staring at the black screen for a few seconds, I tried to mentally prepare myself. After one more deep breath, I pressed the side button. The screen lit, and it revealed that I had several missed calls, voice messages, and text messages. My heartbeat began to rapidly pick up its pace.

Deciding to view missed calls first, I noticed I had too many to count from Marcus. Just seeing his name on the screen made nervous butterflies flutter in my stomach. There were a few missed calls from Jeremy as well. That led me to believe that Marcus went by my place as I expected. Thankfully, I was at the hotel then and here now. I wouldn't have been able to handle the sight of him. I viewed the text messages without reading them. There were several from him and a few from Jeremy. Deciding to skip Marcus', I viewed only a couple of Jeremy's messages.

JEREMY (6:00am) yesterday: What's going on Mia?

JEREMY (8:30am) today: I'm worried. Call me. Please.

Oh God, I wonder what Marcus said to him. Placing the phone to my ear, I hesitantly listened to Jeremy's voice messages. "Mia, I don't know what's going on, but Marcus was just here. He was … I never seen him like this. He's going crazy. He said the two of you had gotten into a huge argument, and you left. *Mia*, please call me. I want to know you're safe."

The next two were similar, but on the third one, Jeremy was leaving a message, "Mia, can you please call me," when my entire body froze as I heard Marcus in the background, "I will not leave, Jae. I have to hear she's okay!" Then Jeremy said, "Dude calm down, I'm trying to find out. *Ugh*, Mia, please call me. I need to know you're okay. *Please*."

Maybe because I wasn't expecting it, or maybe it was the desperate need in Marcus' tone, but hearing his voice made my heart skip and pick up in speed. I felt faint hearing him. I decided to wait to actually hear Marcus' messages. If I couldn't handle that little piece, there was no way I was ready to hear what he had to say.

Biting on my thumbnail, I sat on the couch a little longer and wondered if I should pick up the phone and call Jeremy or shoot him a text to let him know I was ... *What am I?* I'm not okay. I'm definitely not fine. Sara was still in the kitchen, so I decided to call Jeremy privately from the closet-sized bedroom.

I nervously paced in the small room as the phone rang. I was going to hang up on the third ring when Jeremy eagerly answered the phone. "Mia?" I could hear the fear in his voice.

"Yes." I whispered.

Sighing in relief, he said, "*Jesus*, Mia, I've been freaking out! Where are you? Come home."

Stopping, I sank into the futon. "Jeremy, I'm fine. Well not really, but I'll be fine. I can't come home yet. I'm not ready to face him."

He was silent over the phone for a second. "Yeah, he's here you know, but asleep. He won't leave. He sleeps by the door, hoping you'll walk in soon." Letting out a deep breath, he continued. "Are you sure you're okay? Do you need me to bring you anything? Some clothes? Any of your things?"

"No, um, I'm afraid he'll somehow follow you. I'll buy whatever I need. I'm not sure how long it will be before I'm home, Jeremy, but I'll keep you updated. Just let him know that you spoke with me, and that I'm okay. Maybe that will keep him out of your hair."

He lowered his tone to almost at a whisper. "He's waking up now. Okay, I'll let him know. Love you, be safe."

Swallowing back tears, I whispered, "I love you too, Jeremy." He ended the call.

****

After a quiet dinner with my mother, I hibernated back in the bedroom. I felt extremely bad. I knew she was trying, but it was so hard for me to try back. I couldn't laugh at her jokes or engage in conversation. I was too distracted. My mind would wander off when she began to talk. I thought of Jeremy and how he was handling Marcus. I also wondered if Marcus was drunk at this very moment.

Before me, he didn't know how to handle his emotions, so he poured them into drinking. Then when he met me, he poured them into sex. Now that he didn't have me, did he go back to drinking, or was he still pouring his emotions into sex but with others? That thought upset my stomach.

I sat on the bed, my back leaning against the wall, with my knees up against my chest. I knew I shouldn't do it. I knew that I'd just be setting myself up for another night of full-blown tears, but I couldn't help it. Placing the phone on top of the pillow, I laid my head next to it, and lowering the volume, I heard his voice through the speaker as I listened to his messages.

The first message was right after I left him. "Mia, please come back. We need to talk. *Please,* don't drive while you're upset. Please call me. I love you so much." He choked on the last sentence.

"*Mia,* I'm sorry. I'm so sorry. I wish I could go back and change everything. I wish I could make it better. I know I fucked up. Please call me back. I love you."

"I know you don't want to speak with me. I completely understand, but please let me know you're okay. I can wait till you're ready to speak to me. Just please send me a text. I have to know you're safe. Please don't shut me out. I love you so much, Mia. Please. I'm begging."

The next few were similar with him apologizing and pouring out his love for me. Listening to his broken voice made my heart ache. The most recent message was not long ago. I left my phone in the room after speaking with Jeremy. Marcus called during dinner. He called after Jeremy told him that we spoke.

He spoke in a low tone. His words broke my heart as I heard the sadness in his voice. "I spoke to Jeremy. He said he'd talked to you. I'm *relieved* you're safe. I thought maybe something might have happened to you." He paused and continued in a raspy, out-of-order tone. "Mia, I know you *hate* me. I know there's *nothing* I can do to change that. I just want you to know that *you* and our *peanut* mean everything in this world to me. Without you, I'm nothing. I will always be here for you, no matter what, and I know it's best the two of you stay away from me." I cried along with him on the last sentence. "Make sure to tell our baby that his father loves him every day of his life, just like I will always love you *every single day.*" The call ended.

Burying my face into the pillow, I sobbed in soft, painful screams.

I had to tell him.

CHAPTER TWENTY-FOUR

After listening to that message for the hundredth time, I worked up the courage to send Marcus a text message over two weeks later. I told him that I needed to talk to him and to meet me at a coffee shop near the university.

A public place should prevent us from breaking down *hopefully*. A week ago, my mother picked up my vehicle from the hospital parking lot. Still not having the courage to go home, I decided to stay with her until today. Packing the few things I had left, she sat on the bed and watched me load my small duffel bag. She looked sad that I'd be going back home.

"Sara, thank you, again, for all of this. You know you're welcome to stop by my place anytime." I wanted her to know that just because I was leaving didn't mean it was the last she'd see of me.

"I know. Hey, my niece, well, your cousin, will be moving here from Philly. She'll be staying with me awhile until she can find a job and get herself situated. She's close to your age. Maybe we can all go out for dinner, and you can show us around?"

I softly smiled. "Yeah, that sounds nice." Not really. Don't get me wrong. I was looking forward to slowly meeting my mother's side of the family, but I didn't want her to meet me while I was in this state of mind. I still needed time mentally before I could get back to being me. I wasn't sure I'd ever be me again. Only time would tell. After placing the bag in the trunk of my car, I hugged and thanked her again.

When I pulled into a parking spot, my stomach fluttered with butterflies in anticipation. Then when I got there, I didn't think I could do this. I'd wanted this in a public place because I was afraid of how I would react when I saw him in person. Now I was afraid that I'd collapse in front of everyone. He had a right to know, and he deserved to be told in person. Taking a long deep breath, I exited the car, and in a slow steady pace, I made my way to the café. Arriving a half hour early hoping to sit and wait for him, I stopped in my tracks when I saw him through the glass wall. He was already there.

Biting my lip, I studied him. He hadn't noticed me. It had been over two weeks, and from this distance he seemed slimmer. His hair was a mess, though an adorable mess. He wore jeans and a navy blue fitted shirt. His hands were folded together on top of the small table. He stared down at them while his leg nervously bounced.

Running his hand through his hair, he began to mumble something then spread his hands as if speaking with someone sitting in front of him. No one was there. Shaking his head, he sank his face into his hands. Both legs were bouncing now.

At that moment, I was going to turn around and walk away, but after rubbing his face, he looked my way. His entire body froze when he laid eyes on me. His lips parted and eyebrows creased. I tried to swallow a few times, but my throat was too dry. He slowly brought his arms down to the table, and his eyes remained locked with mine. Looking down, I broke from his stare. Unhurriedly, I made my way through the glass door and to him.

The entire few seconds it took me to finally reach him, I thought of how I should greet him. I wondered if I should kiss him or hug him? Either way it would have felt awkward, or was I more afraid that once I hugged him, I wouldn't let go?

I took the easy way out and just slid in the seat across from him. Not bringing my eyes to his, I waited as we sat in silence. The leg bouncing had stopped, and I watched as his hands and fingers spread and pressed down on the table. His fingernails turned white with the pressure. It was like he was keeping them from reaching out. He cleared his throat before speaking, and even though the familiar sound of his low deep voice pulled me in, I kept my eyes down. "Hi," was all he said. It was short, yet there was so much more behind it.

It worked, that simple word forced my eyes up and to meet his again. Both of our chests moved in a matching rhythmic speed. I shied my eyes away, looking out into the parking lot away from him. I couldn't look into those eyes and break his heart with the news I had. I began to ache, knowing that I would have to relive the emotional heart-wrenching pain all over again. Lifting my hands from my lap, I laid them on the table and looked down at them. We were a mere inch away. His fingers flexed, I stilled, and with my reaction, he brought his hands under the table, rubbing them along his thighs.

"Would you like something to drink?" His voice was low yet steady; I knew it was an attempt to get me talking. I nodded. "Tea?" he asked. When I nodded again, he stood and walked over to the front counter to order our drinks.

Exhaling deeply, I stared at his back as he stood in line. I wanted to run up to him, throw my arms around his neck, and tell him I love him so much and that the past couple weeks had been nothing but miserable without him. Then I thought of all the lies, my brother, his still working for that *man,* and I couldn't bring myself to do it. He looked over his shoulder, and a very small, crooked smile formed when he saw I was staring. Pressing his lips together, he glanced down and then focused back on the line.

Tearing away, I blankly stared out at the trees. I knew this was going to be hard to do. Even though I practiced over and over how and what I was going to say, each time I cried. In person, it would be even harder, and I knew my tears would take over, and it would be so difficult to concentrate on what I'd practiced.

Marcus returned, sliding into his chair. He placed the tea in front of me. Looking up at him, I gently smiled. "Thank you," I said softly. He nodded while taking a sip of his coffee.

Closing his eyes, his eyebrows came together. He seemed to be thinking, and then before I could say anything, he placed the cup aside and brought his hand to mine. "Mia, I miss you so much." He breathed out as if he were holding it in the entire time.

Searching my face, he remained still. His touch shot warm, familiar electricity through my veins. "I miss you too," I admitted. I did. It wasn't a lie. His eyes grew wide with hope, but I couldn't lead him on. "*But,* that's not why I'm here, Marcus." His brows furrowed with confusion.

Attempting to swallow again, I bit my lip, trying to think of the best way to say this. There was no best way. No matter how I said it, it would destroy him. "Marcus, I asked you here because I thought you had a right to know in person." Looking down at our joined hands, my eyes stung with tears.

He gently squeezed my hand. "The right to know what?"

I brought my eyes back to him, "A right to know that the night we'd gotten into the argument, that night I bled a lot. I called Dr.

Lee, and when I arrived at the hospital ..." I paused to hold back my sobs as the tears rudely escaped my eyes. Still keeping his hand locked to mine, he brought the other against my face, cupping my cheek. He repeatedly stroked his thumb along the moisture. I closed my eyes, allowing slow steady breaths to calm me before opening them. "Marcus, I lost *our* baby. I miscarried." I cried.

"*What*?" He shook his head, not wanting to believe what I just said. He searched everywhere in our area, letting out deep breaths, taking in the words, the loss. Fixing his gaze down on our hands, panting, he cocked his head to the side, studying our hold. "It's my *fault*," he whispered.

Squeezing his hand tighter, I lowered my head, trying to fix his eyes with mine. He didn't stare at me. "Marcus, it's no one's fault."

His eyes finally met mine, "*Oh* yeah? Then how did it happen?"

Shaking my head, I slightly shrugged. "Dr. Lee said anything could've happened: lack of nutrition, stress, *anything*, Marcus."

"You were always stressed because of *me*." He pointed at his chest with his free hand. "You were always worried about *me*: scared every other night, afraid that something would happen to *me*. Then the whole Romeo and Lou situation and the documents you found ... all because of *me*, Mia."

"Marcus, I ..." I couldn't say anything to that. Yes, it was true I was always worried sick about him, but to blame the miscarriage on him was too much. I couldn't allow him to think it. It wouldn't be fair to him. "Marcus it is not your fault. Things like this happen all the time; it's normal. I'll be fine, and so will you."

"You went through it on your own? You must've been scared, and I wasn't there. I was ... *ugh*." He shook his head disgusted with himself.

The anger I felt towards him slowly drifted away as I looked into his wounded eyes. Yes, my body was the one that physically went through the changes of carrying and losing our child, and yes it would take time for me to physically and mentally heal. But I knew he fell in love with our child the moment I told him I was pregnant. His love grew even more when he saw the peanut-shaped body on the ultrasound. This was just as hard for him as it was for me.

I wasn't exactly sure what I was doing; all I knew was that we couldn't stay in here any longer. I stood, his hand still with mine, and began to move towards the door. He followed behind me as we slowly walked out of the café and into the parking lot. Spotting his all-black, tinted Mercedes, I headed towards it. Once we were by his car, I leaned against the back-passenger door and pulled him into me. Wrapping my hands under his arms, I hugged him tightly. I wanted to comfort him. I wanted him to comfort me. With his arms firmly around the middle of my back, we did just that for a long time. We said nothing, did nothing—just soothed each other.

It was bizarre how out in the parking lot even while people walked by minding their business, this felt more private to me than in that secluded, tiny shop. Not bothering to see if anyone was staring at us because at this moment I truly didn't care, I closed my eyes and sank my head into his chest. I took in his *oh-so*-familiar lingering scent, allowing myself to savor this moment, not sure how long it would last, but knowing that it would eventually have to end. He did as well when he lowered his head, burying it into the base of my neck.

A tiny painful sigh released from him as he tightened his arms around me. The slight movement lifted me to the tip of my toes, causing the side of our cheeks to lightly brush. The brush of his growing beard was a strange feeling. His face, always smooth and freshly shaved, now pricked with tiny hairs. I didn't mind though, allowing him to gently tickle my smooth skin with the hair. He slowly brought his head around, pressing his forehead to mine, and the tips of our noses brushed. His lips faintly parted, and the warmth of his breath throbbed against my chest.

My eyes traced the lining of his full lips; the ends of his perfect, pearly white teeth barely showed. My eyes slowly made their way up to the dent on his upper lip, up to the tip of his nose, to his cheeks, and then to those gorgeous big, brown eyes. He was watching me watch him. I lost air for a second as he brought his chin out, his lips inches away from me. "Marcus," I whispered in a way to stop him, but I didn't pull away.

"*Please*, Mia." Closing his eyes, he pressed his soft lips against mine. A tingling sensation shot through my core at his touch, and it warmed as he slipped his tongue through my parted lips. I closed my eyes to savor this too. *Oh,* how I'd missed those lips, that soft stroking tongue, and his greedy kisses. I brought my hands around his neck and pulled his kiss in deeper. His small, gentle groan vibrated against my lips. His hand quickly left my back, and he reached in his pocket, all while never moving his lips away from mine.

An alarm beeping sound went off, and then I heard his car doors unlock. In a swift movement he opened the door, leaning me against the open space. Not second guessing, I bent down into his backseat, pulling him on top of me. On his way in, he shut the door, only taking his lips away from me for a mere second.

He returned his mouth to my face, spreading gentle stroking kisses along my eyebrows, my eyes, my nose, down the side of my cheek, and my jawline. When he reached my lips again, he mumbled in between breaths, pulling away gently to list everything he'd missed. "I love you so much. I've *missed* you so much, Mia. I miss your *scent,* your *lips,* your *touch,* the way your hair falls against your face ... the way you *smile.* I've missed you so *fucking* much, especially," pulling away for a second, he cupped my face with his hand, and narrowly stared into my eyes saying, "those eyes—those *beautiful* eyes. I've missed looking into them every morning when I wake up and every night before I fall asleep. I have done *nothing* the past two weeks but dream of your eyes."

I closed my eyes as a single tear escaped and rolled down the side of my face. His thumb wiped it away before he continued to place several gentle pecks against my lips. On the last peck, he kept his lips firm against my mouth, and his tongue once again found mine, twirling in delicious delight. I knew I had to stop, to not lead him on and let him think that we were okay because we weren't. But his words, his touch, and his lips momentarily persuaded me to cave in, to briefly break down that wall I slowly began to build once again.

I told myself over and over again in my head as he slowly slid his hand up my shirt that this was what we needed—that we both needed to comfort each other—that we needed this last *goodbye.* We needed *closure.*

I moaned against his lips when his hand reached my aching breast. Neither one of us was able to hold it any longer. We quickly ripped our clothes off, and he sank into me, relieving the pain in my inner thighs. My body trembled as I felt the fullness, the hardness. I realized that I needed this, that I needed him at this very moment. "*Mia* ..." He groaned, dipping his head into my neck, leaving feather-like kisses along my collarbone.

"I love you." He choked in pain as he continued in soft, gentle thrusts, joining our hips. My entire body ached with longing for him, wanting him, and I eagerly wrapped my legs around his hips pushing him in deeper. "*Oh* Marcus, I've missed you so much. I love you." I moaned into his earlobe. My confession ignited him, and he picked up pace. Crushing his lips to mine, his tongue reached far back into my mouth, and I sucked on it, craving his taste.

Our bodies, damp with sweat, trembled with the sensation, trying to hold on to every peaking moment. Eventually we both gave in, allowing our bodies to release the aching tension. Breathing heavily, he lay flat on my chest.

I stared at the roof of his car, trying to control my breathing as well. *What the hell did I just do?*

I began to squirm underneath him, and he sat back on the heels of his feet, watching as I sought to find my clothes and throw them on. "Mia, what are you doing? I thought we …" I stopped half way through putting my shirt on and turned to look into his puzzled eyes. I led him on: He didn't think of this as a goodbye. He thought of this as rekindling our relationship.

Biting my lip, I slowly rolled the shirt down. "Marcus, I'm sorry for leading you on."

His head snapped back. "Leading me on? What do you mean *leading* me on?" He brought his fingers to the middle of his stomach. I didn't say anything since I was afraid to say the wrong thing. He gulped in a mouthful of air when he finally realized what I meant. He tilted his head, and his shoulders slumped. "But you said you missed me too. You said you loved me!"

Shifting and lifting my legs, I sat as he was, facing him. "Marcus, I love you so much. I will *always* love you. And yes, I've missed you. I will *always* miss you, but too much has happened to go back to the way we were. Don't you *see* that?"

With his head still tilted and his hand still at the pit of his stomach, his chest heaved in and out, and his growing painful expression felt like a knife just stabbed my heart. "And this? What was this!" he snapped, his hand leaving his belly, sprawling along the seat where we just made love.

My heartbeat began to speed up at the tone of his voice. He was beginning to get angry. I didn't blame him. It was wrong of me to make him believe for one second that we were back together.

Slightly shrugging my shoulders, I looked down ashamed. "It was for comfort, I guess, closure."

"Really?" With his jaw clenched tight, he quickly grabbed his shirt and tossed it on, not caring that it was inside out. Straightening his legs to the floor of the car, he adjusted his jeans. Once they were secured at his waist, he zippered and buttoned them. Opening the door beside him, he glared at me. "Well, I hope you got your fucking *closure.*" The door slammed shut after he stepped out. Startled by the loud noise, I quickly stormed out of the car.

He was walking down the parking lot at a fast pace. I had to jog to catch up to him. Where was he going? It was *his* car we were just in. When I was finally close enough, I reached out and grabbed his arm. "Marcus, please don't walk away. Talk to me."

He stopped, turned, and looked down at me. "Why? What's the point! If I poured my heart out to you at this moment, would it make a difference? Will it change your mind? Will you take me back?"

I wanted to, but I couldn't. *"No."*

"That's what I thought!" Pulling from my grip, he went back to walking down the lot.

Hurriedly rushing back to his side, I began to feel angry. "How could I? After what you did? You lied to me, *remember*? You kept a secret from me. You knew my brother. *Worst* of all, you know who killed him, yet still you work for *him!*"

He stopped again. Biting his lip, he turned to face me. Lowering his head until he was only inches away from my face, he looked me straight in the eye. "Yes, and I'm *sorry* for that. I knew that it would be hard for you to accept it. Can you only imagine how difficult it is for *me* to work for *him*, knowing that he *killed* my father?"

I froze, tilting my head. I studied him, trying to rationalize what he just said. "Are you saying that Lou Sorrento murdered your father?" His eyes grew baffled as he realized he gave away something he wasn't supposed too. Straightening, he shook his head, and turned walking back to his car. He picked up the pace at almost a jogging speed.

"Marcus!" I yelled after him, I had to run. Meeting up with him once again, I brought myself in front of him, placing my hands on his shoulders to stop him. I'd never been more confused in my life. If Lou killed Marcus' father, why would he still be involved with him? He's obviously trying not to let me in. "You're shutting me out *again*, Marcus. This is why our relationship was the way it was. You kept things from me. That's how someone loses trust in another by keeping *secrets*."

"My *secrets*, Mia, are meant to be kept hidden because in the end, they could potentially harm you." Shaking his head, he looked away from me. "Maybe you're right. Maybe this should just be what it is ... closure." He brought his eyes back to me, and tears sprung to my eyes. *This* is it. This is finally the end.

"I will always love you, Mia. You're the love of my life." Cupping my face with both his hands, he brought his forehead to mine. "No minute will ever go by without a thought of you. If I can't have you physically, you will always be a part of me spiritually in my dreams and memories."

He was leaving me. "I love you, Marcus." I sobbed.

Bringing his lips against the side of my mouth, he mumbled, "I know, *baby*. Thank you for loving *me*. Thank you for showing me what *true* love is. I will *always* cherish you for that."

Before I could protest, he was gone, leaving me alone in the middle of the parking lot with aching tears. *He* left *me* this time, and it felt like the earth swallowed me into its core: I was buried alive and suffocating.

I'm not sure how I made it to my car. I'm not sure how I found the keys and entered the vehicle, and I'm not sure how I made it all the way home. The entire ride was a huge haze. My entire life would never be the same. In fact my future looked like nothing but one huge block of blurriness.

CHAPTER TWENTY-FIVE

When Marcus left me standing in the parking lot, I was sure my life was over and I wouldn't know how to breathe or live again without him. Well, there I was thirty days later, and I was still alive and still breathing. A day hadn't gone by without my mind drifting off to him. I still cried sometimes, but I was a little grateful it wasn't every night anymore. The first two weeks were hard, *really* hard. Jeremy had to fall asleep with me to make sure I didn't suffocate with my face buried in the pillow as I sobbed till I drifted away.

He spent a lot of time with me, and I was grateful for that. It made Stacy extremely jealous, and soon they broke up. I felt horrible. I told him to go win her back, that I was fine, but he assured me it was more than just me. He also said that if a girlfriend of his couldn't accept his being there for a friend, then she was no girlfriend at all. I loved him for that also. He was just too good to me. Honestly if it weren't for him, my mother, and Megan, I wasn't sure I would've made it this long.

Megan is my cousin who moved here from Philadelphia. She was staying with my mom, and although her upbeat, bubbly personality was totally the opposite of mine, we hit it off right away. We're similar in age, and I was helping her fill out college applications. She was able to find a job as a cocktail waitress at one of the local night clubs. Megan was beautiful: she was tall, slim, had light brown hair and the lightest brown eyes I'd ever seen. I wasn't sure if they were hazel, but they turned to a small hint of any light color she wore. She came over to my place a lot, and I was sure it was because she had a thing for Jeremy. He, of course, didn't mind her company as well.

The three of us became close, doing everything together. We watched late movies, went shopping, and went out to dinners. Though they kept my mind occupied a lot, there was always something missing. They would crack jokes, and I would watch them goof around. I was the third wheel, never chiming in on their jokes and never laughing at them either.

Megan said I needed to lighten up and get loose. If she only knew the person I was before Marcus and I broke it off, maybe she would understand. I never told her about Marcus. Well, she knew that I had gotten my heart broken and that I was trying to heal from the aftereffects. Jeremy and my mother made sure not to bring him up in any way, afraid that I would run into the other room crying. Seriously it was ridiculous.

This was the last weekend before school began, and I knew that I would be swamped once Monday came around. This was Jeremy's last year, and he would soon graduate, pass the bar, and go off on his merry way to become a successful attorney. I knew he'd be a great one. He wanted to practice contract law. I thought it was boring, but he had an eye for viewing documents and catching things that most people would miss, and he was at great negotiating.

I wasn't sure what type of law I wanted to practice once I finished. Maybe I'd start off in general law, doing a little bit of everything until I found out what I really wanted to do. I was viewing my roster that came in the mail. Criminal Law II and Ethics were my courses that semester. Fun ... *not*.

"I have a *great* idea!" Megan burst through the door. Her ponytail swung side-to-side as she made her way over to me by the kitchen island. Raising my eyebrow, I watched as she threw her purse on top of the counter. She had a habit of coming in without knocking. I guess it was my fault for not locking the door.

"What's your great idea?" I asked, placing my roster down.

Jerking straight up, she pressed her hands together with the biggest   oh-my-God-no-one-could-possibly-be-this-happy   grin. Shaking my head, I allowed her to continue. "We are going to Club21 tonight!" She began to do a jumping-up-and-down dance.

"No!" Okay, so maybe I kind of overreacted, but there was no way I was going to *that* club. No way at all.

Her hands fell to the counter, and her lips pouted. "*Why*? I thought it would be great before you started school."

Shaking my head, I was not backing down. "No, and out of all clubs why did you choose that one? Why can't we go to where you work?"

"Because I called out sick tonight, so I could take you out. Besides, a co-worker of mine told me about Club21. Her cousin works for the owner, so she was able to get me VIP tickets." She flashed that smile again as she pulled out two tickets from her back pocket.

"What's her cousin's name?" Okay, so maybe I shouldn't care, but I did wonder if it was someone I knew or someone that was possibly new or his *ex*-assistant. *Grrrgh.*

"I don't know, but she's going to be there. Her cousin is throwing her a birthday bash. She really wanted me to go, and I thought it would be nice to take you out." She pouted again. "Oh come on, Mia, you act like an eighty-year-old woman sometimes. You need to go out and have *fun*. You're only twenty-four. *Gosh*, I would hate to see how you act when you're thirty!"

I most certainly do not act like an eighty-year-old woman. I gave her a wicked glare for that rude comment. I'm just more laid back. Y*eah*, that's it laid back. I'd rather sit at home, reading a book, or watching a movie, sipping on wine or coffee far away from the outside cruel world. *Oh* my God, I do act like an eighty-year-old woman! Narrowing my eyes at her, I watched as she placed her folded hands under her chin, pouting her lips and widening her eyes. She was giving me the most pathetic puppy face I'd ever seen. She even went as far as to whimper like a crying puppy.

"*Fine!*" Giving in, I rolled my eyes again.

She squealed and ran to my side, jumping up and down. "Oh we are going to have so much fun!"

I shot a pointed stare and brought a finger up. "*But* if I say let's go, you have to promise me we go. Promise?"

"Of course, Mia, but I'm sure you're not going to want to leave. I heard it's a really nice place. Come on, let's go *beautify* ourselves. *Oh,* and I'll need to borrow something of yours." She bit down on her lip and then giggled. I shook my head, and we headed to my bedroom to beautify ourselves. I just hoped that night would go down smoothly.

****

"This is called a *club*. In here you can act your *age*."

Megan's sarcastic tone ripped through the pounding music and through my hazy daze. Since we walked in five minutes before, I had done nothing but search around the dance floor, by the bars, up towards the VIP rooms, and everywhere else to see if I could find anyone I recognized. Well, I was more eager to see if I could find *one* person I recognized; I could care less about anyone else.

"Huh? What? Oh, yeah, I know." I returned my attention to her, and she rolled her eyes before grabbing two shot glasses from the bartender.

She handed me one. "Here, this should loosen you up." Tossing her head back, she chugged down the shot without hesitating. She scrunched her face for a second and wiggled her shoulders. "That was good!"

Shrugging, I saluted with my glass and chugged back the shot. The warm liquid soothed my throat but burned once it reached my chest. I shimmied like Megan, hoping it would help the burn. It didn't. I was also sure by her amused expression that I made a sourpuss face. "Atta girl!" she shouted over the loud music.

We took a few more shots before heading to our VIP room. Nothing was different: it was exactly how I remembered it. Megan's co-worker, Jasmine, was completely hammered by the time we entered. Her cousin, the one who works for the DeLuca firm, was there as well. To my surprise, I didn't recognize her. Thank God! She probably worked in one of the other departments.

After some shots and a few Cosmos, I was beginning to loosen up. I hadn't felt this *good* in a while. The room was occupied by fifteen other girls. Jasmine wore a pink and zebra print sash with "Birthday Girl" printed in glitter across it. Her tiara was slanted on her head. It had been straight at one point during the night.

The other girls were close to my age, and I was surprised to learn that we had a lot in common. Who knew that girls were actually *fun* to be around? As the night progressed, I bravely danced with them on the dance floor, took more shots, played karaoke in our private room, took more shots, danced some more, and had more shots!

Before I knew it I was laughing, *really* laughing. I hadn't had this much fun since ... Well I couldn't even remember when I had this much fun! I was being myself again—something I thought would never happen. It was as if the cure was tequila, music, and a girls' night. Could it be possible that my life would go back to normal? Could I eventually go a day without crying over him? And then it hit me—no, not a reverie—the aching and pounding of my bladder. Standing, I made my way to Megan and grabbed her arm. "I have to go to the bathroom, come with me!" I yelled over the music. She nodded and grabbed her clutch.

No matter how modern and huge a club is, there is always a line at the ladies' room. I was considering going to the first level where the dance floor was. Though not wanting to chance losing my spot, I stayed put. Staring at the men's bathroom across from me, I even highly considered walking in. There was no line, and I had yet to see anyone go in or out. Megan must've sensed my thoughts as she stared also at the men's bathroom door. "You thinking what I'm thinking?" I nodded. "Come on then." Grabbing my arm, she dragged me across the hall. Stretching her other hand, she reached for the door. Before she was able to touch it, the door swung open. Losing balance, she released my grip and fell into a firm athletic male. Megan's scared-then-pleased expression forced me to burst into laughter. She giggled as she flexed her fingers along the muscular bicep. Looking over her shoulder at me, she wiggled her eyebrows. It made me laugh even harder. She finally looked up at the man she had landed on, and I followed her gaze.

My mouth dropped, and I stood frozen. My laughter instantly came to a halt, and I believe my heart stopped beating.

"Hello, Mia." The familiar voice brought my chest back to life and sped up my heart. Extending his arms and firm grip around Megan's shoulders, Jimmie pulled her away. She looked up at him and then back down at me.

Standing between us, she studied me as I stared into his light green eyes. "Do you know him, Mia?" She asked, pointing her thumb over her shoulder. When I nodded, her smile broadened, and fixing her attention back on him, she patted his shoulder. "Good, so you don't mind if we hit the men's room? The ladies' room is kind of occupied." She thumbed the long line of females.

"Knock yourself out. It's empty." He stepped aside, holding the door open for us to go in.

She jogged into one of the stalls. He was holding the door for me, and I looked up at him again. "How are you? How's Elle?" I really wanted to know how they were doing, but my head was screaming, "How's your brother doing?"

"I'm good, and she's doing well. She asks about you all the time. She brings up this girls'-day-at-the-mall thing a lot."

Oh my God. I forgot all about that. "Oh no, I'm so sorry, Jimmie! I promised her before Marcus and I—"

Cutting me off, Jimmie said, "Don't worry about it, Mia." I looked down ashamed. "Uh, I've been trying to get a hold of you. You're a difficult woman to get a hold of these days."

I brought my eyes back to his. "Well, I changed my number."

I had to do it. Shamefully, I have to admit that I never memorized Marcus' number. He programmed it himself on my phone, and since then I just searched his name when we contacted each other. Though after our break-up, I didn't trust myself. I was afraid that I would send him late-night texts or "accidently" call him and hang up. It made the healing process more difficult, so I got a new phone and a new number in the hopes that it would keep me from thinking of him. It didn't work, of course.

He nodded. "Mia, can I talk to you in private?"

Biting my lip, I hesitated. My buzz was beginning to wear off. That wasn't good. I nodded. "Sure, let me just use the bathroom, and then we can talk."

"Okay, I'll wait for you here."

I trotted into one of the stalls, passing by Megan as she washed her hands. "Who was that hottie?" she asked.

Lifting my dress, I pulled down my thong and peed. *Ah*, that felt good. "Some guy I know."

"Was he the one that broke your heart?"

"No, his brother was." I mumbled as I pulled my underwear back on and flushed the toilet. Opening the door, I found her leaning against the counter, arms and legs crossed. I made my way beside her and washed my hands.

Turning her head, she looked at me. "Are you going to be okay with him alone?"

I didn't realize she'd overheard our conversation. Then again he kept the door open, and our voices weren't extremely low either. Shrugging, I walked towards the hand dryer. "Yeah, he's safe. No worries."

She nodded.

After my hands dried, a man walked in and gave us the am-I-in-the-right-place look. We giggled as we walked out the door. Jimmie was leaning against the wall when we exited. Megan hung her hand around my shoulder and leaned in to whisper. *"Oh my God,* he is truly gorgeous. Maybe you should put a good word in for me."

"Megan, he's like ten years older than you." Although Jimmie didn't look it, he was. He was thirty-three, and she was my age.

"So, I *love* older men. They're more experienced." She winked. I couldn't do anything but laugh at her. "Okay, well I'll meet you back in the VIP room, but if you take too long, I'll be looking for you with a police escort and all."

Laughing, I lightly slapped her arm. "I'll be fine. Go have fun." She glanced at Jimmie when she passed him, noticeably eyeing him up and down. He laughed and shook his head at her boldness. She was too much. Still laughing, he looked over at me and slightly smiled.

"You look good, Mia."

"Thanks, Jimmie, you don't look so bad yourself." I said, nudging his arm with my elbow.

We walked down the hall of the second level of the club, passing by several VIP rooms. I followed him till we reached the very end. He entered a room, and I followed behind. To my surprise, I had never been in there before. It was different than the others. Double in size, on one end there was a sectional and flat screen TV set up, and on the other end there was a long dining table large enough to fit over ten people. There was also a small kitchenette along the wall, complete with a stove, dishwasher, fridge, and a very small counter space.

Jimmie took a seat by the edge of the sectional. I walked over by the glass wall overlooking the dance floor. Crossing my arms, I watched the crowded club as couples danced and a group of women in one corner celebrated a bachelorette party with the bride-to-be wearing a veil and taking shot after shot. In the other corner, a man and woman were practically having sex with their clothes on by a private table. It dawned on me as I watched my surroundings I had never seen Jimmie here before, nor had I heard him talk about coming here.

"I never thought of you as the clubbing type," I said, turning to finally face him.

He raised a brow. "I don't do clubbing."

"Then why are you here?"

Tilting his head, he stared at me for a moment. It was a look of surprise that I didn't know. "We come here either before or after a job to discuss plans."

Ah. *Wait,* so that meant Marcus came to the club a lot then. Huh, I guess there was always something new to find out. Nodding, I made my way over to the sectional and sat opposite from him. "So what did you want to talk about?" Hopefully I sounded casual.

"Well, for starters, I wanted to say how sorry I was to hear about the *miscarriage.* I know that must've been hard." I nodded. Jimmie and Jeremy were the only two that knew about the pregnancy before the miscarriage.

"Also, I wanted to say, uh … Marcus told me he kind of slipped some information to you about Lou and our father."

Standing up preparing myself to leave, I looked down at him. "Don't worry, Jimmie; I won't say anything if that's what you thought." I knew it. He was trying to cover his ass.

"No, no. Please sit." Glaring at him, I warily sat back down. "I wanted to explain it to you in a way without giving too much information."

"How come you can do that and Marcus can't?"

Rubbing his hand through his buzz-cut hair, he exhaled deeply. "Well, because Marcus doesn't know how to say something without giving too much away. And around *you,* he's weak Look, he didn't ask me to speak with you, if that's what you think. I offered to talk to you for him, but he refused, and I'm slowly growing desperate. He's out of control now, drinking constantly, careless on jobs. I don't know how to handle him anymore."

"*Oh?*" I thought of that night when Marcus came home completely drunk. He was so different. It was as if someone else had taken over him. He must be miserable, and for him to be careless on a job means he doesn't care if his own life is taken. My heart fluttered at the thought.

"Yeah, look, I'm just going to say this in the simplest possible way. A few years ago, we received information that Lou was responsible for our father's death. At first we didn't believe it because he's practically family. Well the more info we received, the more evidence was built against him. That's when I met your brother. He was privately working on the Sorrento's file for years, trying to take them down. His sergeant wanted him to stop working on the case, but he grew addicted. See the Sorrentos are *very* careful: they watch how they spend their money and who they do business with. But Lou only trusts two people: Marcus and me. He'd never think we'd turn on him. So we began to work with your brother. It grew irritating at first. We gave him a great deal of evidence, but he said it wasn't enough to take Lou down. It was just enough to take some of the Sorrentos down. He said that for this kind of case, you needed years of evidence and piles of documents, so the feds could step in and take over. Anyways, we grew impatient, and your brother grew sloppy. That's when Lou started looking more into your brother. When he found out he worked as a Boston detective, he took him out and told us *we* had to be careful whom we talked to because the entire time we were clueless about him. I'm truly sorry about your brother, Mia.

"We didn't know Lou was going to do it. He took it upon himself. If we had any indication, we would've warned Michael. Trust me, we would have."

Blankly staring at him, I managed to speak, "So you tried to set Lou up?" He nodded. "And what happens now?"

Looking down, he lightly shrugged. "We're working on that." Meeting my gaze again, he pressed his lips together and creased his eyebrows.

"What do you want me to do, Jimmie?" I asked. There was a reason he was telling me this: a reason why everything made so much sense now even though there were still so many black holes that needed to be filled.

"Talk to Marcus. When he's with you, everything is better in *his* world. Now he's lost."

Nodding, I stared at his face again. "Okay." I let out a deep breath. "Okay, I'll talk to him."

Jimmie walked over and wrapped his arms around me in a tight embrace. "Thank you so much, Mia. Everything is going to be okay. Trust me." I wasn't sure if he was trying to convince himself or me.

We ended our hug and made our way towards the door. We stopped when the door handle jiggled and the door swung wide open. My heart sank when I saw him. Marcus was in black pants and a white button-down shirt with his latest accessory, a bleach-blond, overly-tanned chick with her arms wrapped snuggly around his neck. He leaned her into the inner doorway as they sloppily made out. I wanted to throw up. I studied them in disgust. He seemed to be getting *by* just fine to me! I snapped my head at Jimmie, and he closed his eyes and mumbled, "Fuck."

I heard the female giggle, and I turned back to them. Marcus turned his head, and his grin widened when he saw Jimmie. "Hey, Bro ..." Then his head moved, and he spotted me. Extending his neck, he blinked a few times. When he realized it was me, his mouth dropped open. Trying to swallow, he pulled away from the girl. Leaning his hand against the door, he tried to keep himself balanced. He was completely trashed.

After a few seconds, he adjusted his flickering eyes. "Mia? You look *beautiful*." The last word was a slur. I barely made it out.

My eyes flashed from him to the girl he'd just sucked face with. Her orange complexion, fake blue eyes, and her bleach-blond hair, which I was sure was also fake, stared back at me. She tilted her head to study the woman he just complimented. Her size D boobs with any slight movement would pop from her extremely tight and short pink minidress. Her overly plump lips covered in pink lip gloss, which were far too light for her orange complexion, smacked together as she chewed on gum.

Reaching for her hair, she curled a piece of extension with a finger. "She's cute, is she going to join us, Marky?" Her bubbly, high-pitched Boston accent brought my anger level from a *five* to an easy *twelve* within two-point-five seconds. What made it worse was the name she called him. Hearing the nickname his family used on her lips placed a fireball in the pit of my stomach.

Oh, I was beyond pissed. Snapping my head back in his direction, I crossed my arms. "Really!"

It took him a moment to process what was going on. He stared at me forever before he looked back at her and laughed. *He laughed!* "Oh, no, sweetie, she's not joining us. I think you should go, though," he said to her.

"But I thought we were having fun, Marky." She pouted.

Arrrgh! Throwing my hands in the air, I yelled, "Oh, by all means, don't let me spoil your fun!" I stormed between the two of them and headed down the hall.

"Mia! Mia! Come here." I looked over my shoulder as I continued to quickly walk down the hallway. He was stumbling side-to-side trying to run after me. *Ugh,* he was pathetic.

"There you are, are you okay?" Megan gripped my arm and studied my angry appearance. Looking behind me, her eyes grew. "*Oooh.* Who is that fine piece of ass?"

Rolling my eyes, I snapped. "Let's go!"

She narrowed her eyes. "Do you know him?"

Glancing over my shoulder, I looked in the direction of her goggling eyes. Great, all three were behind me: Jimmie, Marcus, and the plastic chick. "No, he's just someone I *used* to know." I growled.

"Oh come on, Mia!" Marcus wiggled his brows. "You know you know me a little better than that." Biting his lip, he flexed his hips, swinging his arms in and out. *He was air humping!* After a few pumps, he stopped, laughed, and pathetically tried to straighten his posture.

"You're a dick!" I couldn't stand him!

Laughing, he moved in closer to me, reaching for my arm. "Come on, baby. Let me show what you've been missing."

Yeah, that did it. I think I was beyond my boiling point. In my best impersonation, I mimicked his beach-blonde's Boston's accent. "Oh why would you want me, Marky, when you can have Boston Barbie!"

Plastic chick didn't dig my comment. Cocking her head to the side, she put her hands angrily on her hips. "Are you, *like, offending* me or something?"

Laughing once at her stupidity, I thought about whether I should even answer her. "No, not at all, it's *like* a compliment to be called Boston Barbie or *something.*" I spit sarcastically.

Straightening her position, she smiled. "*Oh*, okay." Then she giggled.

With my eyes and mouth wide open, I faced Marcus. "REALLY?" You could've done just a tad better Marcus, seriously!"

"Come on guys. Let's take this out of the hallway." Jimmie chimed in. Marcus snapped his head in his direction.

He sneered. "Butt out, Jimmie. I think you've done enough. Matter of fact, what were the two of you doing in a locked room *alone*?" His face turned serious, and his eyes were beginning to grow sober.

Jimmie grew angry with the accusation. "Are you *fucking* kidding me, Bro? You need to get that shit out your fucking head. We were talking about you!"

"Huh? Funny, she won't even talk to me about *me*, how did you manage that?" Marcus' mocking expression faced me again.

"You won't talk about *yourself* to me! That's why you left me, remember?" I burst.

His eyes grew with anger. His stare was frightening, but I stood my ground and made sure to not show one moment of intimidation. Megan, though, was scared, and she inched over to my side. Grabbing my arm, she began to pull me back. I stood in place, so she stopped pulling but kept her fingers firmly locked around my arm. Jimmie moved toward Marcus and placed his hand against his chest.

Marcus hovered out of his brother's reach. Lifting his finger, he pointed in my direction. "You left me! *You* left *me*, Mia!" Breathing heavily, he glared at me. "I cared for you. I still care for you!"

Crossing my arms, I laughed once. "Oh *yeah*, well if I didn't run into you just now, what were you going to do with her? *Huh*?" I asked, nudging my head in Barbie's direction.

He slightly turned to look at her. Then rolling his eyes, his gaze met mine again. Smacking his lips to one side, he grew cocky. "I was gonna fuck her!" Sprawling his hands in the air, he nodded at my stunned expression. "Yeah that's right, *hard* too! But the entire time I was going to think of you!"

Gawking at him, my heartbeat raised. "How fucking romantic!" I couldn't believe he just admitted to that!

"Well what about you? *Huh*? What were you doing here? Trying to find someone to take home tonight?" He raised his eyebrows, arms still spread apart.

"You know, Marcus, I wasn't thinking about it, but that's actually a great idea! I'm sure I could find a man here willing to hook up with me tonight. As a matter of fact, I'm going to randomly choose a tall, tan, sexy, *fuckable* man as we speak. Have a great fucking night!" I turned on my heels and stormed down the hall.

He snapped. "The hell you're fucking … Over my dead fucking body, Mia. Mia!"

Turning my head, I looked over my shoulder; Jimmie was manhandling him. "Watch me!" I yelled and disappeared down the hall with Megan.

CHAPTER TWENTY-SIX

We exited the club. Breathing in the cool air, we walked down Boston's midtown strip in silence. Taking in what just happened, I couldn't believe him! My anger was tripling. I wanted to go back in the club and smack him across his head. That was why I couldn't be with him. That was why we weren't meant to be together. All we did was argue and fight. It wasn't worth it. My night began perfectly and ended in a nightmare. *Ugh*! I wanted to scream.

Megan hailed a cab, and we slid into the backseat.

"*Wow*, so I take it that was your ex, huh?" She spoke for the first time since we left the club.

"Yeah, can you see why we're not together anymore?" I mumbled.

"*Well*, you can see he still *loves* you, and you *clearly* still love him."

When I turned my head, she lightly shrugged at my pointed glare. "Didn't you just witness what happened? How could that possibly be love?"

Shrugging again, she stared out the window. "What do I know? I've never been in love before."

****

The next day I called Jimmie. I wanted to let him know that I didn't blame him for last night's episode. I knew Jimmie would blame himself. He apologized on behalf of Marcus and assured me that he didn't leave with the girl. He said Marcus left her at the club alone, and he stormed off home. I wasn't sure if Jimmie was telling the truth or not, but I didn't care. Marcus DeLuca had put me through enough pain, tears, and heartache.

I was done crying over him. *Well*, okay, I cried last night and this morning, but I was trying to stop. It was so hard. Even with everything we'd been through in the last three months, I still loved him. Any outsider looking in on our relationship would call me stupid and naïve.

At one point I believed in our relationship. Now it was ruined. I would never love a man again, nor would I ever trust again. Though I knew I was strong and one day I'd be able to get over this, for now I'd just have to deal with it. Before hanging up with Jimmie, I promised him that I would take Elle this weekend for my promised girls' day out. He said it wasn't necessary, but I insisted. It was the least I could do for her and for Jimmie.

After hanging up the phone, I exited my room. Megan was sprawled across the couch knocked out. Jeremy was by the kitchen island making coffee. He saw the look on my face and slid the coffee he made for himself over to me. "Rough night?" he asked.

Laughing once, I just sipped on the cup. I closed my eyes when I inhaled the freshly brewed coffee: my second most favorite scent in the world. My *first*? I sighed when I thought of him again. The headache from this emotional roller coaster known as Marcus DeLuca seemed to get worse. Seriously, it was so bad I could actually hear a knocking sound at this moment. I looked up at Jeremy; his eyes trailed to the front door. The knocking happened again. *Oh*, it wasn't me; it was the actual door.

"I got it." Megan said while yawning. She stretched as she stood and happily skipped over to the front door in nothing but a t-shirt and lace panties. How could she possibly be so damn happy this early in the morning and after a night of drinking? I envied her for that.

She opened the door, and her smile broadened as she tilted her head. "*Oh*, you're even more beautiful sober."

Jeremy and I glanced at each other with furrowed brows and then back at the door. "Is Mia home?" Marcus' straightforward tone sounded in my ears.

This could not be happening! He could not possibly be here, especially after last night. He has a lot of fucking balls, showing himself around here.

"Um, *yeah*, she's here, but I truly doubt she wants to see you at this moment." Megan giggled.

I didn't see the humor.

Angry as I mentally relived last night's scene, I jumped from my stool and stomped over beside Megan. Pushing her aside, I grabbed the door. "What do you want, Marcus?" I made it a point to sound stern.

His scent hit me like a ton of bricks. My most favorite smell in the world lingered between us. The scent of his bath soap from his freshly taken shower mixed with his cologne. He smelled so good it was sickening. "I wanted to apologize for last night. I didn't want it to end like that."

Slapping my hand on my hip, I tilted my head. "Marcus, we ended a month ago, so last night was not an end to anything."

Looking down, he shoved his hands into his front pockets. "I don't want to argue, Mia." Glancing back at me, his face was unreadable.

"Neither do I. So that's why you should go."

"Come on, Mia, can we please talk?" he begged.

"No, I'm done, Marcus. I'm *so* done." I closed the door, pressing my back against it so that I slid down to the floor exhaling. My eyes closed as I buried my hands into my face.

There was one soft knock against the door, a sliding sound, and then his voice pierced through at a lower level as if he was on the floor as well. "I'm not giving up, Mia. I'm not going anywhere. I won't go. I refuse to not fight for us this time."

Shifting my body so that my mouth neared the crack of the door, I whispered. "Marcus, please just go. I'm *trying* so hard. It's difficult already. It's bad enough that I think I can't let you go."

"Then don't, Mia, *don't*. Please just give me another chance."

Tears stung my eyes. "I can't."

"I'm not leaving. I don't care if it takes you a lifetime. I'm not giving up."

Sighing, I stood and walked away and headed to my room. I threw myself in bed. He'd eventually go. He couldn't stay there forever. *Why was he making it so hard for me?* I hated him for that.

****

Taking the longest nap ever, I woke to the smell of cheesy pizza. I was starving since I skipped breakfast and lunch. I washed up in the bathroom before going to the kitchen. When I entered, Jeremy and Megan were whispering to one another. They seemed to be having a serious discussion. They both looked up at me as I entered. The fresh box of pizza was still closed. I opened it. Ah, it smelled so good. Grabbing a few plates out the cupboard, I placed them on the kitchen counter.

When I glanced back up they were both staring at me. "What?" Their eyes fixed on each other and back on me. "What?" I asked again, irritated.

Megan pressed her lips together before speaking. "Marcus is still out there. He paid for the pizza. He refuses to go." She bit her lip.

"So?" I tried to act as if I didn't care. Deep down, I did care—though I wouldn't show them that.

"*So*, he's been sitting out there all day and hasn't eaten a thing. I'm not sure if he's even used the bathroom, Mia," Jeremy chimed in. I glared at him, annoyed by his sympathy for Marcus. Whose side was he on, anyway?

"There's a gas station down the block. He can use the bathroom there." Both of them widened their eyes, surprised by my lack of compassion. "What!"

Tearing their eyes away from me, they dug into the pizza. I grabbed my slice, and slumped onto a kitchen stool and began to munch into the warm cheesy bread. They sat in silence, eyeing each other. I watched them as they gave slight shrugs and sympathetic expressions to one another. Oh, come on! Since when was Marcus DeLuca a saint! Did he magically win them over during my eight-hour nap? So what if he'd been sitting outside this entire time without food, water, and a restroom. He deserved it. I hope he starves!

Alright, that was mean even for me. Ugh. I jumped off the stool and grabbed another plate from the cabinet. Placing two slices onto the plate, I looked at their pathetic faces as they stared at me with hopeful eyes. Rolling my eyes, I stormed toward the front door. When I swung it open, Marcus was sitting across from me. His head leaned against the wall. Arching my eyebrow, I walked over and shoved the plate onto his lap. He smiled. I said nothing but turned on my heels and stormed back into my apartment. Slamming the door behind me, I went back to eating my pizza. Jeremy and Megan both with crooked grins continued to munch on their slices as well. We ate in silence.

****

After dinner, we stayed up for a while, watching re-runs of a comedy series. I laughed at certain scenes, but it was the fakest laugh I'd ever heard. Jeremy even raised his eyebrows at me a few times. I was caught. I wanted to enjoy the show. I really did. My mind drifted to Marcus sitting out on the hallway on the uncomfortable hardwood floors. An ounce of me began to feel sorry for him, but then my mind would drift off to last night's scene, and the sorrow I felt would be overcome with anger.

It was beginning to get late, so Megan left for home. Jeremy stayed in the living room watching TV, and I went to my room to prepare my things for my first day of school. As I laid out my clothes, laptop and textbooks, I started to wonder if Jeremy took out the trash. Maybe I should take out the trash. No, it wasn't an excuse to see if he was still out there—*maybe* a small one.

Deciding to check anyway, I walked over to the kitchen. The trash wasn't full. H*mm*. Pulling the bag out of the can, I began to walk through the apartment trying to find trash anywhere in sight, emptying both bathroom trashcans into the bag, also the bin in my bedroom. There, that was full enough to take out. After I donned my slippers, Jeremy walked out of his bedroom as I was getting ready to exit the door.

"What are you doing?" he asked.

Startled, I lifted the trash bag I held in my hands. "Oh, uh, the trash was full," I said.

He stared at me questioningly. "*Yeah*, I emptied it this morning."

Shrugging, I smiled. "Really? Huh, oh well, I'll go dump this one."

Smirking, he said. "I'll do it."

Quickly turning around, I brought my arms up to stop him. "No, no, you got it last time. I don't mind."

Chuckling, he shook his head and entered the kitchen. Taking a deep breath, I opened the door. Sure enough, DeLuca was sitting in the same spot. His eyes were worn, but grew hopeful at the sight of me. With my best stern expression, I swiftly passed him and made my way down the stairs. Once I exited the door, I breathed in the fresh cool air. This was getting ridiculous; he couldn't possibly keep this up every night. Dumping the trash into the dumpster, I made my way back in.

When I entered my floor, he was still sitting on the hardwood surface. Rolling my eyes, I hovered over him with my hand on my hip, looking down. His eyes looked up. "What are you doing, Marcus?"

A simple smile crossed his face. "I told you, Mia. I'm not going anywhere until you talk to me."

"There's nothing to say, Marcus. Go home. You're wasting your time."

Lowering his head, he shook it. "Nope, I'm not going."

Rolling my eyes again, I stormed back into my apartment. He couldn't stay in that hallway all night. *Who the hell did he think he was?* Besides it would get chilly. Ugh, rummaging through my linen closet, I pulled out a quilt and pillow. Walking back out front, I opened the door and threw them on his lap. "This is only because I don't want a frozen dead man in front of my door when I wake up. And I'll leave the door open, so you can use the bathroom, but that's it! Only to use the bathroom! I refuse to have my hallways smell like piss. And wipe the grin off your face, DeLuca! I'm not doing this to be kind. I'm looking out for my tenants."

He pressed his lips together to hold in his laughter. *Ugh!* Why did I even bother to give him the stuff? Walking back in, I closed the door behind me without locking it. This was going to be interesting. I wondered how long it would last—I was sure not long at all. I locked my bedroom door though in case he tried to sneak in.

CHAPTER TWENTY-SEVEN

Day One

I woke up the next morning refreshed and peaceful. It was the first full night's sleep I'd had in a long while. Even though Marcus was not in my room, something about having him a few feet away was comforting. That scared me a little.

Today marked a new day, and I decided the moment I awoke that I would not allow anything to ruin my day, not even Marcus. I was actually excited to start school as I began my morning ritual. Something about the familiar surroundings of Harvard made me secretly squeal.

After showering and humming, yes, I was actually humming, I threw on my sweats, school logo t-shirt, and a red cap. *Ah*, this feels more like home.

Jeremy was asleep. He would begin his first class on Wednesday, so I made coffee for one and quietly sat on the stool, eating my breakfast. Once I was done, I placed the dishes in the sink. Grabbing my backpack, I headed out the door.

Marcus was standing before me, freshly showered and newly dressed. He had the biggest grin on his face as he held up the folded quilt and pillow I gave him last night. I studied him; he was in jeans and a blue t-shirt. He must've left early this morning to shower, change, and come back. Narrowing my eyes, I snatched the things out of his hand and placed them on top of the couch. *Did he even sleep here last night?* Walking out the door, I briskly passed him and hurried down the stairs. I could hear his footsteps behind me.

After exiting the building, I picked up speed. It was a nice morning, and I wanted to walk to school. His pocket change rattled as he hurried behind me to keep up. Feeling his presence beside me, I closed my eyes for a second and inhaled. *He will not ruin my morning; he will not ruin my morning.* I lowered my cap when I felt his stare. From my peripheral vision, I could see the huge smile stretched across his face. *Why was he so damn happy?* Ignoring him, I continued at the same pace; he managed to keep up.

"Ethics, huh?" he asked, pointing at the textbook I held tightly secured against my chest. I quickly glanced down and then straightened again. I nodded as I refused to speak or look at him. *Yes*, I was giving him the silent treatment. Maybe he'd get the hint.

"I did very well in Ethics. Maybe I could help you if you run into any problems. Well I'm sure you won't, but if you do ..."

Snapping my head at him, I laughed once. I rolled my eyes and focused on ahead of me. He did well in Ethics? I snorted. Maybe in the classroom and the legal world he aced it, but when involving his relationship and personal life, his ethics sucked big time! He must've sensed my thoughts because the rest of the walk he remained quiet. Still not leaving my side, he took it upon himself to walk me all the way to school. Once we reached the building, I hurried inside, not glancing his way or saying goodbye.

The rest of the day went very well. Surprisingly, I enjoyed both my Ethics and Criminal Law classes. When it came to school, I was always attentive, making sure to scribble everything down. *Yeah* I was that student! Since it was the first day, though, I allowed my mind to drift away at some point and think of Marcus. *What was his plan?* To bug me every day until I gave in? Couldn't he see it wasn't that simple? Our relationship was nothing but a mere emotional, dramatic roller coaster.

I couldn't help but think that in just over four months we'd been through so much more than most couples who'd put in years into their relationship. Being with Marcus DeLuca was draining, frustrating, confusing, and *extraordinary* all at the same time. It didn't make sense. Our relationship didn't make sense! We both had our issues, and two wrongs surely did not make a right.

After school, I met with my mother and Megan for dinner. Megan had exciting news as she was going to begin classes next week at the local community college. I was so excited for her. She skipped college straight after high school in the hopes of "finding" herself. Now more eager than ever, she was majoring in Interior Design with a minor in Business. My mother also shared great news: she was able to find work at a local clinic as a medical assistant. With their exceptional news and my first day of school, we celebrated with a few glass of wine.

That evening, Marcus was seated across from my apartment door as he was the night before. He stared at me when I walked past him. The hope in his eyes was slowly beginning to fade. Not saying a word, I grabbed the quilt and pillow from the couch and handed it to him. He smiled gently, and I went back to prepare myself for the next day.

The next few days were similar. He would greet me with a bright smile early in the morning and quietly walk by my side to school. At night, his smile faded when I briskly passed him, though he was hopeful every day. I was beginning to get used to seeing him, and although I acted sternly by not saying a word, my heart ached for his not giving up. Even with the many eye rolls, snorts, and cocky attitude I was giving him, he didn't budge, and slowly my guard was beginning to fall.

****

Day Five

I awoke to day five, feeling a slight pinch in my stomach. Marcus had worked so hard in getting my attention, and I enjoyed our quiet walks to school together. My attitude wasn't fair to him, so I decided that today I'd be nicer. Today I would give him a shot. *Though*, today he wasn't there. His gorgeous dimple didn't greet me this morning. The quilt and pillow I laid out were sprawled out across the floor instead of neatly folded in his hands. My heart hitched at what could have kept him away. Then my mind reared towards Lou. I'd bet my entire life Marcus had a job that he couldn't keep away from.

I didn't have class today, but I made my way to the university for the study hall. The entire time I couldn't concentrate. Right when I was beginning to cave in again ... *Lou Sorrento*, that evil man had such a hold on so many lives. If I were to ever see him again, I was sure I would end up behind bars for murder.

After "studying," I went back home. It was almost noon, and I figured I should get ready to take Elle out to the mall. It looked like it was going to pour today. The earlier we went, the more likely we'd miss the rain. When I turned onto the second floor of my building, Marcus was sitting across from my door with the quilt neatly folded and the pillow next to him.

His eyes widened when he saw me walking down the hall. He probably thought since I didn't have school I would sleep in. Getting to his feet he stared at me as I approached him. He was wearing last night's clothing: dark blue jeans, a white shirt, and black boots. I eyed him up and down. His eyes looked worn; he hadn't slept. *Yeah, he was on a job.* Shaking my head, I continued to glare at him. "Don't you have work?" All week he hadn't been at the office, or at least I thought he hadn't.

Pressing his lips together, his eyebrows pulled in. "I can skip work. I own the firm." He lightly shrugged.

Tilting my head, I further studied him with my arms crossed. "*Huh*, yet God forbid you miss a job with Lou, right?" Looking down, he said nothing. Just what I thought. I stormed back into the apartment.

****

Elle was ecstatic when I pulled into the driveway. She practically ran into the car, tightening her tiny arms around my neck. Tears stung my eyes. I felt terrible for abandoning her. I knew she felt extremely close to me. I'd shut her out when things went bad for Marcus and me, and I wanted to punch myself for doing that. It wasn't her fault, and it wasn't fair to her either.

Kids never forget, but they surely forgive easily. I wish I could easily forgive and forget.

I treated her to shopping and lunch. Then we enjoyed a manicure and pedicure. Is it bad to say that one of my best friends was an eight-year-old? Yeah, I knew I was pathetic. Elle was too adorable not to love. Her enthusiastic, selfless personality gleamed through her eyes. She loved everyone and everything. Seriously, I could give her dollar-store bubblegum, and she would jump up and down because I thought of her.

We sat in our massage chairs beside one another, and I listened as she went on about school and her new teachers and a few boys that she had an eye on in class. I laughed, and she giggled, confessing her puppy love.

"Mia, what do you think of the colors of teal and yellow?" she asked.

Turning to look at her toes, I noticed she had chosen a bright pink polish. Maybe she was thinking of changing her mind. "I like the pink, Elle, but yellow and teal would be pretty on your toes also."

She giggled. "No, for the wedding, silly." My eyes squinted, and I stared at her, wondering what she was talking about. Her smile broadened, "Uncle Marc said I could be the flower girl. So when grandma was looking over colors last weekend, she thought teal and yellow would be pretty colors for a spring wedding. Since Uncle Marc said you didn't want a fall wedding."

My heart dropped. He hadn't told his family about our breakup. I couldn't say anything. I just nodded and slowly turned my head blankly, staring at my own toes. I hadn't spoken to Theresa in over a month. Wouldn't that be strange to her? "Elle, what has Marcus said about me not being around lately?" I asked curiously.

"That you've been really busy with getting yourself ready for school, and now that you've started you won't be around as much. Is that why you haven't been to any of the Sunday dinners? Uncle Marc hasn't been to them either."

I nodded again, speechless. I'd been walking around miserable for the past month for all to see, and he'd been lying to his family this entire time as if everything were okay. Did he think I would run back into his arms and we would start where we left off? This man, he's … Ugh! He's beyond frustrating.

When we left the mall, it was pouring. We had to stand in the entrance before working up enough courage to run to my car. Elle and I were drenched when we entered the vehicle. We laughed, not bothered by our soaked clothing. The entire drive I couldn't stop thinking about Marcus and his continuing lies. He made it look so easy.

Elle's voice cut through my thoughts when I pulled into her front driveway. "Mia, this was the best girls' day ever! We should do it again." Her damp body pressed into mine before hopping out of the dry car and into the pouring rain. I watched as her little legs hurried into the front door, and she waved at me before entering. I smiled and waved back.

I sat in the car for a few seconds, staring at the closed door and listening to the sound of loud thumping noises from raindrops against the rooftop. Sighing, I put the car in drive and slowly removed my foot from the pedal. As I looked up, I slammed on my brakes when I saw a figure standing in front of my vehicle. It was

Marcus; he was drenched and motionless staring at me. I shifted the gear to reverse. When I looked in my rearview mirror, I saw that his car was behind mine. I was trapped.

Irritation filled me. "Move!" I yelled, pointing my hand over the window. He didn't budge. I yelled it a few more times from the top of my lungs, but still he didn't move.

Taking the necessary steps, I exited my car. Angrily, I stormed around the front of my vehicle to face him. Standing a few feet away, I allowed the rain to drench my body. I stared at him as I breathed unevenly.

The rain pulled and tugged at his shirt as he stood tall, his shoulders broad and slightly hunched over. His arms were slightly bent at his side, and his legs were partly separated. His shiny black hair was made unruly by the rain, and his chest heaved in and out rapidly as he stared at me. "What are you doing, Marcus?" I yelled over the loud, thundering rain.

He shrugged. "I don't know! I don't know what to do anymore. I have to do something to get your attention!"

Angrily, I brushed some hair away from my face. "You didn't tell your family about us!" My arms fell to my side.

"Because I wasn't ready, Mia! I was still hoping that ..." Moving a few inches closer, he brought his hand in the air. "I still had the slightest hope that you would take me back."

Shaking my head, I gawked at him. "Why? Give me one good reason why I should?" After pulling away another lock of hair from my face, I crossed my arms.

I stood in place as he moved in closer and said, "Because we love each other, because we deserve to be happy, and because we're miserable without one another."

I stared at him lost in thought. "You call this love, Marcus! We constantly fight, we hurt each other, we lie, and we keep secrets. How could you call that *love*?"

Looking down, he shook his head. The rain, now dying, dripped down his olive skin and clothing. His shirt clung to his chest, defining the muscular tone. Placing his hands to his hips, he stared at the ground for a while. I watched him as we both were at a loss for words.

Finally glancing into my eyes, he walked over, and his body hovered over mine. My heart hitched at the proximity. "I'm not perfect, Mia. And our relationship may not be perfect to *you*, but it is to *me*. You will never find one couple in this world without problems." He tossed his hands in the air. "*Hell*, I bet there's another man right now on the other side of this planet, standing in the pouring rain, fighting desperately for the woman he loves."

Our breathing grew as we studied each other, searching for something. Cupping my face, his expression grew compassionate as he continued to speak. "Yes, we fight, who doesn't? But I wouldn't change any of it—nothing, not even your attitude." I sucked my teeth and rolled my eyes.

Smiling, he continued. "See, like right there. I love you so much. *Please,* give me a chance to prove to you that this time around we could be happy. Let me prove to you that we are *meant* for each other. I'm so sorry for hurting you. Give us another chance, and I promise I'll never hurt you again. I promise that I will make you happy. *Please?*"

"Marcus," I whispered. Staring into his pleading eyes, I brought my hands to his face. Why did he make it so hard for me to walk away? I loved him with all of my heart, and I would give my last breath for him. Though we walked a path that many would run away from, could I continue to walk it with him? "I'm *scared*." I confessed. I was afraid—afraid if I caved in I would set myself up for failure.

Letting out a deep breath, he pressed his forehead down to mine. With his eyes closed, he whispered, "That's what love is ... It's scary not knowing what's expected, but I know it'll be the *best* frightening love we've ever had."

Seconds or minutes went by as I stood watching him. I loved him so much, and I was miserable without him, but could we do this? If this wasn't love, then I wasn't sure I wanted to experience love at all because what I had with him was something no one could ever replace. Without further thinking, I wrapped my arms around his neck and pulled him to me, locking our lips together.

His lips spread into a smile, and he slowly lifted me and tightened our embrace. We stood in the rain tangled with one another.

I wasn't sure where our paths would take us, and although this felt both wrong yet so right, this time around I knew one thing for sure: as we gave ourselves a second chance, I had no choice but to be *cautious*.

EPILOGUE

Lou Sorrento

Taking a long-needed puff of my fine Cuban cigar, I leaned back on my chair as I watched the cloud of smoke dissipate into the air. I needed to get to the bottom of this fucking mess ASAP. If Marky kept giving me the fucking run around, then I'd have no choice but to take it upon myself.

Speak of the fucking devil. He stormed through my office doors with his clothes drenched. Eyeing him suspiciously, I thought he seemed fucking anxious.

"What's so fucking important that I had to run down now?" He snapped.

He'd been getting a little rowdy these past few fucking days. I clenched my teeth and dabbed the tip of the cigar against the ashtray. Cracking my neck, I straightened in my chair to look at him. If he wasn't family, I would've fucking cracked his head with the back of my hand.

I breathed deeply to keep myself from exploding. My temper's something that gets the best of me, so I'd start off in a nice way … see how it went. "Why the fuck are you soaked?"

His arms spread as he looked down at his clothes and back at me like I'm the fucking dumb-cock fuck. "It's pouring out, what else could it be?" His arms slammed back to his side.

"You don't own a fucking umbrella or something?" He was pissing me the fuck off.

"What do you want, Lou?" he snapped. Marky had grown a lot of fucking balls!

It was time to show him who the fucking boss is! "I want to know." I was now out of my chair hovering over my desk, and I yelled from the top of my lungs, "WHO THE FUCKING RAT IS!" He didn't fucking flinch. He was standing there staring at me like I had lost my fucking mind. This kid was going to give me a fucking heart attack!

Lowering my voice, I pressed a finger on top of my desk and glared at him. "You've been giving me the fucking runaround for the past few months! There have been FBI scumbags sniffing around my fucking warehouses! Either you find out who the rat is, or I'll do it myself, Marky." I cocked my head, burning my eyes into his. "Unless you know something you're keeping from me?"

Letting out a deep breath, he looked me square in the eye. "I don't know shit. I've been dealing with personal things, but I'm back on track now. I'll find that rat for yah. Can I go home to my girl now?"

Ever since he's been with that fucking girl, he's been one loose fucking canon. I stared at him for a long time. Laughing once, I adjusted my suit jacket and sat back in my chair. "That's fine. Go back to Mia. Tell her I said "hi" by the way." *Oh*, he didn't like that *mmmh.* His jaw clenched when I said her name.

I smirked at him. "You have another week. If I don't have my rat, you're off the job."

Marky nodded, turned, and walked out the door. Vinnie walked in right after, closing the door behind him. He slowly walked over. Once he approached my desk, he reached into his inner leather jacket pocket, removing a large yellow envelope. He tossed it to me, and I grabbed it from the wood surface it just fell on. Smiling, I looked up at him. "Is this everything?"

"Yeah boss, everything you need to know about her."

"Good, good. Do me a favor. Keep a close eye on Marky. I want to know his every whereabouts."

"Sure thing boss. Anything else?"

"Nope, you did a great job, Vinnie. Make sure Stacy pays you before you leave."

Vinnie nodded and headed out the door.

Grabbing the envelope, I pulled out all the documents. The first document I saw was a picture of Mia Sullivan. She sure is fucking beautiful. The next document listed everything about her: past employment, residence, relatives. Squinting my eyes, I took a better look at her siblings. Well I be damned. Michael Sullivan.

Motherfucker!

Snatching the phone, I made a quick phone call. "Hello, yeah it's Lou. I need you to do me a huge favor. Meet me here at six.

Thanks." After ending the call, I re-lit my cigar and took another long puff as I continued to rummage through the documents.

If Marky thought he had one up on me, he was clearly fucking mistaken!

BONUS SCENE

As a bonus scene, I thought I'd show you what *Disastrous* would have been like from Marcus' point of view.

CHAPTER ONE: MARCUS MEET'S MIA

I fucking hated my life. Every day I woke up and thought, "What the fuck! Couldn't I've been spared today?" Yep, it's pathetic, but it was true. What's even more pathetic was that my brother found me less than a month ago sprawled out on the bathroom floor with a bottle of brandy in one hand and an empty bottle of pills in the other. I wimped out and tried to leave this corrupt world in the easiest way I could think of. He rushed me to the hospital and managed to keep that shit out of the media and from our family. I still don't know how he did it.

After that, he wanted me to see a therapist. *Me? A therapist!* He was fucking losing his mind. I refused to sit on a couch and spill my *feelings* to a cock-sucking stranger and have him help me deal with my *"issues."* FUCK that!

My life consisted of dealing with other's *bullshit* instead of my own. I was an attorney—number one in Boston according to the Boston Lawyers' Magazine, four years in a row. I was also a fucking sidekick for one of the largest Italian mafia families in the city, the Sorrentos. Yeah I know a lawyer by day and fucking mobster by night, who would have thought?

Anyways, that's where I was heading, to one of my meetings with some of the guys. We would meet at my club before a job to go over details and shit. I had a huge headache and could barely keep my eyes open from lack of sleep, but I'd take care of that with a nice glass of brandy.

Jimmie, my brother, still gave me shit for drinking, but he would butt out of my business and leave me be, especially because he was the one that put me in this fucking mess to begin with. He's lucky he's family because he was due for a pistol whipping a long time ago.

I pulled into the back private lot of Club21 and turned off the ignition. Taking a second for me before going in, my head slumped against the headrest. I let out a deep breath as I rubbed my temples with my fingertips. This was going to be another long night. Well, I thought I might as well get this shit done and over with. I exited my car and headed for the back entrance. Luckily, that night, we were just going over details on a job scheduled for the weekend, so I should only have been an hour or so tops.

After I knocked on the door twice, it opened. Vinnie was behind it and nodded at me as I walked in. "Hey boss," he mumbled.

"Hey, Vinnie, is Jimmie in yet?" Knowing my fucking brother, who was always late, he wasn't here. I couldn't blame him though. He always had to wait for the sitter to watch Elle: his daughter, my beautiful niece.

"Nah, not yet, he said he's gonna be a least an hour late."

Cock-sucker. I knew this was going to be a long night. I nodded at Vinnie and headed into the club. I was greeted by numerous people when I entered, and I gave the best charmed expression I could.

I needed a drink.

Heading towards the bar, I spotted Lora. She was a good looking woman. I've slept with her numerous of times, and I knew she'd let me in again. All I'd have to do was nudge my head toward the VIP room, and she'd squeal like a fucking teenage girl. She spotted me. Smiling seductively, she made her way over.

"Hey, gorgeous." she said, holding a tray with one hand and dragging the other through my hair.

I gave her my famous crooked grin. That shit made the chicks fucking wild. She bit her lip, and I knew she was going crazy right then. "Hey Lora, I thought you were off tonight?"

She placed the tray down on the bar and looked at the bartender, placing her order before answering me. "Paige, can I have a Grey Goose and tonic and a Cosmo? Thanks. Yeah, they needed me. It being the last day of school for most universities, they knew it would be packed."

I looked over her shoulder and spotted Jeremy immediately. I knew he was there by his signature pussy drink. Jeremy's father designed Club21 and my office building. He's the best at what he does, so Jeremy and I became kind of close in the process.

He was with a woman though. I didn't recall him mention a girlfriend before. From a distance, she looked attractive, and even from behind the table, you could tell she had a nice body. She seemed out of her element, looking around uncomfortably. I ordered three shots for their table and told Lora to tell them that I would join them after I greeted a few people.

Lora swayed her hips over to them, and I watched from the bar as I sipped on my drink. For some reason, I was drawn to the table. I watched as Lora set down the shot glasses and the woman next to Jeremy snapped her head to him. She looked upset as Jeremy tried to explain something. Without a moment's hesitation, she grabbed her Cosmo and gulped it down. *Fuck* that was sexy! Jeremy grabbed her hand. He seemed to be soothing her. I assumed she was with him. I took a few more sips of my drink and continued to watch. She relaxed as Lora hurried and handed her another drink.

For the next hour, I stood at the bar, greeted a few people, and secretly spied on Jeremy's table. I wasn't exactly sure why, but I found her facial expressions interesting. She seemed bored and kept drinking to entertain herself. Even when two additional people joined their table, she looked as if she were just being friendly for their sake.

Jeremy stood up and walked over to the end of the bar. He didn't spot me. He approached a blond-haired chick and led her to the dance floor. *Huh.* I realized she wasn't with him. The couple from the table also headed to the dance floor, leaving her all by herself.

She raised her hand at Lora, who walked over by the bar to grab another Cosmo. She was going through her phone. Lora grabbed her drink, and I quickly stood from my stool and followed behind. Lora placed the drink on the table, and I stepped beside her. I stared at the woman before me who had yet to acknowledge my presence. She quickly grabbed her drink and took a long swig. Her lips curled into a smile as it went down.

"Um, good evening, Mr. DeLuca, would you like your usual?" Lora formally asked. Around others she used my last name, but when we were alone she wasn't as formal.

Without taking my eyes off the woman gulping her drink, I said, "Yes, that's fine. Thank you." Lora seemed angry and stormed off. I didn't care about Lora anymore the moment I was greeted with the most unique emerald green eyes I had ever seen. I lied to myself earlier when I said she was attractive. She wasn't. She was absolutely fucking BEAUTIFUL. I forced a smile, trying to hold my composure. I had flutters in my stomach, can you fucking believe that! Actual fucking butterflies in my stomach. I never felt that shit before. She gently smiled, and it was breathtaking. *Calm down, DeLuca; you've been around gorgeous women. Not this fucking stunning.*

Oh my God, I felt a hard-on forming, so I hurriedly slid through the seat before she spotted it. I scooted over until I was near her, and I instantly caught a whiff of her scent. Fuck. She smells like cherry candy. *Who fucking doesn't love cherry-flavored candy?* I fought the urge to lunge over the table and attack her lips. I wondered if she tasted like cherries. *Okay, get a grip!* I told myself. I turned and nodded at her. Her shaky hands instantly rushed under the table. She was nervous. That's cute. *Did I just use the word cute?*

I smiled at her. I had to know who she was, so I blurted out, "Hi, I'm Marcus DeLuca, and you *are*?" Great, dickhead! That didn't sound forward at all. Lora handed me my drink, so I grabbed it and took a sip to calm my own nerves.

"Hi, I'm Mia, Jeremy's friend." She tilted her head and glanced towards the dance floor. I looked over, quickly nodded, and took another sip of my drink. I had this urge to not drink around her, afraid that she'd judge me. *What the hell was I talking about? S*he just chugged down like five Cosmos. *Did that make me a stalker because I knew how many drinks she had?* Fuck. I'm acting like a little bitch.

Mia? It fit her perfectly. Why does it sound familiar? *Oh* wait. I leaned in and folded my hands on top of the table, keeping them from reaching over to touch her face. It looked so soft. "Are you Sullivan? Mia Sullivan?"

She bit her bottom lip. I couldn't help but stare at those lips. They were perfect in every way: glossy, full, plump, juicy, kissable lips. My semi-hard-on turned full blown hard.

She finally glanced at me, and at that moment for only a mere second, our eyes locked. I knew I wanted to know more about Mia.

She was so beautiful, nothing like I'd ever seen, and she was here, sitting next me. "Yes, how did you know?" she asked, breaking my thoughts.

I stumbled over my words like a fucking dick, "Oh, ah, Jeremy mentioned you a few times. Also, I texted him earlier, to see if he knew you. I've heard a lot about the highly-recommended first-year law student, Mia Sullivan." I tried to make up for it with my playful, flirty grin.

"Yes, that's me, I ... I didn't apply, Professor Johnson applied on my behalf. He handed me the acceptance letter for the interview this morning actually." She didn't give me the response I usually got from other females. Was she not interested? Maybe she did have a boyfriend. I just nodded again, trying to come up with something else to get her attention. That's when Jeremy approached. Douche bag.

"Hey, there you are! I see you met Mia."

"Yes, we met." Thanks for cock-blocking. *Cock-blocking?* I wasn't trying to get in her panties. Well, I wanted to, but not just yet.

"So, Marc, sorry I can't hang, but I kind of have this chick that wants to hook up." He pointed his thumb to some girl by the bar. I took a quick glance and looked at him, hoping that Mia didn't have to leave as well. He faced Mia. "Mia, I know you had too many drinks tonight. Will you be okay getting home? I'm going to take a cab back to this chick's place. Also David and Michelle left like ten minutes ago. Are you going to be okay taking a cab home? I can wait for a cab with you if you like."

I watched her expression slowly grow angry. You could tell she wanted to snap at him but restrained from doing so, so I blurted out the first thing that came to mind. "I'll drive her." Mia quickly glared at the drink in my hand. "This is the only drink I've had all night. I'm fine. I can drive her home. Go ahead, Jae, get out of here." So I lied—it was my third drink tonight, but I was good to drive. Jeremy thanked me, kissed Mia on the cheek, *lucky bastard*, and left.

She watched Jeremy run away. Angrily, she picked up her drink and chugged it down, slamming it against the table. I held back a laugh. She was so wasted. Not looking in my direction, she slid across the chair and stood. My heart seriously stopped. Not only was she stunning she had the most curvy, hour-glass, thick-in-all-the-right-places body. I adjusted the bulge in my pants before quickly sliding in the opposite direction, made my way to her side, and grabbed her arm to keep her steady.

My breath hitched as I quickly eyed her up and down. Her dress was tight and short. I had this urge to hide her from everyone's sight. I wanted her all to myself. *What the fuck. All to myself?* She wasn't some toy you could just keep hidden in your room to play with as you please, you dick wad! Slowly, I was getting pissed at myself at the thought, then another came to mind. Jeremy was willing to let her go home alone in a cab dressed like that. Was he fucking slow or something?

"Hey, you don't have to take me home. I'm fine with taking a cab. Thanks anyway." The sound of her sweet voice pierced through my building rage for Jeremy. She began to tug away from my grip. I tightened it, not willing to let her go and began moving forward.

"No, I'm taking you home. What kind of man would I be if I let you go home completely drunk in a vehicle where a cab driver could possibly take advantage of you?" Peeking over my shoulder, I risked another glance at her. "Especially in that dress." *Shit*, I just sounded like a super douche bag control freak. I picked up the pace, moving us through the crowd, hoping she didn't hear me through the pounding music.

Nope, she heard me, and she didn't like it either. She yanked her arm away from my grip. I turned to face her. With her hands now on her hips, she tried to maintain her wobbly stance. "And what? Shall I get in the car with you, a *stranger*! What if *you* take advantage of me?" She yelled over the music. She was so fucking cute I couldn't help but laugh. Shaking my head, I grabbed her arm a little firmer to keep her from falling.

Proceeding through the crowd, I led her through to the back. She covered her eyes with her free hand, blinded by the hallway light. As I continued down the hall, I could hear the loud clumping noise of her heels and feel her swaying side-to-side. "You can't even standup straight on your own, and you want to get in a cab? *Didn't* you heard about those four females in Boston within the last year? All four were too drunk and were driven home in a cab alone but never found again!"

She tried to pull away from my grip again, but I restrained from her doing so. "Yes, I heard! And I can't stand straight because my heels are too high, thank you very much!" Oh, she was feisty. I wondered where she was from. She didn't sound like she was from Boston. I kept myself from laughing.

"I don't understand why women put themselves through that torture." Glancing over my shoulder, I slowly eyed her up and down, tracing her entire body with my stare. *Shit*, I didn't want her to think I was trying to get in her skirt. Think of something quick, DeLuca. "And you'd look just as good in that dress in flats." She would have—hell she could have worn a trash bag and still pulled it off.

After grabbing my car keys and giving advice to Vinnie about dealing with the meeting tonight, we walked out the door. Once we got to my car, I settled her into the passenger seat, and she fastened her seatbelt. For the twenty-second walk around the car to the driver's side, I had the fucking biggest smile on my face, and I couldn't figure out for the life of me why.

As soon as I stepped into the car, I put my game face on. "So where to?"

"You don't know where I live?" she mumbled.

"Why would I?"

She rolled her head and stared at me with those big beautiful eyes. "Do you know where Jeremy lives?"

"Yeah." I answered, captivated by those eyes.

She yawned, and her small round nose and eyes squinted. It was adorable. "We're roommates."

Huh? That caught me off guard. "Oh, he didn't mention that."

"I can tell."

Nodding, I put the car in reverse and managed to keep my eyes on the road. It was difficult to do. My car filled with the scent of cherry candy, and I breathed in the fragrance peacefully. At one red light, I chanced a quick glance at her, and she was passed out. She even slept beautifully: her face content, her head leaning against the headrest facing me. Her arms were crossed over her lap. I looked down at her bare legs and fought every impulse to trace my fingers along her thighs. If she could have read my mind, she would have clearly thought I was a fucking pervert.

I finally approached her building and found parking directly in front of it. After turning off the ignition, I stared at her for a few minutes. She looked so peaceful I didn't have the heart to wake her, but I couldn't sit in here forever. Well I would, but when she woke up and caught me staring at her, she'd think I was some type of weirdo.

Forcing myself out of the car, I made my way to her side and opened the passenger door. She didn't move an inch. Kneeling down, I gently shook her. She moaned, rolling her head against the headrest in my direction. Her eyes popped open, and she smiled at the sight of me. I couldn't help but smile back. I lifted my hand and touched the side of her cheek. Skimming my thumb along her cheek bone, I noticed that her skin was so soft and delicate. "How you feeling?" I asked.

"Like crap," she mumbled. I laughed, stood up, and reached my hand out for her to take it. At first she was hesitant, but eventually she took it. Once on her feet, she stumbled forward into me. My quick reflexes prevented her from falling. Lifting her head, she giggled. It was the most engaging sound I'd ever heard. I would have done anything to hear that sound again. Her hands were pressed against my chest, and my body began to tremble. *What are you a little bitch now? You've been touched by plenty of women before,* but not this one.

"Well are you just going to stand there or lead me to my room?" She flashed a flirtatious grin. I lost my breath for a few seconds, and then before I could blink, I quickly helped her up the stairs and to the front door of her apartment. She removed her keys from her clutch and sloppily made her way through the door, throwing her clutch on top of a table.

I followed closely behind her with my hands held up near her back in case she fell. She was mumbling something while pulling on her dress. "Shit, I can't get this thing off. Could you unzip the back for me?" She whimpered when we entered what I thought was her room.

Wetting my lips, I hesitantly inched closer. Her long, wavy hair was in the way, so I brushed it over to one shoulder, sweeping my fingertips along the back of her neck. I had to bite my bottom lip down to hold my composure. Taking a deep breath, I swallowed hard. Very gently and slowly, I pulled down on the small metal zipper, tracing my finger all the way down her back. I smiled when small round goose bumps formed against her skin. Once her entire back was exposed, she turned around.

Smiling, she slowly slid her dress down her curves, allowing the fabric to fall on the floor. My heart raced, watching her stand there in nothing but a lace strapless bra and matching panties. She was without a doubt the most beautiful woman I had ever seen. Her eyes traced down to my visible hard-on, and she smiled. Lifting her gaze back to me, she attempted to move forward but lost balance and fell back into her bed, laughing.

I rushed over. Grabbing the dress she just took off, I threw it on the bed and kneeled before her. She sat up and stared at me as I took one of her legs and rested her foot on top of my thigh. When I yanked off her heel, she moaned with pleasure. I smiled. I still didn't understand why women put themselves through the pain. I yanked the other shoe off and began to rub her feet. I wasn't sure why, but the small moaning sounds she made turned me on.

Pulling her feet away, she leaned forward and ran her fingers through my hair. I closed my eyes, feeling an electric sensation pulse through my veins at her touch.

When I opened them, she was inches away from my face. Her eyes were searching mine, and I wanted to lunge at her. "Your hair is so soft. It feels nice," she whispered. I wet my lips in hopes it would control my heavy breathing. Her eyes caught my lips, and she stared at them. "Your lips are nice too. They look soft. I want to feel them." She inched in a little closer, and her lips just about touched mine when I pulled away.

I couldn't do it. If she were another girl, I would've hit and run, but there was something about her that was different. She made me have fucking butterflies for God's sake, and when she touched me, a tingling sensation ran from the roots of my hair straight to the tip of my boner. It didn't feel right to use her. For the first time in my life, I wanted to do something right and get to know her.

Her head cocked back, disgusted with the rejection. Failing desperately to stand, she stormed over to her nightstand and mumbled a few curses. She opened the drawer and reached for something, and then a buzzing noise went off. "Oh screw it, I'm too tired." She mumbled then the buzzing noise went off, and she tossed whatever she was holding onto the side of her bed. She threw herself in the bed, huffing and puffing.

I held back a laugh. Getting to my feet, I walked over to her bedside. I stood over her, staring into a lovely face. "I'm sorry. I want to kiss you, but …" She rolled her eyes and crossed her arms.

"Please save your lies for someone else. I'm used to being alone anyway."

Alone? How could this beautiful, smart, breathtaking woman be alone? She swallowed hard, and at that moment her eyes filled with tears, but she held them back. I wanted to crawl in the bed beside her and hold her. She wet her lips, and then tightly shut her eyes.

I watched her for a few minutes until she was fast asleep. As soon as I knew she was completely in a deep sleep, I pulled the sheets up to cover her shivering body. Without a moment's hesitation, I leaned down and planted a small kiss against her lips. Something happened when I kissed her. It was just a small pathetic kiss, but I felt this pulse against my chest once our lips touched.

Gently rising, I walked backwards out of her room, watching her and kicking myself in the ass for not staying to watch her awaken. *Mmmh,* she would be nice to wake-up to every single morning.

Once I reached the living room, I passed the table and spotted her clutch. I needed an excuse to see her again, and I knew that it broke every tough-guy man code alive, but I stooped down to the lowest level and grabbed her purse. *Yeah,* I needed an excuse alright, and what better way than to say she left it in my car.

I had to see her the next day. I had to know her: where she was from, her likes and dislikes. My mind was racing wanting to know who Mia Sullivan was. And for the first time in my life, I was happy to wake up tomorrow to find out everything about her.

ACKNOWLEDGMENTS

Mom, thank you for always believing in me, and although I've repeated several times, "You're just being nice, because I'm your daughter," you're the one person who always pushed for my dreams. If it weren't for your continuing to push me, *Disastrous* would have never been read by others. Also thank you for reading every chapter as it was written. I loved our morning talks about the characters as if they were real because in my mind they are!

To my husband, Babe, thanks for putting up with a dirty house, laundry undone, and take-out food for months. I know it was difficult for you to give up our date nights for my late-night writing. You stuck it out and encouraged me the entire way. What would I do without you? You're my rock.

Jess, my baby sister, thanks for helping me brainstorm on title ideas and encouraging me.

To my M7, I am the luckiest girl in the world to have such beautiful, extraordinary women in my life. Thank you for always encouraging me.

Thank you to all my family and friends, who didn't judge me when I finally worked up the courage to tell you about my passion for writing. The love and support I received from all of you pushed me harder to get this done.

Dave Goldhahn, you took my vision and blew it out of the water. The cover is absolutely beautiful. Thank you for being patient with me.

Theresa Wegand, you are truly an amazing and sweet person. Thank you for the advice and the wonderful work on editing, proofreading and beta-reading *Disastrous*. I was blown away with your professionalism and quick feedback. It would have never been completed without your special touch.

Jenny Aspinall, you have such a big heart, and the love you have for books allows authors like me to write them. I've never met anyone like you, and I'm so privileged to have crossed paths with you. Thank you for all of the love, support, and feedback while beta-reading *Disastrous*.

Sali Benbow-Powers, wow you are such an amazing, sweet and lovable woman! I loved your Google stalking frenzy to find the perfect images that would suit my characters! Thank you as well for beta-reading, the feedback, inspiring words and support.

Lori Francis, I love your sense of humor, though you are also such a beautiful woman. Thank you for the encouraging words, beta-reading and all of the feedback on *Disastrous*. I take it back: you cannot borrow Marcus, but I'll think about letting you have Jeremy for a night.

And last but surely not least, thank you to the readers for taking a chance on *Disastrous*. I hope you enjoyed it!

ABOUT THE AUTHOR

Emmy Montes was born in Puerto Rico but raised in Philadelphia, Pennsylvania. She currently resides in Philadelphia with her husband, Alex, and their English bulldog. She has a Bachelor of Science degree in Legal Studies. She works full time as a paralegal for a mid-size law firm. Although she loves the legal field, writing was always her passion.

Her first love for books began with the Goosebumps series as a child. After that she read anything and everything from poetry to short stories. She was passionate about the fictional world and intrigued by the way an author could pull you into a story with just simple words. As a hobby she started writing her own poetry, daily journal entries, and short stories.

She actually dreamed of being a journalist and even went as far as researching colleges to earn a degree in Journalism. At the time, major newspaper companies and magazines were having budgets cut, and after careful thought she settled on another major. When she finished her degree, she felt like something was missing. She continued to write for several years, working on different story ideas, but never finished. *Disastrous* is her first novel.

Connect with Me Online

Email: auth.el.montes@gmail.com

Facebook: E.L. Montes

Goodreads: E.L. Montes

3672766R00157

Printed in Great Britain
by Amazon.co.uk, Ltd.,
Marston Gate.